CW01277050

Suffol
County Coun
Libraries & Heritage

You may keep this title until the last date stamped below or the date given on your receipt.
Providing it has not been reserved by another library user, you may renew it by visiting any Suffolk library, via the world wide web or by telephone. To renew your loans by web use **www.suffolkcc.gc.uk/libdirect** [illegible]
To [illegible]

THE FIRST BOOK
OF THE TREVU TRILOGY

By

F J WARREN

30127 06789376 3

Front cover design courtesy of Justin Hubbard

This novel is entirely a work of fiction. The names, characters and incidents portrayed in it are the work of the author's imagination. Any resemblance to actual persons, living or dead, events or localities is entirely coincidental.
F J Warren asserts the moral right to be identified as the author of this work.

Copyright F J Warren 2006

All rights reserved.

No part of this publication may be reproduced, stored in a retrieval system, or transmitted in any form or by any means, electronic, mechanical photocopying, recording or otherwise, without the prior permission of the author.

ISBN 1846852080
978-1-84685-208-4

British Library Cataloguing In Publication Data
A Record of this Publication is available
from the British Library

Published 2006

by Exposure Publishing
An Imprint of Diggory Press
Three Rivers,
Minions
Liskeard,
Cornwall,
PL14 5LE
UK

WWW.DIGGORYPRESS.COM

SUFFOLK COUNTY LIBRARIES & HERITAGE	
HJ	28/09/2006
F	£8.99
	3M

For Mother

ACKNOWLEDGEMENTS

The author wishes to thank her family and friends for their encouragement before, during and after the completion of this work.

Special thanks to Iris, Linda, Jennifer, Susan and especially Justin for his enthusiasm and invaluable assistance.

CHAPTER 1

HE was cold, hungry and more than a little afraid. It was not because of the advanced hour or the loneliness of the location but what the response to his fevered knocking on the old wooden door would be. The wind howled again, whipping the heavy muffler from his face and allowing the driving rain to soak into his neck cloth. He swore under his breath and finally gave up his useless knocking. Walking around the small, tumbledown cottage he peered through the windows into the hollow darkness and finally, finding himself at the back he hammered on the low door that led from the cottage directly unto the small hay meadow. There was no light and no sound.

"Waste of time," he muttered angrily to himself and turned away to retrace his steps up the path, past the tumbling stream, to where he had tethered his horse.

"I'll be back tomorrow," he shouted defiantly over his shoulder at the windswept property but his words disappeared on the wind so he trudged purposefully on leaving the isolated cottage to its own reflections.

It was half an hour later before he reached his home after a wasted search along the many rutted tracks that led to the little village. Davy, the head groom, came running from his cottage at the back of the stables. He had been on the look out for signs of his master's return but the figure that dismounted did not look in the mood for conversation.

"I got'n sir," said Davy, "Best go in and get yourself dry, sir. Bitter wind blowing the rain right through 'ee." Receiving only a grunt in acknowledgement he caught the bay mare by the bridle, turned her and led her off in the direction of the stables.

His master mounted the low step that led to the house and entered into the small, dark hallway. The main house had been built three centuries before and had been added to as his ancestors had seen fit. Consequently, the impression given was one of a rabbit warren. The house was composed of different styles of architecture going back to Tudor times. As generation succeeded generation they had, if the occasion and wealth allowed, built another room but had never bothered to align either roofs or walls. On the inside of the building this had left low ceilings and gloomy rooms that had steps leading down to them, low doorways that tall owners had to duck under to get through and then paradoxically large, well-lit rooms with small stairs leading to them with high doorways, but as Redvers removed his sodden clothes he noticed none of this.

This was the house he had been born in, its unusual architecture was a part of his own growth and he saw nothing wrong in its construction. Stamping the wet from his boots he descended a dark passage, lit by a single candle in the wall sconce and headed for the small parlour at the back of the house.

On the threshold his dark sombre eyes met the sparkling twinkle of the grey eyes of his wife. Her delicate brows lifted in question but no word came from her full, generous mouth.

"She wasn't there," muttered Redvers. "There was nobody at home and I could determine no sign of life. The fire must have been out so dark it was within," he muttered then added desperately, "God alone knows where she can be at this time of night."

He walked towards the log fire and spread his hands to the warmth. As he did so the worn wicker basket, set on the small parlour table emitted a low wailing. Immediately his wife arose and bent over the tiny bundle resting inside it; a tender smile spread across her face as she picked it up and commenced to rock it gently. Lulled by the warmth of the room and the pleasant rocking sensation the baby resumed its interrupted rest. Redvers gave it only a cursory glance.

"I don't know, Penelope. It could be mine, or it could be some other's b...," catching himself up he cut short his sentence and avoided her eyes.

"It doesn't matter," said Penelope placidly, "He is here now."

"Don't be a fool woman! We are not going to keep it. Tomorrow as soon as practicable I'll go down to Sardi's cottage and make her take it back" he said angrily. "Get Hannah to look after it for the night, feed it and ... and what have you. She won't mind another one temporarily and then, on the morrow, it can be returned."

Again Penelope's brows lifted. In the face of her quiet composure, Redvers lost any of his own that remained.

"Oh God, Penelope! Don't look at me like that, woman! I mean . . . ," he was almost shouting now, but to steady himself he took a deep breath and then plunged resolutely on.

"I apologise now that it may be mine and that I should have brought this embarrassment upon you but by this time tomorrow it will be back with its mother and we need never mention the matter again. I'll . . . I'll give her some money to clothe and feed it with. Make it right with her ... somehow." An expression of pain descended upon her face and, chastened at the sight of it, he crossed the room to bring himself to stand before his wife still rocking the sleeping child in what seemed to him a possessive embrace. She schooled her features bravely and mastered them enough to portray the impression of a wife seemingly unconcerned with the struggles that were consuming her husband, and balked by her silence he suddenly spoke as if the words were torn from him.

"Forgive me," he said and bowed his dark head.

Penelope smiled to herself and then stretching out her delicate hand, and placing it under his strong jaw, gently raised her husband's head until her eyes met his with an understanding look.

"What I failed to give you, you have given me. What is there to forgive?" she asked him composedly.

Stricken into silence at her words his only answer was to bow his head in shame again.

The following morning at breakfast, Penelope appeared serene, giving no indication of the turmoil that had invaded the quiet farmhouse on the previous evening. Of course the servants had talked and were talking now but she cared not. When Penelope had awoken that morning she felt that the crushing years of failed childbearing had drifted away and at last her life had been given back some meaning. She had asked after the baby from Hannah, her serving maid, as soon as she had come downstairs to the dining room to partake of breakfast.

"Don' 'ee worry 'bout tha' liddle mite," beamed Hannah. "Took a good feed and then went sleep almost t' once." Nodding wisely, she vouchsafed, "They d' 'ave special strength when they come by the back door . . . so t' speak".

That the baby in question had undoubtedly arrived in the house by way of the front door was not for Hannah to question. A mother of five, all but one still alive, she had known no other man than her husband but she had a love of children, particularly babies, that forgave them their parentage.

They were the true innocents in this world she maintained. The parents, well they were a different matter. Carnal pursuits had led them astray when they should have known better but having a soft spot for Captain Redvers, whom she had known since they were children together on the farm, if his by-blows ended up on the front door step late at night it was not for her to condemn. She supposed, with a pang of regret, that the offending mite would be returned to its mother or failing that sent to an orphanage. He was a little dark skinned to be sure but not so that you would notice; and he was still an innocent babe for all of that.

That Hannah was convinced of the baby's parentage, Penelope was well aware. She herself knew that the custom of leaving unwanted children on the steps of the father's house was common practice in this part of West Cornwall. Most of the offending infants were promptly packed off so that no scandal could attach to the family but some were kept. The girls became servants and the boys farm hands or stable hands, with minimal wages and even less respect they invariably became the lowest creatures in the hierarchy of servant culture. A few - a very few - had been accepted into the families of their fathers but this practice was not an assurance of a happy outcome. Despised by the wives, hated by their half siblings, they suffered miserable lives. Sometimes their mothers entered the household as servants, to shut the door on the gossips for good. On Sundays these families, bastions of respectability in their individual communities, dressed themselves in their finest and with their servants filled the little churches praying for forgiveness for their sins and avowing love to all their neighbours, however lowly their state. After the service they returned to their houses, the unwanted children were regulated once again to their lowly positions within the family and the stigma of non-relenting gratitude imposed upon them.

Penelope shuddered at the thought and she determined that the poor innocent that had arrived so miraculously in her household would never be placed in that position. All her married life she had longed for children. Miscarriages and still births had followed each other with relentless regularity. Redvers' love for her slowly died as each tragedy ensued. His adoration for her finally withered when the doctor told him, as the last stillborn child was laid in its motionless crib, that there would be no more children for Penelope to bring into the world. She bore it well, never remonstrating with him when, reckless with grief, he ranged the countryside following his fancy be it another man's bored wife or some obliging whore. Never by one look did Penelope let him know how hurt she was by his lack of affection for her. Neither did she allow the knowledge that he had made himself the talk of their small tight-knit community, and in so doing had turned her into an object of pity, to defeat her. Her pride in herself held her up against the storm of despair that beat against her. Penelope Trevarthen was still the undisputed mistress of Trevu and, it was the Captain's wife that the local farmers and gentry doffed their caps to - not those others. Her kind heart had even learned to forgive her erring husband for well she knew that if she had given him a son and heir then his love for her would not have been dissipated on any other women that crossed his path.

"It would have been so different," she told herself sadly, "He would never stir from my side again."

Her thoughts were interrupted as the door was thrown open and her errant husband stood in the doorway, a look of frustration on his handsome face. In his middle thirties he gave the appearance of a man at least ten years younger but of late the care lines had begun to show. He had felt frustrated by the turn his life had gradually taken. When Penelope had finally been defeated by her body and he knew that he would never sire a child with her his slowly diminishing love for her had died. He was ashamed of himself that he could care so little for her after so many years together but he could not help himself. Now, the final insult: the small, unwanted bundle, left at his door. The conclusive tragedy to a life that had held so much promise. In all probability it was his child, his son, but how could he claim it for his own without bringing shame and disgrace upon Penelope and the family name? The child's colour could never be hidden or dismissed for he had fathered a half caste, - a mulatto - for his small, insular world to snigger about and laugh at. The child would have to be well hidden, he reasoned, an orphanage or some such institution, far away from the locality of Penzance. Concealed from sight and unable to further taint his already tarnished reputation by its unwanted presence.

Sardi, the child's mother, was the daughter of a freed slave and hailed originally from Bristol. Coming to the far west as a serving girl, she had evoked no small amount of interest from the local males as soon as she appeared in the village. No woman as exotic as Sardi had ever been seen in these parts. She was possessed of a dusky, sultry skin, huge dark expressive eyes and an Amazonian figure. Redvers found her irresistible, along with most of the local male population, for she caused a sensation wherever she appeared. With her head held proudly, she seemed to be indifferent to their interest. Like a trout enticed by a mayfly this circumstance only served to whet Redvers appetite the more. He wooed in earnest and finally, he won her. Many delightful hours had been spent in her company of an evening. He forgot his troubled life in the warmth of her embraces but his stolen happiness was not to last. Abruptly - without a word of explanation, Sardi ended their love affair. The mine captain's wife, formerly oblivious to her servant's private life, suddenly turned her out of the house and it soon became apparent why she had followed this drastic course: Sardi was with child.

The local women nodded their heads wisely and not without a malicious pleasure, for gossip had been rife at the sight of Captain Trevarthen's bay mare regularly hobbled at the back of the mine captain's imposing house. "Bound to 'appen sooner nor later," they muttered behind her back, but Sardi, a noted needle woman and seamstress, was undaunted, and took in sewing through a local dressmakers in Penzance. The local farmers wives and other females of consequence from in and around Penzance, although not bothering to recognise her in the street because of her colour and condition, passionately desired the garments that Sardi's deft fingers could make for them and their money paid her bills and the rent of the cottage she had obtained. When her time came she had paid the Doctor and the midwife from her own funds. A strong woman, she was soon up and about after the birth and was often to be seen walking to Penzance with her packed and finished dresses in her arms and a small, living bundle strapped across her broad back like a bolt of cloth. She continued her life regardless, with an inner strength so rarely found in the females living in that locality, bound as they were by the conventions that shackled their lives. Sardi had been stared at all her life so, undefeated by the disaster that had befallen her, she stepped out boldly into the world, giving the impression that she could not be cowed by any thought or deed directed at her by any of the local people. However, even the meanest of them held a grudging respect for her although they took great pains not to show it. The only local who showed her an equal regard was the wife of her former lover and that was the only time that Sardi had felt herself humbled. When they met upon the road Mrs. Trevarthen had never failed to acknowledge her with a warm smile and a friendly greeting.

Now, her baby had been left on Trevu's doorstep, with neither a note nor a sign. Redvers knew well that Sardi was able to read and write, yet no letter of explanation had been left. Before meeting Sardi it had never occurred to him that someone from such a lowly position would possess even a modicum of education. Serving wenches were not among the lettered members of society as a rule. He was intrigued and upon enquiry found that she had received a good education when her family lived in Bristol. Lying in her cramped bed, and cradled in her lover's soft embrace between her sheets of coarse linen she dreamily recounted details of her past life to him. Her father, a notable carpenter, had paid for her schooling with the money he had earned working in the docks. She laughed as she recounted the information that her mother had thought it a waste of good money; but Sardi was their only child and she acquiesced to her beloved husband's wishes. With the accomplishment of reading Sardi won herself a position with an old local Jewish seamstress of some repute. Soon her natural talent and aptitude began to reap rewards for the seamstress and she was promoted. She not only cut, sewed, copied and designed clothes but she kept the accounts for her employer. This pleasant state of affairs lasted for two years, until her father was killed in an accident in the street. A runaway team, maddened by fly, had mown him down as he crossed the entrance to the docks on his way home from work. Her voice faltered as she told him that her mother had never recovered from his death and at the funeral the rain that poured without stopping from the skies wrapped the heartbroken widow in its steely embrace. She caught a severe cold, then pneumonia and with hardly any struggle at all she was gone. Sardi found herself left alone at seventeen, but paid two sets of funeral expenses and, resolutely, returned to her work only to find that her employer, ageing and prey to infirmity, had decided to sell the business. The new owner needed only one sight of Sardi's dark skin before turning her off.

"Bad for business," he had proclaimed, and Redvers felt the tremble of hatred that Sardi could not control at the memory of her harsh treatment.

With her money running low, Sardi gained employment under a mine captain, who had lately returned with his wife from South America. He was heading for a tin mine in the west of Cornwall. His wife decided that to arrive with a servant - and an unusual one at that - would give them some social standing in their new locality. People were always impressed by what you possessed she had reasoned.

Sardi's tale only served to increase Redvers' sympathy for her, and her confidences had given him a feeling of great pride. So much so, that with the shock of his own dismissal from her life he had been hurt more than he could understand.

Even less could he comprehend why this proud and accomplished woman should have chosen to leave her precious baby with only the pealing of a bell to announce its arrival into Redvers' household. He wished that he had tried harder to contact her but his pride had been wounded when she had decided to end the relationship. For Redvers, pride had always been a sustaining influence.

Annoyed that he had spent the hours since dawn trying to contact her, he returned, angry and frustrated to his home after a fruitless search. Her cottage was empty so he had travelled into Penzance but could find no trace of her there, either. The stage had already departed and there was not a person abroad that morning that had been able to tell him if a dark skinned woman had been travelling on it. A post chaste had been hired for Bodmin but that had been acquired by a set of young squires to enable them to attend a hanging. Sardi had completely disappeared - out of his life and the child's.

"There is no trace of her," he explained to his wife. "The cottage is empty for she has paid up her rent with the Widow Tregolls."

"Did anyone see her?... Question her?" asked Penelope in her quiet voice.

"I have met not one soul who has seen her and even if I had how many people would have ever bothered to speak to her?" he said exasperated, and added in a despairing voice, "Who cared for Sardi?"

"You did," answered his wife, with no hint of malice.

At her soft words and gentle tone he hung his head in shame and could not bring himself to look at her face. After a short silence he heard her seemingly unperturbed voice speak his name again. From her place at the breakfast table she calmly enquired of him if he had eaten.

"Yes, I ate in Penzance - at one of the inns," he replied in an angry growl, but he sat down suddenly at the table and grasped her hand. Full of remorse he considered how his life could have come to such a pass. When his time in the military had to end, through a family disaster, he had thrown himself into the challenges with which he had been presented.. Gradually he cleared the mountain of debt that the young couple had been burdened with. However, as their lives together progressed their lack of children had driven them apart and now when he needed to talk to her the words would not serve him. He looked up and caught her quiet gaze upon him.

"I ... Sardi never told ... I didn't ...," he stumbled apologetically and his words trailed into the air.

Broken Bonds: The First Book Of The Trevu Trilogy

"May I say something, dearest?" asked Penelope, a wistful smile playing upon her lips.

He nodded.

"This child may or may not be yours. I will never question you about its paternity. However, it's undoubtedly Sardi's, for no child of that colour could have been born to anyone else in this vicinity. It has been left, possibly, on his father's doorstep. Who can be certain?" she smiled, "and but for us it is all alone in the world. We could send him to the orphanage or leave him with Hannah until he grows to a suitable age when he could be useful about the farm. Such things are not unknown. It will cause comment for a little while and then another scandal will take the gossips fancy. Or," she paused and drew a deep breath, "or . . . we could bring him up as our own child."

"Don't be absurd, woman!" exclaimed Redvers, shocked into disbelief by her suggestion. "Take him in as a member of our own family? The servants will trumpet the circumstances of his birth all over the neighbourhood. From the Land's End to Plymouth too, belike!"

"My dear Redvers - they will have done that already. If the good people of Penzance do not know already, I, for one, will be very much surprised," she announced with an amused smile. He stared at his wife open mouthed. How could she sit so calmly beside him, accepting the biggest scandal ever to fall upon her.

"He is an innocent child, Redvers. The circumstances of his birth, his colour, his lack of a mother, . . . and a father," she continued quietly, " none of these things can detract from this defenceless child's innocence. I have brought five dead children into this world," she murmured, tears filling her eyes. "Can I have the chance, at last, to hold a child against my heart? Possibly your child, but a poor innocent, none the less. I beg of you, dearest, do not deny me this small prospect of happiness."

He started to shake his head but still she pleaded.

"Please Redvers. I ask it of you not for myself alone."

Redvers sighed, smitten into silence by her desire. "Where is the child now?" he asked, after a subdued silence, "Has Hannah brought him to work with her? Perhaps we had better see him again before anything is decided in this matter."

Within ten minutes a beaming Hannah entered the parlour cooing into a small, gurgling bundle of soft, white linen. Hannah gently lowered the child into Penelope's arms and another pair of arms appeared from the swaddling and began to thrash the air in excitement at the sound of her voice.

"Hello, you handsome fellow," cooed Penelope, "What a happy young man you appear to be this morning." Suddenly the child reached out one small hand and grasping Penelope by the finger, placed it in his small pink mouth and began to suck contentedly. A smile of pure delight flooded Penelope's face; Redvers, shaken to his soul, thought that she had never looked so beautiful. He bent his head to look upon the face of the young interloper who had wrought such a change in her and was intrigued to see that the eyes of its mother were regarding him so trustfully. Finding himself consumed by guilt, he heard his wife's soft voice gently dismissing the servant. As the door closed quietly behind her Hannah heard her mistress's voice plead softly.

"Please Redvers. Please."

The baby discontinued his sucking and now started to gurgle happily again, kicking his sturdy little legs, and waving his arms about delightedly, as if his immature life had been given all the pleasure that his little body could contain.

"No," said Redvers, and shook his head sadly, "No, Penelope," but as he reached his hand out to caress her face, with its dispirited expression, his own finger was hastily grasped by the contented infant. He looked down in amazement at the happy child, and then lifted his eyes to his wife's face and noted her expression. She was sitting so calmly, holding the precious child so tightly, and with a look of such entreaty on her face that of a sudden he felt himself consumed with a surge of love for them both.

He sighed again, "I cannot go against you dearest," he admitted contritely, "It shall be as you wish."

The gurgling, contented infant shook his finger happily, almost as if the child and the man were shaking hands to seal a contract.

CHAPTER 2

THE cockerel careered across the farm yard pursued by a noisy gang, composed of the old farm dog and a small vociferous boy of about five years of age. The dog had the advantage of the boy in that he could run faster but he knew he was committing an offence so he ran with no small degree of caution with its head hung low and making surreptitious backward glances in case the pursuers became the pursued. The boy, unhindered by such feelings of conscience, chased his feathered quarry without fear of condemnation. Cornering their squawking prey in the bottom of a disused pig sty he was just about to pounce when he noticed out of the corner of his eye that his erstwhile companion had left him to catch the indignant fowl on his own. Too late he spotted the tall dark shape and the encircling arm that swooped upon him purposefully. His conquest was abruptly ended as he felt himself lifted high into the air. Kicking and screaming he protested loudly but to no avail. His body was twisted around until he was face to face with his assailant.

Redvers pursed his lips. "What have we here?" he queried. "A chicken catcher. Well, well. What punishment shall we use on this little felon?"

"I didden catched it. So I didden be naughty." replied the child with innocent logic, confident that he was to receive no punishment for his offence. If it had been one of the farm hands that had caught him, a swift cuff around his head would undoubtedly have been his reward, but safe in his father's arms he had no fear of retribution.

Redvers laughed his deep, throaty laugh.

"Perhaps Mama will have something to say about that. She will certainly have something to say about these spoiled clothes. Let's see if I can get the worst of this mud off the young gentleman's shoes before we go in, at the very least," and he sat the young offender down on an old granite trough and began to wipe the mud from the soiled footwear. This labour safely accomplished, he hoisted the child into his arms again and with his long, purposeful stride headed towards the house.

They found Penelope in the kitchen supervising the creation of the evening meal. Hannah, now promoted to cook, was bemoaning the fact that some of the apple tarts she had left cooling on the sill of the open window had mysteriously disappeared. A little chuckle, hastily cut short, seemed to indicate the likely culprit. Three pairs of eyes turned upon the smallest member of the group.

"Paul?" enquired Penelope.

The little boy meeting those speaking eyes, at first grinned but then dropped his gaze and looked shamefaced before his mother's pained expression.

"Nice 'n tasty, Hannah," he mumbled, "but I sorry I didden ask furst."

He struggled to free himself from Redvers grip and ran to Hannah and buried his curly head in her floury apron. She bent and, clasping her rough hands around his face, kissed him fondly.

"You'm a liddle devil, Master Paul, but I d' love 'e for all that," she sighed. He returned Hannah's kiss with fervour and then turned and ran towards

Penelope, his arms outstretched. Swiftly she bent to catch him in her loving embrace whilst telling him what a naughty boy he had been. Noticing his somewhat bedraggled appearance she enquired if he had been up to any mischief in his absence from the house.

Paul considered for a moment if it was wise to tell his mother about the chase of the cockerel across the farmyard. He adored her and he knew there would be no beatings for any action he ever undertook but he hated to see the disappointed look on her face. Recently he had broken her favourite vase by trying to hit it using a small bow and arrow fashioned for him by one of the farm hands. He had been all too successful and succeeded in his aim with his third arrow. Penelope had told him he was a very naughty boy and had sent him to his room, but when he came down later and stood shamefaced before her she had swept him up and covered him with kisses telling him all was forgiven. But he had seen the look on her face as she had gazed at the shattered fragments of glass that lay on the carpet and knew that he had been very bad indeed.

Of course, his father, had been told of the incident and had promptly taken the bow and arrows away from him, telling him he was going to have them destroyed. The offending arms were destroyed only to be replaced two days later by a much stronger bow. Redvers and Paul had disappeared into the orchard to try their prowess with this new weapon. His father had impressed upon him that he was not to use it anywhere near the house. They made a solemn pact which had to be amended only once; one of the farm hands found an arrow sticking out of the pasty that he had taken from his [1]crowst bag, and placed at his side on the low hedge upon which he sat in order to consume his meal.

"I chased the white cockerel," he confided to Penelope, looking guilty, "but 'tis all right 'cos I didn't catch 'en."

"Only, my dear son, because I caught you first," said his father, his soft voice shaking with laughter.

Trying not to laugh herself, Penelope tried to admonish her so cherished young rascal but even she could not control the giggles that were threatening to ruin her homily. Hannah, feeling no such constraint, laughed heartily.

Once more Paul was subjected to Penelope's kisses and then presented with a fresh pie and another hug from Hannah. He preceded his parents from the kitchen to the small back parlour, hopping and skipping all the way. Redvers, his arm around his wife's waist, laughed merrily at his antics. However, on reaching the parlour, the boy's high spirits dimmed slightly as he saw the space left by the glass vase so effectively demolished by his marksmanship. That very afternoon he was to go to Penzance, with his father, to find a suitable vase with which to replace the glass target. He was not looking forward to the visit, partly because of the crime that had caused it but also because of his dislike of the town; its inhabitants always seemed to stare at him and to whisper behind their hands.

The streets bustled with people and his father, holding tight to Paul's little

---

[1] Crowst: midmorning break for food.

hand, doffed his hat at various locals and chose not to notice their disdainful glances. Although his little son felt the pain of their rejection he kept his mouth firmly closed. After successfully finding a replacement for the vase his father supervised the wrapping of it and its eventual packing into the bag that he had so providentially brought with him in which to convey the precious replacement to its new home. Paul, bored by the proceedings, sauntered towards the open door and looked out upon the momentarily deserted street, hoping to see something of interest. Almost immediately he heard a man's loud voice shouting frantically; "Stop thief! Stop that boy someone!" and Paul's eyes opened wide to see a young lad, his clothes hanging in tatters about his emaciated body, running barefoot as fast as he could along the street and clutching in desperation a small loaf of bread to his thin chest. Behind him a middle aged man, well built and with a very red face, pursued him doggedly but he stood no chance of catching the runaway for the thief was fleet of foot as well as quick of hand. The boy turned his head to see if he had outrun his pursuer when he missed his footing and he came crashing down in the mud of the road. Hastily he scrambled to his feet but his chance for escape had been lost; the man was upon him and grabbed hold of his arm and with his other hand began to lay about the youngster without a care. Paul jumped as a voice barked authoritatively behind him.

"Stop that at once!" and his father filled the shop doorway with his tall frame and stared in disgust at the actions of the boy's assailant.

"Damned if I will!" retorted the man angrily, but it was noted that after a final vicious blow to the boy's head he dropped his hand, still holding the thief tightly by a thin arm in his strong grasp. The lad, Paul noted, was clutching grimly the filthy, crushed bread to his chest and his face with its cold, blue eyes blankly regarded him for a moment. He was older than Paul but very thin, in marked contrast to the young Trevarthen's sturdy frame, and his face was suffused with red where the man's blows had found their mark.

"What crime has he committed that you should beat him so?" asked Redvers. Then he saw the dirtied loaf that was grasped so tightly still, and knew the answer before ever he heard the account of it.

"Stealing sir! From my shop! Bread it was an' from under my very nose an' 'tis not the first time he has been about these tricks, but 'twill be his last. Stealing bread, the stuff of life! They should hang him for sure for that offence," and only then did Paul see the look of fear that swept across the boy's face. But it lasted only a moment for immediately a bold, impassive expression hid any feeling that the lad felt from the eyes of the outside world.

Redvers regarded the scrap of humanity inscrutably. There were so many of these waifs around, for Penzance was a port after all and many sailors took their pleasure there. A spot of colour flamed his cheeks as he remembered his own time, prior to his young son's arrival into his life, spent in the company of certain females of the town. Nevertheless he enquired if the baker had any knowledge of the boy's parentage, for he looked so young and his heart ached to see his undoubted poverty.

"Some whore's bastard sir, that's all, sir!" the baker announced dismissively, and then cried out in pain as the boy summoned up all his puny strength and kicked him on his leg.

"Damn you, you filthy bastard! Best for you if you'd been thrown down a shaft at birth!" and he let forth another expletive and began again to hit the child until he found his upraised hand caught in a firm grip.

"That will do!" ordered Redvers. For a moment it looked as if the man would shake himself free of Trevarthen's grasp but something about the determined look in Redvers' face made him falter. Slowly he lowered his hand and was released. Redvers felt in his pocket for some coins and produced them.

"I'll pay you for the bread then you can release him," he announced calmly. However, his offer was refused, as the baker assured him his consideration would be wasted. The boy knew no other than to steal and his deliverance from the town would be a boon to many of its inhabitants. Before Captain Trevarthen could stop him, he nodded a brief farewell and turned away, hauling the struggling boy with him.

Paul and his father watched as the pair disappeared into the throng of people busy about the street.

"Dada?" asked his son in a worried voice, "What that man goin' do with the poor boy?"

Redvers tried to answer brightly, determined to shield his beloved son from the horrors that the world had shown him, and tried to reassure him that probably the boy would be told off most severely and maybe beaten some more. But as he explained reasonably to Paul - the lad was a thief after all.

"I d' steal from Hannah but nobody d' beat me like that," gasped his son forlornly, tears filling his eyes in distress at what he had seen. He gulped as he announced worriedly, "The bad man said he would hang 'en." Redvers assured him that such a young child would not be hanged but even he had difficulty repressing the shudder at what he imagined would be the boy's fate. He reasoned that the wretch had committed a crime after all and should undoubtedly be punished for his offence, but the unfairness of life gripped his heart as surely as it had taken hold of poor Paul's. He bent down and picked the distressed boy up into his arms, soothing him gently but again they heard raised voices and the thief's running feet headed as purposefully as before down the street. A stand of goods was displayed outside of the next shop, a grocer's, and almost before Paul and Redvers could comprehend what it was that they had seen, the boy dived for the sanctuary of the cloth that covered the trestle, on the top of which various goods were displayed, and wriggled from view. They appeared to be the only ones to have witnessed his disappearance and when his pursuer, now almost apoplectic with fury, arrived on the scene Redvers calmly pointed to the alley situated just across the street and had the satisfaction of seeing the man head off in the direction of the harbour. His face was expressionless as he returned the adoring gaze of his relieved son, and when he threw some coins down at the side of the trestle he noted with satisfaction how quickly a small, grimy hand shot out to retrieve them. A face appeared where the cloth drooped from the side of the wall and two clear, blue eyes regarded the couple in shocked amazement. Redvers turned again to go into the shop and so it was only his son that noted the lad's hasty scramble from within his hiding place.

He grinned conspiratorially as the beaten and panting scrap of humanity availed himself of an apple, shooting Paul a smile of pure mischief as he did so, before he made good his escape into an alley that led in the opposite direction from that taken by his pursuer.

On their way home, with the new vase safely packed into the saddlebag, Paul, who was perched before his father on the neck of the rather frisky bay mare, considered asking a question. He was not quite sure how to ask it and squirmed slightly.

"What's the matter, Paul? Uncomfortable? Soon be home, now," assured Redvers in a cheery voice.

"Why do people keep looking at me when we go town?"

The grip on the child tightened slightly. "Well, . . ." his father began and then sought for an answer. He knew full well what the boy had meant. People had been staring and talking ever since they had taken Paul into their household and openly accepted him as their child. He considered lying to him but he could not bring himself to do that for he had always known that this moment would come. That it had come upon him so soon was to be regretted but alone with the boy perhaps now would be the best time to talk of his beginnings. His son, unable to wait longer for his answer, proposed a reason of his own.

"Is it 'cos my mother was a black lady?" asked Paul suddenly.

Shocked by the sudden revelation, Redvers hands jerked at the bridle and the mare, surprised by this movement stopped for a moment. He kicked her on and attempted to compose his features into a placid expression that in no way expressed his feelings.

"Who told you that?" he asked, deliberately trying to keep a calm tone in his voice.

"Oh - William 'Enry and Alfred and . . . ," he answered, shooting a quick glance at his father's impassive face, "and Minnie and Katy in the dairy and Dick, her shiner. Some of the others who 'elped with the 'ay making and that Mrs. Darvey who came when Hannah 'ad 'er las' baby. She called me a liddle Darkie' but Hannah 'eard 'er and telled 'er to mind 'er mouth."

Stunned, Redvers realised that most of his work force that had any communication with the boy had taken it upon themselves to provide him with the tale of his birth. His dark brows drew together in an angry frown - there would be words of his to set the beams ringing in the kitchen and the rafters in the barn when he got home.

"Well - yes - It is quite true," he answered lamely.

"I was lef' on the doorstep - in a vicar basket," Paul announced importantly. "So you an' Mother took me in for your very own. Katy said I was some lucky 'cos most folk don't want babies lef' on doorsteps and black one's 'specially and that I should be . . . gra ... graf... graful," he ended triumphantly.

Dumbfounded, Redvers considered how best to explain exactly what had happened that stormy night over five years ago. The boy seemed completely happy with the circumstances of his arrival and of his colour. His only concern was that people outside of his home and family had stared at him so. He was so young, only five, how would it affect him as he grew older, when he no longer had two doting parents to confide in and be consoled and supported by? The malicious gossips would enjoy themselves then, taunting and ridiculing him. In his mind's eye he could envisage the old crones of the recently vacated market town passing on their wicked comments to each other in their calculated high whispers, making sure that every word was to be heard distinctly by the intended victim.

"Why, Paul your colour does not matter for, after all, you are loved for who you are and not what you look like," he replied serenely, and then asked gently, "Do you understand, my boy?"

The little boy wrinkled his nose and thought for a long while before replying, "I s'pose so Dada, but maybe one day it'll wash out an' I shall be white like you an' Mama," and he rubbed the back of his hand vigorously until his father's large hand covered his small, puny one and stopped him.

"Never wish for that Paul, for Mama and I love you as you are and wish for nothing to change about you. If when I look into the stables of a morning the horses had all changed colour I would not think them better horses, would I?"

"Mmmm .... not if they d' still go good," replied his son reasonably.

"Well, there you are," announced Redvers, unable to keep the note of triumph out of his voice, "You keep ... um ... going good and we shall think none the less of you and if any of those silly, old fools that stare at you so should tell you different take no notice. They are too blind and stupid to see your worth," he concluded firmly.

Satisfied with this explanation Paul snuggled back against his father and they resumed their journey. However, on their arrival at Trevu, Redvers found Penelope in the garden and lost no time in telling her of his recent talk with Paul. For one brief moment she looked worried by his account of their conversation but then she smiled slowly.

"I think our son has a good head on those tender, young shoulders," she remarked softly. "We have no cause to worry. 'He'll do', as Hannah is so fond of saying."

"Myself, I think he gets his good sense from his mother," remarked her husband proudly and fondly, and then seeing the swift look of consternation in Penelope's face continued. "His kind, loving, forgiving and besotted Mama," and stretching out his hands he pulled her to him.

"Besotted?" she enquired coyly, raising her twinkling eyes to his face.

"Utterly," he laughed and kissed her on the lips.

"Me too," said a chirpy voice from the gateway, "me 'ave kisses too," and erupting into the garden clasping a limp bunch of bedraggled pink campions skipped Paul.

"For you," he said presenting his offering to his mother, "for your new glass ... ," he sought for the right word, " ... fing," he submitted lamely.

"Why Paul, how lovely," beamed Penelope. "Did you pick them yourself."

He nodded proudly.

Penelope curtsied elegantly and said, "Well, I think this the finest bouquet that has ever been presented to me, and you certainly deserve a kiss for it."

This act accomplished, Paul retreated to the kitchen in search of his beloved Hannah. Penelope took up the roses that she had been busily cutting for her new vase and determined to put them in the small dark hallway instead. That their magnificence would not be appreciated there did not worry her at all. In the comfort of the back parlour Hannah brought them tea and some of the small cakes which she had hidden from Paul. Redvers was about to leave the parlour to go to his office to check over some papers, when, Penelope, busily arranging the somewhat dejected posy in her new vase looked up from her arrangement and said, "Redvers, I almost forgot; John Williams from Wheal Sankey will be calling tomorrow morning. He called earlier when you were out."

"Did he say why he wanted to see me?"

"No. But it was most noticeable that he did not seem to be very happy about something," she noted.

"More problems with flooding, I expect. That mine has been nothing but a curse since it opened. It only made a good return in its first year and since then profits have been minimal. Last month John said that they might try for a new lode so I suppose he will be after more money," he remarked, "I shall have to leave off overseeing the ploughing of Holly field until he has gone. I'll send Daniel in my place, he will keep them straight," but before taking himself off he suddenly smiled and pulled her into his arms and kissed her again.

John Williams, Wheal Sankey's mine captain, approached the big house with trepidation for two reasons; Captain Redvers Trevarthen was an imposing figure of a man, tall and slim but with broad shoulders and a formidable temper if things did not go his way. The progress of the Wheal Sankey Mine was not as favourable as had first been prophesied. The returns were not as good as had been expected and the mine was prone to flooding at regular intervals. This meant a lot of capital investment and as Captain Trevarthen was the sole owner it was inevitably to him that John found his footsteps leading. To ask a man to reinvest his non existent profits in the hope of a good return was easy if it was a new mine, but Sankey had closed before and had only been reopened because of the geological survey that noted that the old seam had been badly worked. At first they had struck lucky but once the seam had been worked they had to find another lode and quickly. Captain Redvers would soon tire of throwing more money down that enormous shaft. Now he had to ask him to finance the additional timbering and possibly for the erection of another whim. However, if the tin was there as had been foretold, the income would be considerable. The market was high and tin was making a good return, so with luck Captain Redvers should be well rewarded for his investment.

Suddenly, a small, dark, curly headed boy appeared as if from nowhere, hotly pursued by a dairy maid. The boy had in his possession a precariously held kitten.

"You'm come 'ere Paul Trevarthen and bring that pesky cat wid 'e," ranted the dairy maid, in a shrill voice.

Not seeing John Williams, Paul ran headlong into him and was knocked to the ground. The kitten attempting to escape delivered a nasty scratch to the boy's face but to no avail, for the young lad was determined that he was not going to be released. As John bent to help the child to his feet he noticed the tear stained face had a large red mark running down one cheek upon which the kitten had scored a bloody line.

"She goin' 'ave 'n shot," sobbed the boy, "so I grabbed 'n an' run".

John Williams, a father of four lusty boys and one girl, expertly consoled him and with a wink of reassurance to Paul, removed the writhing kitten from his hands and placed it in his capacious coat pocket, effectively hiding it from view.

Katy, the dairy maid, panted up to them. In a breathless voice she continued to shout at Paul, who faced her defiantly but was glad to be in the stranger's company.

"You'm wait. Yer father 'll 'ave 'e this time. Cheekin' me like that an' then runnin' off with that bleddy kitten. Give 'n 'ere t'once. Davy 'll put 'en going fas' 'nuff afore 'e 'ave a chance t' stick 'is face in a bowl of cream again," she vowed.

"I think it must 'ave run off Miss 'Ocking when the boy fell," said John soothingly, waving his hand towards the flower bed at the front of the garden, "probably in that flower patch over there."

"I'll get 'en don' 'e worry," she muttered turning towards the flowers, but as an afterthought she swung around upon the boy and shouted threateningly at him: "an' don' 'e think I finished with you either you liddle . . . liddle dirty bl...."

Her threat was left unfinished as an angry voice boomed from the doorway.

"Katy! That's enough. Get back to your work. I shall speak to you later."

The outraged dairy maid immediately dropped a curtsey and headed for the dairy at fast as her legs could carry her. Woe betide anyone when the master used that tone of voice.

Trevarthen, visibly angry, walked forward and placing his hand gently under Paul's chin lifted up the battle scarred face to his scrutiny.

"Dear me," he said quite calmly, "we have been in the wars have we not Paul?"

"No harm done Captain Trevarthen sir, 'e's a brave strong lad, 'e'll do," remarked John, and reaching into the pocket retrieved the offending feline and returned it to Paul, who grasped it protectively.

"Nobody want it so can I keep it?" sniffed Paul. And then remembering his manners: "Please."

"I'm sorry Paul, but if it has found its way into the dairy it will be impossible to keep it out now. Perhaps it will be for the best if it is got rid of as soon as possible so that it can cause no further trouble."

His son's face expressed disappointment, disbelief and finally anger.

"No!" he said firmly, "Nobody d' want 'n, jus' like nobody wanted me but I was lucky 'cos I got wanted 'n I d' want this kitten." For once Paul looked mutinous as he scowled up at his father.

A look of exasperation settled on Redvers normally enigmatic face. A problem was looming that Redvers could well do without.

John Williams coughed. "Excuse me Cap'n, but if you was agreeable I would be glad to take the little fellow off your hands - um - the cat that is sir. See my little maid is very lonely and she d' love to 'ave a little cat all for 'er own. Twouldn' be no trouble in our house, sir. When 'tis grown 'e can be a mouser for us. Handy thing a good mouser."

"Well, Paul, what do you think of Mr. Williams taking this kitten home for his daughter? She would be very pleased to have it and it would have a good home."

Paul studied John Williams thoughtfully for a moment.

"Can I come an' see it sometimes?" he asked.

"But of course you can," said John, "and very welcome you'll be. My maid's a lonely child. She'll be glad to have your company."

"All right then," said Paul and promptly passed the kitten back to its new owner. Returned to John Williams' pocket the kitten decided he had enough excitement for one morning and snuggled down to go to sleep.

Redvers, looking relieved, took John by the arm and led him into the house, and sent the boy off to have his hurts tended to by Hannah. When Paul was out of earshot he expressed his gratitude. "Thought I was going to have quite a battle over that," he remarked.

John laughed, "E's some boy and no mistake, sir. Goin' be quite a character when 'e's growed."

Redvers felt a tremor of pride run through him. To have his son so unreservedly praised was unusual. Apart from Penelope and Hannah no one openly admired the boy. People kept their thoughts to themselves in his presence but he was well aware that, because of his colour, few people regarded Paul as the right sort of child to bring into a family. This part of West Cornwall was parochial in the extreme, anyone strange was deemed unsavoury: Jews, Gypsies, blacks and Catholics were all considered to be of the lower orders. Paul's christening raised most of the eyebrows in the district, including those of the vicar, and even his own lawyer had tried to dissuade Redvers from adopting the child for his own.

"People will talk, Captain Trevarthen, people will talk and it will be the boy who will suffer," said Bosence.

With John's praise perhaps the balance was beginning to shift a little, and there might come a day when Paul would take his place in society as a respected member of it.

"Well, John, what matters have we to discuss to day?" asked Redvers, putting the thoughts of his son to the back of his mind.

It was as he had presumed; the mine needed more money invested in it. Williams, like the geologist, was convinced of a good lode but it would need extra finances in order for it to be worked properly, the main problem being the almost continuous flooding. They talked for an hour, his mine captain, putting a good case until Redvers finally agreed to finance another three months work.

"We'll find 'n for 'e , sir, don't 'e worry 'bout that," avowed John, "and now that Wheal Glasny is worked out we ought be able t' pick up that new pumping engine at a good price."

"Well, John, I'll leave it to you - just send the accounts to me and we'll see how things stand at the end of the quarter."

John touched his cap and turned to leave but Redvers accompanied him to the front door, discussing the state of mining in general as they went. Paul appeared from the recesses of the kitchen and suggested that he go with Mr. Williams to deliver the new kitten to his daughter, but his father pointed out John might not be going home immediately.

"Course 'e is," said the little boy, "Can't take the kitten down the mine, can 'e?"

The men exchanged amused glances and it was agreed that as John would be returning to his home at once it would be perfectly all right for Paul to go with him.

"I'll drop 'im 'ome again after we've 'ad a bite to eat if thas' no trouble," he said, "an' if the boy don' mind eating with we."

"Oh, I can assure you that Paul will eat anywhere and anything but I don't want to impose upon you and your good wife."

"Pshaw, my missus can make a meal out of nothing, she'll be glad to see the little fella an' my maid will be thrilled with the kitten. I'll bring 'en back safe 'n sound, dussen worry, sir," and clasping the delighted boy by the hand they set off down the drive.

CHAPTER 3

JOHN Williams lived in a small cottage, on the outside of the village, which lay at the end of a lane that led through a small wood. His large family fitted into it with some difficulty and with them all present it gave the impression of bursting at the seams. His sons were all older than Paul but treated him in a most friendly manner and his daughter, Sarah-Jane, who was of the same age, was as enchanted with their guest as she was with his unexpected gift. John's wife, a large, permanently smiling woman, welcomed him wholeheartedly into her family and proceeded to find him a place at the table, then presented him with a large plateful of food and told him to eat up like a good boy, which feat he accomplished in a very little space of time. John invariably finished his meal with a smoke of his clay pipe so the children were sent outside to play. The boys soon found that Sarah-Jane and Paul preferred their own company and left them to play in the woods.

"Sarey-Jane 'ave 'e got a name for the kitten?" asked Paul shyly.

"Not yet," she replied, "What do 'e think I should call 'en?" and as a thought suddenly struck her she asked, "Is it a girl or a boy kitten?"

Perplexed the little boy furrowed his brow before replying, "I dunno," but after a pause he vouchsafed the information that, "Your father said it could be a mouser when it 'ave growed so why don' 'e call it that."

Sarah-Jane wrinkled her little nose and considered this for a while.

"All right," she confirmed, "Mouser 'tis."

Looking through the window at the two children Mrs. Williams turned to her husband and said, "Well, 'e might be a bit dark skinned but 'e's goin' be some 'ansome fellow when 'e's growed up for all that. 'E'll break a few hearts when 'e start t' get around. Jes' like his father I shouldn't wonder."

"The Captain and his missus are doing a good job with 'en," observed John, "so don' 'e worry 'e'll carry on like 'is father did. They'll keep 'n straight."

"Oh, I spec'late they'll try," said his wife before adding knowingly, "but I reckon they'll 'ave some job with 'en. Anything as good looking as that liddle chap is going t' be will be a sore temptation for most of the maids 'round 'ere."

"Jes' like I was," he chuckled and grabbing his wife around her ample waist planted a smacking kiss firmly on her mouth.

"Oh, guss on with 'e do," laughed his wife and disengaging herself pushed him through the door.

"Time to go young sir," he called to his young charge, still laughing at his abrupt dismissal by his wife. At his call the two children got up reluctantly from the grass and headed towards the door, the tired and sleepy kitten cradled gently in his daughter's arms.

"I'm goin' over t' the mine after I've dropped you off 'ome so I'll saddle up me 'ole mare an' take you up afore me," John announced, smiling brightly down at the little boy. For answer Paul beamed at him for the young lad thought that this was a most delightful idea; riding anything was an improvement on walking as far as he was concerned. He said his goodbyes to Sarah-Jane and Mouser, thanked Mrs. Williams very properly for his meal, and was delighted to be told that he was "Welcome anytime." Perched up before John he headed home, waving until they were out of sight of the mother and the daughter, who was waving just as furiously at the departing figures. For the rest of that day Sarah-Jane played with her gift, a soft smile never leaving her lips.

From that day on Paul became an expert at getting himself invited to their friendly house. Sometimes his father dropped him off on his way to town but mostly it was his mother who took him in her pony and trap. Penelope often stopped for a cup of tea with Mrs. Williams, glad not only of the company but to see her son accepted so readily into a local household. At other times she took Sarah-Jane up into the trap and they would go for a drive along the lanes and tracks around the village. The girl thought this was wonderful, but it was Paul's company she liked most of all and would have been quite prepared to walk through the worst of the moor just to have him as her companion. They had become fast friends from the first hour of their meeting and preferred each other's company to that of any other child in the village.

The lode that John Williams was so desperately seeking was finally found but it was of copper and not tin. However, being a good seam, and copper making a far better return than tin, the revenue from the lode soon began to pour in. In the first year alone the Trevarthens found that their original investment had increased twenty fold and Redvers decided that some of the income should be put aside for Paul's future education. His father wished him to attend his old school at Helston but Penelope had taken it upon herself to provide him with his first essay into schooling and being a well educated woman, was able to teach him quite competently. She also softened the strong dialect that he had used from the time he had learned to speak. Mixing with most of the servants and farm hands had meant that he had picked up their way of speaking quite naturally, but Penelope knew that it would not do for him to continue to speak with such a strong dialect, not if he was to take his father's place when the time came. She offered to teach Sarah-Jane along side her son for, as she explained to Mrs. Williams, she was sure that Paul would benefit from having a companion of his own age when at his lessons. The children revelled in each other's company but it was most obvious that Sarah-Jane, although a diligent and willing scholar, could not match Paul's prowess. He far outstripped her in every lesson and Penelope could not keep her pride from showing in her smiling face as she recounted to her husband the strides that her dear son had made each day.

"Penelope you are too blinded with admiration to see any fault in him. Admit it, for Paul has so bedazzled you with his winning ways," Redvers laughed.

"Not at all!" she rejoined swiftly, "and dear Sarah-Jane shows great promise but everything comes so easily to Paul and he is forever reading now. Indeed, I consider it one of his greatest pleasures and achievements. As to being blind to his faults, he will not practice at the piano as I would like him to do but if I sit with him he seems to enjoy it the more."

"No doubt because you are there to praise him the more for his efforts. He has a most wily way of capturing your attention," he informed her and laughed at her blushing denial.

However, when shown some of the work that his son produced, Redvers had to acknowledge the truth of his wife's claim for it was indeed of a most exceptional standard and far in advance of what could be expected of a child of his tender years. As their son's knowledge increased his height seemed to be attempting to keep pace with his educational attainments. He appeared to be forever growing out of his clothes but his energy and enthusiasm meant that by the time he required new clothes his old suits had needed a considerable amount of mending, as he cared not how torn and muddied he became as soon as the children were allowed to leave their lessons and play. On one memorable occasion Davy had to drive Hannah into the town in order to purchase a new dress for Sarah-Jane, for the one she was wearing had become badly torn when, at her companion's insistence, they had decided to play in the barn and the upturned points of a discarded [2]evil caught in her hem as she had attempted to follow Paul in leaping from the open barn door onto a hay cart left invitingly below them in the yard. When the two forlorn children presented themselves before Penelope her face whitened with shock with their muttered explanation. They exchanged surreptitious glances and Paul was promptly dispatched to his father's office to face retribution for his foolhardiness. Chastened by his telling off, he returned subdued to his mother who had great difficulty in keeping her hands at her sides at the sight of his sad little face. Although Paul never attempted to lead Sarah-Jane on such an exploit again he was not averse to leading her into the dirtiest, but to him most exciting, parts of the farm. His poor mother found herself so often having to explain to Mrs. Williams her daughter's bedraggled appearance, for upon her arrival at Trevu she had always looked such a picture of cleanliness, that she purchased a quantity of suitable clothing, and before ever Sarah-Jane sat down to her lessons she was dressed in her 'Trevu clothes' in order that she could present a pristine appearance when returned to her doting parents. Sarah-Jane followed in Paul's hasty footsteps with slavish adoration and although she did not enjoy to chase the pigs and attempt to sit on them as her playfellow was wont to do or to climb trees, or even to jump the little streams in the lower meadow -a feat she was unable to accomplish - she never refused to follow where he led. Penelope sighed and always ensured that Hannah had arranged for there to be plenty of hot water available on the children's return, so frequently did the pair arrive at the house covered in mud and dirt. Sarah-Jane thought it most pleasant to be placed in a hot, sweet smelling bath, and to be washed and petted before the warm fire, but from the yells and complaints emitting from the washroom next to the kitchen her erstwhile companion did not enjoy the experience quite so much. Penelope would smile and shake her head fondly as the two children were cleaned. After being reunited they would exchange mischievous grins and beguile Hannah into giving them some of her baking, for Paul was always adamant that he was starving and could not possibly wait for his tea.

In Paul's eighth year Sarah-Jane's brothers offered their services to Captain Trevarthen to teach his son to swim. At first Penelope wished to

---

[2] Evil: a four or five-pronged manure fork.

refuse their offer but Redvers took her on one side and patiently explained that living so close to the sea it would be an advantage to their son if he could swim, and he would no doubt enjoy the experience.

"John's boys will take great care of him Penelope, never fear," Redvers told her reassuringly. So one sunny afternoon Paul happily ran alongside his older companions, clambered down the cliff track and found himself on the beach of the little cove that bordered that part of the farm. At first he found the experience daunting but he was nothing if not brave, and although, frequently, he surfaced from beneath the waves coughing and spluttering he made promising headway. After a very few lessons he gained in confidence and was soon able to swim a considerable distance for his age. The oldest brother, William John, treated him most kindly and when he felt that Paul would be able to accomplish the swim led the way to the small outcrop of rocks that lay on one side of the small cove. Paul was consumed with pride when finally his feet found a purchase on the rocks and he heaved himself out of the water. It had been a hard and tiring accomplishment but he grinned at his friends with obvious delight. Soon a swim to the rocks became an established part of the swimming lessons. On their return to Trevu the boys were always provided with a tea and their merry laughter echoed around the old house. The exercise only served to increase Paul's appetite the more so he grew accordingly, and once again young Master Trevarthen would find himself in Mr. Murdoch's establishment for another fitting for a new set of clothes.

Although confident in his own surroundings it was most noticeable that he did not enjoy his visits to Penzance as most of his contemporaries would have done. Protected by the warmth surrounding him in his home his appearance in the town seemed always to be accompanied by whispers and he was ever aware of the looks of obvious disgust that were so pointedly directed at him. Paul was mindful of his father's advice not to be disheartened by the disapproval of the townsfolk, but his natural sensitivity could not be dismissed so easily. Taller by far than the local boys of his age he dreaded meeting with them in a group for they took boldness from being together and would shout insults at him quite happily. He did his best to ignore them but still found it an unsettling experience. Walking at his father's side on one such visit, they were heading up the street when he heard the all too familiar phrases being directed at him. Pointedly ignoring their cat calls and derisive shouts he continued on his way, but turned his head when he heard raised voices followed by a cry of pain. His eyes widened in surprise as he noticed that one of the group lay on his back in the road and that standing over him was the very boy that had been caught stealing the bread that day long ago. The previously raucous band were smitten into silence for the lad, although still thin and dressed in a tattered assortment of clothes, had attained a good height for his young years, but it was not just his stature that frightened them into obedience. The lad seemed incapable of not having his wishes obeyed for he had not only a menacing air, but acted as if he expected that his authority should be recognised. Glancing at Paul, he smiled briefly and Redvers son, with a wave of recognition, smiled back before turning to his father to tell him just who it was that he had caught sight of, but when they looked around the strange lad had disappeared. They saw only the chastened group of boys, with their former leader sitting in the mud of the road and rubbing his chin with obvious distress. Paul turned away from the spectacle quickly for he was unable to control the grin of satisfaction that spread across his face.

Meanwhile running for his home, a stolen pie tucked under his filthy shirt, the blue eyed protagonist, allowed himself a smile. He could not comprehend why he had taken a liking to the coloured boy for he was nothing to him, and in his young life he had never come across much which he wished to admire. But he liked to see the father and son together, for not having a father of his own he valued the sight of their obvious regard for each other. Putting such thoughts from his mind he arrived at the filthy cottage that served as his home and, running into the house, produced his stolen gift for his mother. This lady, dressed in clothes far superior to any than those she had ever provided for her son, looked at him unseeingly from within a gin sodden haze. It was apparent that her child had many of her features including the magnificent blue eyes that regarded him so blankly. She had no use for food, it was drink she craved, so she took the gift and threw it onto the dirt of the floor before catching hold of her son and beating him with a Malacca cane left behind by a previous admirer. He made not a sound and suffered his punishment manfully but when she had finished, retrieved his broken and dirtied pie and retreated to a corner of the room. Carefully brushing off the worst of the dirt, he sat himself against the wall and consumed the filthy meal like a scavenging wolf finally allowed to avail himself of the remnants of the carcass discarded by the others. His blue eyes, unaccountably full of admiration, followed his mother around the room as she staggered from side to side looking in cracks and holes in the walls to see if any bottles had been left unfound, for she had a habit of hiding her drink away from the many customers that frequented her establishment.

"Got any money Joey?" she shouted in frustration after a fruitless search.

"No, Ma," he replied quietly.

She launched herself upon him and for no other reason than for his lack of funds beat him again and finally threw him from her so that he fell in a heap on the floor.

"Well get some, ya bleddy fool!" she swore at him and kicked him in his ribs in disgust.

"'Ess, Ma," he answered and quickly scrambling to his feet headed from the house and began to run towards the town to see what largesse he could steal on his mother's behalf. His neighbour's eldest son, Edwin Nance, stopped him briefly and enquired after his mother but Joey told him that she was gin soaked and not in her right mind.

"S'pose Sally did that to 'e," he said putting a hand under Joey's chin, and raising his bruised and marked face to the light.

"She didden mean it, Edwin. She can't 'elp it fer 'tis the drink makin' 'er do it, an' I can't stop 'cos I got go fer get 'er some money," answered the boy with the merest hint of distress in his voice.

Edwin sighed and fished in his pocket for his few remaining coins. He counted out a small amount from his meagre hoard into his hand and passed them over to Joey with the information that Abel Hawken had a quantity of geneva that was being sold cheap for it was of poor quality, so the boy thanked him gratefully and sped on his way.

Clutching two precious bottles in his arms, one purchased the other procured, he returned to his home to receive yet another thrashing by way of thanks from his mother. After enjoying a drinking session she fell asleep. For most of the afternoon she lay in a drunken stupor on the floor but by nightfall she yawned and awoke. Scratching her head through her mass of tumbled brown curls, she stretched voluptuously, and after a while she noticed her son sitting patiently with his back to the wall and regarding her with a soft smile on his lips.

"You bin' there all af'noon, Joey," she asked, and yawned again.

"'Ess Ma," he answered with a smile, for he thought it his duty to stay and protect her whilst she slept.

She returned his smile and picking up the half empty bottle of gin took a long drink of it before wiping her hand across her mouth and dragging herself upright, swaying slightly as she stood on her feet.

"Come 'ere!" she ordered. Immediately he got to his feet and stood before her, even though he was unsure if she wished either to hit or hug him, but the night was upon them and it was time for her to earn her trade so she pulled him towards her roughly and hugged the thin, tortured body fiercely. "Yer some good boy, Joey," she breathed and felt him tremble in her arms in appreciation of her praise and grateful to be held in her embrace. She could not help but smile fondly to herself at his response. They stood wrapped together for a short while, then she pushed him from her and set about preparing herself for a walk through her haunts to see what profit the sight of her undoubted charms would elicit from the men frequenting the inns and taverns that abounded in that area of the town.

"Get out my sight if I d' come 'ome wi' a customer mind!" she warned him coldly, "They don' want no brats aroun' when they get back 'ere."

"'Ess Ma," he replied softly and returned to his seat by the wall and watched in admiration as she tidied herself in anticipation of her visit to the town. She combed the heavy mane of her hair; her brown curls tumbled over her shoulders and down her back. Catching up the shining coils she twisted them into a knot on the top of her head. She brushed the dirt from her dress, adjusted her clothing and with a final shake of her shoulders, tilted her chin and without a word of farewell, let herself out into the black of the night.

The boy sat unmoving and considered if he should go to see his friend Likky Skewes, or go over the road to the Nance's cottage to see if Mary Nance, Edwin's mother, had any food that she wished to share with him. She would have, he knew, for since his earliest memories Mary, even with her large family to feed, had always found a meal for him from somewhere no matter how straightened her own circumstances invariably were. It was a poor, abandoned area in which to be raised but he knew no other and he appreciated the quality of the few people who had attempted to help him in his struggles to survive. However, he would not move from his post, for in spite of his permanently gnawing hunger he preferred not to leave the cottage until he was sure his mother had returned safe home. She would be drunk as always and if alone would abuse him cruelly; but he cared not. So he waited patiently for his mother's return, knowing also that if she was accompanied by a man he would be thrown from the house and the door barred to him. As the night stretched on his eyes slowly closed and his head fell forward onto his chest as he snatched some sleep. Awakening from another doze he blinked owlishly for a moment before getting up and going to the fire that he had lit for his mother so that the house would be warm on her return.

Carefully he whittled at some wood with his knife and after enticing a response from the meagre fire he added some more broken pieces of timber to the smouldering pile. As the flames leapt up, the door crashed open suddenly. Turning hastily, the glow illuminated a tall, swarthy man, with heavy jowls and a squat fleshy nose standing in the doorway with his arm holding his mother's waist possessively. She blinked at her son, a drunken grin across her handsome face.

"Whas' 'e doin' 'ere?" the stranger asked in annoyance, his words slurred with the drink he had consumed, and he stared at the boy and then swore at him with a sudden, ferocious anger.

"'E's goin', e's goin', don' 'e worry 'bout 'e my 'ansome," promised his mother and completely disregarding her son she began to entice her lover towards the stairs that led to the house's solitary bedroom but before she could reach it the man had begun to pull savagely at her dishevelled garments and in spite of her laughing, drunken protests, he succeeded in exposing the top half of her body to his obvious pleasure. Joey, distressed as always at the sight of his mother disrobed and mauled in the arms of the various males that crossed the threshold, fled from the house and when he had finished running found himself down by the harbour, the shaking of his thin body proclaiming the inevitable result of the emotional strain to which he had just been subjected.

After some effort he controlled himself and turned his footsteps in the direction of the fishing boats to see if by chance he could find some fish that been missed when the catch had been unloaded. He searched to no avail but it kept him occupied for well he knew his mother had no desire to catch sight of him before late in the morning of the following day. Finding some nets piled against the wall he yawned and settled down to sleep before the fishermen found him.

He drifted into a dream in which he found himself in a large room with expensive furnishings and where tables groaned with vast quantities of food; roasted chickens, sides of beef, haunches of venison and golden crusted hams nestled beside sumptuous pies, tantalising puddings and bowls piled high with a myriad of fruits, filling plates and dishes all across the length and width of the table. This scene was entrancing enough, but it was the sight of his mother that thrilled him the most as she appeared to him bedecked in the finest silks and velvets, her hair beautifully dressed and coiled, sparkling jewels shining and flashing around her neck and in her ears, with her arms extended lovingly towards him, a laughing smile on her beautiful face. In his sleep he sighed and smiled with pleasure at the wondrous sight before him.

Young Master Trevarthen stood obediently still as his new suit was placed on his tall frame. Paul's visit to Mr. Murdoch's was not occasioned this time so much by his growth but by the fact that he would soon be sent off to his new school, so a quantity of clothes were required to accompany him. His father smiled proudly as the tailor helped him into his new coat and praised the tall, well built boy, for his stature and the way he set off his new suit. If only his other customers could make their clothes look so fine as Captain Trevarthen and his young son invariably did, sighed Mr. Murdoch.

"Not long to go now lad before you'll be peacocking around Helston with all your new friends," he said proudly as he brushed down his creation across the boy's strong young back.

"No sir," replied Paul quietly but had nothing further to add.

"Nervous eh?" announced Mr. Murdoch, "Don't worry lad you'll soon get used to it, you mark my words. Pity that Squire Tregurthen's boy, Arthur, left last term for he would have been a bit of company for you. Still clever lad like you will soon find your feet." He continued talking all the while, a most irritating habit that Paul had become used to over the years, but when they left the shop he flashed a smile of relief to his father as they strode away in the direction of the inn where they had stabled their horses. Redvers stopped to speak to various people as they made their way down the street but few if any of them acknowledged his son. Respectable matrons shooed their fair daughters past them quickly for the father's reputation alone was enough to account for the disgust on their disapproving faces. But it was the sight of Paul, handsome child that he undoubtedly was, that they had no wish for their impressionable young girls to linger over. It would not do for the likes of the Trevarthens to think themselves approved of by the strict society in which they lived but, even behind the disdainful faces, their minds could not completely lose sight of the knowledge that the young Paul Trevarthen would one day become the richest bachelor in the neighbourhood. Coming to terms with that fact was a sobering thought for many of Penzance's social circle and certainly those who had a brood of girls to establish comfortably. Still, the Trevarthen brat was only twelve; it would be a while yet before his parents would have to put their minds to finding him a wife.

At the stables their horses were brought out by two willing ostlers expecting - and receiving - good payment for their offices. Slowly father and son began to make their way out of Penzance heading homewards. Before they had left the town's environs a well dressed man in his mid thirties, with black hair tied in a ribbon, a full flowing moustache, flashing dark eyes and an almost permanent grin on his face, advanced towards them on a showy chestnut mare. His companion, a well built young lad, followed in his wake on an excitable grey. He was well attired but less richly, and unlike the older man his face was expressionless. His hat covered his glossy brown curls, also tied neatly in a ribbon at the nape of his neck, but under the brim large, blue eyes stared at Paul. The men and boys passed wordlessly by each other, Redvers only acknowledging by a nod of his head the ostentatious bow that the other man delivered him from his saddle. Paul puzzled to himself that, somewhere deep in his memory, he knew the fellow who rode the grey but he could not think from where, so kicked his horse on to keep up with his father. After a while Paul's natural curiosity got the better of him and he asked his father who the stranger was. Redvers, slowing his horse, told him that he answered to the name of Barnaby Rickard and that although he was born into a good family advised him sharply that his son was not to have dealings with the fellow if ever he should come across him in the town.

"Why ever not father?" asked his son, in surprise.

"He is a smuggler Paul, and 'twould not do to be seen in his company for those sorts of people bring trouble in their wake; they are forever being watched and pursued by the preventatives. It follows, therefore, if you should be seen talking to him, then you will be deemed to have dealings with him and afore we know it the whole of Trevu will be swarming with damned customs men," he muttered angrily.

"Have you ever had dealings with such men, Father?" asked Paul innocently.

Redvers threw back his head and laughed, "Good Lord no!" and then he regarded his son seriously, "and I have told the work force that I would prefer them not to make friends of smugglers either for 'tis not the smuggling, it is the fact of having the suspicion laid against you that causes so much trouble."

Paul considered this information seriously, before asking, "What about his son? He seemed known to me from somewhere but I can't place him."

"Rickard has no son to my knowledge but I must admit I paid little attention to the lad. Perhaps you have seen him around the town, Paul? Whoever he is 'tis a pity he can do no better for himself than to go about with that man," he said severely and considering the conversation at an end he told Paul that they had best head for home for he did not wish to be late to sit down to dine, for it was a circumstance that always annoyed him.

"Another drink, Barney?" asked Abel Hawken gratefully. He had managed to stock his cellar again; his casks had been running low and he was prepared to allow Rickard as many glasses of brandy as he wished to consume. Unusually for a smuggler Rickard had a fair way of doing business and, although he undoubtedly made himself a good profit from his dealings, he always charged a reasonable price for the goods he had delivered and he never failed to supply drink of superior quality than any Hawken had been able to purchase before. For that fact alone he had cause to be thankful. The smuggler's method of working was to ensure that the goods were safely stored. Methodically he visited each inn and house that wished to purchase from his well hidden, illicit store, took their order, arranged a night for their purchases to be delivered and then returned at a later time to collect his money. In the event that anyone would be foolish enough not to pay, reference was made to Matthew Tregaro's recent demise at the hands of some unknown assassin, and with a swift look at Rickard's companion's impassive face, the appropriate payment would be immediately delivered into the smiling smuggler's outstretched hand.

Barnaby Rickard shook his head but smilingly declined the offer. He turned to his companion and catching his eye signalled to him that it was time to leave, so waving farewell to the appreciative landlord he got up from his seat by the fire and sauntered from the inn, closely followed by the gangling youth who seemed permanently at his side, almost like a shadow.

They returned to the stables and collected their horses and slowly made their way out of the town without a word being exchanged. Stopping once along the road to Gulval, to ensure that they were not being followed, they arrived at the little cottage that Rickard permanently rented and where he resided when in the county. After unsaddling their horses and seeing to the needs of their beasts they let themselves into the house and Barnaby took a taper to the fire and lit the candles. He looked up into the inscrutable face of the youth at his side and smiled again. A woman's voice from upstairs called out, "Barney?" softly. He went to the bottom of the stairs and called up to his wife that all was well before he told her to rest easy for they could get their own supper. Quietly, they took bowls from the dresser and helped themselves to the thick stew that was cooking slowly at the side of the fire. When their meal was finished Barney took down a bottle of brandy from the mantelpiece, and poured a liberal amount into two glasses and they seated themselves on either side of the fire and appreciatively consumed their drinks.

Barney smiled reflectively at the enigmatic face of the youth who sat and stared into the flames so rigidly. Thinking back it was difficult to say who had found the other first. They had come into contact when the boy had tried to rob him, but his strange appearance had drawn Rickard's eye to him long before then. Emaciated, barefoot, dressed in tatters, filthy brown hair cropped untidily but with, intriguingly, a face so inscrutable it was impossible to read the thoughts behind it. It was soon apparent that he was of limited physical strength as was proved when he commenced his attempt to steal from Rickard. The smuggler, correctly assuming that the boy would wish to rob him because he was wearing such fine attire, had been ready for the essay and had no trouble in overpowering the lad, but feeling the bones hidden beneath the torn and filthy shirt he was filled with compassion for the youngster. Having no wish to see the impoverished lad hurt further, he tied the struggling boy's hands together firmly and smiled into the blank face with its blue eyes wide open with shock and fear, and threw him up before him on his horse, before transporting the living bundle to his home. On arrival Barney's wife, a homely woman much disturbed by the boy's poor appearance, presented him with a bowl of hot soup and some bread - to the tattered wretch's obvious amazement for his face lost its blank look completely. At first he seemed incapable of movement, merely holding his meal in shaking hands, but of a sudden he took himself off to a dark corner and consumed the meal rapidly and noisily. Barney and his wife exchanged worried glances for he seemed to have the habits of an animal, but when Mrs. Rickard stood by the tureen and extended her hand towards the boy, enquiring if he could eat some more he got up immediately and passed her the bowl. With another piece of bread and the steaming bowl clutched in his claw like hands, he raised his shocked blue eyes to her face and was heard to mutter a swift word of thanks before retreating once more to his corner.

From then on the abundance of food that was given to the poor unfortunate on a daily basis was all that was needed to keep him under their roof, but it had taken them a long time to gain the boy's confidence. Phoebe, Barney's wife, took on the task of improving the lad's appearance. Strangely, for such a filthy looking individual he seemed to appreciate being clean, and it was most notable that within a very short space of time he undertook the responsibility of washing himself and combing his own, now neatly trimmed and clean hair. His table manners improved due to Mrs. Rickard's insistence that his meal was placed on the table in a set place. Although, in the beginning he still grabbed his plate or bowl before heading for his corner, they merely installed a small cupboard in his bolt hole so he no longer had the use of it. Perplexed, he stood to eat for a week, regarding them both warily, but gradually he inched closer to the table and when, one evening, he actually sat with them they could not forego to exchange congratulatory smiles. Both of the Rickards, were most fastidious with their eating habits and it was soon apparent and appreciated that after watching them at their meal he began to copy their actions.

Barney had made enquiries around the town about his acquisition and had discovered his name. Joseph, or more usually Joey Bolitho, but when he was told the details of the lad's past life a grim smile had crossed his face for, unofficially, he was thought to have committed a murder; and only then did Rickard consider that providence had played a part in their meeting that night, no matter how strange the circumstances. The smuggler had searched high and low for an accomplice to guard him in his activities, for he could not be forever aware and had need of someone to watch out for him; for in his profession he played a most dangerous game. He had noted from first sight how the boy's face registered almost nothing but that his eyes were everywhere and missed not a thing. With someone of this demeanour at the smuggler's back he could go abroad safe in the knowledge that the youth would be his eyes and would act as a deterrent to anyone foolish enough to go against his master; for it was understood by all who knew of Joey's former life that he had indeed killed his mother's lover to avenge her death at that man's hands and were it not for his neighbours maintaining his alibi he would have been hanged for it.

Until meeting Barney, the waif had lived a most precarious existence for in his impoverished circle there were few enough of these friends who could help him. Of any that did, Barney discovered, Joey would share what little he had managed to procure, and that was little enough, for he had always to scavenge food and steal whatever he could find, wherever he could find it. Under Barney's care Bolitho found himself allowed to eat as much as he liked and for the first time in his life he had been given his own clothes to wear. Tall for his age he began to put on weight and grew rapidly, and, slowly and cautiously, began to treat the smuggler with a degree of respect that in his brief life he had never offered to any other man. The Rickard's smiled proudly at the change they had wrought in the youth but the transformation had not been completely successful for since that first night when the poor, emaciated boy had been brought into the household there had been only the one thing that they could not get Joey to do. Of his former life he maintained a complete and stony silence, and neither would he listen if either of them made mention of his mother for he would immediately place his hands over his ears and turn his back on them. As he had grown older they had come to a tacit understanding, and had stopped asking him any more questions about that time for it was apparent to them both that behind that expressionless face was a pain of such intensity that the boy's only recourse was to bury his feelings deep within himself.

Patiently Barney waited for Joey to adapt to his new surroundings and life but he made such progress that, within a year of their first encounter, the same lad, now almost unrecognisable, was entrusted to be his master's guardian and set forth to accompany him about his business. Barney, a tall man himself, considered ruefully that in a very short time he was to be dwarfed by a giant when he made his progress around the local inns and towns! Rickard's foresight had been justified for Bolitho's appearance had the desired effect upon his associates. Although still little more than a boy, the cold eyed, impassive youth's reputation had gone before him and combined with his natural attitude of authority, Barnaby Rickard soon discovered that his methods of working were no longer queried by the hot headed lads that so often made up the disparate groups of smugglers that he used.

Dismissing his memories, Barney sighed and tossed off the remains of his brandy before getting up and returning to sit at the table where, reaching into his capacious pockets, he removed a quantity of leather purses. He emptied them and after counting out all of the money they contained, he placed the greater part into the largest of the bags before passing over a more than fair share to his accomplice and received a quietly spoken word of thanks in reply, followed by a glimpse of his companion's rarely seen smile.

"Don't give it all away, this time Joey, no matter how sorry you do feel for the widow Tregaro. She got a sister married to a rich farmer over to Sennen so she'll see she all right, understand me boy?" Barney told him authoritatively, and fixed him with a firm stare, for he had heard the tales of the young woman's surprise at finding a purse of money on her doorstep when she answered the knock of an unseen caller. The boy blushed quickly and then nodded his head before he raised his arresting blue eyes to his master's face.

"Didden like think she was lef' t' manage all alone," he explained quietly and then added knowingly, "Thas' 'ard t' do."

"I know 'tis Joey and I know that you above anybody else would understand that. However, she's young, with no children. There's a comfortable farmer over to St. Just got his eyes on she tho' so there's no need for you to take her troubles on your back. You did what I asked you to do, lad, and well I know, if you do not, that if you hadn't we'd both be swinging from a gibbet by now for Tregaro would have told all to the Excise men, for he was ever a detestable and scheming fellow. I appreciate what you did Joey but 'tis no good for you be giving away all you own to every widow and orphan that come your way or else you'll end up wearing the same sorts of rags you had on when I found you," he said severely, before adding in an even stronger tone, "You hear me boy?"

"'Ess Barney, I 'ear 'e!" he replied, and a shamefaced look swiftly crossed his face.

"Good lad!" said Barney relieved at his response, and grinned at him. Stretching and yawning, he patted Joey on his shoulder and advised him to get to his slumbers; they had to be away early in the morning for they were bound for France again. So Joey nodded then stood up and damped down the fire before following his master up the stairs to his own sparse but adequately furnished room. When he got there he took great pains to hide his money away carefully, for in spite of Barney's kind and fair treatment of him older habits than the ones he had picked up from the smuggler and his wife still remained with him.

As he climbed into his bed he resolved to do as Barney had told him but, nonetheless on the morrow, when he got to the harbour, he determined that he would search out Edwin and send him home with some coins for Mary and the family.

He yawned, for he was most tired; it had been a long day for they had visited many inns and houses since they had left the house that morning. Before he fell asleep he recalled with a pang of regret how young Paul Trevarthen had failed to acknowledge him as they passed each other on the road. But then, he mused, sleepily, it would always be easy to identify the Trevarthen boy but the same could not be applied to him, and a sad smile curled his lips, for now he realised that, with the all care and attention that had been lavished upon him since he had joined Barnaby Rickard's household, even his poor, dear mother would have failed to recognise him. As he brought his mother to mind, slowly and silently in the solitude of his own room, he gave vent to the feelings that he kept forever hidden from the world and tears poured from his eyes until the protective arms of Morpheus dragged him away from the nightmare of his former life.

CHAPTER 4

THE dark boy stared forlornly out of the window, down which the rain trickled with cascading rivulets of water and sighed. Nothing happened to brighten the long days of school for him and the weather only helped to increase his sense of loneliness.

He had expected to like school as he had enjoyed his lessons with his mother and he continued to study avariciously. Undoubtedly the cleverest pupil in the school this feat had not endeared him to his fellow classmates. The majority of them hated him for he was not like them; his intellectual abilities highlighted their own ignorance but his colour filled them with repugnance. The teachers sided with the pupils and together they formed a veritable army against whom he had continuously to battle. By having a different colour skin he had become the object of much derision amongst his fellows and the teachers would always find an excuse to beat him. They felt offended by his ability for, they reasoned jealously, why should this coffee coloured by-blow prove the locals boys to be so lacking in educational attainment?

His parents visited regularly but the joy of seeing them again and hearing of his home and his old playmates was soon overshadowed when they eventually left and abandoned him in this dark, forbidding place, leaving him awaiting their next visit or, even better, the start of the holidays. Perhaps he should have told them how miserable his experiences of school were but knowing that they thought they were doing their best for him and were so proud of the scholarly work he produced, he took great pains never to let them know of his unhappiness. Life at school left him depressed and morose so he studied harder than ever, for in his distress it was the knowledge and life that lay within the covers of the books he read that allowed him to escape from the forbidding prison in which he found himself.

The sound of a door banging at the end of the corridor broke into his thoughts, and he turned quickly to see James Hoskin, a classmate, who like Paul was the object of much bullying, come running down the passage hotly pursued by three older boys. Immediately Paul's sympathy was aroused for although the boy had never attempted friendship with him, for fear of retaliation from the other pupils, he had never treated Trevarthen as the others had done.

"We'll have you, you whelp," called out the largest bully.

As Hoskin rushed past Paul he brushed his sleeve and fleetingly turned his tearstained, frightened face towards him. On a sudden impulse Trevarthen stepped into the middle of the corridor effectively blocking their path.

"Leave him alone," he said defiantly, as Hoskin's pursuers came to a halt in front of him.

"Ha! The little whelp has got himself a champion. Master Mulatto, no less!" laughed Dick Bray, the oldest and the ringleader, for as the Headmaster's nephew he felt emboldened to do as he pleased about the school. With a movement of his head he motioned Trevarthen to move out of his way, but the request was denied for the dark lad merely folded his arms and stood four square to them.

"Leave him alone," he repeated in a calm voice.
"Who's going to stop us?"
"I am," said Paul quietly.

The boys looked at one another and laughed gleefully; a chance to maul the blackamoor in such a deserted place was not an opportunity that came their way often enough. Of course, they had managed to attack him periodically throughout his school life but they had had to be circumspect about it. The masters turned a blind eye to most of the beatings that came Paul's way from the other pupils but they had never been allowed to continue them for long, for the boy's father was rich, and if he took his son away and made a complaint, various local families might reconsider sending their sons to their establishment. Anyway, reasoned the bullies, the boy was poor sport for he rarely made attempts to defend himself. So believing that his reticence to fight had not altered and that he was merely exhibiting some incautious bravado they surveyed the corridor to establish that no masters were present. Judging themselves to be free from restraint they pitched in upon Trevarthen with reckless abandon but soon discovered that they had erred seriously, for the seemingly unthreatening giant appeared to have no wish to be mauled by them. Paul had never been known to defend himself overmuch, the odd half-hearted punch was all that he had ever thrown in all the time that they had been his tormentors at school, but this was the day when they discovered that Trevarthen could deliver a punch, indeed a surprisingly good one. He could also wrestle, and he threw them all with consummate ease. In a very little time all three boys were on the floor, hurting in various places; one was suffering a copious nosebleed. However, Paul was still standing, a little breathless and his knuckles were bruised, but that seemed to be his only injury and what was the most worrying to them was the impression that he appeared to be quite content to continue the altercation should they wish it.

Dick Bray, he of the bleeding nose, muttered threateningly at his conqueror; "Just you wait, you filthy swine you, you'll pay for this. I'll bet when he hears about the way you set upon us my uncle will thrash you within an inch of your miserable little life." They picked themselves up and retreated, in no very good order, to find Mr. Clymo and to regale him with the tale of their woes.

Trevarthen watched dispassionately as they headed back the way they had come, albeit in a less confident manner, looking fearfully over their shoulders at him in case their conqueror should decide to pursue them. Hearing a noise behind him Paul turned and noted the frightened face of James Hoskin peering at him from around the edge of a door.

"You'd . . . you'd better run for it. Clymo will truly thrash you for this," he told Paul worriedly.

"Let him," returned his saviour, "It won't be for the first time. He has always managed to find some excuse to punish me whether I deserved it or no. At least now I've given him good cause," and he gave a hollow laugh before asking the boy why they were chasing him.

"Oh - they just enjoy picking on me. I'm small and . . . not very strong, so they feel they can abuse me whenever they want. Once they know that you are different they make your life a misery," sighed James.

Trevarthen grinned, showing his white, even teeth.

"Don't have to tell me that Hoskin. They've been doing that to me since the day I came through these doors."

"Don't you care?" asked James, not without a certain amount of envy.

"Not any more," said Paul evenly and grinned, "they lose by it, not me. Oh, I agree I have to put up with the beatings but I've got a thick skin as well as a dark one," and he grinned again. They turned to walk along the corridor for they both knew that the bell was soon to be rung for afternoon lessons. Paul continued, "I've been here for four years, and am soon to leave for I have no wish to attend University as father wishes me to return to our farm. In spite of my treatment here I have obtained a good education whilst half of those bullies cannot even write their own names properly, even though the masters have tried, again and again, to beat some learning into them." Staring into the far distance, he snorted in disgust and added, "I have met people like them all my life. Forever making fun of the dark skinned boy because he is different. Well, Hoskin, I believe that being different is a thing of quality for it cuts one out from the dross. My father told me that I am worth knowing for who I am, not what I look like."

James Hoskin considered this for a moment, and then said, "That was well spoken Trevarthen, but they'll do you down for all of your fine words."

"Pooh," scoffed his companion, "Let them try." He made to turn away but of a sudden turned back to stand in front of Hoskin and tentatively held out his hand, in return the boy grinned broadly and shook his hand delightedly. So in great companionship they made their way down the corridor.

It was during the next lesson that Paul was called to the headmaster's study. As he got up to leave he was aware of Dick Bray's malicious leer but he calmly ignored it and made his way from the room, oblivious to the low murmur that buzzed around him. He had expected to be savagely beaten for Mr. Clymo had taken an instant dislike to Trevarthen on sight, but that day the headmaster had indulged his taste for brandy and this only added fuel to his temper. He beat Paul so badly that he drew blood, but almost to the end his victim made no sound. When he had finished his savagery he dismissed him with a venomous grin. Unable to return to his lesson, it was some time later when James Hoskin found him leaning against the wall of the school yard, his face contorted in agony. Gently placing Paul's arm around his neck he led him to the washhouse and with much care sponged away most of the blood that was even then causing the shirt to stick to his back, hoping his actions would make Trevarthen's sufferings easier.

Paul gave him a wan smile, before gasping, "Thanks Hoskin. I tried not to give in to the great bully but I had to howl in the end for I thought I could bear no more. God but he has flayed me this time!" He drew a deep breath, pulled down his shirt and struggled painfully into his coat before standing upright. "Well, we had better get to our lessons I suppose unless we want to bring another a thrashing down on both of our heads, or more properly our backs." and he managed to achieve a small, wavering grin.

Slowly they moved back across the courtyard, with Paul gratefully leaning on James's shoulder, until they reached the classroom. Mr. Armitage, the Latin teacher, raised an eyebrow at their late entrance, but he had heard of

Mr. Clymo's boast that under that dark skin Trevarthen's blood flowed red because he had seen the colour of it. He had been shocked by his headmaster's laughter for it was not in the Latin teacher's nature to wish to inflict such punishment on his fellow man, so he merely directed the boys to their places and continued on with the lesson. Surveying the group of pupils, most of whom had precious little understanding of the work in front of them, he knew there was one amongst them who was an outstanding scholar and so he found himself staring at Trevarthen, wondering how the lad could continue to go through his school life with the almost relentless mistreatment that he received from the pupils and teachers alike. Fellows from rich families usually had a good time at school for the others would wish to make friends with them, but Trevarthen's dark skin had set him apart and his natural friendliness had been muted and hidden. Withdrawing into his school work his exceptional abilities were soon evident for all to see, and as the years progressed he became far more able than any of his teachers, including himself, he had to admit with a rueful smile. He had even suggested to Captain Trevarthen that his son should think of going to university but the boy's father had shaken his head and stated that he expected his son to return to the farm for it was no wish of his that Paul should leave his home. In vain did the Latin teacher point out to him the benefits of a university education - but to no avail; when he broached the subject with the boy himself he met with an even more determined attitude and for reason the boy said he missed his family and would not be swayed by any of his arguments.

Looking up from his book his teacher watched Trevarthen working easily at the translation he had been set but was surprised to see that he appeared to be frowning. Knowing Trevarthen's expertise he could not believe that the piece set would be giving a scholar of his abilities any problems, when before his horrified gaze Paul's head slumped forward and he slowly slid from his chair to the ground and remained there in a heap on the floor.

"Ol' Master Mulatto has fainted sir!" sneered Edward Hendy who was sitting in the seat next to Paul and let out a loud guffaw which the rest of the class, with the exception of James Hoskin, joined in and turned into a hearty chorus of laughter.

"Stop that at once," shouted Armitage and slashed the nearest boy across the face with his cane.

A surprised silence fell in the previously raucous classroom, for Armitage was probably the only teacher in the whole school who would never seek recourse to the cane for punishment. Into the sudden stillness a timid knock was heard on the door.

"Come in," bawled Armitage as he strode across the room to where the boy lay collapsed on the floor.

One of the junior masters entered and searching the room found Armitage trying to lift Trevarthen back into his chair. He immediately crossed the room towards him and completely ignoring the master's struggles with his pupil calmly repeated his message.

"Excuse me sir, but Trevarthen's father has called for him. Trevarthen is to pack his things immediately and return home. His mother has been taken ill and it is thought that he should be there," he said and then he gave an embarrassed cough and added, "Not expected to last if you know what I mean sir. Mr. Clymo wants him to attend them in his study at once."

It was only at this moment that he noticed that Mr. Armitage was trying to hold the boy up in his chair, and realising his predicament, suddenly bethought himself of a useful suggestion. Tapping the master on his shoulder he announced that he would take himself off to get some water to throw over the boy, adding helpfully: "Tough sort these darkies, don't you know," and so saying disappeared out of the room before Mr. Armitage had a chance to call him to task over his thoughtless words. Returning a few moments later with a jug of water, he was about to throw it over Paul's head when it was wrenched out of his hand by the infuriated teacher.

"Fool!" he muttered and proceeded to put the jug to Trevarthen's lips. "Paul, here lad," he said gently, "Come, try to drink some of this."

Taking out his handkerchief, he dipped it into the jug and proceeded to wipe Paul's face. Slowly the youth became aware of his surroundings and he opened his eyes but it was a moment before they lost their dazed look.

"I . . . Your pardon, sir, . . . I . . . ," Paul stammered and then gave a low groan.

"Clymo wants to see you in his study, lad. I'll get someone to help you to walk there for you cannot manage unaided," he told him solicitously.

Paul raised a weary eyebrow and bravely tried to grin, "Another beating sir?" he queried and noted that the master blushed and lowered his gaze.

"I think it is bad news from home for your father has come for you," said the master, unable to face the youth's disquieted expression.

"Mother?" asked Paul anxiously, and in spite of his injuries he struggled to his feet although he had to make use of Armitage's shoulder to steady himself.

"I . . . I think so lad. Best to get along now," he said, in a sympathetic tone, and then turned and searched the room before calling out, "Hoskin, here, Hoskin! Help Trevarthen to Mr. Clymo's study," and helped him take Paul to the door where he added vindictively, "and if Captain Trevarthen wants to know why his lad's in such a bad way - tell him the truth, by God!"

Luckily for Paul, his father had not travelled by horseback but had arrived in his carriage. Redvers did not know that there was no possibility of his son returning to his home by any other means, he had merely brought the carriage because it would give him a chance to talk to him before he was to see his mother. Penelope had been taken ill so suddenly that his first thought was to bring her beloved son to her side.

Dr. Simcott had informed him that he must face the likelihood that his wife was going to die for she was very weak and did not have a strong constitution. The thought that she should pass away without sight of her beloved Paul cut at his soul. It was the least he could do to have their son brought to her bedside. Torn between staying at her side and sending a servant to collect his son he determined to tell him the sad news himself so he had the carriage put to and set forth for Helston immediately, leaving his wife sleeping peacefully.

On entering the headmaster's study, at first he did not realise how sheepish Mr. Clymo looked for his only concern was to see his son. When

Paul staggered into the room supported by a frightened looking lad the colour drained from Redvers face for he was in very little doubt that his son had been the recipient of a vicious beating. Upon enquiry, the headmaster looked worried, and began to mumble that Trevarthen had been the instigator of a fight and that he had beaten three helpless boys severely. The look of disgust that settled on the father's face and the contempt with which he had heard the tale made Mr. Clymo's voice take on a whining note for it was obvious that, knowing his son, Captain Trevarthen believed not a word of his explanation. With stony calm Redvers crossed to his son's side and carefully removed his coat, and then with Hoskin's help, lifted the back of his son's bloodstained shirt. The sight that met his eyes appalled him for Paul's back was one mass of red wheals. The anger that was rising in him would have been the same for any man who had suffered such a beating let alone for a sixteen year old boy. Picking up Clymo's bloodied cane he turned in cold anger on the headmaster and before he had the wit to run from the room proceeded to beat him so soundly that the man thought his last moment had come.

"And if you would wish to lay this matter before a magistrate I could not give a damn!" shouted the Captain when he had finished, throwing the cane at the moaning, huddled heap in the corner. He turned and gently placing Paul's arm around his neck and with the assistance of the lad, Hoskin, they slowly helped his son to the carriage.

"I'll pack up his bags for him and see them sent on to you sir, and I am most sorry for your troubles sir," Hoskin told Redvers sincerely before turning to his friend and adding, "Thanks Paul for all you kindness to me and for what you have suffered today on my account."

Paul smiled gently, and holding out his hand they gave each other a brief handshake before wishing each other farewell.

When his father asked for an explanation he was told of the fight that his son had with the boys and upon further enquiry Paul related some of the horrors he had experienced during his time at school. His father shook his head sadly, and clasping his son's hand expressed the desire that he had been told before of what Paul's life had been like for he would have been taken away immediately. His son assured him it was of no importance and merely smiled resolutely at his father. During the journey home the rocking and jolting of the coach tried Paul severely but he determined to brave it out for his father's sake, not wishing to add more distress to the sadness that was clouding the Captain's eyes.

"We must hope for the best Paul," Redvers told him bravely although his voice wavered as he added, "but the Doctor does not give us much hope."

"Mother has great strength, Father," said Paul calmly. In some cruel way the pain helped him not to give in to his own emotions for the thought of losing his mother was ripping the heart out of his body.

Rain was falling softly by the time they arrived at Trevu. Davy ran from the stables to let down the steps but Redvers was before him and turned to help his son, but Paul assured him that he could manage himself. Nevertheless, he was glad of his arm to lead him into Trevu. In the hallway they were met by the Doctor with a grave expression on his face.

"'Twill not be long, Captain Trevarthen, sir, I'm sorry to say," he said in answer to Trevarthen's questioning look and shook his head sadly. Redvers bowed his head in despair, then bethought himself of Paul so turned to his son and holding his arm helped him up the stairs.

"She's bin' askin' for you both sir," called a grim faced Hannah softly from the landing.

When they arrived in the bedroom it was obvious to both of them that Penelope had not much time remaining. She rallied on seeing them, and caressed Paul's sad face, asking to see his smile in her weak voice. He grinned at her in adoration and she sighed with pleasure at the sight of him and told him what a handsome son she had before turning to Redvers with a smile. Her voice was the merest thread as she told them how much she loved them, called Paul her most special treasure, thanked her husband for his love and devotion and asked that they should kiss her goodbye, before lapsing into a coma. They sat beside her bed each holding a hand and waited out the hours of her last moments without saying a word until, just before midnight, she gave a gentle sigh and without seeming to feel any distress, died.

In grief and pain Paul collapsed and Doctor Simcott, still in attendance, treated his physical hurts with a salve and Hannah helped him to his bed. Redvers stayed alone with his wife for a long while until the warmth slowly left the hand he was holding so desperately. Finally, he begged her forgiveness, whispered his goodbyes, before kissing her cheek then, sadly, left the room.

Hannah came in to see Paul before retiring herself. He was lying on his side so as not to put any pressure on his back and on coming up to the big bed she noticed that his eyes were open. Resolutely, she smiled into his face, and smoothed back his hair which had fallen across his sweating brow.

"Try an' sleep, Master Paul. You'll feel better in the mornin'. Don't 'e worry now. No more goin' back to that 'ell 'ole for 'e. The mistress would have been heartbroken if she 'ad known that was 'ow they treated 'e, the poor liddle soul," she said, and all the while her tears were falling down over her round, ruddy cheeks to dash unhindered down the front of her dress.

"Father?" gasped Paul, "How's Father?"

"Taken it pretty bad, sir, pretty bad. I left 'en in the back parlour. Didden seem like 'e wanted to talk much. Jes' sat there starin' at the fire. Now," she added trying to sound brighter, "come on, Master Paul, you get some sleep."

"Yes Hannah, yes, of course," and he tried to smile reassuringly at her.

Hannah left the room but after a short while Paul painfully dragged himself to his feet, and with no small difficulty headed, for the door. Quietly he crept downstairs and made his way towards the small back parlour. At all other times this was always his favourite room, for his mother had loved it so because it faced south and the sun streamed into it all day long. They had often been alone together in that room and he remembered fondly how he had played with his toys, or read his books, or learned his lessons at her knee. It seemed to him that all the most treasured moments of his life with his mother were bound up in that one room.

Gently pushing upon the heavy oak door he saw his father, slumped in the chair by the fire. Crossing the room slowly he bent painfully and placed a comforting arm around his father's neck. At first Redvers seemed unaware of him for he was staring blankly at the fire, but then he turned and looked him full in the face and his son's heart was wrenched by the unbearable sadness etched on his face.

Stretching out his hand he grasped his father's hand in his own and squeezed it gently. Redvers stared, saying nothing, remembering a morning when that same hand - much smaller then - had fastened upon his finger and how its owner had fastened upon his heart. He recalled how the entry of that small babe into the lives of the disillusioned couple had turned them both back towards each other again. Their rekindled love was infinitely more precious than anything they had had before. Redvers had fondly imagined that he and Penelope would still be sitting in that small parlour twenty years hence and now in the space of two days, the dream was gone, dead like the gentle woman whose love had perpetrated it.

He had a duty to comfort the boy; put his own loss to one side and give all his attention to his son. Tears were slowly trickling from Paul's sad eyes as Redvers leaned forward to console him but found his words choked by the convulsive sobs that racked his own body.

"Paul! Oh Paul! How am I to go on without my precious love?" he found himself crying, "Without my dearest dear."

The boy knelt and put his arms around his father's shaking body and attempted to console him but his voice failed and he gave himself up to his own heartbroken sobs.

Hannah, disturbed by the creak of the stairs as Paul descended them, softly opened the door and found father and son locked in an embrace of mutual despair. Quietly, she closed the door, and returned to her room, but on passing the bedchamber in which the dead woman lay she entered it slowly and went to stare again upon the peaceful, gentle face. Penelope lay with her soft blonde hair tumbled about her, looking as if she was sleeping, her lips locked in her usual serene smile, and Hannah felt that she had only to speak and that the Mistress would open those twinkling grey eyes of hers and start refreshed upon another day.

"Don' 'e worry, Mrs. Trevarthen - my liddle pretty - I'll be there for 'en, for 'en both," she whispered sadly and with a final caress of the golden tresses she turned back the way she had come and left the room.

It was only to be expected that there would be a large gathering at the funeral for the Trevarthens were a well known local family.

"A good woman gone before her time," murmured the old biddies at the graveside, who had long ago whispered behind their hands at the goings on at the big house, but they mourned her passing just the same.

At the church gate Redvers and Paul stood side by side thanking the mourners for attending. For Paul, to be the recipient of pitiful glances and kind words from people who had previously not a kind look or a good word for him was a touching irony. "Did you have to die, Mother," he thought sadly, "to make me welcome here." He hastily removed the thought from his mind, for the people were genuine in their grief - some were even crying. He glanced at his father standing tall and rigid at his side, shaking hands and muttering his thanks mechanically to each individual and could not imagine how they were going to continue, either of them, without Penelope's love to surround and protect them; but he knew that they would have no choice in the matter. Fate had decreed in her cruel way that they must continue without her.

"I am so very sorry, Paul, for your loss" said a small voice from below his chin.

He looked down to see Sarah-Jane's crestfallen face. Tears were sparkling in her gentle green eyes.

"Why, Sarah-Jane, how kind of you to come," he said and for the first time that day achieved a small smile.

"Father and Mother and the boys are all here," she said, "for we wished to attend for she was such a lovely woman, Paul, truly lovely," and with a final squeeze of his hand she moved quickly away, dabbing at her eyes with her handkerchief. His eyes followed her as she moved off and then, recalled to his duty, turned to face another of the mourners that headed the long line that led from the churchyard.

When Redvers and his son returned to the empty house with their servants they found themselves at a loss as to what to do. Hannah taking control, whisked them into the back parlour, where a large fire was burning, and told them their lunch would be on the table in the dining room in no time at all but if they preferred she could make up the small table in the parlour.

"Whatever is the easiest for you, Hannah," replied Redvers, "we will not require much and do not want to put you to any trouble."

"C'mon now sir, no trouble at all," vouchsafed Hannah. "I'll bring it in 'ere, for 'twould be a shame to leave that lovely fire."

They seated themselves at the small table, the one with Penelope's precious vase set in the middle. It sparkled as it caught the sun streaming from the large windows and Paul found himself staring at it remembering the accident with his bow and arrow that had destroyed its predecessor. It stood forlorn and empty, for no one had placed flowers in it since his mother had died, and her son felt as forsaken as the vase.

CHAPTER 5

A WEEK later Redvers received a letter from the board of governors of the school, informing him that no action was to be taken against him in the matter of Mr. Clymo. It had been decided that the headmaster should give up his post and it had been offered to Mr. Armitage who would be writing to Paul at a later date. The governors concluded their letter with condolences on the loss of his wife and the sincere hope that Captain Trevarthen would have no wish to take the matter of his son's punishment further now that the man who had inflicted it was no longer in authority at the school. Redvers sniffed in derision and tossed the letter to Paul.

"Well, that damned man can inflict his perverted cruelty on no other man's son at least," sneered Redvers.

"Armitage is a fair man," said Paul thoughtfully, after reading the contents, "and methinks he will not abuse his position."

Paul had received a letter himself from James Hoskin offering his sympathy and again thanking him for defending him against Bray and the other bullies and hoping that he was recovering from the beating inflicted upon him by the headmaster.

Paul was indeed recovering, and as the weeks passed, his natural exuberance began to show itself again. He was young and healthy and found, not without some degree of shame, that he was adjusting to the loss of his mother and that the first oppressive pain of her death was gradually receding. He felt guilty that he could wake up and be glad to greet the new day. The youth considered that he should have no joy in life now that the woman who had taken such care of him and who had had such pride in him was no longer there, but in a strange way he felt that Penelope's presence was still surrounding him. Going into Penzance on his own to purchase some books, he had found that people no longer seemed to stare at him in the same way. Now, when they looked at him they inclined their heads with a smile or even said, "Good day, Master Paul," in a most friendly fashion. He noticed also that the various little girls who often accompanied some of the proud matrons were no longer so little and that some of them even smiled at him. Oblivious to his own good looks he put this strange occurrence down to pity, but he returned their smiles none the less for in spite of his treatment in the past he had a warm and friendly nature.

On one such visit to Penzance he was just about to enter the booksellers when Mrs. Carter and her daughter Joanna appeared in the doorway and, having made their purchases, were about to leave. He stepped back and politely doffed his cap to them, expecting no more than the smallest acknowledgement in return for that lady had always been the most vociferous in her disapproval of Paul and his family. To his surprise, Mrs. Carter smiled fondly whilst her daughter dimpled and blushed rosily at him. Paul returned his hat to his head and was just about to pass by when Mrs. Carter struck up a conversation with him in a most friendly manner.

"Why, Master Paul, how nice to see you out and about again. How is your poor father, now? Such a shame to lose his dear wife like that and she no age at all. You are to tell him that he must come to call on us and you are to come as well, of course. So lonely it must be for you both in that great racketing house of yours. Most welcome you will be Master Paul, most welcome," she simpered, feeling foolish to address the young man so condescendingly after all the years in which she had been in the forefront of condemning him and his family so vituperatively.

"Thank you kindly," replied Paul politely, hoping that his amazement had not transferred itself to his expressive face, and added, "I will pass on your regards to Father for he is sadly drawn as can only be expected, but I will certainly tell him of your kind thoughts and pass on your invitation. Thank you again," and saying his goodbyes to both of them in turn he doffed his cap again, favoured them with a small bow, and proceeded to enter the booksellers.

After he had bought his book he turned into Chapel Street and was soon accosted by other acquaintances who made similar conversation with him as had been exchanged with Mrs. Carter. His natural charm and good manners meant that it took him a full hour to reclaim his horse from the inn in which it had been stabled and he returned home in a somewhat bemused state. He had no explanation for his sudden popularity; he had not been brought up to be a proud boy and it had never occurred to him that the various matrons of Penzance had decided that, in spite of his colour, he was going to be one of the biggest catches - if not the biggest - in the Penwith area. Allied to this was his handsome figure and undoubted good looks. He was as tall as his father and was still growing. He had soft brown eyes, a straight nose, black, slightly arched brows, curly black hair held back by a ribbon at his neck and probably the most winning smile in the county. The matrons consoled themselves, hypocritically, with the fact that he was not so very dark after all and if he was good enough for Penelope Trevarthen to take into her home, scandal and all, then they were none the less charitable. The thought that the young gentleman in question would undoubtedly inherit the Trevu estate and all its vast income, (including the revenue from Wheal Sankey, undoubtedly the best mine for miles around) played not some small part in their plans, but they were too proud to admit that.

On his return to Trevu Paul found his father seated at his desk leafing through a pile of papers. He faithfully passed on all of the messages and invitations that had been received and watched with a puzzled frown as his father slowly smiled.

"And you are invited as well," chuckled Redvers, "How Penelope would have appreciated this turn of events."

"Yes, but is it not strange, Father, because they had no time for me before?" puzzled Paul. Redvers raised his brows quizzically at Paul, noting that in spite of his youth he had the beginnings of a handsome young man.

"Did it not perhaps occur to you that all the people who spoke with you were the mothers or, in some cases, the parents of . . . er . . . shall we say promising young daughters," he queried and watched in amusement his son's puzzled frown.

"Yes . . . I suppose they were . . . but what is that to say to anything?" he announced, unable in his innocence to follow his father's train of thought.

"These respectable matrons of our locality are looking to the future, my son. In short, Paul, they are considering your very self as a potential partner for their unmarried daughters," remarked Redvers sagely.

At first his son looked shocked at his comments but then laughed so much he had to sit down. The fact that he should be considered as a marriageable proposition in so many households he thought a most amusing notion.

"But, Father," he gasped, "I am far too young to be thinking of marriage."

"Penelope and I married when she was seventeen and I was twenty," Redvers remarked with a fond smile on his lips.

His son's eyes opened wide in astonishment. His father was over fifty now, although he carried it well, but that he had been married at such a young age came as quite a surprise to him. Closeted away in an exclusively male society as he had been he had never given marriage a thought, much preferring study to thoughts of his future life. However, as he considered the knowledge of his father's early marriage, it slowly became apparent that the young men in the surrounding district all seemed to marry at what seemed to him quite a young age. Unmarried females in their twenties were quite a rarity unless of course they failed to please the local bucks for some reason or another. With a shock he realised that he was almost seventeen himself having been born in the November before arriving at Trevu in the following January. Another couple of years and it would be considered quite an ordinary occurrence for him to be thinking of settling down with the female of his choice. This fact sobered him.

Amused, Redvers smiled at his worried frown before surprising him yet again by enquiring if at any time his mother or anyone else had taught him to dance. His son's look of astonishment almost made him laugh out loud.

Paul shook his head and informed his father he thought such an accomplishment quite unnecessary.

"Well, I suppose I had better get someone in to show you a few steps," observed Redvers prosaically before saying with a reminiscent smile, "Haven't danced for years for Penelope was not so very fond of it because her father was a bit of a puritan and did not encourage her to do so. In fact, if it were not for her mother I doubt not that your poor mother would have ever left the vicarage. Mrs. Symons was well aware that Penelope had great beauty and was determined that she was not to be wasted on some little country parson, having to pinch and spin for every penny. We met at the Truro Assembly dance and luckily my father had arranged dancing lessons for all of us: Ben, Jack, myself and sister Caroline. Now there's a thought," he announced, breaking off his narrative suddenly. "Your aunt Caroline - she had a great fondness for dancing and could show a pretty ankle. She's the one to do our business for us. Damned if I will not write to her today."

"Caroline - I mean Aunt Caroline - who is Aunt Caroline?" asked Paul in bewilderment, "and who are Ben and Jack."

Redvers regarded his son thoughtfully for a moment. His wife and son had become his whole world to him, so much so that he had never talked about any members of his family to Paul. He considered for a moment how best to explain to his son about the family that Paul, for one reason or another, had never heard of.

"Well," he began, "Caroline is my younger sister, Ben was my eldest brother and Jack was three years older than me. Ben died after a hunting accident and so Jack was to be the squire. Father, knowing that Jack was to succeed him, made no objection to my joining the army and so I set off to make my fortune. On leave one summer I met your mother, whose father had been sent to a parish just outside of Truro. Father wanted me to marry a local girl but my heart was set on Penelope and in the end he relented. Jack was already engaged to marry the lady who is now Mrs. Carter."

Paul eyes opened wide with surprise and he gave voice to his disbelief.

"Oh - she was quite a beauty in her day. Had lovely brown ringlets and a very good figure. Let me see - where was I? - Oh yes - Jack. Well, your uncle Jack was a bit of a devil. He had plenty of money and took to gambling. His only problem was that he had no success at it," and he sighed sadly, but continued with his tale. "The debts began to pile up. Your grandfather, my father, remonstrated with him but to no avail. At one stage it looked as if Caroline's dowry would disappear along with the farm. I was stationed away at the time, a young married officer totally besotted with his young, beautiful bride. We were so very happy, and I had not a care in the world apart from the threat of war on the horizon. Anyway I received the news of Jack's death about two months before I was due to be posted abroad. I had to sell out, pack up and Penelope and I came home to Trevu." He gazed moodily at something in the distance. "That was when Penelope lost her first baby. She was distraught but I had not the time to notice and I was of no help to her; too busy coming to terms with Jack's death, whilst trying to console father. Of course, father blamed himself for the loss of his son, said he'd been too hard on him and so on, but who's to say?" He lapsed into silence; lost in his private thoughts until his own son's question brought him back to the present.

"How did Jack, I mean - Uncle Jack, die?" Paul asked nervously.

Redvers considered for a moment and then replied, quite abruptly, "Blew his brains out! He was in debt to such an extent he could not see a way out of it. Father never got over it and died about two months after Jack. In a way it was as if he just wanted to die for Jack was always his favourite," and he smiled as he recalled his brother to mind. "Such a jolly, devil-may-care fellow, always up for a lark."

"So," he continued determinedly, after a moment of reflective silence, "Penelope and I found ourselves all alone in this house, surrounded by debts, and naturally our marriage began to suffer. Your mother never complained, of course, for it was never part of her nature, but I felt so frustrated at being thrown into what I saw as an impossible situation that I had never looked for. However, I had no choice but to take off my coat and get down to work and so slowly I began to get the estate under control. Providently one of the mines father had shares in came in with a good lode and the revenue helped to pay off some of the debt. I reorganised the farm, altered some of the practices, rented out the Tremelling part of it to bring in some more revenue, worked from sun up to sun down," he said and looked angry for a moment, but picked up the thread of the tale and continued in a gritty voice. "Eventually I got things back in order and succeeded in paying off Jack's creditors and the rest of the debts that had accrued. Meanwhile Penelope produced child after child. Most were born dead," he paused and Paul saw the pain in his face, "some lived for a day, and then there were the miscarriages. She sustained it all with no complaint - just a lost wistful look on her face. At last, with her final stillbirth, Doctor Simcott told us that she could have no more children."

He fell into an abstraction for a while but then he recalled himself and continued strongly, "That did for our marriage, Paul, for I could not face pretending a love for her that I no longer felt. So, to my shame, I ranged abroad, as it were, following my fancy and making myself presentable to various ladies of the district. Widows, disgruntled wives, women of a certain profession, although I never dallied with single females," and raising his eyes to his son's face added, "until I met your mother, Sardi."

"Sardi?"

"Your mother's name. A most admirable woman, Paul," he reminisced. The youth listened in a daze as his father recounted a hitherto unknown history of his mother. It was almost too much for him to comprehend.

"I never talked of her out of respect for my dear Penelope. It was wrong of me I know but I thought it better so," he ended simply. His son nodded, understanding his father's predicament.

"And Aunt Caroline? Why have I never known of her? Why has she never been to see us?" he enquired softly.

"Ha!" snapped his father, and gave a grim laugh, "Pride, dear boy, pride. When I was busy having my affair with your mother she had heard news of what was going on. She had married a rich lawyer called Crebo and at that time lived in Falmouth. Presenting a picture of outraged virtue, she arrived, swathed in silks and bedecked with jewels, and told Penelope exactly what she should do to bring me to heel," and he laughed at the recollection.

"What did mother do?" asked Paul, wonderingly.

"Showed her the door, and sent her packing with a flea in her ear. Then after you arrived in the household she turned up unannounced just before we were formally to adopt you. Taking one look at you she announced arrogantly that if we were to make you a member of our family she, for one, would not accept you as her nephew and would never cross our threshold again. Very virtuous she looked too, as I remember," he remarked, an amused glint in his eye.

Intrigued his son asked, "What did you say to her?"

Redvers, with a wicked smile playing on his lips, replied: "What did I say? Absolutely nothing! Penelope did not give me the opportunity for she expressed her desire never to see Caroline again, nor any other member of my family so lacking in the milk of human kindness. Your aunt flounced from the room, her skirts swishing around her, and has never crossed this threshold again. From then on until she died Caroline's name was never mentioned in Penelope's presence. However, about five years ago, Caroline's husband died and, unbeknownst to my poor sister, Crebo had been sailing too close to the wind for years. Caroline, never having bothered her pretty little head to find out where her husband had got his finances from, had no idea and had spent freely and wildly. Suddenly, the widow Crebo and her daughters were reduced if not to penury, at least their circumstances became certainly straightened. She sold the Falmouth house and moved to smaller premises in Truro and then she wrote to me asking for financial assistance. I considered telling your mother but thought better of it." He smiled at his son and informed him, "so for the past five years I have been paying your aunt an allowance to enable her and the girls to continue with some semblance of the social standing that she thought due to the name of Crebo and the former Miss Trevarthen. Aunt Caroline will teach you the rudiments of dancing Paul, do not worry about that, whether she likes it or no. She is, after all, under an obligation to me."

"I do not know that I should like to be taught to dance by this unknown aunt. If she insulted mother I think I would rather not have her for a teacher, thank you father," said Paul stoutly, his lips set in a grim line.

"Paul, Paul," said Redvers soothingly, "Do not make Aunt Caroline's mistake and let pride rule you. You may one day find yourself in need of help and succour can come from quite unexpected quarters I can assure you. I, poor sinner as I was, needed help when you arrived on my doorstep. I could never have foreseen that it was to come from my own wife and, for a certainty, I would never have believed that she could become to me more than she was before."

Taking note of Paul's mulish expression, Redvers regarded his son with an equally determined glint in his eye.

"I will write, Caroline will come, and then we will see what transpires," he pronounced decisively.

Barnaby Rickard waited for his companion to return to the house, all the while sitting in his chair by the fire. The clock on the sideboard had struck midnight some time ago but still he remained in his place. When he heard his horse whinny from its stable and the answering call that came he got up in a leisurely manner and, taking down two glasses from the cupboard along with the bottle of brandy from the mantelpiece, he poured out two liberal amounts. Placing one on the table and taking the other with him he returned to his seat by the fire. In a short while the door opened and he looked up into his accomplice's enigmatic face.

"Late tonight, Joey?" he remarked quietly, but the tall youth merely vouchsafed an affirmative and taking off his hat, picked up his drink and took his own seat opposite to his master.

"How goes the book learning then, Joey?" Rickard asked, and looked into his companion's face and noted with a small smile the blankness of his expression.

"Very well," rejoined the young man tersely.

"If you think you've enough learning it would be appreciated if you read to us of an evening, for Phoebe and myself are partial to that," and noting the swiftly raised eyebrows, added, "Perhaps something from the bible might be appropriate considering who has been teaching you!" Joey's cold blue eyes were now fixed firmly on his face, so he added, " 'Tis not everyone that has a vicar's wife to instruct them after all."

If he expected a reply he was to be disappointed for his companion merely turned his head away and studied the fire enigmatically. Thwarted, Barney cleared his throat before continuing in a serene and steady tone.

"Perhaps that passage where Moses received the ten commandants. I'm sure you'd find something there to interest you," he remarked quizzically.

"Thou shalt not kill?" enquired Bolitho and raised his eyes to his master's face, lifting his brows derisively as he did so.

"I considered 'Thou shalt not commit adultery' more appropriate, under the circumstances, young man," countered Rickard and for answer this time Joey blushed fiery red to the roots of his hair. An accomplishment indeed, for even Barney found it difficult to put the young man out of countenance.

After a long silence during which time the youth took the opportunity to compose his features, Joey asked in a subdued voice: "'Ow long 'ave 'e bin' aware of what bin' goin' on?"

"About a year I suppose," replied Barney matter-of-factly. He took a sip of his brandy and considered the young man before asking him if the lady's husband was himself aware of what was happening under his very roof.

"Too busy ministerin' to 'is flock," snorted Joey, "thas' 'ow it all started 'cos 'e was away so much an' Muriel was lonely."

"Muriel?" queried Barney.

"Thas' 'er name," answered Joey and added sharply, "Well, I couldn' keep callin' 'er Mrs. Barnicutt," and he blushed again as he added, "under the circumstances."

His companion nodded and agreed that was indeed the truth and went on to inform him that he had thought it prudent not to tell his wife of how their lodger was spending his time, for she would not have approved of his conduct, but not a trace of embarrassment crossed the young man's face at his speech. Barney's next words altered his countenance, however, for they succeeded in making a scowl appear and Joey's cold eyes burned with anger.

"With the Reverend Barnicutt one of my best customers, Joey, I'll not have you putting my business in jeopardy! For that reason," he said angrily, "this liaison will stop! You may inform Mrs. Barnicutt on Friday when I call to arrange the delivery for her husband and his friends."

"An' if I refuse to do this?" snapped Joey.

"If you refuse I will turn you from this house without a second thought, my lad! I had assumed that you would grow weary of her for she is ten years older than you, but you seemed lost to all possible consequences. If you will not see what a liability you have become to me with your actions then I no longer wish your services in my employ," Barney told him boldly, "and that is my final word on the matter!" He got up angrily and took himself off to bed without even wishing his companion a good night.

The young man's eyes followed him resentfully as he made his way up the stairs, before tossing off the remains of his brandy and moodily sat in his chair with his brows furrowed and his cold eyes glinting in the firelight. Rarely since he had been taken into the smuggler's household did he have his will thwarted. Everything he complied with had been an improvement to himself and he would be the first to acknowledge that fact, but he was angered by his master's attitude. It was not that he had an overwhelming passion for Muriel Barnicutt, or for that matter did she for him, but they obtained pleasure from each other's bodies; the vicar's wife because her husband did not wish to spend his time in her company and himself because he enjoyed being in the arms of a washed, sweetly scented woman. He had dallied with less salubrious females, naturally, for when first his feet led him down that path his innocence had not imposed a bar on his activities. Barney had never referred to any of his past liaisons, although he was well aware of what pastimes the red bloodied young man that shared his home was engaged in, but Joey had assumed incorrectly that he had no idea with whom. A smile crossed his face as he realised that, in spite of his wisdom, if his master imagined he had spent only a year in Muriel's fond embrace he was much mistaken. Joey had hardly learnt his alphabet before he found himself subjected to her unbridled passion, and, since it was Rickard himself who had arranged for him to learn to read at the vicarage, he had attended regularly for his lessons for nigh on four years. His reaction to her advances was one of shock at first but he was not tardy in accepting the pleasures she wanted him to indulge in. A long sigh escaped him as he wondered if he was prepared to lose all for the sake of a woman that he held in small affection but to whom he was exceedingly grateful, and then he considered how comfortable his life was compared to what it could have been, and he realised with a jolt that had he been left as Barney had found him he would probably have been dead long ago. He sighed again, and with his temper cooling, he felt in his pocket and brought out the book that he was currently reading. Shifting his position to catch the light from the candles, he turned to the page he had marked and began to read for he wished to finish the book before he returned it to his lover. After all, he considered reasonably, with what he had to tell her on the following Friday this was the last tome of hers that he would ever be allowed to borrow.

The following day Joseph Bolitho, with his mask like face, watched carefully as Barney talked with a certain sea captain down by the harbour. The captain was gesticulating wildly with his hands, but it was not to him that Joey was paying the most attention, for by the harbour wall a young man sat with a clay pipe dangling from his mouth. This was not the first time that Joey had taken note of this particular fellow and had followed him about frequently, discovering all about him and marking most particularly with whom he conversed. Oblivious to Bolitho's interest in him, the fellow seemed to be most interested in the two men although he was trying to conceal this fact by knotting ropes, but his eyes would not leave them be. As Rickard glanced in Joey's direction he took note immediately of what his lackey had directed him to look at by a slight nod of his head. The smuggler turned back to continue his conversation with the captain and, placing a hand around his shoulder in a friendly fashion, walked him some yards further on before stopping to resume his conversation. The listener at the wall, nonchalantly dropped his rope, stood up and stretched and then as if drawn by a magnet strolled slowly down the length of the wall until he was again able to hear their words, but after a few minutes they concluded their conversation. Barney and the captain shook hands and went their separate ways, the captain to return to his boat and the smuggler let his steps lead him up an alley that led to the poorest part of the town. Knocking out his pipe, before putting it in his pocket, the young man bethought himself to retrieve his ropes before hurrying off so as not to lose sight of his quarry. All was deserted as he left the harbour save for two fishermen idly mending their nets with their bone needles and talking over the day's catch. He had not far to go to observe his quarry for Barnaby Rickard appeared to be standing still at the end of the alley as if waiting for someone. Hesitating briefly, unsure whether to continue his pursuit, he stopped and thought for one strange moment that a shadow moved; he looked behind him but all was deserted as he well knew. A few moments later, Rickard made his way down the alley again, and looked first into Joey's cold, blue eyes, that registered no emotion and then down to the ground where a man lay with his own eyes opened wide with surprise, across his throat a gaping gash from which his blood was pouring onto the cobbles. No word was exchanged but Bolitho picked up the man's knotted rope and looped it loosely around his victim's neck so as to hide what had taken place. Then he hauled the corpse upright and placed its arm around his own neck. Catching hold of the still warm hand he proceeded to walk away in search of a deserted cottage, of which there were plenty in that part of the town, knowing that should anyone enquire he had only to say that the man was incapable due to drink. Finding an appropriate house, deserted by its inhabitants, he hid the body away from prying eyes to wait for his return at nightfall when it could be disposed of silently, either weighted out to sea or more probably down a shaft.

When Joey returned late that night to the house in Gulval, his boots were wet with sea water, but Barney said not a word and merely passed him a full leather purse. Bolitho murmured his thanks and, taking the glass offered to him, sat in his chair and consumed his brandy before picking up his book and commencing to read. Even Barney found it difficult to repress a shudder at the sight of his coolness, though his own life of crime had hardened him to most things. Soon after Rickard retired for the evening but Joey, engrossed in his book, read on into the small hours. When he retired himself, he took his usual pains to ensure that his payment was well hidden, but apart from that he seemed to have not a care in the world, and after climbing into bed he was soon fast asleep.

CHAPTER 6

A WEEK after writing to Caroline Crebo, Redvers sent his carriage to Penzance to pick up his sister and her three daughters from the stage. They had wanted to take a post chaise but, as her brother had not offered to pay for this form of transport, Caroline had thought it prudent not to ask as it would not be the best way to ingratiate herself into her brother's good books. She was determined to make a good impression on her brother and did not want to mar her chance to find herself taken back into the family. The boy might prove to be a problem but this was her opportunity for herself - as well as the girls - to be grasped with both hands and not to be discarded for want of a little effort.

Paul watched their arrival from the upstairs window that looked out over the garden at the front of the house with deep foreboding. A middle aged woman descended from the carriage looking very much like a younger version of his father. She was quite tall for a female and had a very haughty cast to her features. She had dark hair and eyes like his father and the daughters all resembled their mother in that they all had a similar cast of countenance. They were very pretty but they all looked bored and did not appear to relish their visit to their uncle overmuch. He noted that they were all dressed in what looked to his unpractised eye to be very expensive garments of silk, in his aunt's case, and the finest muslin, in his cousins. Although his aunt was correctly attired in black the quality of the dress was obvious even to him. Paul supposed that he was meant to go down to meet them and wondered if he should wait until someone was sent to fetch him but decided that this would be a churlish action on his part. Taking a deep breath, he walked down the stairs and turned his steps purposely towards the front door. He arrived just as his father had finished greeting his sister. Their salutation appeared to be somewhat perfunctory, the slightest of pecks on the cheek between brother and sister, and the curtsies dropped by his cousins to his father expressed the merest civility. Steeling himself he waited for someone to notice him. That someone was his aunt. She looked him over as if he was a prize racehorse, and he felt self-conscious under her direct gaze, until she spoke in a tightly controlled, even tone that expressed no emotion.

"Well, well, Redvers! I am most agreeably surprised. Never would I have thought it possible that such an unprepossessing infant could have turned out so well," she said and with these daunting words she extended her hand and moved regally towards her nephew, her silks rustling crisply with every step.

"How do you do, Aunt," said Paul and bowed formally.

"Hmm. Most creditable, Redvers, most creditable. He undoubtedly has an air. Good-looking too and will become a fine figure of a man 'ere long," she remarked and proceeded to introduce him to her daughters. Upon sight of Paul the girls had all miraculously lost their bored looks. They regarded him with wonder, looking as he did like their idea of a bronzed god. Unaware, as usual, of the effect he was having upon these females, or indeed any young female, Paul greeted each cousin in turn with simple courteousness. Aunt Caroline nodded her head and addressing Redvers barked her approval.

"Such a pleasure to meet a young man who makes no attempt to beguile every young female that he meets."

Her nephew could have told her that he had no wish to beguile any of his cousins. They might be smiling adoringly at him now but he had not forgotten their expressions when they had arrived. His aunt's treatment of his mother still rankled and if Penelope had cause not to like this woman then he saw no reason to be of a different persuasion.

A luncheon had been prepared for them in the dining room. The room was hardly used these days as Redvers and Paul much preferred to eat their meals in the cosiness of the back parlour, but neither of them wished to sit through a meal around a much smaller table with what were in effect, to Paul at least, four strangers. Redvers and Aunt Caroline sat at each end of the long table. Paul, with the eldest cousin, Cecily, seated beside him and with the other two girls, Julia and Sofia opposite them. The younger members ate in total silence unless spoken to but Aunt Caroline kept up an almost constant babble of small talk. Redvers contributed very little to their conversation and Paul produced only monosyllabic answers to any questions that were addressed to him.

As soon as the meal was finished, Aunt Caroline expressed a desire to converse with Redvers alone and sent for Hannah to show the girls to their rooms. Having ascertained that the house contained a piano - and to Caroline's agreeable surprise - a music room, Paul was despatched by his aunt to find some music suitable for dancing.

"Nothing too sprightly, Paul," beamed Caroline, "Julia's fingers are not as nimble as mine, although I blush to admit it." Her nephew noted that she neither blushed nor looked in the least modest concerning this statement but was glad to get away from the stifling atmosphere.

The idea of having to be taught to dance had not appealed to him in the first place and, having now met his aunt, he was appalled to think that he was to receive instruction from this forceful woman. However, he dutifully leafed through the sheet music that was kept beside the piano and having nothing better to do sat down and idly played over some of the tunes to himself. He was a very competent pianist; Penelope having taken great pains with him when he was younger to ensure that he had practised regularly. She had had a great love of music and as he had adored her above all other females he would do anything to please her. Admittedly there were occasions when the lure of the outside world appealed to the young boy far more than playing his scales, but this was always counterbalanced by being alone with Penelope and being the object of her undivided attention.

Unaware that anyone had entered the room, he continued to play, losing himself in the pleasure of playing one of his mother's favourite pieces of music. At the end of the piece he jumped as a round of applause greeted his efforts. His aunt and cousins had quietly entered the room whilst he had been playing and had all seated themselves on the high-backed chairs that were placed along the wall.

"Well done, Paul, most beautifully performed. Penelope's influence no doubt. Your poor father, although embed with a good voice, has never been of a musical persuasion. Our father employed the best music teacher for me, of course, but he only had the boys taught to dance, to improve their social chances as he put it, and that is what we are going to do for you." She beamed at him and then continued in a voice of steely determination; "I suppose we had better start with something simple as your father tells me that you have had no instruction whatsoever. A sad state of affairs in a boy rising seventeen I must say. Never mind. We will soon rectify that."

Rectify it she did. By the end of two hours she had taught Paul the steps of three country dances. She was beginning to enjoy herself, for the boy had only to be shown the steps once before he knew them and his natural athleticism lent grace to every movement of his body. She noted with approval that her daughters were equally impressed with his efforts and they vied with each other to partner him; he was, after all, a most handsome young man and their uncle's only heir. Caroline was determined to please Redvers, for she needed his money more than ever as her daughters would need to be dressed in the latest fashions in order to impress the local young men of Truro. Unaware of her thoughts, Paul merely followed her directions without complaint, but he was still resentful and was glad when the dancing lesson was over. However, if he thought that he was going to be left alone by his new relatives, he speedily discovered otherwise. His aunt took his arm and demanded to be shown around the garden before the light dimmed. The garden in late September was looking a little faded, its summer splendour had gone, but there were plenty of flowers and shrubs to be admired.

"Of course, dear Penelope loved her garden so," Caroline remarked and felt, with a slight start of surprise, the young man stiffen beside her at the mention of his stepmother's name. Having already discovered from Redvers that his son had been told in no uncertain terms just why it was that she did not visit and that Penelope and herself had not seen each other or communicated for sixteen years, she could well understand that he would side with his adopted mother. Obviously, her nephew had held Penelope in great esteem. She considered that this would not be so surprising, for there were few woman who would have undertaken to raise their husband's bastard as if it had been their own, and even fewer who would have done so when his colour had been taken into consideration. She turned and regarded the tall, handsome young man with a quizzical smile playing on her lips. His colour was actually not so pronounced, she observed, although it was apparent that he had a darker skin than was normal. But it did not detract from his appearance, in fact in all fairness it added to it. She considered him thoughtfully, and as if feeling her glance upon him, Paul turned and faced her with a slightly sullen pout to his lips.

"Do not look so, Paul, it does not become you and is most disturbing to young females. Charm, dear boy, charm and at all times. Young females like to be put at ease, scowling at them will not achieve that effect. Do you understand me, Paul?" and she rapped his hand playfully with her fan.

"Perfectly, I thank you, aunt, but what if I do not want to charm these unknown young females? What then?" asked her nephew, evenly.

"Why then you will be a great fool. Consider your situation Paul. To put it plainly you are, as you are well aware, not as other young men. Firstly the colour of your skin marks you out as different from others in this locality; also you were adopted into your family and, although looking at you it is apparent that Redvers was your father, those eyebrows, the shape of your nose and those cheek bones, are all his, you were not born in wedlock and not every family would be willing to have you as a member of it," she announced brutally, completely unconscious of the cruel ignorance of her words.

Paul, immured to insults, pounced and the words were out of his mouth before he realised what he had said, "Just so Aunt, after all I have had experience of that from my father's family already, have I not?"

Caroline had the grace to blush. "Hmm - touché Paul," but she added tartly, "Learn to curb your tongue in future if you want to have an easier passage through life".

She turned abruptly, removed her hand from where it had rested on Paul's arm, and headed back towards the house, the silk of her dress swishing angrily around her. Paul, abandoned in the middle of the path, considered if he ought to go after his aunt and apologise, but then he decided against such an action. He had had quite enough of swapping pleasantries with her for one day. The sun was setting over the wood at the end of the valley and he considered its quiet beauty before turning up the path and retracing his steps. His father met him in the hallway, a small satisfied smile on his face. "My poor sister has developed a headache and has had to retire for the night. Well done, Paul, for we can eat in peace tonight," he laughed.

His son grinned, but pointed out that the daughters would no doubt expect to sit down with them for their evening meal.

"Sent them up a tray to their room. Damned if I am going to sit down with those mindless little ninnies if I can in anyway avoid it!" remarked Redvers, not without a wicked smile. Paul laughed gleefully at his father's expression.

"For how long must we put up with their company?" queried Paul, "I am heartily bored of them already and wish that they were gone. I have learnt the steps of three dances already - surely that is enough?"

"Patience, my son," soothed Redvers. "I am afraid you will need to learn more than three dances to impress the females," and he could not help but smile at his son's quick scowl. "They are needed just at present - but I can assure you that as soon as my sister has accomplished her mission I will encourage her to leave using all the powers of persuasion at my disposal."

They laughed companionably at his remarks, and linking arms, headed to their sanctuary of the back parlour.

The next morning they all met again at breakfast. Caroline appeared to have forgotten the hostilities between herself and Paul and set out with great determination to endear herself to him. She realised that she would have to tread carefully, for he was no fool, and he possessed a natural reserve that could not easily be broken. It would be necessary for her to proceed upon her mission with due care. Paul was determined to learn his dance steps as quickly as could possibly be accomplished; the sooner to have his aunt depart for her home in Truro taking those silly, mindless daughters of hers -whose presence he detested with a passion - with her. In this he was defeated because of Caroline's determination to ingratiate herself into her brother's good books. Paul's dancing prowess came a poor second to her need to put her finances upon a better standing. Consequently she made her nephew perform the same dance over and over again finding small faults with each of them. Naturally Paul began to look sulky and was taken to task.

"Smile, Paul, smile! Your partner must be made to feel as if you were glad of her company and not that you were wishing yourself twenty miles away," she ordered brusquely.

Her words did nothing to remove the sullen look from Paul's face and as his father chose that moment to enter the room he seized his opportunity and immediately released his partner, Julia, from his light grasp and crossed the room to his father's side.

"Bow, young man, bow," rapped out his tormentor. "You must always bow to your partner at the conclusion of the dance, however abrupt the ending might be," ordered Caroline, in a hard, firm voice, and Paul turned on his heel and bowed stiffly to his cousin.

Redvers felt a great deal of sympathy for him but knew that to free him from his dancing lessons would in the end do the lad a great disservice, for he well knew from his own youth that young females loved to dance and the better their partners could dance, the more they were pleased. After all he remembered fondly, he had met his beloved Penelope at a dance and although dancing was not something that she had a particular fondness for, it was the only opportunity she had of meeting young men. He sighed, but realised that Paul would have to buckle down to it and learn, as he would also have to learn to make himself pleasing to the girls' mothers. Making a good impression at a social evening would open doors to him that otherwise might have remained firmly shut in his face. In spite of the expression on his son's face he determined that although Paul might not like it, learn to dance he would. Inwardly steeling himself, he smiled briefly at Paul, and turned to address himself to his sister. However, as he had a great fellow feeling for his mutinous son, he sought to give him some small particle of solace, so he remarked reasonably:

"Caroline do not be too hard on your young pupil. This must all be rather strange to him for Paul has not been brought up in a family given over to much socialising, don't you know? Penelope preferred to stay at home and never looked to entertain on a grand scale," and he added not without a touch of malice. "She was never one for the grand occasion or the lure of the ballroom. We preferred it so."

"I am well aware of that," retorted his sister, "but the boy has to learn how to conduct himself with propriety when in company. He has need of presenting himself in a pleasant manner, as should most young men, but in his case his manners need to be more winning than most. He is, as I am sure you will have to admit, at a distinct disadvantage."

Momentarily stung by her callous speech Redvers pointedly remarked, "Methinks, his prospects will endear him to many, dear Sister."

"Naturally, my dear Brother," flashed Caroline, "but that will be to no avail if he cannot first impress people with his ease of manner and charm. He cannot face the world with only his inheritance to recommend him, as well you know, otherwise why have you need of my services?"

Redvers sighed; he could not argue with that. Caroline was quite right for Paul would soon find that for him to make a path in society and for some future family, as yet unknown, to be prepared to entertain his suit, it would require a great deal of effort on his son's part.

Paul, listening to their conversation, became aware that his wish to escape from the hateful lesson was not to be granted and, his anger grew so that he began to look even more mulish. Nevertheless he was determined to make the attempt and sought to hint at his displeasure at his treatment.

"Perhaps I shall be able to perform the steps with more alacrity if I could have a break from my instruction now," he pleaded, with a flash of his winning smile. " I would like to pick up a book I have on order from Samuels in Penzance. It should have arrived by now and I could resume my lessons after lunch." He was sure he would be able to while away quite a bit of time in the bookshop.

Redvers began to shake his head but was interrupted by his sister, who seeing an opportunity to visit Penzance suggested that Paul's proposal was actually a good idea, she immediately announced her intention of continuing the dance lesson at a later time and proceeding to Penzance with her nephew and her daughters. The disappointed look on his son's face prompted a sympathetic smile on his father's. Paul had not foreseen the consequences of his suggestion and did not appear to relish the proposed visit to the town in the company of his relatives in spite of his release from the hated dancing. In his innocence he had achieved one object only to have it replaced with what was to him a far worse prospect, but Redvers instinctively realised that for his son to arrive in Penzance in the company of Caroline and her daughters would in no way detract from his standing in their society. In fact, the knowledge that, if Mrs. Caroline Crebo - the former Miss Trevarthen of Trevu, was prepared to be seen in the company of her nephew it would lend much authority to his son's position in Penzance's stiflingly structured society. Much to Paul's obvious disgust the suggestion was agreed upon and the carriage ordered to be brought around. Still determined to be difficult, Paul expressed a desire to ride his horse. Caroline, recognising that Paul was annoyed by the usurpation of his Penzance trip and not wishing to provoke him further, became conciliatory and told him that this was an admirable idea for, although, the carriage could seat five, it would be much more comfortable for all of them if he would be so kind as to be their outrider. Thwarted, Paul could do nothing less than to fume inwardly and to comply with his aunt's wishes.

In Market Jew Street he began to wish himself back at the hateful lessons as his aunt, her hand upon his arm, proceeded at a slow and infinitely stately pace the length of the street. Chancing upon various acquaintances she introduced her daughters in turn and made sure that Paul played a part in each of the conversations that ensued. On approaching the book shop, he suggested that he should go in by himself to obtain his book and to meet again with his aunt as soon as his mission was accomplished. He grasped at a chance to while away some time among the bookshelves that lined the walls, but his aunt promptly forestalled him:

"Certainly not," she avowed strongly. "We will all stay together for we are giving the people of Penzance a most favourable impression of ourselves. You will realise the need of this when you start to attend local functions, Paul.

Closeting yourself away with your books and shutting yourself up in Trevu with your father will not do your cause any good. You have to present yourself to society as an acceptable member of it. This means not only that you have to follow the manners of society but also that that you are to be seen to be held in the greatest respect by all members of your family. Your appearance in Penzance today, accompanied by your father's sister, who is not unknown in these parts I would remind you, will not harm your credit in the least. In fact my presence in your company will do your standing a great deal of good." Suddenly, she nipped his arm lightly, and said in a whisper just loud enough for him to hear; "Smile, Paul, I see Inez Carter approaching. Such an influential personage in this town," and then affecting a start, she cried out in a delighted voice, "Inez, my dear, how wonderful!"

Paul stood back as they exchanged kisses and waited patiently as his aunt and Mrs. Carter introduced their respective daughters to each other. Mrs. Carter greeted Paul in an equally friendly manner and enquired after his 'dear Papa'. Paul, in his mannerly fashion, made a suitable reply. The little group exchanged pleasantries again and they moved on after the two women had announced their intention of calling upon each other in the not too distant future.

The morning dragged on and Caroline's nephew suffered greatly for, although he had been able to obtain his book, he had been given no opportunity to browse in the bookshop as he had intended. His aunt took great pains to see that he was outside the shop and continuing their procession as soon as his tome had been purchased. So completely foiled in his attempts to get away from his aunt was he that he soon discovered, paradoxically, he could not wait to return to his home and the resumption of the dreaded dance tuition. He suggested tentatively that it was time to leave Penzance, but his aunt would not hear of it and entered a linen draper's to have a look at some materials as she desired a new dress to be made up. Her daughters, thrilled by the materials that were displayed on the shelves, giggled and sighed amongst themselves, but Paul fumed in frustration.

The manageress was all charm to what could well turn out to be a potentially valuable customer, for she reasoned acutely that the formidable stranger had three daughters and she was aware, with a sweep of her professional eyes, that the clothes that they had on their backs at the moment must have cost a pretty penny. As she moved to the back of the shop to collect some more books of patterns for her clientele, she glanced at Paul with a puzzled frown on her face. Aware of her glance he stirred uncomfortably, but his aunt called the attention of the manageress to her so the shopkeeper retraced her steps with obsequious rapidity, and the moment passed. His aunt was showing an interest in some dark lavender silk: She explained - quite unnecessarily - that she was in deep mourning because of the loss of her sister-in-law, she thought it appropriate to be out of full mourning by December and would then have a need of a half mourning dress of lavender silk. She enquired of the proprietor what other suitable colours had she in stock, and was assured by her that she would be receiving some new materials within the next two weeks. She proceeded to explain that she had a most acceptable agent in London who made purchases on her behalf from the merchants of the capital and also of that other great trading port Bristol. Perhaps, she asked artfully of Mrs. Crebo, if she would be able to call again, at a later date? It would be no trouble, she assured her, to send a message to her when the fabrics arrived for she was certain that the lady would find something to suit her. If the lady wished, she could send off a letter to her agent that very night by the mail with instructions to purchase materials that would be acceptable to her discerning eye. Charmed by her consideration, Caroline thought that this would be an excellent idea, so she proceeded to furnish the manageress with her address, informing her as she did so that she expected to be in the locality for another month at least, an announcement that annoyed her nephew greatly. He noticed that the manageress looked startled when his father's name was mentioned but surmised that perhaps she had been one of those accommodating woman that his father had admitted he had dallied with in the past. That would account for her puzzlement at seeing him in her shop for it was unlikely that she did not know who he was by appearance alone, but as the woman continued to talk to his aunt he was intrigued to learn that she did not know the area very well as she had only been in Penzance for two months, having previously had premises in Plymouth. As soon as Caroline's business was completed she whisked him out of the shop and he soon forgot about Mrs. Martin's interest in him by his aunt's declared intention of taking him to a tailors. At this point Paul, told his aunt if they did not make haste they would be late returning for their meal and, he pointed out testily, that his father did not like to be kept waiting for his lunch. Although he did not realise it this was a masterstroke on his part. Caroline had no intention of offending her brother as she was well aware, from past experience, that her personality and somewhat forceful manner would not be acceptable to him for long.

   They arrived at Trevu to find another carriage waiting in the driveway. Paul was forbidden to take his horse to the stables himself and had to hand it over to Davy, as his aunt ordered him to accompany them into the house. Noticing his mulish expression she advised him to remove it at once lest he wished to incur her wrath. He smiled grimly at her and she continued to berate him until they reached the withdrawing room, where they found Redvers, making small talk with Mrs. Emily Daniels and her daughters, Mary and Jane. Redvers greeted the appearance of his sister and her little group with relief. Caroline and Emily professed delight at seeing each other again after so many years. They remarked smilingly to each other what beautiful daughters they both had and what an age it had been since they had attended their first dance together. Paul winced as they both laughed artificially and then heard to his dismay that his aunt would call to see them, for she expected to stay at Trevu for quite a while. His son noted that his father received this information with despair, but that the smile he bestowed on his sister was stoical if not saintly. However, Redvers smile broadened in spite of himself when Mrs. Daniels turned her attention to his son. Paul had need of all his natural charm to remain mannerly in the presence of so patently false a woman. She insisted that a place be found for him on the settle beside her eldest daughter, for she prattled on, she was sure that they would find lots to talk to each other about. 'What was that he had in his hand?' 'A book! How diverting!' She proceeded to inform them that her own dear Mary was a great reader. 'Dear Mary' assumed an expression of fear and despair at this remark for a swift glance at the title of Paul's book had confirmed her suspicion that it was written in Latin. However, to the relief of both parties, they did not have long to exchange pleasantries, for Mrs. Daniels, a stickler for correctness was soon on her feet, shaking out her skirts, and declaring that she was delighted to have met up with 'dear Caroline' again and that she had not realised how much 'dear Paul' had grown. They must all call on them soon, including the 'dear Captain' and his son, "the dear, dear boy," as she referred effusively to Paul. Waving her goodbyes she shepherded her almost voiceless daughters from the room and back to their carriage.

Redvers, could contain himself no longer, and as soon as he heard the front door slam shut behind his uninvited guests he went off into a howl of laughter. Caroline regarded her brother indulgently, but advised him to get used to having his peace shattered by such visits, for she had had a most busy morning in Penzance.

"What of it?" gasped Redvers, trying to get his breath, "they will not wish to see me. I am sure you will be more than a match for them on your own."

"They might not be too disappointed at your lack of appearance but Paul has to be present," she asserted and directed a firm look at her nephew. This was too much for the young man and she was given evidence of the temper that Paul could not always hold in check.

"Well I am not kicking my heels indoors waiting for a parcel of your waspish old cronies to come and chat over past times with you, and bringing their stupid, empty headed daughters along and expecting me to entertain them, I can assure you of that!" he flamed.

"Guard your temper, Paul," said his aunt, remarkably unmoved by his outburst. She moved towards the settle and seated herself elegantly, and then patted the space beside her. "Now come here and sit beside me and let's have no more examples of that sulky boy's temperament if you please," she pronounced firmly. He looked to his father for support but Redvers was unable to look him in the eye and lowered his gaze, so with a scowling face Paul walked briskly across the room and sat down abruptly.

"That's better," smiled Caroline. "I know you find all this very irksome; but I cannot fail to impress upon you once again that you are at a severe disadvantage and you have to make more of an effort than most young men of your age." She smiled sweetly at him, and then informed him that perhaps they could leave their dancing to later in the day. Determined to hang on to some of his independence he announced that he would decide for himself what it was he wished to do. He would get some food from the kitchen and spend some time fishing down by the brook; his angling success would decide when he returned to the house and no other reason. So with a look of chagrin on his face he stiffly bowed to them all and marched out of the room, slamming the door behind him.

Caroline sighed.

"It will take time, Redvers, but he will learn, he will learn."

CHAPTER 7

THE bay mare cantered into the yard and Redvers dismounted and passed his reins to Davy as that stalwart ran from the stables. The letters from the mail office were stuffed into his coat pocket and he hurried into the house to distribute them. There was a letter for the three girls from their father's sister in Falmouth, two letters for his sister - one from Truro and the other a note from the Penzance linen draper, Mrs. Martin - some business letters for himself and, unusually, two letters for Paul.

The tinkling of the piano informed him where to expect to find them all at this hour of the morning. Entering the music room quietly he watched Paul perform his part in the dance with his cousin Sofia. Although the youngest of Caroline's daughters she was certainly the most vivacious and, if it had not been for Paul's grim face they would have made an enchanting couple as they danced together.

Caroline, becoming ever more adept at handling Paul's recalcitrance, suggested that he should try to look as if he was enjoying himself although she realised that is was very difficult for him. At her remarks a tight smile appeared upon Paul's lips.

"That's better," beamed Caroline, marking time to the music and directing her nephew's steps at the same time in a most determined fashion. Cecily finished the piece and the dance came to an end. Sofia curtsied and Paul bowed and then stood stiffly as he waited for his aunt to suggest that another piece of music should be found to accompany them in yet another dance. Redvers seized the opportunity to give his obviously seething son a small measure of relief from the proceedings.

"I have the mail from Penzance and, wonders upon wonders, every person has received a communication, although in my case they seem to be mostly bills," smiled Redvers indulgently.

At his news his nieces shrieked and whooped. Paul looked puzzled, for he rarely received mail, but his aunt appeared as if she had expected nothing different. The letters were distributed accordingly and Redvers left the room to go to the front parlour which served as his office. The girls retired to a corner and laughed and giggled amongst themselves, delighted to receive their aunt's letter, for it was sure to contain much detail of the goings on in and around Falmouth. Caroline's neighbour had written asking if she was to be away from her home for some time, would she consider letting her house out as her sister's family wished to visit for a few months and were looking for a property to rent. Naturally, if Mrs. Crebo should be returning quite soon she would get her husband to look elsewhere but had thought of her immediately, but she did not wish in any to offend her and would quite understand if Mrs. Crebo did not wish to let out her property. The letter went on at great length about the social life that Caroline was missing in Truro - sadly flat she was informed - and that her neighbour had been afflicted with her rheumatics again but was trying a new medicine from Doctor Veale, who was such a gentleman, and was quite hopeful of the outcome.

Caroline folded her letter and glanced across at Paul, busily reading his own letters with a deep frown across his brow. She pondered her neighbour's request in hidden delight for if she could rent out her house for, three or even six months, it would provide her with a good income for the season. After all, she pondered to herself, she would need plenty of dresses for her daughters' next year and as she would be chaperoning them herself, she would need to appear to advantage and to do that she would need to have money. Paul, although still irked by their continued presence, was beginning to accept them in his home and, although he kicked over the traces occasionally, he dutifully accompanied her on her progresses around the district and was always civil to all she had him meet even if, as she well knew, he hated every minute of her social manipulating. Her second letter contained a list of details of the materials that were now at the shop in Penzance. If Mrs. Crebo would like to call on Tuesday next, Mrs. Martin's agent, the person responsible for procuring all the materials, would be present and would be most willing to take instructions from her as to what her requirements would be. Mrs. Martin concluded with the acknowledgement of what a pleasure it would be for her humble establishment to have her custom and hoped that they would be granted a visit from her on the day in question.

She looked up at her nephew as he folded his own letters and excused himself. Caroline was about to ask him where he was going, but decided against it for he was looking grimly determined and she had no wish to pry into his business too closely. Redvers would enlighten her presently if it would be of interest to her, of that she had no doubt, for her brother was beginning to rely upon her most noticeably where matters concerned Paul. Well, she knew that he was most struck by the number of people who now found time to call upon them and the way in which his son was being treated. It was all so different from when Penelope had been alive. Caroline pointed out to him, that Penelope, with Paul's best interests at heart, had protected him from the very people it would now be necessary for him to mix with. Redvers began to acknowledge the force of her argument. Caroline, seizing the moment, continued sweetly that Penelope had been quite right to protect Paul for by giving him a stable family life he had felt cherished and wanted, and consequently he had benefited from her care and attention of him and, it was most apparent, that it was Penelope who had been responsible for turning him into such a fine young man. She went on in this vein to Redvers whenever she thought her words would have the right effect and acknowledged to herself, with satisfaction, that they frequently did. So she would let Paul have his time with his father because she knew well that her nephew was finding it increasingly difficult to get his own way with him. Caroline had accomplished that and was quite prepared to bide her time.

"Well girls, how are things in Falmouth at your aunt's house?" asked Caroline brightly, and was speedily told all the latest gossip.

Meanwhile Paul was trying to make headway with his father concerning one of his letters. He was hopeful of making some progress because his father had had good news concerning another of his business investments and this always put him in a good mood. Paul's first letter had come from James Hoskin, recounting school gossip and telling him how well he was doing at his lessons now that Dick Bray and Mr. Clymo had left. Mr. Armitage was proving to be an excellent headmaster and that school had become a most enjoyable experience for the boys. Even the food had improved, he enthused, and he had grown another two inches. He finished with the wish that it would be possible for him and Paul to meet again soon and urged him to write to him with his own news.

The second letter came from Mr. Armitage himself. After passing on his good wishes to Paul, and to his father, he enquired of Paul if he would be in a position to do some work for him. Before being elevated to the position of headmaster he informed Paul, that he had taken on the task of a Latin translation of the works of a minor Roman poet that had to be completed before the following March for a publisher in London. Having recently married a widow of his acquaintance who had a family of two small children, he was finding it most demanding with his new responsibilities, both his new family and the school were taking up a lot of his time, to commence the work. Would Paul possibly take up the task on his behalf, he wondered? He would willingly pass on the money from the proceeds of the sales to Paul for he had no intention that the work should be done for nothing. Paul was delighted with Mr. Armitage's request for two reasons. Firstly, having hated his time at school, he was, perversely, missing the discipline of study and, secondly, he would have a good excuse to cut down on the visits and dancing that he loathed. Of course, wisely, he did not mention this latter reason to his father.

Redvers was not overly impressed with the idea for as he told his son,

"You certainly do not need the money, Paul, you have to admit that?"

"Of course not, father, but I do miss my studies. Mother gave me such a fondness for it," his son pleaded but did not mention that he would enjoy the time to himself that it would give him even more.

"I cannot believe that you can actually want to spend your time translating Latin. I hated any such thing when I was at school I can remember and did all I could to get out of it, too," and he laughed reminiscently.

Paul smiled with him. With a little more effort on his part he believed he could get his father to comply with his wishes.

"Can I at least write to Mr. Armitage and tell him that I am prepared to give it careful consideration and will let him know by the end of the month whether I can undertake the work or not?" enquired Paul making no attempt to hide his enthusiasm.

"Well . . . Well, yes, I suppose so. Come to think of it, it would be a shame to waste your fine education, after all for it cost you enough did it not?" smiled Redvers.

They both laughed and Paul feeling well satisfied with the outcome of their talk, left and found his way to the kitchen just in case Hannah had been busy doing some baking. This dancing lark gave him a good appetite at least he reasoned. Hannah greeted him with obvious delight for, with his time so circumscribed by his aunt, he could not visit as often as he would have liked to do.

They spent a pleasant half an hour chatting and Paul managed to acquire two of Hannah's saffron buns, which she lavishly buttered for him, while they were still hot. Their time together was cut regrettably short for Lizzie, the serving maid, interrupted them to recount that Mrs. Crebo was a looking for him and that she wanted to see him in the back parlour, if he would be so obliging as to attend upon her there if it please him.

"If I please, indeed," snorted Paul, but he knew he would have to go. Planting a buttery kiss on Hannah's cheek and flashing his beaming smile at her by way of goodbye, he bounded out of the kitchen and headed towards the back parlour. At the door he stopped and, taking out his handkerchief, wiped his mouth and then carefully brushed any crumbs from his coat.

He knocked on the door and hearing his aunt call out for him to enter twisted the handle and went in. His aunt was sitting with her back to the window for, unlike his mother had been, she was not fond of the sunlight as it did not show her skin to perfection. This was not her favourite room in the house anyway, as she preferred the formality of the withdrawing room. Informing Paul that she wanted to visit Mrs. Martin's on Tuesday she would be obliged if Paul would accompany her, if she would not be putting him out, of course. She was certain that he would not mind, for he would not wish to see his aunt go to Penzance unaccompanied. As to her daughters she considered it so much the better if they should stay behind, for they would chatter so and she wanted to spend some time examining the cloths and materials without having them always exclaiming over trifles. Of course - she pointed out with a smile - whilst she was upon her business he would be able to go to his bookshop again, for she knew how fond he was of his books. Paul did not feel inclined to go with her but she deftly parried all his protests and excuses with good reasons for his presence. All those lovely Penzance girls would be able to roll their eyes at him she informed him and, noting his swift look of annoyance, she countered swiftly by informing him that she would not be able to stay long in the street. 'Perhaps he could browse in the bookshop and meet his aunt at a later time?' she suggested kindly. His presence was required to carry her parcels for he was such a fine, strong young man, and she continued in this vein for some minutes. Eventually he gave in, knowing full well that even if he appealed to his father to send one of the farm hands in his place his aunt would easily find an objection to it. The following Tuesday they set off early and, although they did not need to take the carriage, his aunt had insisted most vociferously on this conveyance for Mrs. Caroline Crebo was not going to be seen bowling into Penzance in anything as common as a pony and trap.

However, upon their arrival in Penzance she was as good as her word and allowed Paul to visit his precious bookmaker's unaccompanied, but on her strict instruction that he was to present himself at the linen draper's promptly at ten o'clock. He took out his pocket watch and checked the time - it would give him half an hour in Samuels. The longest time he had spent there since his aunt's arrival. He smiled at her gratefully and parted with his aunt outside of the entrance to Mrs. Martin's shop and sped on his way to his destination, his head full of books.

Meanwhile, Caroline stepped regally into the establishment and proceeded to the counter. Mrs. Martin came bustling in from the back of the shop, looking somewhat flustered. She smiled a greeting and professed herself delighted that Mrs. Crebo could attend her humble establishment. In response to Caroline's question she confirmed that all the new materials were available but as yet they had not been put on display. She enquired if Mrs. Crebo would very kindly follow her through to the storeroom at the back of the shop, where they had been placed temporarily before being displayed in the shop. Her agent was there and was perfectly willing to take any instructions that Mrs. Crebo had for her. Caroline followed in Mrs. Martin's wake and entered a brightly lit room, piled high with rolls of materials of every hue. Standing in the middle of the room with her back to the door and bent over examining a batch of particularly fine silks was, from her fine figure, a tall, youngish woman wearing a beautifully cut dress of grey silk, with a high collar down which cascaded black, curly ringlets. Mrs. Martin made the introductions with a worried look on her face and she had good reason for the Miss Brown that turned to face Caroline was a sultry dark skinned young woman. Mrs. Crebo felt the floor jolt beneath her feet. Looking into her nephew's eyes she was well aware just who it was that stood before her in that Penzance store room. Miss Sardi Brown stepped forward majestically, her hand extended.

"How do you do, Mrs. Crebo, it is pleasure to meet with you," she said brightly but nervously - and then smiled Paul's beaming smile.

For once in her life Caroline was bereft of speech. Desperately pulling herself together she tried to fathom how it was that the woman who had not been seen in Penzance for nigh on seventeen years should be standing so tall and proud before her. It was a nightmare, not only for her but Redvers, Paul, all of them. She struggled until finally she found her voice.

"What are you . . .?" she began but then remembered herself and turning to the shopkeeper gave her a tight smile and said dismissively: "Thank you Mrs. Martin; that will be all for the time being. I expect that you have business in the shop."

After making sure that Mrs. Martin had left the room she turned again to Miss Brown and enquired in a hard voice, "Well, what are you doing here? Why have you returned to this town?"

"I am indeed Mrs. Martin's agent, Mrs. Crebo, ma'am. When she told me that you were most interested in purchasing some fine silks and other fabrics I arranged to visit her. Mrs. Martin is hoping to get herself well established in this town, but as you can imagine I had another reason for returning."

"Showing your face around here will soon ruin any chance of Mrs. Martin expanding her business," Caroline snapped and then added angrily. "Have you considered the consequences of your foolish action.?"

"Of course, Mrs. Crebo," replied Sardi defensively, "for I enter and leave these premises at night, and always heavily veiled. I can assure you that I shall be returning to London as soon as my business here is completed. I have no wish to stay longer than is necessary ma'am," and she added quietly: "I wish only to see him again. Is it so very much to ask, Mrs. Crebo, ma'am?" and as she looked into Caroline's eyes the despair and emptiness wrenched her shallow heart. For all her hard heartiness she could not fail to recognise the pain in her look.

"Why now? Why come back here after all these years? Why leave your son in the first place?" the questions tumbled despairingly from Caroline's lips.

Paul's mother turned her face away, wringing her hands convulsively, her voice shaking as she replied. "I left him because I loved him. I knew that Redvers wife would love and care for him as I would never be able to do, ma'am, for I had reason to believe that a woman who could meet me on the road and smile so generously at me would be as generous to my little boy. I was right," she said defensively, " for she took him in and cared for him in spite of you all - did she not?"

"She took him to her heart as no other woman would have done," agreed Caroline, "that is for sure. She loved him as a mother. Redvers was too frightened at first, even to accept the boy was his responsibility, but first Penelope and then the child won him over. He's been his son's slave ever since."

Sardi flinched but let the thoughtless remark pass. In her life there had been worse, much worse than that said to her and about her.

"May I see him?" she pleaded and urged desperately, "He need not see me, for I can stay in this room and not even enter the shop. After all this time . . . just a glimpse . . . ," but she could not continue for her voice broke on a sob.

"No! It is impossible! Consider your son, at least. What possible good would it do him? Paul knows only that his mother left him as a babe in arms. He has been accepted here, and he has proved himself worthy of his father's name," Caroline asserted proudly and then in a hard, bitter voice she continued, "He has no thought of you, for I have never heard him even mention you. You cannot be so evil to him now for your appearance in his ordered life will shatter him - so soon after losing the only mother he has ever known - No! . . . It must not happen!" she asserted firmly and made to turn away but Sardi held out her hands in entreaty.

"I beg of you - let me but catch of sight of him, ma'am. I will not call to him, I will not move to touch him . . . I ask only this one favour of you for my life is so empty without him. His father was my only lover, his son my only child. Do I deserve to be punished still further? You cannot be so heartless, ma'am. You need tell no one of this meeting and I can assure you that Mrs. Martin is sworn to secrecy. Knowing my past she recognised Paul immediately but after she told me and I announced my intention of coming to Penzance she became afraid, but I persuaded her to help me. There will be no more visits, ma'am, you have my word on that but, please, please - let me catch just one small sight of him - for mercy's sake," and by now large tears were rolling down her cheeks.

Caroline wanting desperately to refuse this request, and then to turn and walk out of the shop found that she could not. Why did this have to happen? After all her scheming and conniving at getting herself accepted back into her own family, and now, when the rift that had been caused by Paul was almost healed, it looked as if all her plans would be ruined. All her craftily constructed world was falling down around her but even then, amidst what could possibly be a disaster that would affect not just her own life but Redvers and Paul's as well, she found that she could not forbid the mother the one thing that she so desperately craved.

"All right," she said in a low voice, "It shall be as you wish. He is coming to the shop at ten to carry away my purchases - if I can bring myself to make any. You can see the door and the front of the shop from here. Stand and look your fill, but not a word, not a sound. If your son should see you now 'twill ruin his young life and," she added in a more forceful tone, "I think that you would not want that on your conscience."

Reaching out to Caroline, Paul's mother took her hands in her own and pressed them convulsively, thanking her profusely until she resolutely summoned up her courage and wiping the tears from her eyes turned towards the bales of silks. At her side, Caroline mechanically began to pick out the colours and quantities that she wanted, and Sardi cut and calculated amounts, advised on ribbons and lace until at length the list was made up. Picking up one small bale of muslin that Caroline had already arranged for the local seamstress, Mrs. Simmonds, to make up into dresses for the girls, she turned to go back into the shop.

"Remember," she said authoritatively, "Look at him by all means, but if you should try to call out to him I shall ensure that the townspeople will have you run out of Penzance. Feelings will run high, my dear, I can assure you. Your son's father is now held in high esteem, his past forgiven if not forgotten; and he employs many from hereabouts. The people here will not want to see their Captain humbled by the likes of you. Conduct yourself sensibly and it shall be as you wish, but there will be no more such occasions. Your son is ours now - leave him alone and go away - lead your own life far from here, where, please God, he may never come into contact with you. Do you understand?"

"Yes ma'am, it shall be as you wish. I am . . . I am most grateful. I know I have behaved badly to place you in such an . . . an . . . invidious position, but I do most truly thank . . . ," but here she could not continue and turned away to dash the tears from her eyes.

Caroline turned without a backward glance and stalked into the shop, withering Mrs. Martin with a cold stare, but merely asked her to tally up her account and arrange for the bill to be sent to Captain Trevarthen. Mrs. Martin, hastily making the muslin into a parcel, thanked her profusely, well aware that the consequences of her actions on her friend's account could so nearly have lost her Mrs. Crebo's valuable custom and, more than that, could well have cost her the business that she had worked so hard to acquire in the town.

Her valuable customer heard the clock strike the hour and both women awaited Captain Trevarthen's son's imminent arrival with trepidation. As to the hidden third, who could tell what state she was in?

Paul, unconscious of the consequences that his entrance would cause, burst into the shop exuberantly on the last stroke of the clock. His half hour of freedom had put a good deal of his former gaiety back into his step and the broadest of smiles lay across his face. Remembering his manners, he politely greeted Mrs. Martin and turned to his aunt, his eyes sparkling.

"Well, aunt, here I am to carry all your purchases as requested," he said joyfully and, so saying, he held out his strong arms before him almost as if he was greeting someone.

There was a loud crash from the storeroom and Paul, surprised by the sudden noise, lifted his laughing eyes from his aunt's stricken countenance.

"What was that!?" he exclaimed and looking over his aunt's hat directly into the store room continued, "Oh look, Mrs. Martin, a shelf must have broken. There are bales of cloth rolling all over the floor. Shall I go and help to put them back for you?" and without waiting for a reply he took a step towards the storeroom but Caroline's hand shot out and grabbed his arm in a surprisingly strong grasp.

"No!" she cried in a panic stricken voice.

"But aunt . . ." expostulated Paul, "I thought . . ." but his words were cut short.

"Be quiet!" she snapped at him, "Here, take this package. Mrs. Martin is quite capable of dealing with . . . with a . . . a broken shelf. We must go! We must go at once! Good day Mrs. Martin. I will send for the rest of the materials on Friday. See that they are ready."

Bemused, Paul stared at his aunt in amazement, but he barely had time to say goodbye to the manageress before he found himself outside in the street with his aunt beside him, firmly holding him by the arm. She almost marched him back to the carriage and said hardly a word on the journey home; he found himself quite at a loss to explain her strange behaviour.

Upon their arrival at Trevu, Caroline swept into the house and disappeared up the stairs, leaving Paul to stand dumbfounded in the hallway still clasping the package. Cecily, coming down the passage called out to her mother but Caroline replied, sharply, "Not now, Cecily," and this was followed almost instantly by the sound of a door slamming.

Hastily, Cecily turned on her cousin.

"What have you said to upset Mama so?" she said accusingly.

"Nothing, Cecily, nothing. I swear it. When I collected my aunt from the shop she seemed upset and hardly spoke on the way back, not like her usual self at all. I have no idea as to what has happened to discomfort her so. Perhaps Mrs. Martin said something to upset her?," mumbled Paul.

"Well, you had better put the package in the back parlour. Mama will no doubt see to it later - when she is more herself," advised Cecily.

Following her instructions he left the three sisters closeted in the back parlour, trying to fathom out their mother's strange behaviour. Paul, finding himself left to his own devices, decided to go in search of his father and soon ran him to ground in the stables, grooming his favourite bay mare. Redvers greeted his son warmly. "Hello, Paul, your aunt let you off at last, I presume. Do not, I beg of you, inform her that I have been grooming my horse for she does not approve of me smelling of the stables. Did she have her usual parade with you?" he added with a laugh, fully expecting to hear another list of complaints from Paul concerning his aunt.

"No. It was most strange," said Paul and he recounted the tale of his trip to the town and of his aunt's unusual behaviour.

"Hmmn - yes indeed - most strange," pondered Redvers. "Something has annoyed her obviously. We had best be careful - Caroline in a fury is something not for the fainthearted."

Finishing his grooming he gave his horse a final pat and, throwing his arm about his son's shoulders they strolled back to the house, not overly concerned with the result of Paul's trip to the town with his aunt. However,

Caroline did not put in an appearance in the dining room for two days, complaining of a sick headache. Hannah took her meals up on a tray but apart from thanking her Caroline said hardly a word. On the Thursday, she sent for writing paper, and on the Friday the carriage and went to Penzance unaccompanied. She returned with packages of material from the dressmaker's but this time she greeted her daughters in her usual manner and busied herself deciding which of the seamstresses she made use of would have the responsibility for making up which dress for her daughters. By the Saturday Caroline appeared to be her usual ascorbic self. She joked with Redvers, teased Paul, twitted her daughters, but now and again her conversation lapsed. During one such pause Paul stole a look at her from under his lashes and noticed that her normal, slightly vain expression had given way to a worried frown. Catching Paul's eye Caroline looked guilty, like a child caught out in a mischievous act. He found himself smiling at her in spite of himself but she did not return his smile and to his surprise she hastily turned her face away from his gaze.

Sardi, indifferent to the glances of contempt that were directed at her, sighed with relief as the coach lumbered to a halt in the yard of the Lion Inn in Truro. She descended from the coach and shaking out her skirts - for the passengers had to cram one against the other - she breathed a lung full of good air, and then walked towards the coffee room of the inn. Before ever she had a chance to reach the door the landlord's wife appeared and Sardi found herself informed rudely that, 'her sort' were not welcome in their establishment. Sardi, fiercely proud, was undaunted and would have asked an explanation of her when, of a sudden, a stranger spoke in a cool voice at her elbow. She turned in surprise to see a tall, well built young man, with a handsome countenance and the most brilliant blue eyes that she thought she had ever seen, asking if he could be of some assistance to her. Replacing his hat over his dark, brown curls he turned his inscrutable face away from her and asked the landlady why it was not possible for this particular passenger to enter the inn.

The landlady, much discomforted, sought quickly for a reason and, after a moment, informed him that, it was not the policy of her establishment to allow unaccompanied females into the inn. At this the young man turned again to Sardi and bowed, then promptly offered her his arm before saying: "If 'e will Ma'am I would be most 'onoured if 'e will accompany me to dine with me." and smiled a most entrancing smile which only served to make him look the more attractive.

"I am most honoured sir," she replied in her soft musical voice, "but I fear that I am unknown to you and as you are most certainly unknown to me it would not be appropriate, methinks, that we should be seen to dine together." She looked at him severely for she did not wish him to imagine that she was the type of woman that the landlady had implied she might have been.

Unabashed the young man informed her that he was well aware of who she was for he had often seen her son in Penzance. At this information her eyes flew open wide with shock.

"Come ma'am," he continued gently, "fer the time is gettin' short an' e'll soon 'ave be back aboard the coach. If 'tis not the knawin' of me that worries 'e I am called Joseph Bolitho," and he bowed again with youthful elegance.

Something about the man intrigued her for she thought him known to her, but knew that he could not possibly have been, for he was far too young. But if he knew her to be Paul Trevarthen's mother he obviously knew of the Trevarthen family, so she considered that possibly he was one of their workmen. Perhaps, she concluded, Caroline had sent someone to ensure that she left the county as she had promised, so, feeling that this explanation accounted for his sudden appearance, she placed her hand upon his arm, received again his smile and allowed herself to be escorted into the inn - much to the landlady's obvious chagrin.

At their meal she had time to study him and noted his elegant, quiet style of dress, and was impressed with his manners at the table for with his strong dialect she had assumed him to be of the lower orders. With a twinge of shame she realised that she should immediately think the less of him for the way he spoke as others thought the less of her for how she looked. Raising guilty eyes to his face she felt emboldened to ask in what way her son was known to him.

"I seen 'en around the town, Ma'am," he answered briefly and was then asked if he was known to her son, but he shook his head and told her that he thought that was not the case.

"Then why have you taken such trouble to escort me to dine? For well I know my son will never hear of it neither from his family nor, I should imagine, from yourself," she said in a voice in which her sadness could not be completely hidden.

"I didden like the landlady's attitude to 'e, Ma'am," he replied succinctly. The abrupt way in which he announced his reason surprised her and she detected that he had been hurt in his own past at people's perception of himself.

"I would thank you for your concern, Mr. Bolitho, but I can assure you that throughout my life I have suffered in a similar way and have become indifferent as to how I am perceived," she told him, but then added sadly, "and I hope most passionately that my son will learn to do the same."

"Don't e worry 'bout 'e, Ma'am. The Trevarthen's are moneyed people an' yer boy's a 'ansome lookin' chap so there's maids a' plenty in Penzance an' roundabout settin' their caps at 'en," and he smiled reassuringly at her as he spoke.

"Truly? Truly Mr. Bolitho? It is the truth you are telling me?" and as he nodded in the affirmative her son's beaming smile lit up her whole face as she sighed with relief. A rough voice called from the doorway that the coach was almost ready to leave and so, despite her protestations, the young man paid for their meal and then escorted her to the carriage. But here the coachman announced that the lady would have to ride on the roof.

"I have paid the full fare to Plymouth from where I will travel post to my home," said Sardi furiously, "and therefore, I am entitled to my seat in this coach. You have not the right to disbar me!"

For one moment the coachman looked embarrassed, but then he told her boldly that the other passengers objected to her presence for she had been veiled when she caught the coach in Penzance; they had no idea of her colour else they would have remonstrated the sooner, and he would have said more but of a sudden her companion had him by the neck and his back was against the coach, and he began to sweat in fear as he felt the young man's knife pressing against his rotund belly. A Penzance man himself, he knew well the name and reputation of his passenger's companion if she herself did not.

"Richard 'Enry, you d' knaw me an' you d' knaw full well what I'll do to 'e if this lady 'ere don't get to sit in the seat she bin' an' paid fer, right an' proper," his assailant hissed in a vicious voice. Sardi stared, frozen into shock, at his words and the transformation that had come over the young man.

"All right Joey, all right! Easy now Joey! I'll do as 'e say right nuff," he agreed hoarsely and he sighed with relief as he felt the pressure on his neck ease. Coughing to clear his throat, he announced in as brave a voice as he could muster that it was almost time to go and would all the passengers please to climb on board. A man in a black frock coat that proclaimed the minister with a bible clutched in his hand began to complain vociferously and protested at having to sit with a half caste, pointing in disgust to Sardi who tilted her chin bravely back at him, although she was shaken both by the recent events and by the clergyman's wrath. Again the cold voice hissed angrily but this time Bolitho, keeping his hands to himself, addressed himself to the preacher and merely said: [3]"James, chapter five, verse nine, yer reverence." Embarrassed, the minister had to look into his bible to find the relevant passage and, when he did, he looked at Joey in impotent fury and climbed into the coach saying not a word, for to be put to the blush and by such an obviously rough fellow as that was almost more than he could bear.

Sardi shook her head and did not know whether to laugh or cry; for one moment she had thought herself about to witness a murder and the next Mr. Bolitho was quoting the bible - and at a man of religion as well! She glanced into his face admiringly and began to thank him for his actions on her behalf but he waived them aside and, smilingly, named another piece from the bible, before wishing her a safe journey home. Then he handed her up into the carriage and shut the door. The coachman's whip cracked, the horses plunged forward and the coach set off again on its long journey. A little way out of the town Sardi asked most politely of the affronted looking cleric if he would be so obliging as to inform her what Hebrews, chapter thirteen, verse two said. This time the minister did not have to look in his bible but blushed a deep crimson as he quoted angrily: 'Be not forgetful to entertain strangers: for thereby some have entertained angels unawares.' Sardi smiled with deep pleasure at these words, for in spite of Mr. Bolitho's obviously violent nature there beat within him a heart of great compassion. For some strange reason she felt immensely comforted that he should know of her son and also strangely disquieted that, when in his presence, she had the most peculiar feeling that she had met him before.

---

[3] *Grudge not one against another, brethren, lest ye be condemned; behold, the judge standeth before the door.*

Barnaby Rickard, with his business at the Rising Sun completed to his satisfaction, strode happily into the yard and smiled at his protégé who stood staring enigmatically after the departing coach.

"Any problems, Joey?" he asked jovially and was handed a leather purse full of money as the young man replied. "No, only the tapster's waterin' the beer but that tidden our problem." and with his impassive face he followed his master to the stable. Within a short space of time their horses were cantering in the direction of the next of the many inns that they were to visit that day.

CHAPTER 8

THE February sunshine, filtering weakly from behind the clouds, fell through the window and across the desk where the young man sat writing. Glancing up, and feeling the warmth on his face he smiled at the brightening of the sky. He felt quite happy as his Latin translation was completed. Tomorrow his father had promised to travel to Helston and deliver it to Mr. Armitage, and from there Redvers was going on to visit a local farmer who had a bull that he wished to purchase. Although Paul had been asked to accompany him he had declined, mainly as he did not wish to visit his old school again for he felt that he needed more time yet before he could go back there. Clymo and the boy Bray were no longer there but it was not fear of seeing them that held him back, more the remembrance of the long, lonely days and of being made to feel such an outcast. His aunt had made sure that he was no longer received in the same manner by the local people - he should thank her for that at least, he acknowledged with another smile.

He continued with his letter to his friend James Hoskin, but in truth there was not much to tell: His aunt and nieces were still in residence, mainly because Caroline had arranged to rent out her property for six months and had prevailed upon his father for them to extend their stay. They had all managed to survive each other with an arranged truce. With his translating work Paul had found a measure of freedom and his aunt was noticeably less abrupt with him; she would often sit and talk with him quietly. He had found her a most irritating woman at first but gradually they had come to respect each other, although Paul would be the first to admit that she would frequently annoy him and it was a common occurrence for him to lose his temper with her and stamp from the room. James had enjoyed Paul's descriptions of the hours that had been spent learning to dance, and how, worse than all the dancing, he had to learn to make small talk with a load of silly girls.

At Christmas there had been a small gathering of selected neighbours, for it was not considered appropriate to hold a dance since they were still in mourning for his mother. However, the local fiddler had been hired and the piano had been pressed into service. After the quiet but pleasant supper it had been decreed that it would be quite in order for a small dance to be set up for the young people. Caroline and her daughters each took turns to play the piano. Paul found to his annoyance that he did not have a chance to sit down for he had no choice but to dance every dance, well aware that his aunt's basilisk stare would be directed at him if he showed any sign of dissent. Her hours of training proved invaluable; for he was politeness itself to everyone he met. The girls that whirled about the room with him were the cream of the local society and they all wanted to dance, most especially with Paul Trevarthen. The other lads came a poor second. Paul soon learnt the value of those dance lessons. And being young, athletic, and handsome as well as knowing every dance that was performed - better than his partners in most cases - he was well aware of the admiring glances of the girls and the proud smiles of their mothers. At the end of the evening after the last visitor had left for home he was congratulated by his aunt on his performance. She even went so far as to hug him, such was her joy at the way the evening had gone. Her nephew had acquitted himself so well on what was, if not a public engagement, at least a foretaste of the social world with which he would have to mix.

She smiled proudly; for his colour had become irrelevant to all those families who at one time would not have had him over their doorstop. The smell of the money Paul would inherit, along with the properties, combined with his charm and social elegance was sufficient inducement for many a family. The boy could have been a headless monster - nothing would deter those scheming matrons now and nothing could stop his elevation to the status of the most desired bachelor in Penwith, even the county. Caroline's bosom swelled with pride. She had triumphed, and her cup ran over with her obvious pride in her achievement. She looked at Redvers and was delighted to see him smile and bow his head in acknowledgement of her success. Even he could not believe that his young son, the social outcast, could become the coveted idol that he undoubtedly was in the neighbourhood. In the beginning he had chafed at having to have Caroline back at Trevu, but she had certainly known what was best for his son, he had to admit that. Paul had been a problem at first but now he could acquit himself at any public function and had the confidence to address all layers of society. People were also impressed with his scholarship, and some even said the boy would be destined for great things. Redvers felt such a pride as he had never thought possible. When the local squire and prominent magistrate, Sir Joshua Tregurthen had taken him on one side and barked, "A credit to you, Trevarthen, a credit," he thought his heart would burst with pride. He knew that his dear Penelope would have been so proud to have seen her son thus, for she would never have wanted her beloved Paul to live out his life in seclusion in this lonely farmhouse.

Paul, not realising that he had caused such a stir, had enjoyed the evening but he was glad when it was over. He was not particularly interested in any of the girls that he had met for he had known them for quite a while and had found it such an effort to sit and be polite to them and their often simpering mothers. He had to admit that they were nice enough young ladies, of course, but so empty headed and in truth he was not at all interested in the female sex. His favourite female companion was Sarah Jane Williams but he knew he was not in love with her. He merely liked her more than any other girl of her age, but did not see much of her anyway because she had left to work as a companion to Mr. Tregenza's aged mother in a big house in Penzance, where she lived in. She came home every second Sunday and sometimes, if he could get away, he would go down and see her as she was probably his oldest friend, but he had to admit that he would have felt the same about her if she had been a boy.

They would sit and talk in the garden if the weather was fine or in the kitchen if it was not. Mouser the cat would either sit on Sarah Jane's lap or Paul's knees with his head nodding sleepily as the young friends chatted. Sometimes Paul went to see John Williams and his wife knowing full well that Sarah Jane would not be there and occasionally he had gone fishing with John's sons if they were also at home; for apart from William John, who worked in an inn, they lived in as farm workers on various farms thereabouts. Those same boys had taken him down to the cove when he was young and, with great patience and care, taught him to swim. He had a great fondness for them and visited their cottage as often as he could for the whole family were such good friends of his. Of a sudden, his thoughts were broken into as he heard Cecily's voice calling to him from the bottom of the stairs.

"Paul! Paul! Mama wants to see you, Paul!" she shouted in her shrill voice.

He sighed and got up. His aunt could always find something for him to do, he could be sure of that. He considered that perhaps he would go with his father tomorrow after all. At the bottom of the stairs, Cecily was waiting. She smiled winningly at him and slipped her arm through his.

"I think Mama wants to take you to the tailors in Penzance. You are to have a new coat and pantaloons. Won't you look the swell then?" and she laughed up at him, her eyes dancing.

Her cousin grimaced and began to pout. On seeing his expression, Cecily immediately mimicked her mother:

"Do not pout so, Paul, it does not become you. Charm, Paul, charm. Charm at all times. That is better - now - Smile, Paul, smile!" she trilled but the laugh she broke into was cut short at the sound of a sharp voice.

"Quite right Cecily!" snapped her mother from behind them. She had been with Hannah in the kitchen and had only just returned. The two cousins whirled around to face her, each of their own countenances blushing guiltily.

"I will speak to you later, Cecily. For the moment I wish only to talk with Paul," announced Caroline in a crisp voice that did not bode well for her daughter.

"Yes, mama," said Cecily in a subdued voice and dropping a quick curtsey fled the scene and allowed aunt and nephew to confront each other.

His aunt favoured Paul with her most gracious smile; he smiled back but warily, for he had learnt to be on his guard with her. He was even careful about what he said to his cousins, because he believed that they relayed everything he said in their presence back to their mother's interested ears. He could well remember her forestalling of a carefully planned fishing trip that he and the Williams' boys had intended to make. Now, when he wanted to go somewhere, he got himself out of the house and from under her eye by subterfuge, never telling anyone of his destination or intentions. Even so, she was adept at keeping a careful eye on him and often he found that she could thwart his plans quite successfully by arranging a social call at remarkably quick notice. Being at an age when he wanted some independence, his aunt's continued control of him was beginning to chafe. Studying her face carefully he could tell by the look in her eye that, even now, some plan was forming in her scheming mind, so he determined not to let his countenance divulge his feelings.

"Dear Paul," she said and smiled sweetly at him, "I am so sorry to curtail any intentions you may have of going anywhere tomorrow - unless of course you have changed your mind and wish to go with your father - but Mrs. Sampson has asked me to pay her a call tomorrow afternoon and it would be so fitting if you could accompany the girls and myself. Her daughter is such a sweet, kind child, is she not?" Requiring no answer on Paul's part she swept on:

"We will be visiting the tailors in Penzance this afternoon, for you have grown so much you are almost bursting out of that coat, you know. I will be leaving directly after we have dined so you will be ready I am sure, will you not?" and fixing him with a firm stare waited calmly for his acquiescence.

Paul considered whether it was worth his while to resist, but knew that his aunt would have already obtained the consent of his father to any of her plans, so he merely bowed politely and said he would be ready at whatever time she wished.

"Dear, sweet boy," oozed Caroline and smiling graciously whisked herself off in pursuit of the undoubtedly quaking Cecily. Paul felt a certain fellow sympathy for his silly headed cousin.

"A bit more growing in the young gentleman yet, Mrs. Crebo," said Mr. Murdoch the tailor. "He'll be taller by a good way than Captain Trevarthen and he's a fine tall gentleman surely. Just hold out your arm please young sir, thank you. Not set too tight across the back I assume Mrs. Crebo, allow for a bit of growth there. Fine pair of shoulders I must say. Just lift both your arms now, young sir," and he deftly measured around Paul's chest, "would be good at the wrestling if he had mind for it, Mrs. Crebo," and then catching her eye added circumspectly, "but perhaps not."

"He has grown out of the last coat so quickly I would appreciate it if you could allow for some growth, Mr. Murdoch, for he has yet to reach his eighteenth birthday and I am compelled to agree with you that he will be taller yet," affirmed Caroline.

"Certainly ma'am, certainly. Was it the black again that you wanted? Certainly, but not the silver buttons just the gold. Quite right, Mrs. Crebo, a good choice. Much more *comme il faut* as the French say, ma'am," and then changing the subject he rattled on in the same manner: "New people up at Nancemellin now. Quite well off apparently. Retired Sea Captain from Padstow, made his money in the Black Ivory trade so they say; now your waist young sir. Same colour pantaloons as last time, Mrs. Crebo? Excellent choice if I may say so ma'am, excellent choice. A widower with one young daughter, very pretty young lady. Will set the young bucks hearts aflutter around here and no mistake. Now your leg, young sir. Lovely flat thigh on him ma'am. Should sit a horse well I shouldn't wonder. Just the circumference of your hip and we'll be done young sir. There we are. Same number of neckcloths as last time, Mrs. Crebo? Thank you ma'am, thank you, much obliged. Should have them ready for you on Monday next. I'll work on them myself ma'am, you can have my assurance of that ma'am. Captain Trevarthen's account as usual? Certainly, Mrs. Crebo. A pleasure doing business with you ma'am, a pleasure." He was still talking in the same vein as Paul, after shrugging himself into his coat, left the shop with his aunt.

They walked down the street without saying a word but suddenly, Caroline turned, and surprised Paul by saying, "I must apologise on Mr. Murdoch's behalf Paul. A singularly tactless remark on his part I think you will agree. But public sympathy for . . . for," and here she seemed unusually lost for words.

"The slave trade, aunt?" enquired Paul at his most innocuous.

Caroline blushed fiercely, an almost unknown occurrence, and continued in a determined voice.

"Just so, Paul. As I was saying, it is true that the majority of the public do not regard the sl... that profession as a well thought of trade anymore. We shall not be in communication with Nancemellin now that the Misses Bowater's have moved to Exeter. Such refined ladies too and with such excellent taste in all things, such a pity, but never mind. I will have to warn your father though. We would not want him riding over to Nancemellin and then for him to hear the wrong thing from this retired sea captain. He will probably cut them anyway knowing Redvers for your father never did approve of slavery and Penelope was set most firmly against it. I can remember that my brother-in-law's wife fancied owning a little black page boy once but your mother wrote her such a letter. Oh dear - I can still see the look on Beatrice's face when she showed it to me," she turned her face to him a small gleeful smile on her lips.

"It made me proud to have her as Redvers wife, I must admit, when I read that letter," she chuckled at the memory, "What was it now? Yes I have it: 'Nor anyone the right to sell the soul and body of another' was one of the many condemnatory phrases in it that particularly struck me," and catching hold of Paul's hand she continued in a voice burdened with undue humility. "Had I half her strength of character Paul I would have not turned into the silly, worldly woman you see before you now."

Paul was so amazed by this statement that for a brief moment he could think of nothing to say.

"Why aunt, I . . . ," he began and squeezing her hand in return he simply said, "Thank you, aunt, most sincerely."

Caroline gave herself a little shake, "Come now, Paul. This will never do - sworn enemies in agreement with each other," and they both laughed and continued down the street. Stopping at the bookshop she looked roguishly at him and he smiled back. "Only for a moment aunt, I promise," he assured her, and they both entered the shop in complete charity with each other for once.

True to his word Paul selected a book with haste. In fact he knew which book he wanted as Mr. Armitage had recommended it to him when he had sent seasonal greetings to him at Christmas. He was paying for it when the doorway was darkened by a couple entering the shop. Completing his purchase he turned to see a large, tall gentlemen, with a smiling face, very heavily sunburnt, replacing his hat and straightening from the bow that he had just so obviously made to his aunt. On his arm was a young girl of about sixteen with the most exquisite face that Paul had ever seen. Grey, twinkling eyes, and the most beautiful, full lips, a soft pink and white skin and an abundance of blonde ringlets that escaped in profusion from under the confines of her straw bonnet. Paul, his mouth agape, found himself staring at her; for a moment his customary good manners and charm deserting him, then he remembered himself and raised his hat and bowed with his usual elegance. In return she curtsied prettily and gave him such a smile that he felt his heart had melted.

The tall gentleman, however, did not smile at him, regarding him with a look of disgust and Paul was aware of the distinct coolness in his manner, which was so at odds with the smiling face that he had used when he had greeted his aunt. Feeling distinctly awkward Paul looked to his aunt for some silent advice. She merely smiled at her nephew reassuringly and favouring the couple with a slight inclination of her head she took Paul by the arm and led him from the shop.

"Methinks we have met Nancemellin's new owner, Paul," she remarked succinctly before continuing smoothly, "for that girl is most ravishing, as Mr. Murdoch stated but, sadly, she will not be one of your dancing partners for one thing is most assuredly certain," and she turned a most sympathetic smile upon him as she informed him brusquely, "Her father does not approve of you."

Paul refused the offer of a small biscuit from the plate held before him by Mrs. Sampson for in spite of his appetite, he heartily detested those little dainty morsels and found them so difficult to eat. He could quite easily put the whole of one of them in his mouth but knew that he was supposed to take a small bite each time it was presented to his lips. Well, he thought to himself, he could not be bothered to engage in such foolery. Hearing a gentle voice at his shoulder he turned to Miss Lavinia Sampson who had asked him a question.

"Your pardon Miss Sampson, did you ask have I met Miss Petherick yet? I do not think so, in fact I am most certain that I have not as I know no one of that name."

"Oh my dear boy, such beauty and such manners," gushed Mrs. Sampson interrupting them without a qualm. "Her father was a sea captain you know, but she was privately educated in a very select school for young ladies as he was away a lot and her mother had died when she no more than a babe in arms. Such sadness, the loss of one's mother," and she smiled at Paul pityingly, but continued with hardly a chance to draw breath, "and the father, well such a handsome man, not even in his forties. Amassed plenty of wealth too by all accounts. A sea captain with a fleet of ships to his credit. I forget what sort of trade he called it. Oh, I remember now, for it was the slave . . . ," but at this point her voice trailed off. Hastily she changed the subject and twittered on for some moments on the price of candles. "I vow we shall all be sitting in the dark by Michaelmas," she finished and laughed nervously.

"Quite so," agreed his aunt Caroline serenely and rising to her feet said, "I fear we must be going dear Mrs. Sampson, but I must thank you most sincerely for such a lovely tea that you have so beautifully laid out for our pleasure. I am quite undone and can see I will have to look to myself when you call again."

Mrs. Sampson blushed and demurred, whilst they exchanged bows and nods, and made arrangements for another visit and then Mrs. Crebo and her nephew left.

"Mother," hissed Lavinia after the door had closed behind them, "how could you tell him that Captain Petherick was a slaver. Poor Paul must have felt it dreadfully," and she sighed longingly.

"Oh my dear, I know, I know. I could have wished my tongue cut out," admitted a flustered Mrs. Sampson.

Mr. Anthony Tregenza's house was one of the finest that existed in Penzance, being newly built to overlook the bay and so gave a pleasing view of the Mount. Contrary to its pleasant aspect, its interior, although most attractively decorated throughout, with fashionable colours and furniture, had a cold, forbidding feel. Joseph Bolitho, waiting patiently for his master to conclude his business with the house's owner, shifted uncomfortably on the chair he sat on outside of the withdrawing room. Inside, Barney and Tregenza sat and talked over their brandy which, hopefully, would make up part of the order that had been placed with the smuggler. Soon, Joey thought to himself, it would be time to go again to France for in their trade it was always best to keep well stocked with further supplies. Staring blankly across at the opposite wall he did not alter his position as a door banged below stairs, succeeded almost immediately by the sound of a yapping dog, with the noise of its claws slipping and pattering on the tiled floor of the hallway, followed by its panting as it made its way up the stairway which led to the corridor in which he sat. A woman's voice called out firmly, "Bouncer, Bouncer! Come here at once!" but the dog appeared either deaf or disobedient for on reaching the top of the stairs it bounded along the corridor and, on catching sight of the stranger, headed towards Joseph Bolitho barking incessantly. A rather fat terrier, with a short-haired black and tan coat. It did not give Joey the impression that it was pleased to see him, for interspersed with its piercing bark it gave voice to some throaty growls for good measure. On reaching Joey the animal stood his ground and barked and growled; perplexed to find that the man he had at bay neither moved nor spoke but merely looked at him impassively. As he usually elicited some response from any one he chanced to come across, the man's attitude began to annoy him and so he rushed forward and attempted to bite him on his ankle, which was ensconced in what looked to him like a tasty leather boot. Too late did the unfortunate Bouncer realise his mistake for he was immediately lifted off his feet, only to be held in a firm grasp. His barking was curtailed by the man effectively placing his hand over the dog's jaws; thus clamping them together. Bouncer still growled as before but, his strategy in ruins, all he could do was raise his doleful eyes to the man's cold ones and wonder nervously just what it was that the person who had entrapped him would eventually do with or to him.

Another sound, of feet running along the corridor made the man turn his head and this time the terrier noted the small smile that quivered on his lips. Still growling, albeit not quite so defiantly, he noted his mistress's companion hurriedly running along the corridor with her skirts held up to enable her to run the faster and, in so doing, she was showing a most neat pair of ankles. Arriving in front of the man he stood up immediately and, still holding poor Bouncer, bowed to the flustered young woman who was attempting to brush back her brown curls that had fallen from the ribbon which normally held them in place, whilst apologising for Bouncer's shocking behaviour. Holding out her hands for the dog, she raised her clear, green eyes to his face and was surprised to see that the man was smiling; for every time she had caught sight of him previously on his visits to her master's house his face had always seemed set in a blank mask.

"I'll 'old 'en fer 'e Mistress fer I wouldn' want 'en to bite 'e," he said in a soft voice, his eyes admiring every part of her; but she was blind to his regard for her as by this time her gaze was directed solely at the terrier.

"Oh! Never fear for he will not bite me, or indeed any other woman, for 'tis only men that he dislikes so," she told him breathlessly and reached across to take the terrier from his hold. As she did so her hand brushed across his and he felt a tremor of excitement course through his veins at her touch and felt a blush rise in his face. But again the girl did not notice for she was soothing and petting the dog who was growling, but only occasionally; for he did not wish to incur the man's displeasure. Recovering his composure, Joey was about to address the young woman when the door behind him was pulled open and Tregenza and Rickard came out, laughing and joking with each other. On sight of his mother's companion - who was busily dropping a curtsey - Mr. Tregenza enquired of Miss Williams if all was well. She hastily explained that it was but that Bouncer had disgraced himself by attempting to bite Mr. Bolitho. He asked, in great concern, if the dog had been hurt for he would not want his dear mama distressed by any injury to her dog and she assured him pointedly that neither the dog or his guest's companion had sustained any injury.

" 'Twould poison any creature that would bite your man, eh Rickard?" announced Tregenza discourteously and he laughed uproariously, but although Barney smiled in return at his jest he was not oblivious to what he imagined Joey would think to that remark. Miss Williams raised her eyes to Joey with a look of apology on her face, but said not a word and Mr. Tregenza abruptly dismissed her without even glancing at her, so she curtsied again and with a quickly muttered goodbye to the gentlemen turned hastily and strode away along the corridor, still clasping Bouncer firmly in her arms. Out of the corner of his eye Joey watched as her elegant figure disappeared from view but, aware that Barney was about to leave, retrieved his hat and turned to follow him from the house. Completely ignoring Rickard's henchman, Tregenza wished his smuggler a jovial farewell and then returned to the withdrawing room to sample some more of the excellent brandy that he had just purchased; smiling in satisfaction as he realised that eleven more bottles would soon be residing in his cellars.

Outside in the street, Barney looked into his companion's face but his impassive stare forewarned him that Joey had nothing to impart to him, so they continued on their way to the next property that they needed to visit. At the end of a busy day they were returning through Market Jew Street when Joey observed Miss Williams again as she made her way along the street with a considerably happier Bouncer leading the way. Noticing the direction in which Joey was looking, and espying old Mrs. Tregenza's servant, Barney tactfully advised Joey that he wished to visit Abel Hawken for he needed to speak with him on a matter not related to smuggling.

"I'll see you back at the stables, Joey, but there's no hurry for methinks I shall be a good half hour with Abel," and so saying he turned abruptly and headed towards Hawkin's inn.

Joey released from his place, hesitated for only a moment before crossing the street and on catching up with Miss Williams executed an elegant bow. Bouncer, the man's assault upon him still fresh in his memory, gave a small growl but hoped it was not so loud that it would attract the man's attention for he had no wish to repeat his experience of earlier in the day. He noted with disgust that the man had fallen in step beside the young girl but as he was paying him no attention he continued to sniff with pleasure at the many smells that were so delightfully assailing his nostrils along the roadway.

"I would apologise Mr. Bolitho for Mr. Tregenza's remarks to you to day. He seems at times to be completely devoid of manners and his mother also. Money and position does not always lead to social correctness, I have often noted," she remarked coldly. But she was intrigued that Joseph Bolitho should wish to talk to her, for common report would have it to be that he spent little if any of his time being gracious to females of her status; he was reputed far more interested in woman who followed a quite different lifestyle.

" 'Tis not important Miss Williams, ma'am, fer I didden take no notice of the ignorant fool," he told her and smiled himself to see the dimples in her cheeks as she attempted not to smile at his comments. He studied her face and figure for a moment in growing admiration before asking if she would wish to meet with him on her day off, for he would be delighted to accompany her wherever it was that she would wish to go. She turned her face away, so he would not catch sight of her flushed cheeks, before telling him that she would be visiting her parents on that day as she did every time she had leave from her employment.

"I would be 'onoured to escort 'e Miss Williams, ma'am, should 'e wish me to," he offered humbly but she shook her head and politely refused him. Undaunted he continued to talk with her and suggested that he could call of an evening if she felt at all in the need of company. She quashed this plan abruptly by informing him that she was not allowed gentleman callers when residing with her employer, and having little spare time, devoted what she did have to spend it with her friends and family. However, something about the wistful look in her eye intrigued him so he continued to walk beside her, attempting in his most mannerly fashion to encourage her to change her mind. Politely refusing all his suggestions, he finally blurted out in desperation what it was about him that had incurred her displeasure.

"I am not interested in attracting a follower, Mr. Bolitho, so your efforts are entirely wasted," she informed him boldly.

"Surely, Miss Williams, if a suitor should come along wishin' to take a wife an' 'e got money 'nuff to set 'e up in a nice 'ouse away from that grim place of Tregenza's you'd be interested then?" he attempted again.

She sighed and halted her walk, to Bouncer's disgust, and informed him that if such a person had all the gold in the world she would still not be interested in his advances. Rebuffed but still determined; he enquired if it was who he was that displeased her but she shook her head, and he noted with pleasure how her silky, brown curls, fell about her face as she did so.

" 'Tis not who you are, Mr. Bolitho, more who you are not," she told him cryptically and pulling Bouncer around began to walk back the way she had come. The dog followed dejectedly, as did the man for Joey had completely lost his heart to the girl and did not wish to leave her side. During their walk back to the house he tried again to establish friendly relations with her but she was adamant that she had no desire to meet with or even to see him again. At the entrance to her employer's house she wished him a curt goodbye but he caught up her hand and pressed it to his lips and, looking up into her face, gave her sight of his most attractive smile and, oblivious to her previous protestations, announced that he would hope to see her again before long.

"Hope all you will, Mr. Bolitho, for I can only emphasise once again that my attitude is unlikely to undergo any transformation with regard to your good self," and removing her fingers from within his hand she turned abruptly and without a backward glance left him standing in the roadway, gazing after her retreating form in admiration. But even then at the back of his mind he found himself wondering just who the man - that he so obviously was not - might be.

CHAPTER 9

CAPTAIN Trevarthen and Captain Petherick met a fortnight later, on the road from town, the former going to Penzance and the latter returning. They bowed formerly but each regarded each other with distrust. Redvers knew full well of the sea captain's former life and Captain Petherick had been told frequently of Trevarthen's son, the young man he had met in Samuel's book shop.

"Well thought of around here sir," Veale the innkeeper told him. "We don't mind the colour of 'en and that's a fact sir. Go a long way to find a pleasanter spoken young fella than 'e sir. Comin' into his father's fortune and all his property when the time comes sir. Plenty a maids round 'ere got there eye on 'en so to speak. Wen't 'ave to look far for company when 'e's a bit older either. There's a few young widows givin' 'en the saucy looks already, if you know what I do mean sir."

"But the boy's black for God's sake," remarked Captain Petherick, "Don't they mind?"

"Appears not sir. His fortune is the same colour gold as anyone else's see. Thas' the most important colour to they people lookin' for to match up their liddle maids with 'en."

"Well I can thank God I have my own fortune and have no need to seek him out for a prospective son-in-law," avowed the Captain and, downing the last of the beer in his tankard, turned to leave the inn.

"More fool you then," said Veale *sotto voce* and turned back to take the order of another customer.

Now, on the road to Penzance, the respective fathers eyed each other over their horses' ears.

"Good day sir," said Petherick abruptly.

"And to you sir," replied Redvers equally as abrupt.

"Neighbours I believe sir. Live at Nancemellin. Name's Jeremiah Petherick, retired sea captain," he said staring belligerently at Redvers and then, in case he had not been told, he added vehemently, "Guinea Trade."

"So I comprehend, sir," Redvers replied in a calm voice, his face impassive.

"Met your sister I believe. Not introduced, of course. Met in Samuel's book shop. Ah . . . with your . . . your . . . a . . . your son, I believe," he stumbled.

"Quite right, Captain Petherick. My sister, Mrs. Crebo, was accompanied by my son, Paul," he affirmed, still keeping his voice on an even keel.

"Mother black, I presume. Remarkably light coloured for a mulatto, your boy. Still; can't say anything, had quite a few a they meself. Never married one 'tho," he laughed, then considering that he made a good joke threw back his head and laughed even more.

Redvers regarded him with a tight mouth and a steely eye. "I never married his mother either," said Captain Trevarthen, "as I was married at the time."

"Oh ho! So that's the way of it was it? Well, you won't be the first man to pass his bastard off on his wife, sir. There's plenty of them around. Most wives cause a mort of trouble over them, 'tho. Even more so in your case, I should think. Don't yours mind?" he enquired with another bellowing laugh.

"I am a widower sir. My dear wife passed away April last. She it was insisted that Paul be taken in to our family. We neither of us ever regretted it." he stated a look of disgust settling on his features.

"Damn 'e sir," cried Captain Petherick, bristling at Redvers coolness, "Aren't you ashamed of yourself? You can't be any too proud going around with that damned black passed off as your son."

"On the contrary sir, I am most proud of my son. He has no failings in my eyes and, I might add, he has no failings in the eyes of most of the people who have come across him. Here, he is a well regarded young man of the locality. Certainly most well regarded, my sister assures me, by the young ladies of his acquaintance."

"Well my maid won't be one of his acquaintances! I'll make damned sure that their paths won't cross and so I tell you, sir, and to your face too," he shouted, his colour rising alarmingly.

"Then you had better keep your daughter at home sir, for Paul is welcome everywhere. They mind not his colour hereabouts. 'Tis the young man they admire," retorted the Master of Trevu and, touching his whip to his hat, he spurred his horse on and said, "Good day, Captain Petherick," and so passed by.

The guinea trader stared after him with an angry expression on his face before kicking his horse viciously and heading on to his own home.

That evening Redvers, waiting until the young people had retired for the evening, mentioned to Caroline that he had met Captain Petherick.

"And a nastier, more oafish brute I have never met in my whole life before. The man's a damned, hell begotten scoundrel," he said.

"Redvers!" his sister said in a shocked voice.

"Well, so he is Caroline. The filthy swine could not even talk without peppering his speech with disgusting remarks. Damn it, Caroline, I have never considered myself a saint but my life before Paul's entrance into it seemed almost virtuous compared with his!" He continued angrily; describing Captain Petherick in such terms that Caroline was forced to put her hands over her ears.

"That's enough, Redvers," she warned him with a quelling look. "I know you are angry but curb your tongue do, I beg of you. That man is never likely to cross your threshold and if we have to meet him in company I shall certainly cut him. Paul will come by no harm by him, I can assure you, for; as you well know he is too well liked for his popularity to be damaged by anything Captain Petherick can do to wreck it."

So life continued as normal, as Caroline had said it would and, it was proved that Captain Petherick could in no way damage Paul's reputation. They rarely saw them and if they did Mrs. Crebo never acknowledged him or his daughter. However, Paul had great difficulty keeping his eyes off that beautiful young lady and although she tried hard she found it equally difficult to keep her own eyes off Paul. Of course Captain Petherick, as a rich landowner, moved in the same social circle - and a small circle it was - but he soon discovered that the only people who did not have a high opinion of Paul were some of the young lads, who would have preferred Paul to have been small, ugly and poor, so successful was he at getting the young girls to sigh over him. His colour, surprisingly, seemed not to bother these young bucks. The sea master could not believe it and considered them all bewitched by the black heathen. He thought it best not to express himself too freely though, as he did not wish his daughter to be snubbed by the old crones who held sway as the arbiters of taste and decorum in and around Penzance. Determined that he was not going to spoil his little Dorothea's chances in the marriage mart, as he called it, he kept his own counsel. He knew his daughter to be the most beautiful girl that Penzance had seen for a long time. Knew it because all the local young bucks were falling over themselves to dance with her, talk to her, or to call at Nancemellin in hopes of seeing her. Dorothea was bombarded with posies of all different hues, but the Captain was relieved to discover none of them bore the name of Paul Trevarthen. In his efforts to deny the existence of that young man he completely failed to notice that his daughter, on catching sight of that particular gentleman in the street, would always blush prettily and that her eyes and those of his neighbour's young son would invariably meet.

Captain Petherick was far too determined to have his daughter wed advantageously to be in the least aware of his daughter's growing admiration for the handsome fellow, so he continued in his quest to find the man that he could eventually give Dorothea's hand in marriage to. It was a shame, he considered, that Sir Joshua Tregurthen's son had been married a couple of years ago and was out of the running; but there were several eligible young gentlemen around, although he was ever brought back to the realisation that not one of them could hold a candle to the Trevarthen boy when it came to looks, mulatto or no. Then there was the family fortune, for with the mine paying the highest return of any in the country, coupled with the vastness of the Trevu estates and other holdings, Paul Trevarthen would ultimately be the richest landowner for miles around.

"Wicked, wicked," the Captain sighed bitterly, shaking his head over the fact, but alter it he could not.

Conversely, although 'out of the running' as Petherick had stated, it was to be Sir Joshua's son who played a part in Paul's finally getting to meet the Captain's daughter. The Tregurthen's first grandson was born and they were so delighted that they decided to hold a ball in the infant's honour. Of course, anyone who had their feet on Penzance's social ladder had been invited, and as it was the Tregurthen's party, everyone made sure that their gilt edged invitation took pride of place on their mantelpiece and each family moved heaven and earth to enable them to attend the ball.

Naturally, Caroline and her daughters spent a small fortune on their dresses for as part of the Trevarthen household they were all to attend. Paul had to suffer yet another fitting at the tailors, but the highly decorated waistcoat he was to wear and the coat of pale blue superfine, did not lift his spirits. Admittedly, he had never worn such elegant attire but perversely he preferred the more sober dress that he habitually wore, even though his appearance in such fine clothes did nothing to detract from his astonishingly handsome face and physique. Hannah, catching sight of him dressed for the ball, clasped her hands across her ample bosom and, pink with pleasure, exclaimed, "Master Paul, they maids won't be able to take their liddle eyes off 'e sure nuff."

Redvers turned to her and agreed. "Quite so, Hannah. He will outshine every young buck in the place," but his son only blushed, feeling remarkably foolish and hoped fervently that the party would be over the sooner so that he could lay aside his puppet garb and return to his more favoured style of dress.

The Tregurthen's house, rebuilt on the ruins of the fire that almost completely demolished the previous dwelling, was an imposing and substantial building. It had none of the idiosyncratic style of Trevu that Redvers and his son so admired and loved. Squire Tregurthen had spent a small fortune on the house and had - unusually for that area - insisted on what was a classical style: with its pillared porch and pediments and large square paned windows, it looked most imposing but completely lacking in character unlike the old Tregurthen Manor house that it replaced which, like Trevu, relied for its charm on a combination of its former occupants desires and ambitions. However, the lights from the house shone warmly; their rays spread out across the immaculate gardens like a gilded fan and helped to soften the otherwise soulless exterior. The Trevarthen party arrived at the ball with a host of other Penzance families but when Paul, desperately trying not to look self-conscious, entered the ballroom along side his father every young female in the ballroom vowed to dance with him. Cards were flashed under his nose without the slightest degree of decorum, but with his aunt's training now firmly embedded in him, he was his usual charming self to all and, knowing what was expected of him, managed not to have his name placed against only the cards of the prettiest girls and never that of the same girl twice. His aunt, her hawk like eye forever upon him, nodded her approval. Caroline had time to note that her own daughters were all looking remarkably pretty in their new dresses, and as they soon found their cards filled up, she was sure everything was looking set for a quite exceptional evening.

Redvers, never fond of dancing, seized the opportunity to leave his sister in charge of the young people and so had wandered away to talk to some of his fellow landowners when the third country dance started. Paul obediently took his place and bowed to his partner as the dance started. He performed his steps to perfection and as he turned back elegantly after releasing his partner - as the dance dictated - to have his hand taken by another he suddenly realised that the young lady, whose delicately gloved hand had been placed in his own, was none other than Miss Dorothea Petherick. A thrill went through him that he had never experienced before at her touch. He tried to smile but was convinced that he was goggling at her foolishly. Miss Petherick, for her part, knew only that the most handsome young man she had ever seen in her young life was smiling at her in such an intoxicating way that she felt herself tremble. Oblivious to all around them, the musicians seemed to play for them alone, and hand in hand they set out to perform their steps, both feeling and expressing that they were indeed dancing on air. They were soon to be brought savagely back to earth when, after having managed to dance only a few steps, a strong hand grabbed Paul by the arm and pushed him roughly until his back was wedged against one of the columns that held up the ballroom's ceiling.

Captain Petherick's face glowered at him, suffused with anger, "Keep your dirty black hands off her - you . . . you filthy ni...," he shouted into Paul's shocked face. However, he got no further for his daughter rushed across to her father and tried to pull him away whilst crying bitterly, "Father, no! Oh! Please, please let him go. Please father - he was doing no wrong."

"What?" he shouted at her, unable to believe, what his innocent child should be saying, "You! You would have me watch you dance with this black devil? Damn you, I'm your father and I say what manner of . . . manner of . . ." but his speech finished abruptly as he suddenly became aware of Redvers standing in front of him.

"Unhand my son, sir, and then may I suggest that you leave this house at once as you have shown yourself completely unable to conduct yourself with propriety in this company," he said, speaking quietly but those who knew him well could see his hands forming into fists and knew full well the effort he was making at imposing some control over his temper.

"Damn right, sir," boomed a deep voice at his side as Sir Joshua Tregurthen's angry countenance loomed into view. "Never known a thing like it. Get out! Get out and take yourself back home. We don't want the likes of you befouling our town."

Captain Petherick, his hopes for his beloved daughter's conquests lying in tatters about his feet, released Paul as if in a dream and pulling his sobbing daughter after him strode from the ballroom, his face suffused with an angry red stain. As she left with her father at her side, Dorothea turned and directed a look of such longing and entreaty at Paul that the pain in his heart cut into him like a knife. In a dream he found his other arm now held tightly by his aunt's hand and, as he looked in bewilderment into her face, she smiled understandably up at him, but turned and addressed the Squire and Redvers in a calm ordered tone.

"Well done, gentlemen," she purred sweetly and then, pulling Paul towards her said, "Come Paul - a turn about the garden will soon put all to rights, you will see." In a serene and calm manner, she propelled him with great firmness towards the large window that led out to the low balcony and the steps that went down to the lawn. Her nephew was hardly aware of the babble of conversation that broke out behind him as he was led away and Sir Joshua's roaring voice extolling his guests to resume their dance and shouting at the band to: "Play, you fools, play."

Outside in the cool of the garden Paul found himself shaking, so his aunt found him a garden bench and made him sit down on it as he struggled hard to maintain his composure. The abuse delivered to him was to him bearable although it had shocked the company gathered in the room. Abuse was something that Paul had learned to live with, others that witnessed it were the more shocked by it because they had come to admire and respect the young man in their midst. It was not the hateful words that had destroyed the young man's composure; it was the sight of her dear face as she was led sobbing from the house. The pain of Petherick's remarks were as nothing compared to his realisation that she returned equally the feeling he felt for her. His aunt's words broke in upon his despairing thoughts:

"Very unpleasant for you Paul, I know, but 'tis all over now, and you can be assured that he will not show his face around the town in a hurry after such an exhibition as that," she said quietly.

"No - I know he will not," he whispered in a stricken voice and he gulped convulsively as he said, "and neither will she." Unable to contain his pain the longer, he cried, "Oh God aunt! Why did that hateful man have to be her father of all people?"

Realisation of Paul's predicament struck Caroline with a blinding flash. Pushing her nephew under the noses of Penzance's most highly regarded families she had been made well aware by Paul that he had no interest whatsoever in any of their aspiring daughters, but at last he had found someone that he did feel an attraction for. She considered quietly for a moment and then spoke softly to him:

"One's first love Paul - it is - it is so rarely one's last, you know. It will pass even tho' it hurts dreadfully at the moment," she told him sympathetically.

She heard him mutter softly and brokenly, "I've never felt this way about any girl I've ever known, aunt. I . . . I felt like this . . . ever since . . . ever since I first saw her in . . . ," he could get no further for he had great difficulty in mastering his feelings.

"Shh . . . Paul . . . Shh . . . it will pass . . . it will pass," Caroline told him gently and, placing her arm around his shoulders, gave him what poor comfort she could. When she thought he had recovered his composure enough to enable him to rejoin the throng they returned arm in arm to the house. They entered the ballroom quietly but Paul, whether he would or no, was soon surrounded by people, mostly the young men of his own age. They were at great pains to show their unity with him and their loyalty and friendship helped him to face the rest of the evening.

Rumours were rife in Penzance about the incident at the Tregurthen's ball and the talk was everywhere relayed by guests and servants alike, so that soon there was not one part of the town that did not have knowledge of the happenings.

Anthony Tregenza discussed it with his mother whilst they took tea the following afternoon and, as he had been present, was able to supply his aged parent with much desired information on the actual events.

"The Squire was most annoyed for it completely wrecked the conviviality of the evening, Mama, as you can imagine. Old Redvers looked pretty mad, as well," he announced sarcastically before he laughed in a cruel fashion at his recollection of the turmoil in the ballroom.

"Serve him right," announced his mother in her thin, high voice, "for he would whore his way around the town without thought of the consequences," and then broke off to tell Miss Williams that Bouncer, sitting dejectedly on his velvet cushion, had dropped his ball and required it to be returned to him. The young girl patiently put her embroidery to one side and retrieved Bouncer's toy for him - which object he then patently ignored - before returning to her seat and on picking up her frame began to set her delicate stitches again, her face closed and shuttered to her employers. It would have mattered not what her thoughts were for neither had the intention of including her in their conversation.

Broken Bonds: The First Book Of The Trevu Trilogy

"Still if he had not bedded that damn mulatto he would not have the problems of marrying off his bastard, that undoubtedly he will have," she announced in disgust. She continued in her usual foul mouthed manner, "Pity he could not have got a boy on a white woman. That at least would have been more fitting!"

"Well, 'twas not for want of trying if I remember, correctly," her son grinned at her; finding nothing wrong with her speech for he had modelled himself on his mother and thought her a quite exceptional woman.

"Petherick's daughter will come into a fortune so they say. An only child too. Perhaps, we should invite them for tea, Anthony dear," and she raised her calculating blue eyes to her son's florid countenance, with a knowing smile.

"God's life Mama! She is nothing but a child and her father will live for years yet. Still," he said, noting his mother's disappointed look, "I will make enquiries; for with her father's behaviour she has not done her chances in the marriage mart a lot of good in these environs."

"No, more's the pity, for her father made a vast fortune out of slavery. However, he has made it most difficult for the wench to be accepted everywhere, for those damn Trevarthens are most highly regarded hereabout. Still, Anthony dear, 'twould be such a shame if all that money could conceivably go to another - less deserving - gentleman," and she smiled adoringly at her son.

"Mama!" he answered, with a blush, "The girl may not see in me what it is she desires in a husband, although I do consider myself to be quite exceptional; for money and position are mine in abundance," he added with pride, and breathed deeply until the ominous creaking of his corsets, attempting to contain his ample figure, warned him to desist.

"Of course she will admire you, you fool!" cried his mother, angrily, and added, "Apply your magnificent brain for one moment my dear son. What girl in their right mind would wish for the Trevarthen bastard for a husband when the renowned Anthony Tregenza, gentleman of Penzance, is by far the more eligible?"

"I will of course give it my most careful consideration, dear Mama, but," her son added guardedly, "it is apparent that the Trevarthen's have a great deal of sympathy and 'twould not be wise to offend our friends in the town. From what I can glean from their conversations they appear to be siding with the mulatto, don't you know?"

"Personally, I blame that damn Methodist Wesley preaching on and on about slavery. Damn fool; for what are these people good for but to be slaves, eh?" she muttered in annoyance.

"Well, Mama, I do most heartily agree with you but," replied her son, in disgust, "I must tell you that it is reputed that Paul Trevarthen is one of the most intelligent lads in the county, for Herbert Colenso who used to teach him at Helston told Squire Tregurthen he was the best scholar he had ever come across."

"What!" shrieked his shocked Mama, and went on to ascribe his abilities to his father's side of the family although, rack her brains as she might, not one of Redvers long line of ancestors could she bring to mind as having had more than a modicum of academic ability if they had any at all. They finished their tea complaining all the while of the unfairness of life and, after her son had departed, Mrs. Tregenza ordered her companion to take her precious Bouncer for a walk for, "the damn thing has that look on his face again," she announced in disgust.

Outside, in the street, Bouncer, freed from the tedious confines of his prison, trotted along the road in great delight. Miss Williams on the other hand, had recourse to her handkerchief and dabbed at her eyes frequently. But when the tall, brown haired gentleman with the fine blue eyes doffed his cap to her and wished that he might be of assistance in her distress, she raised her green eyes to his face before saying defiantly, "My dear Mr. Bolitho, surely, you have come to realise by now - for I have frequently informed you that it is the case - that there is nothing you can do to assist me or that will in any way improve your standing in my eyes?"

Joey's handsome countenance hid his pain at her words and his attractive smile spread across his face as he said reasonably, "I am ever 'opeful Miss Williams that one day you'll come to see that I am most serious as regards my intentions to 'e fer I do consider 'e a most fine and beautiful lady an' if there is ever any thing I can do fer 'e you 'ave only to call on my services, Ma'am," and even Sarah-Jane could not fail to note the look of adoration in his normally cold eyes.

She sighed heavily, before telling him again that she was not looking to find herself a follower but when Joey, emboldened, asked her why that should be the case, she blushed and was unable to answer him. Shaking her head at him when he asked if she had another suitor he smiled broadly, before he announced his declared intent of calling at her home when next he would be free from his activities and she should have leave from her own employment, for he wished to talk with her most seriously and sincerely.

"I am sorry, Mr. Bolitho, but I have no intention of telling you when next I shall be free to visit my parents and as far as I am aware you are not so well acquainted with me that my home is known to you. Also," she added in a strict voice, "I can assure you that I have no desire to give you this information." If she thought to weaken his determination Sarah-Jane was to be disappointed for he merely smiled at her again and said with a twitch of his lips: "Why Miss Williams, don't 'e knaw who you be talkin' to after all, fer if Joey Bolitho want knaw somethin', e'll find it out easy 'nuff." A flutter, of what she thought must have been disquiet, in her heart made her look up into his face and she studied his features for a while. He was indeed a most good-looking fellow, with remarkably handsome features, a wide mouth with delicately carved lips, a short straight nose, almost black well formed brows, a tanned unblemished face and large blue eyes surrounded by thick dark lashes. There were woman a plenty who sighed over him she well knew, for along with his good looks he had a decided air of charm about him. However, she felt neither flattered by his attention nor interested in his intentions so she merely held out her hand and wished him goodbye in a flat tone, thinking indeed to agree with her employers that the world was a most unfair place, for she would have given everything she possessed to have Paul Trevarthen smile at her in just such an adoring way as Joseph Bolitho was doing at that precise moment. Joey caught up her hand, lifted it to his lips and placed a delicate kiss upon her fingers before wishing her farewell and added with his mischievous smile, "Until we meet 'gain, Miss Williams, ma'am." When she was finally lost to view in the house he turned and walked back to the inn where he had left Barnaby Rickard, in deep discussion with various customers about the goings on at the Squire's ball, for all had heard differing tales of what exactly was supposed to have happened during the obvious disturbance. Getting himself a drink from the bar he came over to sit beside Barney, who alone amongst his fellows noted the warm gleam in his companion's normally cold eyes.

CHAPTER 10

THE bay mare trotted down the lane and pricked her ears at the sight that met her eyes; for another horse stood by the roadside having his near hind leg attended to by a young man who kept his head bent and his back to the road as he worked. She felt her rider stiffen in the saddle and was not surprised to be pulled up alongside the roan contentedly eating grass growing in the hedge. The young man removing the stone from his horse's hoof did not alter his position or even turn his head to see who it was on the other horse, for he already knew just who the gentleman would be that had stopped beside him. Carrying on unconcernedly he turned only when he was addressed by the man whose temper was rising at the rudeness displayed to him.

"What are you doing here, fellow?" he asked abruptly, and watched with growing annoyance as the young man unhurriedly finished his task, replaced his knife and lowered his horse's leg to the ground, gently and fondly slapping the beast's rump before turning to face his inquisitor.

"Mornin' Cap'n Trevarthen, sir," he greeted Redvers, politely, his face impassive.

"Damn your pleasantries!" snapped Redvers angrily, "I asked you what you were doing here?"

"Thought that 'twere obvious, Cap'n, sir, fer I was takin' a stone out me 'orse's 'oof," he answered calmly, his blue eyes steady on Trevarthen's face.

"I could see that, man!" responded Redvers testily, "I wish to know why you are on my property, for I have never encouraged your sort to call and well you know it."

" 'Ess sir, but 'twouldn to see you that I come out 'ere anyways," came the swift reply.

"Damn you man! I will have an answer from you, for if you have come to encourage any of mine in the smuggling trade I will run you off this property afore ever your feet touch the ground," announced the Master of Trevu, angered by the young man's insolence, and he continued in an annoyed tone: "You are I believe the smuggler known as Joseph Bolitho, cohort of Barnaby Rickard, are you not?"

"'Ess sir," replied Joey unabashed and swept the Captain a graceful bow in acknowledgement.

Redvers, in spite of his anger, bit back a smile at the felon's impudence. Summoning his temper to the fore he again enquired Bolitho's reason for being in the locality.

"Come a visitin', sir," answered the smuggler calmly.

"And to whom are you paying this call?" barked Redvers, "for I would know their names, for I will not have my workers to spend their time with you!"

"Tidden one a yer workers, sir," rejoined the young man, his face impassive.

"Don't be so damned foolish man! If they live on Trevu land they work for me, so I will know their names, do you hear?" fumed Redvers, and he was almost shouting now.

"'Ess sir," Bolitho responded but said no more.

Redvers, annoyed with being confronted by a young man who seemed determined to thwart him, pushed his horse forward in a threatening manner towards Bolitho who, impudently clapped his hands under the mare's nose, and in fright the poor animal reared up suddenly and almost unseated her rider. Bringing his horse under control, Redvers, breathing heavily and now in a great temper, turned again to face the young man and as he did so noted the small posy of flowers knotted into the roan's mane, bound by a length of satin pink ribbon. In a flash of realisation he understood that Bolitho had come a courting and, in fairness to the young man, perhaps he would not wish it spread abroad for by reputation he was quite a ladies man with many conquests, although he was known to favour wenches who plied their trade openly above any other. There were no woman like that around here, but looking down into Bolitho's handsome countenance he could well imagine he could steal a young girl's heart easily enough. However, his face impassive, he puzzled as to who exactly it could be amongst his workers who would be the recipient of Bolitho's interest and found to his embarrassment that he could think of many, for at the sight of a handsome face some of the local females could become most idiotic. Bolitho had said the person he was to visit was not one of his workers but there were no women or girls around the locality that were not employed directly on the farms or in Trevu. He was on the point of accusing the fellow of being a liar when he remembered his mine captain's daughter Sarah-Jane and bethought himself that, as it was a Sunday, she might well be on her day off from the Tregenza's household. Considering further he realised that it would be possible for Bolitho to meet her in Penzance and would wish to visit with her on her day off, although he found it most surprising that the dear girl should in any way look with favour on a miscreant of Bolitho's calibre.

He studied the smuggler's impassive face for a while before taking a chance on his conjecture and announcing abruptly, "John Williams is well known to me an' I think not that he would want your sort to call upon his daughter," and had the satisfaction of seeing a quick blush stain the young man's cheeks.

"Possibly, sir, but I shan't knaw 'til I've presented meself will I?" he announced brazenly and, considering the conversation at an end, swung himself athletically into his saddle, politely doffed his cap at his questioner and wished him farewell before proceeding on his way as nonchalantly as if he had been out for a ride on his own land. Before spurring his horse on to the lower farm estate, Redvers watched his retreating figure with annoyance, but even he had to admire the fellow's self-possession.

In the garden of the little cottage at Rose-in-Valley Sarah-Jane sat happily watching Mouser playing with a leaf blowing across the grass. So absorbed was she that only when a shadow darkened the place where she sat did she look up and catch her breath in excitement. The man silhouetted before her she immediately assumed to be Paul Trevarthen by his size and stature. As he had not called for so long, she smiled in uncontrolled delight but the smile froze on her face when she heard her visitor's voice say, "I come a callin' like I told 'e I would Miss Williams," and Joseph Bolitho stepped out of the light and she saw his handsome face plainly with the sun upon it.

"So I observe Mr. Bolitho, but as I am so tired of telling you, it a waste of your time and mine that you should have bothered to follow me all this way," and she got up angrily from her seat and made to enter the cottage with the intention of shutting the door behind her. Joey, swiftly stepped in front of her, and with his most engaging smile presented her with his posy. She sighed her thanks and took it from his hands, and thought never in all his life had it ever occurred to Paul to present her with such a gift in spite of all their years of friendship.

"Well," she announced in a tight, annoyed tone, "You are here now an' I suppose there is nothing for it but that I shall have to introduce you to my family, tho' I warn you Mr. Bolitho you are not such a person to be looked on with favour in my household. We are a law abiding family and wish for none of your persuasion to come amongst us," and she raised her chin and looked at him defiantly, but he only smiled at her the more, so with a sigh of exasperation she led him into her home.

John Williams regarded the young man, who was to him so obviously besotted with his daughter, with a jaundiced eye for he was not the sort of fellow he would have wished for his daughter. Indeed Bolitho was not the sort of man he would wish to entertain under his roof, for he considered smuggling a most foul occupation as it led young men astray and encouraged the locals to drink to access because of the cheapness of the drink supplied to them. But worse than that; the fellow was known as a murderer. He had no wish to converse with him, but politeness forced John to speak to him and he was most surprised to discover that Bolitho could talk sensibly and intelligently and had a more than fair layman's knowledge of mining. Sadly, John concluded that if the man had followed a more law abiding profession he could have welcomed him to his home gladly, for the young man would have made an admirable son-in-law. His wife was equally disappointed that of all the young gentlemen who could have taken an interest in her pretty daughter it should be none other than the most notorious smuggler in the county who came to call on her. Obviously her daughter was not interested in the man, for there had only ever been one young gentleman that she had set her heart on, but even in her disappointment Mrs. Williams had to admit Joseph Bolitho was a most good-looking young fellow and she was not immune to the fact that he had a great deal of charm. He was most well mannered and correct for he stayed only half an hour before taking his leave. At the door he stood with his hand on the handle, waiting patiently for Sarah-Jane to walk him to his horse, and even her annoyed expression as she considered if she could be rude enough not to see him off the premises, made him smile. She walked by his side until he reached his tethered horse and looking into his eyes felt chastened that he should admire her so for she could not love him blinded as she was with her love for another. A smuggler would not be welcomed into her family anyway, for the whole household had been brought up from their earliest day with a great sense of right and wrong and Joseph Bolitho, although he might know the difference between them, cared not about such scruples.

"Please not to call again, Mr. Bolitho, for you are not welcome here either by my family or by myself," she told him coldly and made to turn away from him, but he caught her by the arms gently and turned her about to face him again. She tried to look at the ground beneath her feet but a strange compulsion made her lift her clear, green eyes to his face. Noting the pain behind the smile, she felt consumed by guilt that she did not feel the same passion for the man as he undoubtedly felt for her, but Sarah-Jane had no wish to place herself in a position where Bolitho might believe that he stood a chance for his suit to prosper.

"I can change fer 'e Miss Williams if thas' what 'tis goin' take fer 'e to look upon me kindly," he informed her in his soft voice; but she shook her head.

"Mr. Bolitho: please to understand that you will never come to that place in my heart where you so desire to be. It is impossible and I would sooner you know it now than realise it the later. You will have to look elsewhere for companionship for you will not find it with me, sir!" Giving him a very firm stare she told him sternly, "Do I make myself plain to you, Mr. Bolitho?"

"Most!, Miss Williams but this place in yer 'eart that I'm tryin' to reach 'tis empty I 'ope, fer I desire that in time you will grow to love me Miss Williams as sincerely as I d' love 'e?" he told her simply.

"Mr. Bolitho it is not for you to ask that question of me," she told him angrily and noted with displeasure that he smiled the more at her, but did not realise that even when angered he considered that she looked most attractive.

"Well?" he enquired softly.

"I have not the slightest intention of telling you more than I have already done, Mr. Bolitho, and I would be most grateful if you will leave immediately for I have to help my mother in the house," she cried in annoyance but he did not release her and merely told her again that he would know the answer to his question. She twisted about in his hold but although he held her gently he had no intention of setting her free so finally she relented and shouted at him in reply.

"Yes, Mr. Bolitho, yes! There is another man in my heart and in my dreams but I doubt not that he will ever look to me for love, for he loves another," she told him on an angry sob, "but still I shall wait for him in the hope that one day perhaps he will see sense." This time she noted he could not hide the pain in his face and even his eyes, normally so cold and dispassionate, appeared bathed in sadness.

"Then Miss Williams, we shall jes' 'ave wait together fer like you I don' believe I'm goin' love another my life long the way I d' love yerself," and slipping one hand down her arm he caught up her shaking hand and kissed her fingers before turning and swinging himself up on his horse.

"Yer servant, Miss Williams," he said quietly, doffed his cap and retraced his path through the wood. She followed him with her eyes until he was out of sight and then wiped her angry tears from her face before composing herself and returning to the cottage. Nothing was mentioned by either of her parents of their visitor until they made their way home from church in their pony and trap, but on reaching the road that forked to Trevu her father turned towards her and informed his daughter prosaically. "They be neither the one for you my girl, but methinks the smuggler if he had been a better man would find more favour with me than Paul, for you only got look at that blaggard Bolitho to see 'e, at least, do worship the ground you walk on," but he had not the opportunity to say more for - her nerves overwrought - Sarah-Jane promptly burst into tears.

On his way home Joseph Bolitho's path crossed the Master of Trevu's yet again and he politely doffed his cap at him.

"Cap'n Trevarthen, sir!" he greeted him stiffly, for his morning had not been as successful as he had hoped, but neither had it been as disastrous as he had feared.

"Mr. Bolitho," returned Redvers and noting the smuggler's impassive features wondered how well the young man had fared on his quest, and realised with a sudden shock that, just like himself, if he had not the intention that anyone should know his feelings he would hide them behind his own mask, lest his emotions should show. Whereas his son on the other hand, sighed Redvers to himself, let almost every care and feeling show upon his face like an enraptured Methodist at a bible meeting.

When Joey returned to Gulval he was met by an irate Barney who told him that he had sent Likky to search every tavern and inn in Penzance for him, for he wished to catch the tide that afternoon for France. Joey considered that perhaps now would not be the right time to inform his master that he was seriously thinking of giving up the smuggling trade. He would have to lead Barney along that road slowly for he doubted that he could come up with a reason that would satisfy his master and, at the moment, he had not the wish to inform anyone that he had fallen in love and with a girl who had no more love for him than if he had been a pebble on the beach. So he merely nodded and threw his things in his bag and, availing himself of one of Phoebe's delicious pies set off in his master's wake, eating hungrily as he did so.

In the January of the following year Paul received a small book of poems, bound in vellum, from Mr. Armitage. His name it was that appeared on the spine and inside on the frontispiece and looked most fine. His father, when the book was shown to him, stared at it for a long while and when he did finally speak could only say, "Well done Paul."

His aunt Caroline and her daughters had returned from Truro to spend Christmas at Trevu; and on being shown the book they were most impressed and they congratulated him wholeheartedly. Caroline asked to be given a copy and Paul said he would be writing to Mr. Armitage soon: no doubt that gentleman would be able to get another copy sent on. Paul, now taller than ever, looked down at her and laughed when his aunt told him they had never had an author in the family.

"I am not an author, aunt, merely a translator," he smiled gently.

"Do not prevaricate, Paul," she said; her forceful personality showing itself, "Your name it is that appears in print and that makes you an author as far as I am concerned."

"Yes, aunt," he accepted meekly.

It did not take long for the whole of Penzance to discover that there was an author in their midst for, unable to contain her pride in her nephew's achievement, his aunt Caroline had seen to that. It was soon public knowledge that Captain Trevarthen's boy had had a book published and he rapidly became a local celebrity in the town. Samuel's was besieged with people ordering copies of the book. As the minor Latin poet that Paul had translated had written almost entirely on the subject of love, the young girls who had read the book were enchanted and fell in love with Paul all over again. On a shopping trip to the town with his aunt he was almost mobbed, but laughed it off and told Caroline that he imagined that the furore would soon die down. In that he was proved wrong: Literary society was so taken with the book that the printers had to rush and print further copies to keep up with public demand. Various literary societies sent letters asking him for talks or readings at their gatherings, but he refused them all. Paul was completely bemused; for he could not understand the effect the book was having on people. He did not comprehend that his sympathetic translation of the text could appeal to so many people. Old dowagers and simpering schoolgirls bought copies and sighed over the words in the privacy of their own bedrooms. Young wives bought it to give to their husbands as a token of their love. Old maids read their copies with misty eyes and contemplated the might-have-been.

In the March a banker's draft was forwarded to Paul. When he opened it he almost dropped the letter, so surprised was he at the contents. His father was equally bemused, but promptly took his son to town and an account was opened in Paul's name and the draft swiftly deposited. The manager of the bank was most obliging. Three more drafts followed in quick succession. Paul, in all innocence, had become a person of substance in his own right and by his own hand. He wrote to Mr. Armitage expressing guilt at having had such success with what he considered had been the headmaster's own work. Mr. Armitage promptly wrote back that he considered Paul's translation to be far better that any work he could have produced. As to the idea Paul had of forwarding some of the money that he was accruing as payment to his old teacher; he firmly refused but said that if Paul had a wish for it the school library could do with funds to purchase more books. Redvers advised Paul on a suitable amount to send and suggested that a scholarship fund could be set up to enable any poor boy to be enrolled at the school. Paul thought this an excellent idea. So did Mr. Armitage and arrangements were made to this effect. He also thanked Paul for the magnificent sum that had been forwarded to him to enable him to replenish the several battered books that lay on his library shelves and to allow him to purchase such a large quantity of new ones.

Turning the little volume - that had caused his life to change so unbelievably - over in his hand Paul found his mind returning yet again to his experiences since the night of the Tregurthen's ball. He had spent the summer mostly in his father's company and was most glad to do so, for in the last year they had grown closer together than ever. Their days were full, for there was always plenty to do on the farm. He had learnt to plough under old Daniel's direction, he helped with the hay making, went with the men to cut the corn and when they stopped for crowst he was wrestled to the ground by Davy Tyack, the farm's own district champion. All the while he was using his energy to burn out the desperate loneliness that had never left him since the night of the dance. They visited their friends as before but less frequently, and some of the families that previously Caroline had been at such pains to call on she no longer appeared to wish to visit. When they did go to Penzance - not so often as before he noted - they met all their friends and their conversations continued on as if nothing had happened. At first he had felt uncomfortable, but his aunt would have none of it and pushed him on. When his book was published he was requested to attend all sorts of functions, but his aunt expertly weeded out the unwanted invitations so he found himself gracing only a select number of households, although the attention he received there was considerable.

The Pethericks were not seen in the town for a long time after the dance and few of their former acquaintances wished to visit for the Captain's outburst at the Tregurthen's had offended their sensibilities. On one of his visits to the town Paul did have one brief glimpse of Dorothea as she came out of the milliners, but as she was being escorted by her father he turned away abruptly and made sure that they did not encounter each other. Even then he found himself trembling at the sight of her.

When at the start of last summer Caroline and her daughters returned to Truro, her nephew declined an invitation to return with them. She said that perhaps he was rather young for the Truro season and perhaps he would prefer to come and stay when he was older. He thanked her kindly and was in such good humour with her that he kissed her cheek with more warmth than he usually felt for her when they eventually left. This time Caroline had arranged a post chaise to take them from Trevu directly to their home in Truro, or more correctly she had suggested that Redvers arrange it.

Now almost a year had passed since that fateful dance and if he still longed for his lost love, he was old enough to come to terms with life without Dorothea. He knew that he loved her but he had resigned himself to having to live the rest of his life without her. Several local girls had shown an interest in him but he had never by as much as a look given any of them any reason to believe that he favoured them. He looked for nothing more than friendship.

He sighed and put down the book. Shaking himself from his reverie he decided to visit John Williams and his family. If the boys were at home they might want to go fishing, he thought reasonably. It had been a hot, sultry day and he wanted to get away from his home for a while to take his mind off his troubled thoughts.

However, when he arrived at their little cottage he was disappointed to discover that Mrs. Williams had visitors, for her sister from Camborne had been visiting with another sister in Marazion and had come across to stay for the night. The Williams' boys that no longer lived at home had returned for a visit, only to find that, like their brothers, they had to give up their room to accommodate their aunt, but they did so laughingly with much good humour. The small kitchen was a riot of noise and merriment, but Paul thought it would be too much for him and decided he would make his excuses and leave but William John forestalled him when he announced that he would like to go swimming in the little cove and did any of the others want to accompany him? His brothers all thought it was a most fine idea and noticing Paul's hesitation they urged him to come with them.

"C'mon Paul, go for a swim with we. Cool 'e down after a hot day proper that will," young Mark told him laughingly.

Unsure what to do their high good humour was infectious and finally, Paul considered that a swim would no doubt do him good. So in a short space of time Paul and his friends were making their way up the hill and across the top of the cliff to take the path down to the cove. Once on the beach they undressed quickly and were soon diving from the rocks and splashing about in the water. The freedom the water gave Paul did indeed lift his spirits and soon he was swimming out to catch the waves that would throw him back on to the beach, laughing as much as his friends. They spent a pleasant hour, joking and splashing in the water as if they were all young boys again, but at last they decided it was time to make their way home and reluctantly headed for their clothes that lay in piles on a rock.

William John, struggling into his breeches, turned his head as he heard a sound from the bottom of the shallow cliff to the north of the beach. It sounded like a shout but he could not be sure.

"Did 'e 'ere something, Paul?" he asked.

"I thought so William John but I am not sure."

"'Tis comin' from over there," said Peter and peering into the gathering gloom he shouted excitedly, "Someone's waving to we, look!"

Indeed someone was waving at them. They could just make out a shadowy figure against the rocks that lay at the bottom of the cliff, frantically waving a light coloured piece of cloth. Finishing their dressing as hurriedly as their wet bodies would allow they dragged on their boots and started to run across the beach towards whoever it was that appeared to require their assistance. They arrived breathlessly to find two people: the first, a man lying insensible on his back on a rock with blood pouring from a cut on his head, and the other a girl who was weeping distressfully. Obviously the man had fallen from the top of the cliff and the girl had climbed down after him. However, it was not the sight of the scene of the disaster that stopped the young men in their tracks, it was the recognition of the couple to whom the disaster had befallen.

William John turned immediately to Paul.

"You go 'ome, Master Paul," he said authoritatively, "We can see to 'e and get 'en 'ome."

"No - no, William John. I shall have to help you for it will take all of us to get him back up the cliff. The path is not easy," Paul said quietly, and then turning to Peter and Dick, instructed them to retrieve some of the planks from a pile that had been left on the beach when a local fishing boat had broken her back on the rocks in a vain attempt to beach herself on the sand.

"Hurry," Paul said firmly, "for we will need to tie him to the boards in case he has damaged his back. Mark, you go for Dr. Simcott and bring him to Nancemellin. We will have got him back to there, God willing, by the time you return." Without wasting any more time he took off his coat, pulled his shirt over his head and tearing it into strips with his strong teeth began to bind up the Captain's copiously bleeding head.

In the company of his friends he resisted speech with Dorothea, and so William John it was who suggested to her that she ran back to the house and advised the housekeeper of what had happened. Perhaps she could arrange that they send a wagon to enable them to get her father transported back Nancemellin the quicker?

"Yes, yes, of course," she said still shaking with the fright of what she had witnessed, but she made a valiant effort to control herself and so she turned and, picking up her skirts, ran lightly up the twisting path to the cliff top.

With the aid of the planks and, fashioning ties out of strips of the remainder of Paul's shirt and using the boys' shirts that they had also ripped apart, they managed to make a serviceable stretcher on which to carry the unconscious Petherick. He moaned as he was lifted gently from the rock and placed carefully on to their makeshift stretcher but did not regain consciousness. They each took hold of a corner and with great difficulty managed to manhandle their burden to the top of the cliff, for although all strong young men the sea captain was a well built man himself and their task was not made easier by the gathering darkness. When they arrived at the top they found that not only a wagon from Nancemellin was heading towards them but Redvers and John Williams were galloping towards the little group as well.

Captain Trevarthen; alerted by Mark as to what had happened and also to whom, was met by John Williams on the road for Mark had to return to collect his horse before heading to Penzance to get medical assistance. Redvers glanced worriedly at his son and in spite of the darkness of the hour could make out the look of grim determination on his face. They did not exchange any words and the little rescue group, with the help of Redvers and John Williams, proceeded to place the Captain in the back of the wagon, which had been strewn with loose hay and over which a blanket had been placed. As Paul had correctly surmised they arrived at Nancemellin at the same time as Dr. Simcott and under his expert direction Petherick was taken into the house. To enable him to examine the Captain easily he ordered Mrs. Dennis, the housekeeper, to clear the dining room table and so the boys and men laid the still unconscious man there. Leaving the room, they returned to the hallway and stood in a tight little group, with the boys explaining how the evening's events had unfolded in subdued voices. Of Dorothea Petherick, Paul noted, there was no sign.

Twenty minutes later Dr Simcott rejoined them and informed them of Petherick's condition. "Severe bruising and a nasty cut to the temple - the lump the size of a goose egg, nothing broken 'tho - damned lucky - could have bled to death if somebody had not bound him up - put a fair few stitches in it," he remarked in his usual abrupt manner. "Said you'd carry him to his room - use the blanket, easier. No need to send for the men with you all here."

So once again they hoisted up their burden and successfully negotiated the stairs and deposited the Captain on his bed in his bedchamber. The housekeeper signed for them all to go away and as her son, young Willy Dennis, short on wits but with great strength, was lumbering up the stairs to assist his mother to undress the master, they quietly left the room and followed each other down the stairs.

In the hallway Dorothea was standing, talking to Dr. Simcott. It was obvious he was informing her of the extent of her father's injuries and so they began to edge their way towards the main door. Dr. Simcott turned away to ascend the stairs to deliver a sedative he had prepared for his patient and Dorothea immediately ran towards their small group and began to thank them. She shook each of them by the hand, thanking them most warmly in turn, but when she came to Paul she blushed rosily and seemed incapable of speech.

"I . . . how you . . . under the circumstances . . . I . . .," she stuttered but Paul just took the proffered hand and said quietly and composedly, "Would have done the same for any man, Miss Petherick, no need for thanks I can assure you."

She smiled gratefully at him, but summoning up a better voice said to them all in general, "I shall be sure to tell Papa to whom he owes his deliverance from that dreadful fall. When he fell so quickly I was so sure that he would be killed. Thank you, gentlemen, all of you. Thank you most sincerely," and she smiled at them all radiantly.

They made their way out of the house, and having discovered that the boys had no means of transport except for their own legs, Miss Petherick instantly ordered that the carriage be used to convey them to their homes. She stood in the glow of the silvery moonlight that bathed her and waved them out of the yard. The Williams boys talked excitedly about the events of the evening but Paul sat silently watching until at last her small figure disappeared from view.

Arriving home not long after his father; Paul knew well the best place to look for him and ran him to earth in the back parlour, sitting in front of the fire with a glass of brandy in his hand. He looked up into his son's ecstatic face before lowering his eyes; disturbed by what he had seen. However he made an effort to control himself and announced in a firm, soft voice:

"Help yourself, Paul," and pointed to the bottle on the sideboard. "Do you good after all that excitement."

Paul shook his head and declined the invitation, for he had yet to develop a taste for spirits, but he crossed the room to the fire and sat opposite his father. His eyes were sparkling as he asked breathlessly, "Miss Petherick is most beautiful is she not, father?"

"Most," agreed Redvers quietly, fearful of what next his son would say.

"I . . . I admire Miss Petherick most . . more than any other young woman I have ever met, you know."

"Yes, I know you do, your aunt had mentioned it to me," Redvers told him softly, and noted his son's face darken with a quick blush.

"Do you think . . . Perhaps her . . . I mean Captain Petherick would . . . ," he floundered unable to express himself for in his excitement he was away on a flight of fancy that Redvers knew could never be attained. Gazing sadly at his son, he knew how difficult the words he was going to say would be for Paul to hear.

"I do not think nor do I believe that, in spite of any gratitude Captain Petherick might show to you after your actions of tonight, that he will ever allow his daughter to . . . ah . . . be more than on speaking terms with you in future," stated Redvers. "Knowing the gentleman's attitude to you as I do, I do not think that he will consent to any other form of address, Paul, and so I must warn you. Do not to let your hopes run high in this matter. I am sorry for it but, as I see it, the situation has changed but slightly. Do you understand me, Paul?" he asked gently.

As he watched the light dim in his son's sparkling eyes he wished that he had cut his tongue out, but he was convinced that it would not do for his son to expect more than could be possible out of the unlooked for circumstances that had befallen the boy that night. He continued in his subdued voice, "There is more to think of than that though Paul. Your mother and I had no respect for any that peddled the trade in which Captain Petherick was formerly occupied. Your true mother was the daughter of freed slave, don't you know? Do you think it would be fitting for you, her son and his grandson, to be thinking so warmly of the daughter of such a man as that?"

Paul's head bowed but he mumbled, "She is not like him, father, I know she not. It is not her fault that she is the daughter of such a man. It is not my fault that I am a slave's grandson, either. Should we be punished for what we cannot help?"

"I know, Paul, I know," he sighed, "but you cannot escape your parentage any more than Captain Petherick can his past. You are young, do not break your heart over this, it will pass."

"That is what Aunt Caroline said, but I still have the same feelings for her. Nothing has altered for me father and it has been over a year since I first saw her. I cannot conceive that I will ever feel for any other female what I feel for Dorothea now," he said sadly.

Redvers leaned forward and clasped his son's hands in his strong grasp.

"Paul, my dearest boy, if I could tell you that everything will be as you would want, I would. God knows I do not want you to suffer like this but I cannot turn the world around to suit your needs. Perhaps I am wrong and that man will change but unless he takes the cloth and renounces all his sins I cannot see it and so I tell you. I say this not to disappoint you Paul, but you must understand me when I tell you that your dream cannot be realised."

There was a long silence and Paul slowly withdrew his hands and muttered in a flat voice, "Yes father, I understand you. Thank you for your time," and he got up dejectedly from the chair and moved towards the door.

"Paul, come back, Paul," pleaded his father, "we cannot leave it like this."

At the door Paul merely remarked, "There is no more to be said, Father," and left the room leaving his father staring despondently after him.

CHAPTER 11

AT the end of the week a parcel arrived for Paul from his tailors in Penzance. It contained one new shirt and a note. The note informed him that Captain Petherick was most grateful for his efforts in rescuing him from his fall and that he would be calling in person to express his thanks to all the young gentleman who had made sure of his safe return to his family. By the end of the day Paul had established that each of the Williams boys had also received a new shirt courtesy of the Captain.

"Damn fine ones too," remarked John Williams, "Pity you boys can't save a few more from they there cliffs - you'd 'ave a good wardrobe in next to no time."

"John!" exclaimed his wife laughing and gave him a gentle push.

At Trevu the missive produced no such jollity, but Redvers expressed his surprise at the shirt; more so at Captain's intention to call in person on his son.

"Perhaps he damaged his head more than Dr. Simcott thought," he remarked sarcastically but, on looking up from the Captain's note and meeting Paul's heavy frown, he thought it best not express any further remarks on the subject.

Later that morning the Petherick's carriage made its way slowly up the drive and drew up at the front steps, Paul, trying not to break into a run, hurried towards it. Pulling open the door and letting down the steps with his boyish enthusiasm, he raised his head and noted Dorothea's smile but the awareness of the Captain's hard stare kept his own smile at bay.

"Good morning, sir. Miss Petherick," he said, politely, "Please to come in, sir. We were expecting you," and held out his hand in order to assist Miss Petherick to descend. She thanked him politely, smiling up into his face, and he turned, in a daze, in order to assist the Captain if he should so need it. Petherick's grim expression soon jolted him back to reality but the Captain did need his help to descend from the carriage, for he was still badly bruised and the journey had undoubtedly tired him. So, with the aid of a stick and Paul's arm, the Captain found himself entering his neighbour's home.

Redvers met them in the hall, his face impassive, and suggested that they all proceed to the withdrawing room. Once there, an awkward silence fell upon the company which Redvers saw fit to break by enquiring after the Captain's health.

"Lucky to be here according to Dr. Simcott," he replied in a gruff voice.

There was an embarrassing silence until Dorothea decided to break it by saying in a determined voice, "My father has come expressly as he has something to say to you both, but particularly to P . . . young Mr. Trevarthen." There was another embarrassed silence and Miss Petherick prompted her father by saying, "Well father?" The sea master gave his daughter a fulminating stare, but managed to say with as a good a grace as he could muster.

"I thank you both for your assistance the other evening and to you . . . ah . . . young man . . . I . . . I do most . . . ," he paused and coughed before managing to burst out with, "I do most humbly thank you for saving my life."

Dorothea smiled approvingly at her father before turning to Redvers and stating, "Dr. Simcott says it was only Mr. Trevarthen's quick thinking that saved my father from possibly bleeding to death. We are both most grateful, are we not, father?"

"Yes, ahem, most grateful," mumbled the Captain.

Paul felt his mouth go dry but managed to say, "Quite all right, sir," before adding somewhat lamely, "my pleasure."

Redvers smiled and, turning to the Captain asked him, when Dr. Simcott thought he would be restored to his customary good health again.

"In about a month," answered Petherick grumpily.

"Only if you do not exert yourself too much, Papa," admonished his daughter. "He is so obstinate, he will not follow Dr. Simcott's orders," she explained, with an excited smile directed at Redvers.

Her father looked annoyed; "Acting like a silly old woman. Expects me to sit around all day doing nothing," but winced as one of his bruises reminded him of its presence.

"Yes, Dr Simcott is inclined to insist upon rest as a great cure," agreed Redvers; feeling a fellow sympathy for the injured man and remembering certain accidents to himself over the years that Dr. Simcott had pronounced upon. Conversation was awkward and stunted but Paul cared not a jot, he was trying not to stare at Dorothea like a moon calf but he knew he was doing it anyway and by the way she was smiling back at him, she did not appear to mind. Redvers watched the two youngsters with a feeling of growing concern. Captain Petherick looked at Paul and his face did not appear to convey the impression that he was enjoying himself, he only turned his eye on Redvers when addressed by him.

"Dorothea," Captain Petherick said to his daughter, "we must take our leave. Our neighbours have been most considerate but I should like to go home now."

"Yes father," said Dorothea and although downcast could not keep herself from smiling at Paul even as she rose to leave. Her father stood up slowly from his chair without assistance but he leaned heavily on his stick. His lips moved silently for a moment or two as if considering what to say.

"Well. Goodbye to 'e Captain Trevarthen, sir," he said at last, holding out his hand and then added, "you're a decent man sir, and no mistake, and the boy too."

Captain Trevarthen bowed his head and Paul flashed his smile but a moment later that same smile, now directed once again at Dorothea, was wiped from his face as Captain Petherick informed them brusquely: "Don't expect to come again. I've decided to put Nancemellin on the market and move away. Probably for the best under the circumstances, Captain," and looking directly at Redvers for a moment he resumed: " Probably the best for both our families wouldn't you say?"

Redvers found it impossible to say anything; so wrenched was he by the distraught expression on his son's face. Recklessly Paul pleaded, "Please sir, no need to leave on my account sir. I . . . mind not what you think of me."

"Do you not, laddie?" enquired the ex-slaver grimly. "Well you see I do mind, I mind very much. Rightly or wrongly that's the way of it. Say goodbye to my girl, young sir. It will be for the last time," and turning to Paul's father he asked for his arm to help him from the room.

Paul and Dorothea could only stare at each other in horror, for neither had been aware of the Captain's intention. Holding out his hands to her she rushed into his arms and broke into heartrending sobs upon his breast. He tried his best to console her but equally as broken he found he could not do so. The pleasure of holding his idol in his arms at last meant nothing to him now, for they were soon to be separated when so short a time ago his world seemed full of light and expectation.

"I will talk to him, Paul. Explain how I feel about you. We cannot be parted thus. It is too cruel," cried Dorothea through her tears.

"Oh Dorothea," said Paul brokenly, "I thought it was going to be so different. He seemed almost . . . almost to like me."

Just then they heard her father call her name loudly from the hallway. They looked at each other desperately and then, impulsively, Dorothea reached forward and kissed him passionately on the lips. Paul almost lost himself in the ardour of her embrace, but then all too cruelly he heard her father call her to him again and this time there was no mistaking the anger in his voice.

"Goodbye my dearest," his beloved whispered brokenly, and fled sobbing from the room. Paul, his hand outstretched in entreaty, found he could not follow her.

After seeing them from the premises, Redvers returned to the withdrawing room; a worried expression on his face for he had no idea what to say to his son. He knew himself to be in agreement with Petherick; but he realised the situation was impossible. His son, the half caste and the slaver's daughter; it could never be for his own common-sense told him so and, to give him his due, even Petherick understood the predicament equally as well as Paul's father.

Paul it was who found his voice first. Staring at his father in contempt he announced bitterly. "You agree with him I presume, father. I am not worthy of her or she of me. What a paradox! My god it is so funny, is it not? The infamous Captain Trevarthen unable to accept the slaver's daughter for his little bastard, because his own particular bastard is black - a most rare thing for hereabouts," he ended viciously.

"How dare you!" breathed Redvers, immediately losing his self control at his son's cruel words, "if your mother was alive you would break her heart talking in that way. Do you think this is easy for me, Paul? I would it were different, of course I do, but I wish only to change her father for a better man, not your colour for a white skin. Think better of me than that Paul, I beg of you."

"No!" flamed back Paul, "If you can accept me than you can accept him. What is so different? I have my colour and he his past. Accept them both for I am able to do so."

Redvers shook his head and tried to reason with his son but he could talk no sense into him. Shouting at each other, neither of them heard Hannah quietly enter the room.

"It is a conspiracy between both of you," continued Paul, beside himself with rage. "You . . . you do not want me to love Dorothea because she reminds you of mother. I saw it in your face. Her father does not want his daughter to love me because I remind him of all those poor blacks he bought, shipped, sold, crammed into those stinking holds . . . as if they were bags of sugar or tea. It turns his stomach to look at me but I do not care. And you - I have lived in your white family, with my white father and my white mother and thought I could not be happier, but when I decide to fall in love I must pick someone who needs to be of a purer strain than I am thought to be by most of my acquaintances. All so you can still hold up your head. Captain Trevarthen, the great hypocrite, with his black lover, his sad forgotten wife, and his black bastard that he must look at every day to remind him of his infidelity. Whose the whitest of us now, father?"

For answer, and for the only time in his life, Captain Trevarthen struck his son. He slapped him once, hard across his face. Paul staggered from the force of the blow but did not flinch. Hannah it was that cried out, unable to stop herself. Paul gave an angry sob and ran from the room and Hannah, distraught, would have run after him but Redvers stopped her.

"No, Hannah," Redvers said, but unable to explain himself only repeated sadly, "No, Hannah."

Within the month the Pethericks had left, telling no-one where they had gone. A week before their departure, Willy Dennis had called at Trevu with a parcel for young Mr. Trevarthen and a request. The package contained a copy of Paul's translation and the request was for it to be signed, for Captain Petherick's daughter had obtained the permission of her father for this small gift for her broken heart at least. Paul signed his name and addressed it to his 'Beloved Dorothea' but could not bear to write more, before passing it back to the young servant, waiting with a vacuous expression on his face. Nothing more was heard from their neighbours and, as soon as one of the farm workers informed Redvers that Nancemellin was empty, he could not help but breathe a sigh of relief. At last he thought to himself, his son would be able to have his life return to some form of normality and possibly, after a period of adjustment, he would soon be on the go once again and, would set forth to achieve the great goals in his life that Redvers considered his son so capable of obtaining.

The broken hearted lover, waiting out the time of Dorothea's departure with a heart growing heavier by the day, did not feel his father's relief. Becoming morose and withdrawn he applied himself to his translations and spent hours locked away in his room. He no longer sought out the company of his old friends and would not attend any of the dances and parties to which he and his father were habitually invited. Instructions were left with the servants to say to all callers that Master Paul was not at home for he would attend on no one. Redvers attempted conversation with him, but his son was almost monosyllabic in his replies and Hannah could not even induce him to return to her warm kitchen to sit by her cosy fire and chat away as before. Redvers determined to make his son respond to the life around him, but the harder he tried the more defiant Paul became and, where once there was only a house full of laughter, now raised voices were all that were heard echoing around Trevu's dark passages. Discovering in himself a liking for drink, Paul began to consume vast quantities of it and Redvers, in despair, locked away his brandy and port and strictly forbade the servants to provide any for the young master should he request them to get him some. Impervious to his father's actions; Paul took horse to Penzance and became a regular visitor to the inns and hostelries in the town and around the countryside. Having always ample amounts of money it was not long before certain ladies of the night made themselves known to him, but drunk as he was the boy was not so intoxicated as to fall for their charms. It took clever Polly Vingoe who, displaying great patience by sitting with the sad young man, plying him with drink all the while but conversing with him most sympathetically about the wretchedness of unrequited love, convinced him that he should return with her to her little house. Almost too drunk to walk, he staggered off supported by the redoubtable lady and discovered for the first time in his life that there was one more distraction that he could partake of to help him forget his crushing sadness.

Polly's success was muted somewhat when she discovered that another of her lovers had been watching her progress with the young Trevarthen most carefully and had followed them back to her abode. Paul, drunk beyond sense, was unaware that just as Polly was about to divest his pocket of his remaining wealth a tall, dark haired man entered the room and taking one bill from the roll in the youth's pocket tucked it in between Polly's ample breasts before pulling her to him and kissing her on her pouting lips. She raised protesting eyes to his face and would have spoken but he raised a finger to his lips and directed her to be silent.

"No Polly! Not this one," he admonished her, softly, flashing a warning from his cold, blue eyes, "fer this lamb's too young fer fleecin'," and, with no more words, heaved the insensible boy to his feet, before removing him from the annoyed lady's presence. Negotiating the stairs with some difficulty he successfully arrived in the alley that led off the back of Polly's house. A fisherman returning late to his home, took to his heels at the sight, for in the gloom he could not see who it was that Joey Bolitho had killed this time and wished not to be around to bear witness to the authorities if ever they should come to call. It took all Bolitho's strength to get young Trevarthen into his saddle and he had in the end to leave him slumped over his horse's neck whilst he got on his own horse. They left the stable at walking pace and it was the early hours of the morning before he got the drunken boy back to Trevu, entering the yard so quietly that the stable lad left to await the young master's return was fast asleep in the hay and did not wake, for he fully expected that whenever the young devil would chance to return he would be making his usual commotion as he did so. Bolitho lifted Paul from the saddle and grunted under his weight - for the lad was young in years but a veritable giant of a man for all that - and succeeded in placing him to sleep off his exertions in an empty stall amongst a bed of straw before turning his attention to the poor beast that had so patiently carried his master back to his home. When he had finished he returned to the stall where the young man slept on peacefully, oblivious to his surroundings, and allowed himself a small smile before returning to the yard and quietly walking his horse back to the road. Once there he took off to Penzance as if he had no time to lose and on finding

Polly asleep in an empty bed, removed his clothes and climbed in beside her. She opened her eyes and regarded him with a sleepy smile, and sighed with pleasure as he kissed her lips and neck.

"Don't 'e go to rob Paul Trevarthen, my bird," Joey whispered in her ear, "fer if 'e do I shan't be a callin' on 'e ever 'gain. Understand?" and he saw her nod her pretty head at him before she began to caress his strong, firm body with her soft hands.

"I give 'en a good time, Joey," she informed him saucily, "fer once 'e discovered the way of it I reckon 'e enjoyed 'iself."

Joey laughed and replied, "I 'spect 'e did, my bird, but 'nuff of that 'cos I've come fer me own good time now," and she chuckled in delight and spent the rest of the night happily obliging her favourite bed fellow to enjoy all his desires.

Late the following morning, Paul, his head throbbing entered Trevu's dark hallway leaving a trail of straw behind him in his wake. The foul taste in his mouth had the effect of tempering his normal desire to drink himself senseless whatever the hour of day or night, but he could remember some, if not all, of what had happened to his young body on the previous evening. He smiled in fond reminiscence of what had taken place between himself and the buxom wench that he had found in some tavern and determined to repeat the experience at the first available opportunity. In this respect, he was able to achieve his aims quite easily for he soon discovered that there appeared to be large numbers of young women wishing to oblige him. Preferring to enjoy the experience without having his brain befuddled by vast quantities of alcohol he set out, as his father before him, to enjoy himself in their arms. As soon as Redvers became aware of his son's fresh activities he remonstrated with him most forcibly, but Paul merely raised his eyebrows at him before pointing out that his sermon sounded a trifle hypocritical to his ears. Captain Trevarthen blushed crimson, but persevered in his attempt to turn Paul away from pursuing every female for miles around, but his son had no intention of listening to him and finally his father gave up in despair.

Word came back to Mr. Duncan Ross, the Customs Officer, as he returned to Penzance after leading his men on an unsuccessful attempt at finding the contraband goods that they knew had been landed that night, for they had seen the boat that had been run aground, that Barnaby Rickard had been seen at the front of a line of packhorses on the road to Gulval. They on the other hand had lain in wait for two hours at Morvah, chilled to the marrow by the bitter wind and driving rain blasting into them, because their finest agent presented them with the details with such authority that he convinced them that this time they would finally trap their men. At first the second informer was not believed: the smuggler could not possibly be such a fool as to hide his goods in his own home for Rickard, along with his henchman Bolitho, were known to live in a cottage there. However, the man was adamant that he had met with them and that each beast had at least a keg slung over their backs and he held up his hands with all his fingers extended to show the numbers of horses in the line. Ross, still disbelieving, was persuaded finally when the man told him that they had appeared worried, for Rickard was in a foul mood and had sworn at Bolitho, and not one person assembled in Ross's office could ever remember that Barnaby Rickard had ever been known to do such a thing before. So a bare ten minutes later, Duncan Ross led his gallant band of men out of the Custom's House yard and set off in the direction of the little hamlet. When he arrived there; to his great delight he found assembled in the front of Rickard's cottage ten sweating and panting horses, along with a band of shifty eyed looking men soaked to the skin and vainly trying to keep themselves from getting even wetter by sheltering in the lieu of the cottage.

Dismounting he ordered his troop to check the horses although it was obvious that they had no burdens strapped upon them, but nevertheless they arrested all the men and forced them into a group by the side of the road where the rain ripped into them most cruelly. Advancing upon the cottage, where lights gleamed from the windows, he rapped on the door. It was opened by Rickard himself, wet through and looking most discomforted. Mr. Ross could hardly contain his excitement and with two preventatives behind him pushed his way into the little cottage. Bolitho, from his seat by the fire, looked equally as wet but he merely glanced at them in disgust before turning back to the book that he was reading. Informing Rickard that he knew him to have illicit goods on his premises, and despite the man's protests that the officer was mistaken, Mr. Ross proceeded to search the cottage most thoroughly. Not a proverbial stone was left unturned but after an hour during which they had searched all the rooms, emptied cupboards and drawers, pulled apart the beds as well as searching along the walls and pulling up floorboards in the bedrooms, they could find no trace of any contraband. Mrs. Rickard protested bitterly at the mess that had been made in her house, but undaunted Ross had the men search the garden thoroughly and through the outhouses as well. In the stable they tossed about all the straw, and rifled through the feed bins, but nothing was to be found and even when they returned to the cottage they could not believe that, somewhere in that small place, there did not reside some vast quantity of the finest French brandy that for some unaccountable reason they were unable to see.

"I would know why those horses are outside of your cottage, Rickard," asked the Custom's officer angrily, "for they are lathered up and have obviously been worked hard, methinks upon business for you?"

"Not so sir," replied Barney stoutly, "for they carried tin to Hayle from Wheal Clodgey earlier in the day, but on the way back they broke loose and as Bolitho and I were on our way home from the town we helped to round them up for the tinners."

Sending one of his men to go again and look at the horses, the expression on his face was a joy to behold when on his return the trooper held up a wet sack with the tell tale red stains upon it.

"They be all the same Mr. Ross, sir," said the trooper sadly, for he had been fired with excitement just the same as his commander for they all believed that at last they had caught their most notorious smugglers in the act of secreting contraband upon their property. Dejectedly Mr. Ross ordered his men to release the tinners, and to regroup, and with a resentful apology to the Rickards, standing in the midst of the destruction the troops had caused, they made their way slowly and despondently from the house. Passing the mill with its slowly turning wheel poor Mr. Ross could have wept, for twice in one night he had been on a wild goose chase and, in his despair, he was even beginning to believe that no contraband was hidden within ten miles of the place.

At their cottage Joey and Barney were helping Phoebe to put the scattered household effects back to rights but none of them exchanged a word. Finally, Barney lifted his eyes to Joey's face and apologised for losing his temper with him and for not believing that he could so successfully organise to hide a dozen kegs so skilfully.

"Thas' all right, Barney, fer I was gettin' a bit worried meself. Still they be safe 'nuff now," Joey informed him calmly.

"Shall we move them tonight?" asked Barney, not relishing the prospect of having to go out in the foul weather again.

"No need fer the Preventatives, after a night's sleep 'ill be back 'gain fer a few days yet I 'speculate," laughed Joey, "and it 'aven't bin 'nuff rain to make the river run so fast that the kegs 'ill break loose." Informing Barney that he would pay off the men he pulled on his wet coat and disappeared outside. Soon they heard the sound of the horses slowly making their way up the hill to return to Wheal Clodgey; for tomorrow the men and beasts would have to make the journey to Hayle after all, though they had spent that night carrying a completely different load along a route never before used by them.

"Well, Barney, it has to be admitted that young Joey has got a quick mind for in all the years we have lived here it would never have occurred to us to do what he did to hide our goods," announced Phoebe, and smiled proudly at her husband, for she thought they could both take credit for the way their protégé had turned out to be such a boon to them.

When Joey returned he shook off his wet clothes and thanked Phoebe gratefully for the bowl of steaming soup she passed to him. When he had finished his meal he took up his glass of brandy and sat again by the fire, picked up his book and was soon engrossed in its contents. The Rickards wished him goodnight and retired for the night but as usual the young man sat contentedly reading and did not go to bed until much later. He checked that in their haste to find the contraband the troopers had not dislodged his hidden treasure, but all was safe so he climbed into bed and was soon blissfully asleep.

Outside all was calm and still for the wind had eased and the pouring rain had at last stopped. Only the sound of the mill wheel slowly turning could be heard across the quiet valley, for even with the additional burden of the hidden casks strapped tightly underneath its wooden ledges it continued to turn as unconcernedly as ever.

CHAPTER 12

PAUL entered the house quietly and headed for the kitchen. It was the early hours of the morning and he had had a busy night. He was hungry and the candle he had picked up in the hallway cast his shadow on the glittering pans and bowls hanging from the kitchen's whitewashed walls. Hannah's kitchen always shone like a gilded palace, the walls festooned with the tools of her trade. The fire had been damped down to keep it in overnight, ready to be raked out in the morning and fresh fuel added but some embers still glowed brightly, even at that late hour. Finding some bread and cheese and the remains of a pie he sat down in the chair by the fire and started to eat. He discovered a jug of ale and drank straight from it, not bothering to avail himself of a tankard. 'God he had a thirst on him,' he mused, and no wonder for his latest bedfellow, Molly Pendray, would not leave him alone, pleading for more, telling him her husband would not be back from his fishing trip until the morning.

"Stay Paul," she whined provocatively, "stay an' let me warm 'e 'gain. I got plenty 'a fire in me Paul, don' 'e worry. I wen't let 'e get cold my dear soul."

He laughed, kissed her on her pink lips but pushed her away, got out of bed, pulled on his clothes, threw his money on the table and left. There were plenty of women in his life now and, deaf to the entreaties of Hannah and his father, he ranged abroad most nights. A couple of irate husbands had almost caught him; he had arrived home one night his arms cut about with glass after having to smash a window to get clear, but he cared not. It merely added some excitement to his empty life. He laughed derisively to himself. His life! In an effort to block out the searing pain that continuously racked his body, sometimes he worked on the farm by day but more often that not he spent his time translating his Latin texts. In all truthfulness this was probably the only thing which still afforded him enjoyment. Women gave him no pleasure at all for he just used them to let the steam out of the kettle, as it were.

His father could find nothing to say about his debauchery for how could he tell his own by-blow to behave? Everyone knew there was a time when old Captain Trevarthen had enjoyed himself doing the same thing - Paul was the living proof of that. No, he could not peal that bell over his son's head for he would look a damn fool if he did, Paul laughed to himself. Closing his eyes he breathed deeply and then sighed as he realised, obliging woman that she was, he was getting tired of Molly. There was a woman over to Carleen that he had a fancy for now, for he had seen her in the town with two children hanging off her skirts and had noted the way she had smiled boldly at him. It would not take long to attach her interest in him for he had only to look at them and he knew if they were willing. Musing unconcernedly to himself he imagined that it would not be too difficult to find her; - small place Carleen - not many houses - he could soon find hers - had a rough idea already, and he sighed again.

At the breakfast table Hannah met her master's eye.

" . . . and don't say 'e'll grow out of it again like you d' do 'cos he won't," she continued blazing. "When he lost that Miss Dorothea 'e died inside and we d' all knaw it. Can't strike a spark on ice, sir, and thas' the truth." She sniffed, "Master Paul's no more my lovely boy than the devil's my shiner," and so saying she sat down on the nearest chair, lifted her apron to her face and sobbed uncontrollably.

Redvers pushed away his plate and sighed. Even now he still could not believe that his son would be in love with a girl he had not set eyes on for over two years. Then when he brought her face to mind again he bethought himself he knew why, for the girl's resemblance to his own dear wife and to Paul's beloved mother had played no small part in the adoration that his son felt for Dorothea Petherick. He admitted sadly to himself that if only their children's fathers had not been so obstinate a way through might have been found for the star crossed lovers. Too late now, Redvers had reasoned for the girl was most probably married off with a child of her own. He tried to tell Paul that but had only received a scornful look and heard Paul state coldly by way of reply: "Believe that if you will father - but I believe differently."

"She would believe different of you if she knew the way you were acting now. She would not understand that," Redvers informed him, an exasperated look on his normally impassive face.

"On the contrary, father, I think she would be the only one who could understand," said Paul in an even tone.

Now on the top of all his problems with his son, his dear, faithful Hannah had informed him as he sat at his breakfast that she wished to leave his employ, and in his despair he could not imagine how his household would be able to function without her for since his dear Penelope had passed away she had become the rock to which they had all clung. He thought to himself that he would have to enlist Caroline's help over that matter for Paul would be of no use, so uncaring as he had become. Providentially Caroline would be arriving later that morning, on her own, for all her girls were married now. Quite respectably too and had not given their proud mother a minute's trouble in the process, and had even made her a grandmother, twice over. He wondered idly if Paul would ever make him a grandfather, and in his despair he reasoned that if his son would not change his ways then it was unlikely to be the case. They had thrown every marriageable young girl in Penwith and beyond at him in an attempt to marry him off but Paul would have none of them. Caroline took him to Truro last year before his twentieth birthday and every eligible female in her social circle swooned at the sight of him, but Paul, unimpressed, treated them all to his cold charm and cool civility. Whilst he was there his poor aunt discovered to her mortification that he had an affair with an army officer's wife, and when that gentleman returned on leave, a woman whose husband sold bibles at fairs. One night, in desperation, Caroline waited up for him until four in the morning when he had arrived back at her house with his neck cloth hanging out of his pocket and straw all over his coat. Upon her shouted enquiry he merely said he had got lost and slept in a stable. Enraged, Caroline called him a liar and told him precisely what she thought of him. Paul who had been trained by Caroline always to be civil, smiled sweetly at her, and merely said, "Quite right, aunt," doffed his cap, made a bow and sauntered upstairs to bed. The following day, still fuming she packed his bags and threw him out. The errant son turned up at

Trevu ten days later, with a hole in his hat left by a pistol shot and a tear in his coat a foot long. Of his baggage there was no sign. When asked where he had been, he said serenely, "Here, there and everywhere." The rip in his coat? "Caught it on a nail." The pistol shot in his hat? "Forgot to duck," he laughed.

No; try as they would, sighed Redvers, no one meant anything to Paul anymore, for he regarded everyone in a cold and indifferent way. He smiled only to be civil and charming, but there was no warmth in his expression and no spark of fervour in his eyes. The only female he seemed to have any regard for was Sarah-Jane. He had always a very soft spot for her for she was his oldest friend of his own age. Redvers reasoned that he would have been quite happy if Paul had expressed an interest in marrying her. 'Sweet girl,' he thought to himself, 'very pretty little face - she would do.'

As the door opened noisily, Redvers looked up as Paul, yawning, sauntered into the room. Hastily Hannah got up from her seat, wiping her eyes angrily and resolutely told Paul that his breakfast would be with him in a moment, and bustled from the room, but the youth appeared not to notice her distress and sat himself down at his seat with a look of bored indifference on his face. Stealing an enigmatic glance at his son Redvers felt his heart contract in pain at his loss of the joyous, laughing boy that he had taken such delight in but whose presence had disappeared a long time ago. Now he looked at a young man so cold, so contained within himself that no spark of his generosity glowed to warm the household in which he lived.

Redvers was the first to speak and informed his son that his aunt would be arriving later that morning for she had written expressly that she might visit with them.

"How lovely," replied Paul coldly, and then enquired dispassionately how long a stay his aunt was to make.

"I have not the slightest notion, but she may stay as long as she likes as far as I am concerned, for I shall be glad of some civilised company," replied his father, pointedly.

"Does it have to be this way, Paul? A permanent war between us?" Redvers asked sadly.

"I am not at war with you, Father," he replied quietly.

"Yes you are Paul. Not only with me, all of us who love and admire you. Hannah is heartbroken, and my poor sister dreads having to meet you again. The men hereabouts resent you and hope that it is not their wives you are spending your time with. As to the women," and his son heard him sigh despairingly, "Well some of them want you, whilst the older women are worried that you will be sniffing after their daughters and leading them astray," and after another prolonged silence he added, "You have turned my home into a battleground of worry and fret."

"Do you want me to leave, father?" asked Paul evenly.

"Would you be happier, Paul?" returned Redvers but the question was destined to remain unanswered as, at that moment the door opened and Hannah returned with his son's breakfast. Unusually, unlike his normal unconcerned manner, Paul made an effort and smiled at Hannah as she arrived at his side but she said nothing, merely placing his plate in front of him and poured out a tankard of ale from a fresh jug, and even when he thanked her meekly she did not respond. Instead she turned to Redvers and asked quietly, "Will that be all Captain?"

"Yes thank you, Hannah," but as she turned to leave informed her with a worried smile, "We will talk later if you are still in the same mind."

"Thank you sir. I would like that," replied Hannah gratefully, and she turned and left the men alone again.

"She wants to leave us," explained Redvers and had the dubious pleasure of seeing a look of surprise on his son's normally indifferent face.

"I find that hard to believe, sir, for Hannah seems always to have been here," he said, and then asked, "Has she given you a reason?"

"You are the reason, you fool, for she cannot bear to see you as you are now! We had great sympathy for you when . . . when it happened but your actions since have endeared you to no one," he replied before adding testily: "Well, certain silly women perhaps, but the rest of us are so ashamed of you that you have become unbearable to live with."

"Seems a strange thing for you to say to me father. Do you not see the irony of it?" asked Paul without the glimmer of a smile.

"Certainly I do, but you have so rubbed my nose in my past; I am capable of saying anything to you now. I always felt that you would have been ashamed of me Paul, never did I think that it would come to pass that your own actions should so embarrass me," he told him angrily. He waited for some response but his son maintained his silence. In frustration, Redvers pushed back his chair and got up abruptly and left the room.

Paul's heart tightened within him but all at once he found that tears were falling slowly down his cheeks. He hurriedly wiped his face and as if pursued by ghosts strolled quickly from the room.

Hannah was hurrying from the dining room when she heard the sound of a carriage coming up the drive.

"Captain, Captain," she called, "I think Mrs. Crebo has arrived sir."

"Thank you, Hannah, I'm coming," Redvers called from his office.

Paul, sitting reading a book in the back parlour, heard what had been said and wondered if he ought to go to meet his aunt. He had no particular desire to see her again but it would be expected of him after all. He did not hate his aunt, or any of his family but he felt so cold inside these days it was almost impossible for him to have to be with any of them. He decided that as his aunt would be staying for a while he would show her some of the charm and civility that she had so relentlessly drummed into him. So, with an exasperated sigh, he put down his book, got up from his chair, and ambled slowly towards the front door.

The carriage door opened as he reached the doorway so he held back to allow his father to greet his aunt on his own. Aunt Caroline majestically descended from the carriage, and he smiled to himself to see again the proud way she had of bearing herself, but a slight frown furrowed his brows for she had a most strange look on her face. She looked worried and seemed very unsure of herself and, reasoned Paul, this was a most unusual state for his aunt to be in. Catching hold of Redvers hands, Caroline began to speak hurriedly to her brother and almost immediately his smile of greeting disappeared from his face. He glanced quickly at the carriage, before he turned and looked at Paul, with a worried expression that matched the one on Caroline's face. Paul stood and watched the strange scene nonchalantly from the doorway, but his attention was caught and so his ears strained to catch what was being said between his father and aunt.

"I did it for the best, dear Redvers, but if you do not agree then it will go no further, for I considered that if nothing else will make him come to his senses then perhaps this will," Caroline was telling her brother in an agitated voice.

He presumed them to be talking about himself and wondered idly what plans Caroline had hatched for him now. Another Truro season perhaps? After the last visit and her reaction to his activities, he thought not. Smiling grimly to himself he listened to his father's reply and struggled to understand the meaning of it.

"I . . . I do not know what to say or worse what action to follow!" and then he suddenly cried out, "My God, Caroline, how could you throw this at me now? What am I to do? What am I to do?" he looked from Caroline, to Paul and then back to the carriage with an expression of fear on his face.

Never having seen his father so agitated and behaving in such a way before Paul looked towards the carriage and saw behind the open door the pale green silk of a woman's dress. Probably one of Caroline's daughters he reasoned and then hoped fervently that it would not be Sofia, for her silliness annoyed him so. Perhaps she had done something dreadful and his aunt had brought her to this isolated area, out of the sight of those Truro socialites who could talk and whisper so artlessly. Remembering the cruel words directed at him by the locals from his youth he felt a moment's sympathy for the carriage's occupant, for he was now convinced that one of his cousin's was hiding in the carriage, awaiting his father's permission to descend and hide her shame in his house.

Suddenly, Redvers, without a word to anyone appeared to make up his mind and strode purposefully towards the carriage. Once by its open door he pulled at his necktie and began to speak to the carriage's occupant in a gentle tone whilst his sister watched, greatly agitated, wringing her hands together. Paul was now thoroughly intrigued, and he only looked away when a movement at his side made him turn his head to see that Hannah had arrived from the kitchen and was standing in the doorway by his side. He became even more puzzled by her reaction to the scene for of a sudden her eyes opened wide in surprise. "Oh my God Almighty!" she breathed, staring at the carriage in disbelief.

Quickly Paul turned back to look at what had so amazed Hannah; the sight that met his own eyes transfixed him and the conflicting emotions that ran through him left him trembling with an unexplainable fear for, descending from the carriage, holding his father's hand was a tall, elegant woman. A woman he could not ever remember having seen before but a woman he knew at once. His father was holding her hand so tenderly as if it might be made of the finest china, but his face was unusually pale and anxious and when he turned and looked at his son, Redvers knew he had good reason to be frightened. On the woman's face there was also an expression of fear, but she overcame it and looked at the young man with resolution, a tremulous smile playing on her lips.

Paul neither moved nor spoke but seemed as if turned into a statue, for he had never imagined this moment, and could not believe that it was happening even though, finally, he had sight of the woman who had given him life

The silence was broken by his father who said gently, "Paul, please to come here for I would like to introduce you to . . . to your mother."

Paul, transfixed by shock and fear could not move from where he stood in the doorway. Aware that everyone was looking at him, he felt someone clasp his hand and squeeze it gently.

"Go on, Master Paul," said Hannah simply, "go to 'er."

"I cannot, I cannot," he heard himself say in an agonised voice, and wrenching his hand free he fled from the doorway and back into the house, and they heard footsteps running up the stairs, and finally the slam of a door.

There was another embarrassed silence. It was broken by Hannah who said in a composed, quiet voice, "Shall I lay another place for lunch, sir?"

Redvers, still bemused by what had happened to him, replied, "Yes . . . yes of course," and then turned back to face his former lover and asked her determinedly, "You will do me the honour of entering my home and dining with me ma'am, will you not?"

"I have not come to cause friction in your house, Captain Trevarthen. I can leave if you would prefer it," Sardi replied in her soft, musical voice and he smiled in fond remembrance as he heard the sound of it again.

"No," he replied with firmness, "for I think we are in the right of it." He turned and looked at her and smiled, and marvelled that like a golden statue she should look no older than when he had last seen her. That beautiful exciting skin, with its sultry glow that had never dimmed, the way she stood so tall and proud, the tilt of her head, and his son's eyes. She was smiling sadly into his face and of a sudden he felt that time had whirled about and she was as he had first seen her, a woman of great beauty with a pride in herself that ignored the prejudice she had always had to suffer at the hands of her fellow man. Looking into her face he smiled as he said, "If it please you I should be most honoured to have you sit at my table, dear Sardi," and placing her hand on his arm he led her into his home and escorted her to the withdrawing room. When they arrived he excused himself by saying he thought it best that he go and talk to Paul.

"It may take me a while, for I can understand how shocked he has been at the sight of you, but I will bring him to see and speak with his mother," he assured her in a soft voice and an understanding smile on his lips. He left the room with quiet composure and made his way to his son's room and on reaching the closed door knocked firmly and asked to be admitted..

Silence followed his request; suddenly, Paul wrenched opened the door and stood facing his father with an angry expression on his face. Turning away from his father he stood facing the window that looked out over the drive. Davy was paying off the post chaise and, touching his cap, the coachman turned his horses and returned the way he had come.

"Did you know about this?" he asked his father, curtly.

"No. It was your aunt's idea," replied Redvers slowly, "From the day she left you at my door I have had no knowledge of your mother's whereabouts."

"Has she gone?" asked her son, in a cold voice.

"No," replied his father, "Your mother is with Caroline in the drawing room, waiting to meet with you again. It has been over twenty years since she last saw you Paul," he added coaxingly.

"I have no desire to meet her. I would rather she went away," said Paul, abruptly.

"I expect you would, but she is a guest in my house and you will meet her, Paul. I know she has travelled many miles to see you and you will not offend her," and here Redvers paused considering what next to say, "or me by refusing to meet her."

He watched as his son drew a deep breath but after a moment he turned to face his father and glared at him.

"Damn you!" he swore, and he pushed past his father and marched from the room, trapped in his own resentment. When he reached the withdrawing room he heard the sound of women's voices and stopped, unable to go forward. His father opened the door and placing his hand on his son's shoulder brought him into the room.

Caroline and his mother were seated on the settle, but at their entrance his aunt got up and moved away. Redvers brought his son to stand in front of his mother and, clearing his throat, said in as composed a voice as he could muster: "Sardi this is Paul. I think it is the wisest course that we should leave you now so that you may talk together," and he turned on his heel, took his sister by the arm and escorted her from the room.

Trying not to stare, Paul observed the stranger in front of him. He thought her beautiful for she had such a quality about her; with her soft brown eyes, short nose, and full lips all set off by the velvet brown of her skin, darker in tone by far than his own. As she spoke he felt himself quiver at the sound of her voice.

"Hello Paul," she said in a soft, melodious voice and held out her hand to him and waited patiently. After a struggle he took her hand in his but he was still unable to have speech with her. She patted the settle beside her; a warm, understanding smile on her lips. Again Paul struggled but he moved to the settle and sat down, still unable to believe that the woman that he was sitting beside was his mother. She did not feel as if she was his mother, instead she seemed like a stranger to him.

"I understand that you are feeling upset by this strange meeting," Sardi remarked gently, "for I should imagine this is something you have never envisaged happening to you." Unable to reply he maintained his silence so she spoke for him as she told him she realised how angry and insecure he most have felt on sight of her.

She caught hold of his hand again in her firm grasp and began to speak.

"I have seen you before you know," she began conversationally and told him how she had seen him with Caroline in Mrs. Martin's shop when he was about sixteen. "You have a great look of your father about you, and something of your grandfather too," she smiled fondly and added; "he would have been pleased about that, and very proud of you too." Studying her son, she delighted at the sight of him for he was so handsome, tall and so elegant. Then she praised his academic attainments and told him some of the history of her own father and how he had to strive to better himself when he landed as a slave in the port of Bristol. Her son tried to appear unconcerned with her story but in reality he was devouring every word. After a while she began upon the tale of her own life and now Paul's attention was fairly caught.

"When you were born I knew I could not keep you," she explained guiltily, "for how could I, a poor black woman, ever hope to raise you without the means to give you the opportunities that I believed you deserved? So I took a chance and left you on your father's doorstep. I could not be sure of Redvers, but well I knew his wife would not let me down for there was so much about her that I admired. I had stolen her husband for a while but I could give her a gift that she could never hope to have herself. I knew she would not refuse it." She placed her hand under his chin and turned his face to look into his eyes, which wavered under her searching look, "I think I was right to put my faith in her, Paul, would you not agree?"

"Yes," he replied after a moment's silence, "Yes you were right to believe in her for she accepted your . . . gift with love."

"I have grieved for you every day since, but to keep you would have been unfair. Can you understand why I did what I did, Paul?" she asked him worriedly. But this time there was no reply. Still holding his hand she squeezed it gently, he flinched and tried to pull his hand away but now that he was finally with her again she would not let him go.

"I know you are angry, with me, with yourself - although you do not know why you should be. This is not easy for either of us but we have met now and we will have to get to know each other. I tell you that I do not want to replace the woman you think of as your mother. She brought you up and gave as much of herself to you as she possibly could and I am most grateful, for I think she made you what you are. I should have liked to have known her. Do you think she would have liked me, Paul?" she queried looking all the while into his angered countenance.

"Perhaps," he shrugged, finding it increasingly difficult to talk.

An hour ago he was reading a book, icily oblivious to what was going on around him. Now, he was in the midst of a violent storm that was rampaging through and around him and he found it most difficult to keep his feelings under control. He thought of Penelope, the woman he had always called his mother. Paul wanted her with him to comfort him for the woman holding his hand could not, and would not replace her in his eyes or in his heart. They both looked up as there was a quiet knock on the door. His father strode resolutely into the room and looked anxiously at his son, who could do no more than look at him with a hurt and angry expression on his face.

Taking a deep breath Redvers informed them that lunch was ready and would they come to the dining room. Paul roughly pulled away his hand from his mother's clasp and without saying a word, got up from his seat, crossed the room, pushed past his father and went out, slamming the door as he went.

Redvers looked at Sardi apologetically, before saying sadly: "I am sorry, Sardi, but it is so very awkward for him."

"It is very awkward for all of us, Redvers," she replied in a subdued voice, and lifting misty eyes to her former lover asked: "Will he ever forgive me?"

Redvers, stricken by the pain he recognised in her face, came to her side and put a comforting arm around her shoulders.

"Yes. He loved Penelope so but if he could forgive me for what I did he will forgive you. Not yet - it is too soon - but he will. When he grew older and took on his man's face people told him that he looked like me and it became obvious that I was his father, but he always understood that Penelope could not have been his mother. To Paul, however, she was his mother not just because he never knew . . . never knew another, but because she loved him so," and he sighed before continuing in his soft voice. "It will take time, for both of you, but have patience my dear. Now come, you are a guest in my house and I will take you to dine at my table," and he stood up and, holding out his arm, escorted her from the room.

At the dining table Paul ate his food in silence, taking no part in the conversation but listened to all that was said. Sardi and Caroline informed his father that they had known each for a long time but Caroline had forbidden Sardi to meet Paul when he was younger. He discovered that his mother had become a substantial business woman, owning three shops; one in London and two in Bristol. She had made a success of her life by employing her natural abilities in sewing with the skills of a tradesman. Obtaining quality materials at the best prices, she supplied various linen drapers around the country, whilst on her own premises she had the finest materials turned into fashionable dresses. She had never married, she told Redvers when he asked and there was a long silence. When the meal was finished Redvers suggested that they take a turn about the garden and looked enquiringly at Paul, but his face like a mask, he remained seated and silent.

"I would like that very much," said Sardi and took the proffered arm, and Paul noted in particular the way she smiled into his father's face and his answering smile in return.

CHAPTER 13

THE news that Paul Trevarthen's mother was in residence at Trevu spread throughout Penzance like a spring flood through a river. Acquaintances came from Penzance and the neighbouring farms and took tea with them, as much to see this strange creature as to ascertain exactly what her role in the household might be. Paul sat silent and watched the proceedings with a brooding eye for he was most perturbed that his father might be tempted to reawaken his affair with the woman. Wishing only that she be gone, never to darken Trevu's portals ever again, he hardly spoke with her and pointedly ignored her when in company with her. That his actions were cause for much conjecture, he did not realise but when he caught a pitying look from Inez Carter he thought he could bear no more.

His aunt Caroline watched him rage quietly to himself. Finally she asked him to accompany her to Penzance. He refused but she persevered.

"Paul, come now. You cannot sit in this house day after day and let yourself fill up with anger. Come with me, visit Mr. Samuel's - lose yourself in your books if you must but do not let yourself be eaten up with rage in this way."

"I am not angry!" he shouted at her, his face stormy and sullen.

"Jealous, perhaps?" she enquired tentatively.

"Jealous! Jealous?," he asked incredulously, "Why should I be jealous?"

"Well, your father is paying a lot of attention to your mother, so perhaps you do not like it," she said quietly, her eyes never leaving his face. Looking guilty he declared that he could not care less that his father should be so much with that woman.

"Is that true, Paul?" Caroline asked, and raised an unbelieving eyebrow at him.

Opening his mouth to say something, he thought better of it and stalked from the room, slamming the door behind him. Caroline decided not follow him but sat and continued her embroidery patiently for an hour before packing it away in her needle box. Setting off on her quest to find Paul, she soon ran him to earth sitting in the kitchen in his chair looking at the fire with a brooding expression on his face, his dark brows drawn together in a heavy frown. He looked up as she entered and caught the quick, slight smile that passed between Hannah and Caroline and he frowned the more as he realised that they thought his behaviour most comical.

"Well, Paul.? Will you accompany me to Penzance?" his aunt asked again, but more firmly than before.

"Oh very well," her nephew snapped and got up from his seat and made for the door. When they arrived Paul groaned inwardly to see the press of people about the streets, but resolved to get through what he knew was going to be an ordeal as expeditiously as he could. As he was escorting his aunt it was only natural that, being Caroline, she should stop and speak to various persons along the way. One of the first acquaintances to be encountered was Mrs. Sampson, residing on her own now that her daughter had married. They exchanged pleasantries and Mrs. Sampson enquired most politely after his mother of Paul. The shock of what she had said deprived him of speech for a moment but he managed to reply in an impassive tone that she was very well.

"Such a lovely woman, so accomplished. Quite well off, I hear, and so well conducted for a . . . ," and here she paused and smiled at Paul condescendingly, "for a dark woman. Apparently, so Mrs. Martin tells me, in London members of the quality buy all their dresses from her establishments. Well, would you believe it? Dear Redvers would be a fool to let her go a second time if you know what I mean. It could not be more fitting, could it not Mrs. Crebo, for them to marry? So pleasant for you too, Paul," and after exchanging a few more pleasantries she said her farewells and continued on her homeward journey.

Paul watched her departing form with his temper rising, before announcing in disgust, "How dare she?"

Caroline eyed him speculatively for a moment before replying in a controlled and cool voice. "She dares because the dear lady believes that it would be no bad thing for your father to marry again. Whilst he has been so wrapped up in your concerns he has had no time to consider his own loneliness. I used to think you cared enough for him to notice but then you had time only for yourself and your own loss," she said and noted the guilty look that crossed his face, but he made no effort to find words to refute her accusation.

"Your unreasonable behaviour has been breaking his heart as well you know," she concluded, but this time Paul found his voice and in an annoyed tone informed her: "Do not talk to me of my behaviour! I stand before you now the living proof of his own misdemeanours! I tell you that I do not want that woman in the house and the sooner she is out of it the better I shall be pleased!" and informing her that he was off to the book shop he turned on his heel and discourteously left her standing alone in the street.

Once inside of Mr. Samuel's shop he looked at the books on the shelves but could not see the titles; so blinded with anger was he. The thought that people appeared to contemplate that it would be perfectly acceptable for his father to marry again and that the stranger in his home was thought a most suitable partner appalled him. What about his own saintly mother lying cold in the churchyard? He for one could not forget her and as he ranged up and down the shelves his mind was so full of his troubles that, although he stayed in the shop for half an hour, when he left he had made no purchases. Seeing his aunt, coming out of the Apothecary's shop he gritted his teeth and strode up the street towards her. A young woman sauntered by, giving him a saucy look, but for once he paid no attention. He had had enough of woman he thought to himself sullenly. The woman he wanted more than any other he had ever met had been denied to him, and the woman he had never thought to meet was even now laughing and joking with his father at Trevu. Swearing to himself under his breath, he found himself wishing to be free of the whole tribe of females.

In such a hurry was he to reach his aunt - and so leave the town the sooner - that he did not notice the young woman stepping out of the chandler's shop and almost knocked her down. Reaching out his hand he caught her by the arm to save her from falling.

"I beg your pardon, ma'am!, My fault entirely. I was not looking where I was going," he said stiffly and then with a start of surprise cried: "Why Sarah-Jane, it's you! How . . . nice to see you again."

"Paul!" replied Sarah-Jane with a delighted smiled on her face, "Why 'tis lovely to see you too. Dear Father often talks about you and the night old Mouser passed away. He misses your company, sorely, Paul, for you never come to call these days but I suppose it is rather difficult for you, with your Mother visiting at the moment," she said pleasantly.

"Yes. Yes, it is . . . rather difficult. But I will come, I will come to see you all," he announced determinedly.

"I shall be at home this Sunday," she told him hopefully, "for 'tis my day off from my work. Please to come then for I can assure you, you will be made most welcome." They chatted pleasantly for a few more moments but he noticed his aunt waiting for him at the top of the street, so he made his goodbyes and they parted.

As Caroline had concluded her shopping they returned to Trevu, making little conversation, but she noticed Paul seemed to be in a better frame of mind when he did speak. That afternoon Paul left the house on his own and after returning to dine it was not long before he disappeared again, and once more gave no explanation. Caroline and Redvers looked at each other worriedly but neither made any comment. Sardi it was who told them not to concern themselves unduly for, as she said, "Poor Paul has a lot to think about and has much that he needs to come to terms with."

On opening the door Sarah-Jane looked up into Paul's beaming smile, and her own face lit up in delight at the sight of him.

"Paul? How kind of you to call," she said, and smiled adoringly into his eyes.

"I had two reasons Sarah-Jane," he informed her pleasantly, "one being that I should see my old friends again for I have been most remiss in not paying them any calls and the second was this," and putting his hand in his pocket he withdrew a small kitten, almost in colour and markings the exact miniature of the departed Mouser.

"Oh Paul!" squeaked Sarah-Jane delightedly and held out her hands for the little bundle of mewing fur.

"I think he should be christened Mouser, for surely," said Paul ruefully, looking down at his pocket, "he has christened me," and, displayed for her to see in the corner of Paul's coat pocket, was a large wet stain.

"Paul," said Sarah-Jane hardly able to stop herself from laughing, "off with that coat at once and I will soon have that stain removed for you," and putting the kitten down on her chair she helped Paul out of his coat and began her task of cleaning his coat, chattering gaily whilst remarking how nearly the kitten resembled poor old Mouser. Prudently Paul did not tell her that he had scoured the surrounding countryside for two whole days, until he had found a similarly marked kitten to the one that she had been given as a young girl all those years ago.

"There," she said proudly holding up Paul's coat, "now I will just put it to dry by the fire, and we will go to see Mother and Father for they are both sitting in the back garden in the sunshine," and telling him how pleased they would be to see him she caught up his hand and, holding the kitten in her other, they went outside. They spent a pleasant afternoon together; chatting and laughing at his misfortune with the kitten, who had been christened Mouser the second in honour of his predecessor. Cake and tea produced by Sarah-Jane made the afternoon a most pleasurable experience for Paul and he considered that it had been a long time since he had felt so relaxed and happy. He smiled into Sarah-Jane's radiant face and thought how fortunate he was to have such kind friends. When it was time for him to leave, Sarah-Jane rushed to the kitchen to retrieve his dried coat and walked him to his horse. He promised her that he would not leave it so long before he came to visit them all again, and wished that her kitten should bring her happiness.

"Oh! I am sure he will," she told him happily and suddenly he bowed his head and kissed her soft cheek. Trembling with excitement she heard him whisper, "Goodbye dear friend," and then he was on his horse and trotting away from her down the lane. She stood and watched long after he had disappeared.

Arriving back at Trevu, he bounded into Hannah's kitchen more like his old self than he had been for a long time and, catching hold of Hannah around her ample waist, kissed her on the cheek.

"Master Paul!" she chuckled and flicked at him with her cloth but with no success at hitting him. Observing his mischievous expression she announced hastily, "and don't 'e pinch any of they biscuits."

"Not today Hannah," he told her and, noting the look of surprise on her face, explained that he had been with Sarah-Jane and her parents, adding with playful wickedness, "and she is a very good cook."

This time the cloth found its mark, but Paul only laughed out loud and Hannah beamed to see him so happy, for it had been such a long time since he had behaved in such a carefree manner so much like his old self. In another moment he was gone; and she heard him running up the stairs and the soft thud of his door as it shut behind him.

Redvers, Caroline and Sardi were all seated in the back parlour when Hannah arrived with a tray of tea and cakes, looking big with news, and within a short space of time they were informed of the housekeeper's observations.

"Master Paul come straight in to the kitchen an' kissed me, jes' like the ol' days 'e was sir. Full a' mischief and sparkle. An' knaw where 'e bin' do 'e? - all af'noon too," she said, nodding wisely.

"No, I do not know where he has been," said Redvers, translating for Sardi.

"The Williams' place. Said Sarah-Jane was a good cook," she nodded again, "See what I mean?"

"Yes Hannah, I do but," he answered and he placed his hand on her shoulder, " do not raise your hopes too high, my dear. They have been friends for such a long time now, it probably means nothing."

"Well friends or no, 'e 'ad a great big smile on 'is face an' thas' a fact," and giving him a direct look, turned and left the room.

"Would you disapprove of the Williams girl to be a part of the family, Redvers?" his sister asked forthrightly.

"You always did get straight to the point, did you not Caroline?" he asked laughingly but his face took on a serious expression when he continued: "I do not disapprove if it will make Paul happy but I do not think she is the one for him. I only hope he does not break poor Sarah-Jane's heart," he added, "for she does not deserve that."

"Redvers," sighed Caroline in a subdued voice, "her heart was broken a long time ago by Paul, but he has always been too blind to see it."

Paul put in an appearance at the dining table but it was evident that he was still of the same mind as regards the unwanted presence of his mother in his home. But he was more sociable to them all and Redvers breathed a sigh of relief, for he hated having to dine with his son's scowl permanently on his face. After dining they retired to the back parlour but Paul only made desultory conversation. When Redvers of a sudden asked Caroline to accompany him to the office, for he informed her he had some papers that he needed her to look at, she covered her surprise admirably, for she knew it to be only an excuse on her brother's part to allow Sardi to be left alone with her son. After they left, silence ensued, but Sardi steadfastly regarding her son asked him boldly if he was at last coming to terms with her living in the house. He shook his head and then told her angrily that he would be most relieved if she would leave to enable everything to be as it was before.

"Are you so frightened that with my being here you think your father might ask to marry me?" she asked him complacently.

"Yes," he replied savagely and stared at her angrily.

"I know that you cannot abide the thought of it, Paul, and well I know why, for you do not want me to take Penelope's place in your father's heart. I have not taken it in yours after all, have I?" she enquired of him sadly.

"That is true," he agreed bitterly, "you have not because you cannot! You have come amongst us, disrupting our lives, persuading father into believing that he is in love with you, and trying to make me respect you. As if I could ever forget that you quite happily abandoned me! And were it not for Mama's dearest love and determination, what life would I have led then? Why, the good people of Penzance, who would quite happily have spat on me when I was a boy were it not for her, are now so besotted with you that they even talk of wedding plans for Captain Trevarthen with the mother of his bastard!" He saw her flinch and pressed home his advantage. "Leave me again, madam, for you did not want me before an' I believe 'tis too late now to pretend a devotion that you quite obviously did not feel then and do not feel now." At his hard words he saw the tears come to her eyes and he felt consumed with guilt, for he knew her greatly hurt.

"You cannot forbid and neither will you be able to stop me loving you or your father, Paul, but I did not come here to find a lover. I came to help you to learn to live your life again, without the woman you love but cannot have. It can be done because I have already done it and you, my son, will have to learn to live with that disappointment as I have had to live my life with mine. I think of the two of us I have succeeded to a better degree in doing that. Lost in self pity you have wasted so much of your abilities and talents that we all despair of you. Were it not for the fact that you are my son and that I have loved you all your life I would say that I am ashamed to know you," said

Sardi, and never taking her eyes off his face for one moment she saw the pain she was inflicting upon him, but she determined to continue.

However, her son interrupted her, shouting angrily: "I did not ask you to come here! Better for me if you had not for neither I nor my father have need of you. I am here to love and protect him and the wife he loved, above all others, does not need you to take her place," and she saw his hands clenched hard in the anguish of the emotion he was feeling.

"Then why do you not love and protect him, as you put it? Why must the world revolve only around you Paul? When you could not have the woman you loved you tried to wreck the lives of those around you, those very people who loved you the most. I am here now because it is you and not me that would wish to break your father's heart. As I have told you I did not come back for his sake but for yours. Have I for one moment attempted to step into Penelope's shoes? - no, I have not, because I know in your heart there is room for her alone. Your aunt was so desperately afraid for you that she wrote and asked me to come, because she could not bear to see what you were doing to yourself and those around you, the people who loved you the most. I was the last chance she had to make you see sense. I did not return to marry your father Paul, I came to try and help you. To show you that you have to go on, no matter how bad it seems or how . . . pointless," she stopped and wiped the tears from her face.

In the face of her great distress he felt a sudden desire to go to her, take her in his arms, ask her forgiveness; such was the shame he felt. But he would not allow himself for he was hung all about with the chains of his pride.

Slowly his mother rose from her seat and said, "I have nothing further to say to you, Paul," and left the room without a backward glance.

After a sleepless night Paul sat at the breakfast table, by his father's side and when Redvers asked him if he had resolved anything after talking to his mother, he merely shook his head and turned away in shame. Having no wish to meet his mother again so soon after their argument, he finished his breakfast and, with a brief farewell to his father, left the room. Redvers regarded the closed door with a thoughtful expression on his face and when, a little while later, Sardi and Caroline entered the dining room, he was most keen to point out to them that Paul appeared to be ashamed to meet his mother, which he considered to be a far better sign than his son's previous attitude of undisguised hatred towards her. Sardi considered his words for a moment and then smiled and said that possibly he was right, for she had the impression that during their argument there came a point when his mask seemed to drop, as if he had come to recognise that he had some feeling for her.

"Possibly," nodded Redvers, "but you will find that your son is most stubborn, Sardi. He may know that he wants to like you but he will not allow himself to, at least not for a while yet," and he raised a quizzical eyebrow at her. "I hope you will be prepared to wait for a while longer yet."

She smiled at him bravely and discovered during the following week that Redvers knew his son very well indeed, for it was most noticeable that although Paul was desperately trying to maintain his attitude of coldness towards her, he could not always hold fast to his hard stance. Slowly he began to have short conversations with his mother but only if they were left alone together, for he could not unbend towards her in public lest anyone should comment upon his attitude.

When Sardi asked Redvers if she could place flowers on Penelope's grave, he was stricken into silence, but then he told her that, although he had no objection, he thought she should ask her son. Redvers thought it best that on this particular matter nothing would be done that could in any way offend Paul for he held Penelope in such high regard. So Sardi went in search of her son and found him in the library, apparently reading a book but in reality staring out upon the garden where brightly coloured flowers nodded their heads in happy contentment. When she posed her question he was stunned and felt his heart contract in pain.

"Why? Why do you wish to do this?" he finally blurted out in little more than a whisper.

"Because I owe your dear mother a debt that I will never be able to repay," she answered quietly and watched as his head bowed over his book. At the sound of an escaped sob she put her arms around him and rocked him gently in her arms, and the pain of all he had loved and lost over his short life was finally released. They spent the rest of the day together, talking, crying and laughing. She knew it was difficult for him to accept her in the role of mother, she told him, for she considered that, to him, Penelope was and would ever be his true mother. To Penelope had fallen the burden of bringing up the child that he had been and at her words she noted the grateful look in his eyes and the relieved smile on his lips. Caressing his face with a loving hand, she traced out all his features and said quietly, "I am so proud of you my dear Paul, but I am also proud of Penelope and your father, for truly they have turned you into a son to be proud of and I would ask you to let me share in some small way in their achievement. Will you do me the honour of letting me do that, dear Paul?" and when he smiled into her face and slowly nodded they could neither of them stop their tears from falling and clasped each other as if they could never bear to be parted again.

There had to be a parting, however, for Sardi had to return to London by the end of the month, so Paul and his mother tried to spend as much time as they could in each other's company. On the visit to his mother's graveside he helped her to arrange the flowers he had picked to put there, telling her how his mother had always loved bright colours. Then he looked embarrassed as he realised what he had said.

"I . . . I do not know how to address you, for I mean no disrespect, but," he muttered as he caressed the gravestone fondly, "this is who I think of when I say mother, for I grew up thinking of her in that position and I loved her as a son would a mother quite naturally. How do I address my real mother without casting my dearest, beloved away from me?" he asked worriedly of her.

"Why," his mother replied brightly, "You will call me Sardi, of course," and then added with a happy smile. "I should like that very much, for I think that is how it should be and I would not wish for any other."

His smile of relief and was answered by her own beaming smile and, because it was such a lovely day, they sent the carriage home again and walked back from the Churchyard arm in arm, returning to Trevu with a greater level of understanding than either of them had ever thought possible when first they met. When they entertained visitors now, Paul entered wholeheartedly into the conversation and their friends were delighted that the mother and son had been reconciled, but they also noticed the way that Paul's father also looked at Sardi with a look of warm regard in his eyes. Paul and Caroline noticed his look as well but kept their own counsel; each in their own way were quite content to see the blossoming relationship between the two former lovers.

As the time of her departure grew ever closer, Paul agreed that he would visit his mother in London, but asked if she would not wish that his father should come too.

"If he wishes it I would be most pleased to welcome him to my home," Sardi replied, "but I would leave it to him to decide. My appearance into his life again has been almost as big a shock to him as it was to you, my dearest. I think we all need time to adjust to what has happened in our lives, would you not agree?" and she could not help but notice his look of relief at her words. He had come to love her dearly, but her son would be the first to admit that he still needed time to adjust to having a mother in his life again before he could even think to contemplate the possibility that his father might remarry, even though Caroline and all her acquaintances were convinced that this was a foregone conclusion.

Along the road to Penzance the two young horsemen, friends since childhood, trotted together companionably talking quietly about their recent trip to France. The taller of the two -Joseph Bolitho - was being teased by his friend - known as Likky - about the charms of a certain 'mam'selle' that they had both encountered in an inn whilst waiting for their master to conclude his business with the gentleman from whom he purchased most of his brandy.

"Seemed most taken with 'e Joey an' if I could speak the French as good as you d' do I reckon she'd a bin' takin' with me too fer she 'ad that look 'bout 'er, didden she?" Likky asked enthusiastically, in spite of the fact that his own unprepossessing countenance could not in any way be compared to his friend's handsome one. Likky smiled at Joey's grin, but became suddenly wary when he noted the way his face altered completely as Bolitho caught sight of someone approaching them. Down the road, striding hurriedly along was a young girl, and as she got closer Likky recognised her as the Tregenza's servant, the one Joey had a particular liking for; he would always arrange to be in that part of town when he thought she would be abroad. He was about to question why the servant should be on the road at such a time of day when Joey spurred his horse forward and cantered off to meet her. Hastily goading his own beast to follow on, he reached them as Joey was doffing his cap to the young girl and had a chance to hear nearly all their conversation.

"Mark came to tell me but he had no time to stay, for he had to make for Falmouth to tell William-John, so I had no choice but to start walking. I could not remain, Mr. Bolitho, knowing father was so ill, could I?" and she raised her tearful eyes to his face.

"Course 'e couldn' Miss Williams, but didden they tight-fisted old devils let 'e borrow the coach t' get 'e 'ome the quicker?" he asked and Sarah-Jane understood full well that he was referring to the Tregenzas.

"Mr. Tregenza is adamant that I return on the morrow for he says his mother cannot possibly do without me," she sobbed and hunted for her handkerchief and resolutely blew her nose.

"Likky? Give us yer 'orse 'cos Miss Williams 'ere d' need to get to 'er 'ome fer 'er father bin' takin' bad," Joey ordered him, and although Likky would have protested, one look at his friend's face decided him against such an action. But the young girl held up her hand and shook her head: "I cannot Mr. Bolitho for I cannot ride," Sarah-Jane told him and her tears began to fall again.

For one moment Joey appeared unsure but then, taking off his coat, he laid it across the front of his saddle and shook his foot out of his stirrup, before leaning down towards the girl with his arms outstretched. He told her to put her foot in the empty stirrup and he would lift her up before him and convey her to the cottage. She began to protest that it would be quite all right for it would not take her so very long to walk to her home, but he caught hold of her in a firm grip and she felt herself lifted of the ground; having no chance whatsoever to avail herself of the stirrup in any case as in a moment she found herself seated before him almost in a side-saddle fashion. Joey's roan sidled at the extra weight and, startled, Sarah-Jane gave an involuntary little scream but she was instructed to put her arm around him and to hold on tightly. With a brief word to Likky that he would catch him later at Gulval, Joey set his beast off down the road at a canter.

Unused as she was to travel in such a fashion; the horse seemed to be unconcerned to be carrying an extra load and it was not such an uncomfortable experience as she had assumed that it would be. She thought the worst part by far was to be in such close proximity to a man that she had spent so much time in trying to dissuade from paying her attention, but he held her firmly in one arm whilst in his other hand were the reins of his horse and she had certainly no fear of falling. If the circumstances had been different she was woman enough to admit that she might have found the whole experience quite enjoyable, for she noted coyly that Mr. Bolitho had a most strong, firm body and surprisingly he smelt deliciously of soap.

The miles sped by and when they arrived at the cottage Dr. Simcott's pony and trap were still at the front of the house, so Sarah-Jane was told to remain seated whilst her escort swiftly dismounted, then held up his arms to lift her down. Too worried to notice that she enjoyed the sensation, she was not so remiss as to forget her manners and turned in gratitude to thank the young man for his assistance but he waived her thanks aside and told her to hurry in to her father, adding he did sincerely hope that it was to be good news that would greet her when she got over her doorstep.

"Yes, yes of course, Mr. Bolitho, but I must thank you for I. . . I . . .," she began but then she lifted her tearful face and muttered in trepidation, "Father will be all right won't he, Mr. Bolitho?" and received for answer a most reassuring smile that put great heart into her along with his words.

"Course 'e will Miss Williams. Now, afore 'e do go in," and he took out his own handkerchief and deftly began to wipe the tears from her cheeks, saying, "we'll make 'e look a bit more fittee fer yer father don' want catch sight of 'e lookin' sad, do 'e," and when he was satisfied that she looked presentable told her to hurry along, adding, " 'Tis the not knawin' 'tis the worst Miss Williams."

She clasped his hand in hers briefly in thanks before turning and running to the cottage to be met by Dr. Simcott on the point of departure. Joey was too far away to catch what was said but it was obvious from the delighted look on her face that it was good news that was being told to her and so he put his coat on again, mounted his horse and set off the way he had come. Although he wished no harm to her father he was most thankful that he had been taken ill for Joey's heart was still beating as rapidly as when he had held his beloved Miss Williams in his arms at last.

Paul let himself into Trevu and crossed the hall to where a light showed the shadows in the passage. He knew well where to find his father at this time of night. Sitting in his chair in the back parlour Redvers had his head in a book on fishing, but he looked up as Paul entered the room and greeted him cheerily.

"Been courting, Paul?" he asked a twinkle in his eye. Paul frowned slightly but replied in a quiet voice, "No, I have spent the evening with Mr. and Mrs. Williams, and Sarah-Jane of course."

"John is progressing well, I hope?" asked Redvers. Paul replied in the affirmative and informed him that Sarah-Jane had given up her employment to help her mother to look after him. Catching sight of his father's raised eyebrow he announced in an exasperated voice, "Father, will you get it into your head that I am not courting Sarah-Jane."

"Lovely girl, always was. I have no objection if you want to woo her. You have shown her a more decided partiality than any other girl in the district. What other family gets you across their threshold with such regularity? Poor Sarah-Jane must wonder if you are ever going to propose" replied Redvers, holding his son's eye with an unyielding look.

"She knows that I am not interested in her . . . in that sort of way," he replied stung.

"She might know it but Sarah-Jane must have the patience of a saint letting you toast your toes in front of her fire without a word from you concerning marriage," he remarked and raised an eyebrow at Paul.

"You well know that I am not in love with her and the reason," replied his son firmly.

"All that was a long time ago Paul, and life has to go on. How long are you going to wait for a girl you have not seen for two years, and who has never written, or been touch in any other way?" he asked gently knowing full well how Paul felt on the subject of Dorothea.

"I am not able to give up hope just yet, father. I keep waiting that one day a letter will come or I will meet her again," he told him sadly.

At his words his father put down his book and crossed the room to put his arm around his son and told him gently. "I am sorry Paul, so sorry. I know it has ruined your life for you but there is nothing to be done about it now. Her father, my feelings, they all got in the way but you cannot go on waiting for her to come back into your life. I think it is not going to happen and I think you know it too, deep down."

Paul broke away angrily, "Damn it! Of course I know it. Day after day it is eating away at my very soul. But I cannot look at another woman in the way I looked at her. She was the only woman I have ever wanted to take as a wife. Believe me father I have met many since but they are not the ones I want to marry. If I could find someone I would marry them but it has not happened. Sarah-Jane is a lovely girl but she is not the one and I am sure she does not think that she is. I swear to you that I have never set out for her to feel that way about me nor have I ever given her cause to think that I loved her, at least I hope fervently that I have not," he concluded worriedly.

His father sighed and returned to his seat, and then said, "I am not getting any younger, you have to admit. You will have to face up to your responsibilities and take a wife to keep the name alive. You are the last Trevarthen, Paul. The choice is not yours," he pointed out quietly.

Paul began to pace up and down the room, saying nothing but a muscle twitched at the side of his mouth and his dark frown fell across his face. "I have begun to realise it father but I beg you give me more time. I cannot cold-bloodedly take a wife that I do not feel anything for," he said at last.

"I know," said Redvers, "but you like Sarah-Jane, and she is your oldest friend, can you not even consider her as your wife? She will always want to make you happy Paul, you can be sure of that. She has been in love with you since you were children together. Perhaps she cannot make you happy in the same way but . . ." his voice trailed off as his son caught his eye and shook his head vehemently.

"I am sorry father," he said apologetically, "can we talk upon other matters. I do not want to argue with you but I cannot talk about this for it still hurts too much."

"Of course," said his father promptly and changing the subject, asked him if he was looking forward to his visit to his mother the following week, adding: "London is a fine city, you should enjoy yourself there. Lots of places to visit, different things to do and then the literary societies that you are to be entertained by. I hear you are considered quite a celebrity in the book world."

Paul laughed. "Yes, it should be very exciting, father, and seeing Sardi again, I am looking forward to that. A bit anxious about how I will go on as I have never been in a big city before. Well, I have never been out of Cornwall before and I am sure that I will appear to be quite a peasant in such company," he told his father laughingly.

"Not at all. With your education and brains you will not be in any difficulty. I wonder to myself often how your mother and I, living such a quiet existence could have produced such an exuberant personality as you have turned out to be, but do me one small favour, I beg of you." he said and as his son looked enquiring he added in his soft voice, "Do not stay away for too long for I shall miss you most dreadfully."

"Oh father," said Paul, and reached out and hugged his father to him, "I shall miss you most dreadfully too, but why do you not come with me? I know Sardi would like it, even though she will be coming to stay at Christmas."

Redvers shook his head and said, "I should like you to spend some time together. You can best do that without my shadow in the background. If I do decide to visit it will be on my own, and I shall not have you to hamper my footsteps, I can assure you."

They both laughed and took up seats in front of the fire and chatted comfortably together until it was time to retire for the night.

CHAPTER 14

TEN days later Paul stepped gingerly out of the post chaise that deposited him in front of his mother's house. He stretched luxuriantly, for in spite of the stops he was unused to travelling long distances and his young, athletic and extremely long body had felt cramped by being inside what he basically considered a small box for such a long period of time. Looking around him he was surprised at the size of the building and its garden. His mother told him that she lived in a house in London but he had not expected a newly built house with lots of evenly spaced, large windows and a sweep of steps leading down to a lawn and flower border, the whole surrounded by a large garden. This property belonged to someone of substance so he imagined that his mother was renting it. At that moment Sardi, with a beaming smile on her face, came running down the steps towards him.. Her son turned and ran towards her and picking her up in his strong arms lifted her off the ground and covered her face in kisses.

"Sardi, Sardi," he laughed into her neck, "it is so lovely to see you again. Father sends his love and best wishes."

She laughed merrily, "Oh Paul darling, I have missed you and your father so much," she gasped. "I would never have believed that with my busy life I could have felt so alone. But enough of this; come in, come in to my home and rest yourself for I know well what a tiring journey it is. Johnson will pay off the chaise and arrange for your baggage to be brought in."

Paul became aware of a well built, grey haired man in a very smart black coat standing to one side of his mother. He bowed to Paul and greeted him with great civility. The young man smiled his usual smile but he was surprised to think that his mother had such an imposing servant to work for her, then he thought that perhaps he came with the property. Once inside the house he stopped and gazed about him in amazement. There was a large, well lit hall with a tiled floor and a grand staircase that swept up to the landing and rooms above and everything was beautifully and tastefully decorated. He was reminded of Squire Tregurthen's house, for that had been the grandest house he had ever been in until he had entered this one, but this was bigger and lighter. There were bowls of flowers everywhere: in the alcoves, on tables in front of the windows, and smaller tables dotted by the sofas and chairs that filled the sides of the great hall. Doors led to rooms off the sides and back of the hall. Paul, used to Trevu's dark and forbidding little hall, thought that he had entered a palace. Johnson directed a young footman, or so Paul presumed him to be, to take Paul's baggage up the grand staircase, and at that moment a smartly dressed middle aged woman appeared from a door leading to the back of the house. She was followed by another woman, wearing a large white apron with a mob cap set on her grey curls, and ten young girls wearing a similar uniform. They all formed a line and after his mother had finished talking to the middle aged woman and the young man who had taken his baggage had returned, he found himself being walked down the line of servants, being introduced to them all; starting with Johnson the butler, Steven and Edward the footmen, Mrs. Harcourt the housekeeper, Mrs. Miller the cook and the ten serving and kitchen maids.

Paul felt in a whirl by the end of it. He had never been in a house with so many servants. His mother explained that there were also servants who worked in the stables and garden but he would meet them all later. She then surprised him again by asking Edward to act as Paul's manservant whilst he stayed at the house. Paul looked slightly worried by this as he had never had a manservant before and was not altogether sure what you did with one.

Mrs. Harcourt informed Sardi, that some refreshment had been laid out for them in the saloon. Sardi thanked her, thanked and dismissed the servants and, linking her arm through Paul's, led him into the saloon. Again he had to blink in wonderment at what he saw. The saloon was much grander than the hall and in its large room were more settles and chairs, with an exquisitely worked, large carpet on the floor. Against the far wall was the biggest white marble fireplace he thought he had ever seen. He stood transfixed in the doorway, stunned by the grandeur of what was before him.

"What is the matter, Paul?" said Sardi surprised by his reaction.

"I have never . . . I mean . . . this house, it is so grand, so big. I have never been inside such a building before. I cannot believe that you live here. I do not want to be rude but . . . how . . . I thought . . .," he stumbled on till he could of think of nothing to say.

Sardi explained proudly, "When I left you with your father and mother I returned to Bristol and slowly at first built up a little business with the contacts that I had with the traders and merchants where I grew up. Many of them were known to me through my original employer. I soon realised that dressmaking - particularly high class fashion - and the supply of good quality material were a most compatible concern. It took me a long time, long hours of work, several disappointments but I had ambition and I did not intend to be defeated. Originally I set up an agency to supply material, first in Bristol then wider afield, but about sixteen years ago I set up my first dressmaking establishment in Bristol and after some time I had such a good business that I was able to start another. From then on I expanded into other towns and cities until finally I reached London, buying and selling as I went. Being able to supply the material as well as designing and making the dresses that were offered for sale made sure that I could give my clients the professional care that they demanded. I can assure you Paul that for this care they were willing to pay, and pay highly. They did not mind because the quality of the material, the design of the clothes, and the skill that went into the making of the dresses were all there to be seen. The upper classes have great wealth Paul." She paused and then announced bluntly, "A lot came from their investments in the slave trade." She studied him seriously noting his surprised look, but continued; "and I determined to get back from them, however small, some of what had been stolen from our ancestors. I could not give those nameless people back their liberty, their lives, their homelands, but I should like to think that in their unknown, unmarked graves I, in some small way have given them back some of their dignity. I thought it the least I could do."

"I think your father would have been most proud of his daughter," said Paul seriously, "I know his grandson is." Sardi smiled proudly at his words and smiled even more as her son added; "But I still cannot believe that you have all this," and he spread his arm in a wide circle.

"This and more, Paul. I own property in Bristol as well as the dressmaking shops. The agencies I operate make me a rich woman alone, but the sewing side of the business provides an equally good income and allows me to live in a style beyond most people's imagination. It also allows me to set up various trusts that enable my income to provide for my fellow man, be he black or white, for I make no distinction with the people that I am able to help."

Now it was her son's turn to smile proudly and he put his arm around her and kissed her lightly on her thick brown curls.

"I always considered myself lucky having Redvers and Penelope to bring me up, but I know I would have been equally as proud to have been brought up by you," he told her truthfully.

"Thank you Paul, I shall cherish that remark," she said gently, "but now enough of all this serious talk. We will begin to enjoy ourselves whilst you are here. Where would you like to go? The theatre? The opera? You have only to say."

"The first thing I should like to do," he said smiling his mischievous smile, "is to attack the food I see over there that has been so kindly produced by Mrs. Harcourt."

The next morning Paul was awoken by the sound of curtains being drawn back across the curtain rail in his room. The sun flooded into it and he found himself blinking at the sight of a slight young man advancing towards his bed.

"Good morning sir," Edward said cheerfully, "Shall I place your tea tray here for you sir?"

The half asleep young man nodded and watched as Edward placed the tray on the side table by his bed. Paul struggled into a sitting position and accepted the cup that was being passed to him.

"What time is it please,?" he asked, trying to stifle a yawn.

"Nine o'clock sir," responded Edward promptly.

"What!" cried Paul shocked, and then admitted: "I must have been more tired than I realized."

"The journey no doubt sir," said Edward, then continued urbanely, "Mrs. Harcourt says to inform you that your bath is ready for you in your dressing room and can be kept hot for you for when you should like to take it."

"My what!" Paul almost choked over his tea and then said worriedly, "Mrs. Harcourt is not planning to wash me herself I hope?"

Edward tried to keep his features under control - but he had to grin - although in answer to Paul's question he said that giving Mr. Trevarthen a bath was not one of Mrs. Harcourt's duties.

"I shall give you your bath sir, never fear," he remarked quietly.

"Oh will you. I mean is that what menservants do? I do not want to appear stupid but I may as well tell you that I have never had one before, a manservant that is, and am not quite sure what it is that they do for one," he said honestly.

Smiling at Paul's genuine concern, Edward listed the work that being a manservant involved and won his master's great regard when he mentioned that, having never been one before, he hoped that what he undertook to do for his master should prove satisfactory. Picking up a rather sumptuous dressing gown in dark green silk, embroidered over in gold he added,

"Yesterday you were very tired after your long journey and your mother ordered that you were to be left alone, but to day it was felt that you would prefer to have the assistance of a servant. I have taken the liberty of unpacking all you clothes sir. The maids have ironed your shirts and neck clothes and I have pressed your coat and polished your boots. I hope that this meets with your satisfaction sir," he enquired impassively.

"Why, yes, thank you Edward," replied Paul stunned, but added mischievously, "but do not pamper me overmuch for I shall resist the temptation to go home and you will have to spend all your time running around after me."

"The pleasure would be mine, sir. I hope I shall do nothing to displease you or with which you can find fault," Edward replied with a very serious look on his face.

"Never fear, Edward, I cannot imagine that you would ever do that," and treating his manservant to one of his brightest smiles, finished his tea, got out of the bed and followed him to the dressing room where his bath had been prepared.

Half an hour later Paul arrived at the breakfast table looking as neat as a pin. Although he had never been a slovenly dressed young man in the normal course of events, even he realised that everything about him was, he thought, looking particularly fine that morning. Therefore, on greeting his mother with a smile and a kiss on the cheek he was totally unprepared for her opening conversational remark.

"Dear me," she remarked looking critically at him, "we shall have to buy you a new wardrobe, for sure."

"Why should you have to do that?" he asked in surprise and was reminded somewhat warily of his aunt Caroline.

Sardi smiled at him but continued briskly: "Paul you look very fine, but you are the son of the woman who makes the best dresses in London and uses the finest materials. Although I have no intention of making you into my creation I think you would feel more comfortable in some better quality garments. Therefore I propose that your first visit in London will be to a tailors," and smiled at Paul fondly as a slightly mulish look crossed his face, but continued coaxingly; "Paul, dear Paul - just to please me."

He smiled resignedly but made it plain that he did not intend to spend his days being fitted out for clothes that in his opinion looked very much the same as any other man's.

The tailors that he was taken to was a much larger establishment than he had ever been to in his life and his mother, unlike his aunt Caroline, established what colours and styles he wanted before proceeding to instruct the tailor herself on how she wanted to have the garments made. Her technical knowledge was infinitely superior to poor Mr. Murdoch's, even though he was Penzance's finest no less, and the tailor given the task of creating her son's new clothes treated her with the greatest of respect. Paul was whisked off into a side room and was measured and fitted without any of the superfluous chatter that normally attended a visit to Mr. Murdoch's.

When he returned his mother was supervising the purchase of a rather large amount, or so he thought, of shirts, neck clothes, and stockings. Sardi then produced from her reticule the largest roll of bills he had ever seen in his life and, peeling off the required amount, promptly paid for them. He tried to keep the look of amazement off his face. A small young man carried the large number of parcels to the carriage with them and was given a gold coin for his trouble, whereupon his face lit up instantly and he thanked Sardi by bowing low and repeating his thanks until a shout from the shop recalled him to his normal duties. If Paul thought that they would now return to the house he was speedily undeceived for at their next stop Paul was fitted for boots and shoes before his mother whisked him off to the clock makers where a watch on a gold chain was purchased for him. In fact so many purchases were made on his behalf that they returned for lunch almost wedged to one side of the carriage, so full was it with the results of their foray.

There were still more gifts to come for in the afternoon Paul was presented with his own curricle and pair. He stood breathless in front of the stable block, his mouth hanging open, so amazed was he at the sight of the matching chestnuts and sleek, black painted curricle that he was being told he owned. Matlock the head groom was then instructed to take Paul for a spin to see how he went on. When they returned an hour later Paul glowed with pride on hearing Matlock tell his mother that the Mr. Trevarthen had the softest hands and was more than adept at handling so sprightly a pair. The groom added that he would have no fear of that young gentleman tooling them around the town as soon as he had some of idea of the geography and he would be honoured to go with him himself, it was such a pleasure to be driven by the likes of such a capable whip. Beaming with delight at having her son so praised Sardi informed Paul that if he wished to ride in the park Matlock would go with him to purchase a suitable mount telling him, "My friend Colonel Fleetwood is moving to Herefordshire later in the year and wants to dispose of some of his stable. Matlock informs me that he has several horses that could well suit you for such a purpose but if you would prefer to use the curricle and my carriages instead it is entirely up to you. I think you would enjoy the freedom of riding whilst you are here. It is quite customary to take a morning ride in the park, you know, to peruse a . . . to peruse the opposite sex if nothing else," she ended, her eyes twinkling.

Still stunned by her benevolence her son enfolded her in a crushing embrace and kissed and thanked her but he added in mock admonishment, "Sardi, you are as bad as father in trying to marry me off." Sardi laughed delightedly and after thanking Matlock for his kind offices and even kinder remarks, he linked arms with his mother and they returned towards the house.

A week later Paul was now happily riding his black stallion in the park in the morning or tooling his curricle around the streets in the afternoon. His mother had taken him to the opera and to the theatre and, although he tried not to look like a provincial, he was sure that he did as he appeared to be attracting a lot of attention. At first he had put that down to the colour of his skin, but he had soon realised that his colour was not such a rare sight in London as it had been in Cornwall. London was much more cosmopolitan than any other place he had been in and consequently it was inhabited by a far broader mixture of people. It was soon quite obvious to him that his mother attracted attention, but when he studied the people who were looking at her he soon realised that the men were admiring her and the woman were studying her with envy. His own colour was much lighter and hardly merited any notice at all, so he had concluded that he was considered rather gauche and he tried his best not to appear so awkward in company. Paul, never aware of his good looks, did not realise that the glances and whispers he attracted were to do with his handsome appearance and nothing to do with his delight in being London for the first time.

With all the hours of training his aunt had forced upon him, the pleasant young man gave the impression of being completely at ease in any company. He was aware that girls smiled at him and tried to attract his attention, but that happened in Penzance so he took no notice. His mother seemed to him more beautiful than ever, but in his innocence he did not fathom that the reason for her appearance was that she was glowing with her pride in him and the admiration he was receiving from her friends, acquaintances and servants. The butler took the opportunity, when he was granted some time alone with Sardi, to point out that her young son, having no friends in London, would not be able of his own accord to go out in a large, strange city and make friends amongst young men of a similar age. Perhaps, he suggested suavely, if Sardi could find Paul a companion, with a good understanding of the social life of the city and, more importantly, the pitfalls to be avoided she would solve the problem of his reluctance to leave his mother's house and go off to explore the great, seething, inviting metropolis.

Giving the matter considerable thought, Sardi wondered if a visit to one of her establishments would help to broaden his horizons. Deciding in her business-like way she informed her son of her plans when they met across the breakfast table.

"To go where?" asked Paul in surprise, halfway through his normal large meal.

"With me to the shop," replied Sardi, "I thought you might find it interesting, and because a lot of people come and go you will get to see a lot more of society than you will here."

"But it will just be a lot of women buying dresses and talking about fashion," he moaned, beginning to look sulky.

"Well, we shall see. Finish your breakfast, get your hat. I will be leaving in ten minutes and I expect you to be ready by then," she told him firmly and in a voice that told him it would be no good to argue, and turning to Johnstone asked for the carriage to be brought to the front door.

When they arrived at Sardi's premises he was amazed that it looked more like an expensive withdrawing room than his idea of a shop. Once again he found himself being introduced to a large number of people, the majority of them female. He never ceased to be amazed by the number of people that worked for his mother. At Trevu there were no more than thirty people on the farm and that included the staff in the house. Over twenty people were employed in this shop alone, and Sardi had two more in Bristol as well as a house. He only needed to make a quick calculation for him to be aware that his mother most certainly employed in excess of one hundred people. Paul became rather concerned due to the fact that, as his father's heir, he was considered to be the biggest catch in Penwith, but his mother was obviously infinitely more wealthy than his father could ever hope to be and everyone knew that he was her only son. It did not take him long to discover that she was as interested in getting him married off as his father was for she had raised the subject on quite a few occasions, although she was infinitely more discreet than Redvers had ever been. Her desire for him to get out of the house to mix the more in society was to him an obvious ploy, for surely the people he was going to meet were all going to be females, probably matrons with marriageable daughters in tow. His Aunt Caroline's face suddenly swam into view, and he reasoned he would find himself pushed at another set of females. When would they understand, he thought sadly and angrily to himself, that he had only ever fallen in love with one woman, and that she had been denied to him.

The first six customers that came into the shop were all introduced to him and he was dutifully charming to each of them; he noted with disgust that they were all female. One was an actress, one a well born lady who had fallen on hard times until she became the mistress of a member of the government, two were sisters who had married into the nobility and the last was an elderly, richly dressed lady with her granddaughter trailing miserably in her wake.

Most of the woman stared at him, the actress even told him that she was always looking for handsome young men to act as leading men in the plays that she and her company put on and would he, by any chance, be interested? Paul, steeling himself to be charming, informed her that although honoured by her proposition he was not of a thespian nature.

"Shame, dearie," she said, "such looks, such soulful eyes, such a waste," and she sighed and went off to pick out her dresses.

Presented as Sardi's son to the elderly lady and her granddaughter he bowed gracefully, but Lady Wrothford continued to stare at him until he began to feel uncomfortable. Turning to Sardi she abruptly asked her if she was married. Sardi shook her head and confirmed that she was still and always had been a single woman.

"Bring him up yourself?" demanded the old woman crisply.

"No," replied Sardi serenely, "he was adopted by dear friends and they brought him up. This is his first visit to London."

"Handsome boy. Married?" she asked peremptorily studying Paul's face, much to his discomfort.

"No," replied Sardi with unwearied patience.

"Humph! Having a dance for my granddaughter tomorrow night. Make sure he is there. A young man as beautiful as that appearing at Chloe's first ball will certainly set the town agog," she ordered and then turned away from him and asked, "Dress ready?" and receiving confirmation that it was, followed Sardi to a small fitting room set off from the main one.

Paul was left standing in the middle of the room feeling remarkably foolish. The old lady he found most imposing and if he had been required to speak to her he felt sure that he would have been unable to do so. Looking around for something to do he decided to take a seat at the edge of the room and wait for his mother to return. Ten minutes later the young girl, now dressed in a white gossamer creation adorned in pink rosebuds and satin ribbons, stepped back into the room with her grandmother and Paul stood up immediately.

"Well?" barked Lady Wrothford at him.

Paul looked blank for a moment but, correctly divining that she wanted to know what he thought of her granddaughter's appearance he replied: "I think, your ladyship, that Miss Chloe will be the belle of the ball, so beautiful does she look and," his mischievous eyes twinkled into the young girl's sad, serious ones, "although the dress is exquisite it cannot match the beauty of the young lady wearing it."

"Humph! Pretty, very pretty," chuckled the old lady and turning to her young companion told her to stop blushing and to go and change again. The girl, with a shy smile at Paul, returned to the back room and Sardi and Lady Wrothford were left facing one another.

"What name does he go by?" asked Chloe's grandmother and pointed to Paul with her fan.

"Paul Trevarthen," replied Sardi, completely unabashed by her Ladyship's tone and manner.

"Familiar name. Heard it before somewhere," mused Lady Wrothford, "now let me think. I shall have it in a minute." She wrinkled her brow for a moment and then exclaimed, "Not that damned poet? Is that who you are?" she asked turning to Paul with a hawk like stare.

"I am the Paul Trevarthen that has published various translated Latin works, the first one of which was a book of love poems," he told her in a calm voice, although he found her manner most disconcerting.

"Wonderful!" she exclaimed, "the most handsome man in London and that poet chap as well. Woman have been sighing over those poems ever since that book came out. By heavens, this party is going to be the hit of the season," and turning back towards Sardi she ordered her to come as well.

"Bring that old bore Fleetwood with you. He's been hanging after you for years, he'll jump at the chance to accompany you. His son is down from Oxford so you can make up a party. Arrive for seven, you can dine as well. I want him there," she announced pointing to Paul, "when the Countess of Cleveland walks in with Seabrooke on her arm. Read any of his books?" she asked abruptly of Paul but she answered her own question before he could reply. "Don't bother! Load of drivel," and as her granddaughter returned to her side she announced abruptly: "Well, must go. Come Chloe. Goodbye till tomorrow."

She swept from the room with a speed that belied her advanced years, even her young granddaughter had to quicken her pace to keep up with her. Paul stared after them in disbelief before turning his astonished face towards his mother.

"I am surely not expected to go to her ball?" Paul asked incredulously.

"Lady Wrothford is one of my best customers. It would not be politic for me to offend her. Colonel Fleetwood will be delighted to attend and if, as she says, young Peter is in town he will be good company for you," she informed him briskly. Suddenly struck by a thought she said, "Now, why did I not think of introducing you to Peter before? I am sure that you will get on extremely well." Paul attempted to refuse to make an appearance at the ball but his mother would hear no objection from him, so he submitted to her wishes but with a sulky look which he was told to remove immediately unless he wished to incur his mother's displeasure.

The following evening he met Colonel Fleetwood again and was introduced to Peter Fleetwood his son. Peter was two years older than Paul but he had an irrepressible smile on his face and any shyness Paul felt was immediately dispatched by his friendly manner. Not as tall as Paul he was still well above average height, with light brown hair and light blue eyes that seemed always to be twinkling. Almost from their first introduction they liked each other for, like Paul, Peter Fleetwood had been an only child and so both young men were glad to have found a companion.

The Fleetwood's had taken the Colonel's carriage to Sardi's and stayed to take a small glass of sherry whilst the two young men were introduced to each other. When they proceeded to Lady Wrothford's, Paul was the one member of the party dreading the forthcoming entertainment, for he could not believe that he would be able to conduct himself sensibly in the midst of such a large crowd of people.

Lady Wrothford's town house was yet another revelation to Paul but he schooled his features admirably, for he did not want to look like a peasant on his arrival. It was an imposing mansion set in a square which consisted of equally elegant houses. His host took him by the arm and introduced him to the various members of her family and the other guests that had been invited to dine with her. Although nervous, for he was attracting no little interest, he remained his usual charming self and pretended not to notice the enquiring looks that were directed at him. The meal was sumptuous and when it was finished and the guests for the ball started to arrive there was not a female in the place - young or old - who could take their eyes off him. Paul behaved perfectly, his training second nature to him but he was not sure who he should ask to dance. Daunted to be at his first society ball he took his lead from Lady Wrothford, who glared at him but lifted her brows slightly whenever an approved partner appeared before him. In next to no time he found himself committed to every dance but he had made sure that he had put his name down on Chloe's card for the quadrille. Lady Wrothford smiled her approval with a slight twist to her severe mouth.

When the orchestra started with the music for the first dance, he found his partner, bowed and escorted her onto the floor. Paul had been considered the best young man to dance with in Penzance for Caroline had taught him the steps over and over again, until he performed any number of dances automatically but with a great deal of grace. In London he thought he would soon be outshone by the local males. They were all good dancers, of a much higher standard than the local youths of Penzance, but Paul by his bearing, charm and deftness of foot soon had even these young men looking like clods. Unaware, with his usual innocence, that he was setting a ballroom full of female heart's fluttering he dutifully performed his part in all the dances he had undertaken. Half way through the evening the assembled company went in for supper. Not wishing to lead any of the females into the large room with the tables piled high with all kinds of dishes, he hung back until he saw Colonel Fleetwood with Peter and his mother and went in with them.

Unbeknownst to him, people were being told in no uncertain terms just who this handsome young man was that had suddenly appeared in their midst. At the mention of his name certain females began to fan themselves rapidly and turned soulful eyes in his direction. Trying to remain oblivious to their stares, he was finding it increasingly difficult when a voice at his side suddenly barked at him: "Look at them all! Can't take their eyes off you. Only had to tell a couple of matrons who you were and the news spread like wildfire," Lady Wrothford laughed conspiratorially, "Paul, you're a sensation and at my party too. Damn me but I'm glad I met you!"

Paul, unused to females expressing themselves so forcefully, tried not to look shocked, not only at what she had said but the way in which she had said it. He bowed politely and informed her that it was a wonderful party and he was enjoying himself hugely. He found that a shrewd stare was being directed at him.

"Not with those sad eyes, you're not," her ladyship bluntly informed him. "Hiding a broken heart if I'm not mistaken. Read your poems. Beautiful words. Certainly know how to write about love, you and that Latin chap. Still, have to put the past behind you, now. Handsome looking young man, plenty of charm - not bothering to make use of it 'tho. Won't do y'know? Plenty of woman giving you the eye tonight. Pick any one of them if you want to."

Paul, attempting not to look as discomforted as he felt, regarded his hostess steadfastly but said nothing.

"Humph! Don't want to, do you?" and she tapped him on the chest. "Going to waste, young man, all that marvellous creation your mother and father made. Not right of you to be that selfish, you know. All got to take up our crosses some time. Remember that." So saying she swept off across the room and disappeared into a knot of people by one of the tables whilst Paul was left staring after her in amazement. He turned suddenly as Peter Fleetwood's voice sounded in his ear.

"Never known the old lady chat to anyone for such a long time before. You must have taken her fancy," he said with a mischievous laugh, "But there is one person not so keen on you though," and he discreetly pointed out a fair haired man with a florid complexion on the other side of the room.

"I observed earlier that he keeps staring at me and in a most unfriendly fashion," remarked Paul, attempting not to notice the stranger.

"No wonder," acknowledged Peter knowingly. "In literary circles it's you who wears the laurel wreath. That, young Paul, is your arch rival, Nathaniel Seabrooke." Changing the subject he quizzed Paul on his dancing ability, "Fleet of foot as well as hand. Quite a rara avis, aren't you?" he laughed.

Paul blushed but laughed back at him. Then the irrepressible Peter told him to look at his father making sheep's eyes at Paul's mother.

"She won't have him though," he assured Paul.

"Won't she? Why not?" inquired Paul cautiously.

"Because she is in love with your sire, my young buck, an' I mistake not. She has had half the male population of London after her for years but has never by as much as a look given any one of them the slightest encouragement. No, she's set for life, anyone can see that," he confirmed. "Brought you up, your father, so my old man tells me. Widower now so he says," and he looked at his companion and coughed discreetly. Paul shot him a questioning look back. He reflected for a moment and then said, "Do not ask me, they are old enough to know their own minds," but added, "They have told me that they do not want to rush into anything."

"Would you mind?" Peter asked gently.

"I thought so once but not anymore," he answered truthfully.

People began to drift away and return to the ballroom. The musicians could be heard tuning up, so Peter, announcing to Paul that the hunt was picking up the scent again, linked his arm in his and led him back to the dance to find their respective partners. Paul sought out his host's granddaughter for their quadrille. Chloe blushed rosily at him and he noted that she was looking even more beautiful than when he had seen her last in his mother's shop. The white dress suited so young a girl perfectly, her glossy chestnut ringlets shone, her hazel eyes sparkled and her delicate skin fluctuated with colour in a most attractive manner. Paul realised, with a sobering jolt, that he was admiring her, for he had not done that for a long time. However, he presumed that it was merely the heady excitement of the evening playing with his senses. Bowing gracefully, he led her out to take their place in the dance that was forming, and noticed how much her hand shook in his so he gave it a reassuring squeeze and smiled his radiant smile at her. She smiled shyly back at him and began to relax in his company. Although nervous she was a competent dancer, and with the best dancer in the room as her partner, she began to enjoy herself. When the dance ended he took her hand and escorted her back to her seat by Lady Wrothford.

"My God," pronounced that lady, in her usual abrupt manner, "first time in years I've wished meself a young girl again. I'll send Chloe's copy of your book over. You can sign it for her."

Paul smiled, told them it would be a pleasure and withdrew to find his next partner. As he crossed the room a soft smile crossed Lady Wrothford's granddaughter's face and her hazel eyes followed him admiringly. At the end of the evening he was confronted once again by Lady Wrothford. Looking at Paul she addressed herself to his mother, saying: "Well ma'am, 'tis not only a damn fine dress you can make. Make sure you clear your mantle-piece tonight. Be stuffed with calling cards and invitations now I shouldn't wonder. Got to laugh, set out to launch me granddaughter," and shaking Paul firmly by the hand said, "launched this handsome young fellow instead." Still chuckling she waved an airy goodbye to their party and turned to the next group of people preparing to take their leave.

The Colonel's carriage returned them to their home but Peter and his father declined an invitation to come in. Paul had formed a firm friendship with Peter and had arranged to meet him on the morrow for a morning ride. Before retiring for the night, he hugged his mother and kissed her, telling her truthfully that he had actually enjoyed himself more than he had thought he would. She smiled thankfully and was still smiling fondly at him as he made his way up the stairs to his room. Edward was waiting for him and after he had disrobed, helped him into his night gear that was laid out on the bed.

"Call me at eight, please Edward. Although I am so tired I think you will need to fire a cannon over my head to wake me," yawned Paul sleepily.

"Certainly sir, eight it shall be. Goodnight sir," responded Edward.

"G'night," answered a sleepy voice from the pillow.

CHAPTER 15

BARNABY Rickard eyed his opponent warily for it looked as if he was about to face his last night on earth, for with his henchman, Bolitho, down and apparently dead he had no hope of survival ranged against two men as he was.

Well, he thought, if he had to die he would die fighting, he was a brave enough man for that. So he stood with his back to the side of the boat and waited for them to come on to him. The first of them, the one that had caught Joey such a vicious blow to the side of his head with an oar that he fell like a slaughtered ox to the deck, smiled malignantly and allowed the moonlight to dance upon the blade of his knife, the more to instil fear into his opponent, for all three knew that Rickard carried no pistol and his knife was safely embedded in the planking behind Bolitho's body. When the attackers came upon them Joey's own knife had found a home in the heart of the seaman who had tried to kill Rickard, but even when left without a weapon still he had broken the neck of one man and thrown another overboard, before Calloway had caught him with such a blow that his head exploded into all the stars of the night and he fell senseless to the deck. Now, Calloway edged forward slowly to Rickard and his companion, Rowe, smaller but quicker on his feet seemed unable to contain his glee. As the leader of the little band of smugglers that operated from Polperro he wished to see his old enemy Rickard killed, for then he could control all the contraband that came into the county.

"Never thought I'd be the one to put 'e goin', Barney, but you bin' a thorn in me side fer many a year an' I shall be some glad when yer out a me way, me 'ansome," he jeered maliciously, his puffy, pox ravaged face with its broken nose contorted horribly by his smile.

"You can't run a smuggling operation, Archie, save your soul, for you'll forget to watch out for your men and when you have lost enough of them the others will turn upon you like dogs," scoffed Barney proudly, his eyes fixed resolutely on Archie Rowe's pockmarked face. Advancing upon the one man who stood in the way of all his plans, Archie took out his pistol and, cocking the hammer, pointed it directly at Rickard's heart.

"I don' worry 'bout any bleddy men. Times are 'ard an' I can always find plenty a they silly fools an' if they keep their wits 'bout them they'll live a [4]brave while anyways," he said, his evil leer on his lips, "but thas' more than your goin' do fer .... Ugh!" He had only time for a short cry as Barney's knife in Joey's hand released him from the world. Even before he had fallen his killer had turned to attack the startled Calloway, who like the others had believed Bolitho dead.

Surprised though he had been this man was more alert and he loosed a thrust at Bolitho with his dagger that missed his heart but left a deep cut six inches long in his upper arm. The two men closed and Calloway appeared to

---

[4] Brave: normally good or fine, but in this instance it relates to time and means long or fair.

have the advantage, for of the two protagonists he was uninjured, whereas Bolitho was still concussed from the blow to his temple as well as knifed. Holding each the other's wrist in one hand and their respective knives in the other it would be the strongest of them who would win their fight, for once one man weakened the other could plunge his weapon into the heart of his opponent and so end the battle and a man's life. They struggled fiercely, but Calloway was the stronger and brought Joey to his knees, with his bloodstained knife dripping Bolitho's blood back on to the body from which it had come.

Still the younger man would not yield and with sweat dripping from his brow he summoned all his strength in an attempt to get back to his feet, the better to vanquish his opponent. Calloway's face, inches from his own, breathed his foul breath upon him and Joey felt a disgust rise up within him to think that he could be killed by such a fellow as that. He made a final effort to push the man back, closing his eyes and turning his head away, the better to harness his remaining strength. As he did so Joey was deafened by the thunderous report of a pistol, and even with his eyes closed saw the orange flash of flames, and felt the body opposing him weaken at once and fall from his grip as if it were a marionette with its strings suddenly cut. With the momentum of the strength of his own effort pulling him forward, he fell over the man's downed body and in the illumination from the boat's lights saw the head a mass of blood, and at the sight of it he was whirled back in time to a young boy again. Of a sudden it was her head, with her beautiful face that had been beaten into an unrecognisable monstrosity that confronted him. An image so appalling that he could do no more than as he had done that very morning long ago and, closing his eyes upon his tears, turned his head away and was violently sick.

Barney, not comprehending what it was that Joey could see, dropped Rowe's pistol and ran forward, and catching hold of him, dragged him away and propped him against the side of the boat. When Rickard looked into those blue eyes he thought he looked at a man who had lost his senses, for Joey could only stare at the bloody mess on the deck. His lips moved but he could not utter a sound so appalled was he by what he thought he was witnessing again. When Barney heard Joey's whispered urgent call, "Ma! Please Ma!," rising to an anguished scream, "Oh God! No! No!" realisation dawned on him and he knew then what it was that the young man saw, for of Calloway's face all that was recognisable in the light was the man's ear, from which a gold earring still dangled incongruously and where his face had been was only a bloodied pit.

" 'Tis all right lad," Barney said softly, and placing his brandy flask against Joey's lips, tipped back his head and poured some down his throat. Positioning himself so that he obliterated the sight of his victim, Barney removed Joey's coat and ripped open the sleeve of his shirt to reveal the vicious wound in his arm. A long cut, deep but straight was bleeding heavily, so Barney took his own knife from the youngster's hand and cut the sleeve from the injured man's shirt and, ripping it into strips, tightly bound up the wound. Then placing Joey's coat over his shoulders, got some more brandy down him before turning to the disfigured body and removed it from the wounded man's sight as expeditiously as possible by throwing it over the side. Archie Rowe's body, along with the others were disposed of in the same manner.

Coming back to Joey's side, Barney helped him to his feet and led him to the back of the boat, carefully positioning him beside the wheel. Turning the boat about he smiled with delight as the wind filled the sails and, as it was blowing onshore, it soon brought them back towards the land. Behind them, lay their own discarded little boat bobbing gently on the sea, temporarily marking the watery grave of Archie Rowe and his crew as it did so. An hour later Barney ran the boat aground on the first patch of beach he could find, before turning and helping his companion out of the vessel. Stored in the hold was a considerable quantity of geneva and brandy but it was poor stuff for Rowe had always bought cheap and sold dear.

"We'll leave it for the custom's men to find, eh Joey!" and he smiled into the young man's face and felt afraid for him, for not only was Joey's expression blank but his eyes were as well, for he was still looking back into a past so frightening that he could not break free from its horror. They walked slowly for about half a mile, Bolitho struggling to keep his feet from loss of blood as well as the effects of the blow to his head. Coming across some horses in a farmer's field Barney left his companion leaning against the hedge and set off to catch two of them. They were all haltered and so, hobbling the first with his necktie, he soon caught another for the silly creature, intrigued by what was befalling his companion, ambled up to see what was happening. He helped Joey onto the back of the one and got on the other; letting themselves out on to the road they headed inland. When Barney got his directions from a signpost he breathed a sigh of relief, for they would not have so far to travel before he would be able to get help for his injured companion.

Just outside of the little village of Probus, Barney got off his horse and knocked on the door of a darkened cottage set apart from the other houses along the roadway. After a moment a window upstairs was thrown open and an angry voice, swearing profusely, demanded an explanation as to why he should be disturbed at such a time and by whom.

"Rafe 'tis Barney, Barney Rickard an' I need your help badly. Come down here as quick as you can for God's sake," he shouted up in a hoarse whisper and he went back to Joey to help him dismount, but by this time the injured man had little strength remaining and slipped from his horse's back into Barney's arms. Rafe Bosustow, retired ship's doctor with the Star of Amsterdam: - a brigantine sailing from the West Indies to Bristol - for nigh on twenty years, pulled open his door to be met by his old drinking partner struggling to get a semiconscious man up his garden path. With his help they got Joey into the house and laid him down on the dining room table where he lay like a dead man. Barney provided a hurried but truthful explanation whilst Bosustow expertly removed the hastily applied bandages and exposed a gaping wound. He sucked in his lips but merely commented, "Nasty, very nasty but clean," and availing himself of some gin from the dresser cleaned the wound. He acquired some thread from his late wife's discarded sewing box along with a needle, and expertly sewed up the cut before bandaging it again whilst Joey lay impervious to his ministrations. Examining the bruise on the young man's head, he bathed it in a strong smelling lotion, but did not apply a bandage for miraculously the skin had not been broken. Disappearing into another room he returned with a small bowl and singing, an old sea song contentedly to himself, proceeded to mix a concoction making use of the contents of his medicine chest seemingly at random.

"Lift his head, Barney," he ordered quietly and proceeded to force open Joey's mouth, pouring the resultant mixture down his throat. "That will knock him out, good and proper. Let's have a drink and you can tell me all about your night's adventures in more detail. Damn me if I haven't had such an exciting night since we were almost taken by pirates on the way to Jamaica that time," he exclaimed, laughing at the memory, and after throwing a blanket nonchalantly over Joey's unconscious body, he clapped his arm around his old friend's shoulders and led him off to the parlour where he kicked the fire into life again and broke upon a bottle of rum.

Barney began at the beginning and told him that a meeting had been arranged between himself and the Polperro smuggler, Archie Rowe, on Rowe's boat, three miles off the Saint's Head, as he had been told Archie had a business proposition for him.

"Joey, the lad in there on your dining table, said we shouldn't go for he didn't trust the man, but I've been thinking of giving up the trade and thought myself in a position to sell out my half of the county to the rascal, for he has been doing his damnedest to encroach on my patch for many a long year. When we arrived, Archie was waiting for us, with a grin on his face like a drunken bridegroom's. Well we set to talking and Joey stood back watching for me, for that is what I employ him to do. Damn fool that I was, there were we two against five of them including Archie, with Joey and me without a damn pistol between us for my lad never carries one. He says if they catch you with a pistol they'll do their utmost to find a dead man with a hole in him to pin on you, just so they can have the pleasure of hanging you for the Bodmin traders to fill their coffers at your expense. Anyway, like I said Archie was coming at me all smiles, agreeing with my every word - that made me suspicious for a start - when out of the corner of my eye I saw Joey's knife sticking out of the heart of one of Archie's blaggards. I don't know if he was about to kill me or not but he had his pistol in his hand as he fell to the deck and Joey's too wide awake to make mistakes when there is trouble afoot. Another goes for Joey and I threw me knife at him, but I've not the talent of the boy and the damn thing missed and stuck in the side of the boat. Two pitch in on Joey at once but he sees them off fast enough until Rowe's old henchman Calloway picks up a discarded oar and lays him out with a blow to the head," he took a sip of his rum and smacked his lips together in appreciation before continuing his tale.

"Now, I'm left with Calloway and Rowe and I know well enough my time is up because without Joey I had no chance to save myself for I'm on one side of the boat and my knife is on the other. In the midst of my last prayer I see Joey seemingly come back to life, pull my knife out of its resting place and move so fast that neither Rowe nor Calloway heard nor saw him 'til he'd cut Archie's throat. My lad moved quick enough but Calloway was quicker and went to knife him. He missed Joey's heart but slashed his arm instead, and then they fought for the one to kill the other. That devil Calloway wore Joey down for without any injury he was the stronger, and so I availed myself of Archie's pistol, which he had obligingly cocked when he prepared to kill me and shot at Calloway and succeeded in nearly blowing his head off. I've got to break off this tale a minute Rafe to tell you another one about Joey to help you understand what happened next," and he proceeded to give his companion a brief summary of Joey's first murder and the event that caused it before reverting back to his tale. At the end of it he explained that Joey appeared too shocked to comprehend where he was or what had happened. "Do you think he might have lost his wits, Rafe?" he asked worriedly.

"Possibly," Rafe acknowledged. "Won't know until he wakes up. Still with a past like that it wouldn't surprise me. Pity for he's a well enough looking fellow, but there is nothing can be done for him now. We'll have to wait to see what the morrow brings," and he smiled engagingly at his companion and lifting the bottle and his eyebrow at the same time asked persuasively, "Another rum, Barney?"

In the afternoon of the following day Joey began to groan and Barney called out hastily to Rafe, who had just returned from Truro leading two horses that he had purchased in the market, for the stolen ones had had their rumps slapped the previous night and hopefully, as they had headed off in the direction from which they were purloined, were now somewhere far enough away from them not to raise suspicions. Bosustow entered nonchalantly and went and stood by Joey's head, looking down into his face. Of a sudden Joey's eyes flew open with a start and seeing a strange face he attempted to remove himself from its presence as fast as he possibly could. "All right, lad. Rest easy," Rafe said quietly, and gently but firmly pushed him back down on to the table. Joey blinked at him with shocked eyes but on hearing Barney's voice addressing him he relaxed.

"'Tis all right Joey, for Rafe is a friend of mine," Rickard told him and then proceeded to ask him if he could manage to eat some soup. When he saw Joey nod, he breathed a sigh of relief, for with that sign he knew his protégé had not lost his mind as he had feared. Joey, stiff from a night and a morning lying on a dining table, as well as from the wounds to his body and exertions of the previous night, decided for himself to move from his resting place. Bosustow did not object for he could see the young fellow had a good constitution and in his time as ship's doctor he always found that the ones who wished to go, could, and the ones who did not usually went anyway but to a different place. The Doctor helped Joey to a seat in the parlour beside the fire for although he could walk he could hardly do so unaided. Barney, returning from the kitchen with a steaming bowl of soup and a plate of bread, passed them to Joey and studied him covertly whilst he ate in case the young man displayed any signs of what he had witnessed on the night before, but Joey could not remember any of what happened after Calloway had slashed at him with a knife. So, he was unaware that Barney had shot his assailant, or that he had landed the boat and that they had travelled overland on two stolen horses. Rickard could not believe it, but Rafe took him on one side and whispered into his ear reassuringly, "Seen that sort of thing plenty of times.

Don't ask me how, but if they see something they don't want to they seem to manage to forget all about it somehow and he took a hell of a blow to the head remember. Must have a skull like a block of wood to stand being hit like that anyway," and turning to Joey asked him if his head hurt.

"Ringin' like church's bells at a wedding sir," he replied and Bosustow laughed and left the room, returning shortly afterwards with a glass containing a none too inviting looking liquid.

"Get that down you lad," he ordered, "Won't take too long to help ease off the pain, hopefully." So Joey dutifully downed the liquid and then wished he had saved himself back some soup, for the taste of it in his mouth was most foul and try as he would he could not get rid of it. However, the doctor was right, for after a while the pain in his head began to decrease markedly. Lifting Joey's face to the light, Bosustow studied his eyes for a moment, asked him if he could see clearly and, when he confirmed that he could, turned to Barney and told him that with a proper night's rest he would be able to go again.

"I can go now, Barney. Don' 'e worry 'bout me," Joey told him anxiously, for he knew Barney would wish to get back to his wife to reassure her that all was well.

"Rafe's stable boy has gone on to Gulval with a note for Phoebe, Joey, so you've no need to fret. We'll rest easy for to day and go again in the morning after you've breakfasted. Now, will you stay where you are or do you wish to rest in bed?" he asked calmly.

Joey replied that for the time being he preferred to stay where he was and kept his place for the rest of the day, but availed himself of a bed in the early evening and after a good night's sleep he felt almost back to normal. After having some lotion applied to his injured arm he listened patiently as Barney was told how to cut through the stitches to remove them and when to do it. When Bosustow had finished his instructions they shook hands. The smugglers expressed their thanks, made their farewells and Barney promised to return before the week was out with a selection of drink that would do credit to "George the third's cellars", as he put it.

Barney did not rush the journey home and so it was late that evening before they reached their destination. After falling upon her husband's chest Phoebe fell upon Joey's, and he was placed in his chair as if he had been one of her precious pieces of chinaware and plied with as much food and drink as he could manage. He could not believe how tired he was and so retired almost at once, never hearing Barney relate to his wife what had happened on the boat, particularly the part of the action that Joey could not remember. Phoebe shook her head and wiped away a tear muttering: "Poor lad, poor, poor lad," as she did so. But although never forgotten by either of them it was never divulged to Joey for, as Barney told his wife: "If he doesn't want to remember it, dearest, then I'm not going to be the one to remind him, I'm damn certain of that!"

They sat chatting for a long while and, when they had both agreed what it was they wished to do, decided to broach the subject to Joey before the week was out, for they thought after his recent experiences he would not wish to have to make up his mind as to his future without giving it some careful thought.

Likky and his companion were strolling through Penzance three days later, Joey's face still heavily bruised but not so badly that it marred his looks. Various of his female acquaintances, taking the air after their night's exertions, were calling out to him as he walked along, asking if he had been caught by some irate husband, or similar comments. He took it all in good part and merely smiled and waved at them, seemingly impervious to any of their remarks until he caught sight of Miss Williams leaving the Apothecary's with a shopping basket on her arm. She caught sight of the young smuggler almost at the same time as he spotted her and it was difficult to say who was the most disconcerted. Sarah-Jane had not seen him since he had so kindly taken her to her father's bedside after his first illness and, although she had thanked him at the time, she had never thought that she had been generous enough with her gratitude for - understandably at that precise moment - she had been considerably agitated. Joey, now seemingly the centre of a flood of ribald comments, felt his face begin to redden in embarrassment, but the dear girl was heading straight towards him and besotted as he was he would not forego any opportunity to have speech with her. Upon coming up to her he doffed his hat elegantly and, as he bowed, Sarah-Jane was able to assess the extent of his bruised face. Unfortunately at that precise moment a certain lady, rejoicing in the name of 'Salty Mary' enquired loudly of Joey from across the street,

"Did 'e fall out the bed in yer 'aste to get away afore 'er 'usband come 'ome, Joey?" which question was followed by her extremely loud cackle of a laugh. Bolitho's countenance suffused red where it was not black and blue from its bruising. When he raised his face to hers, her green eyes stared at him in disgust, but still she felt honour bound to have speech with him; with a flick of his head he dismissed Likky so she was able to speak to him privately. Luckily for them both, the cat calls had subsided, for Joey was talking privately to a well dressed lady and would be none too happy with certain women of the town, if they should mar his chances with any female of that quality.

"Dear me, Mr. Bolitho, you are presenting a most colourful countenance to the world today are you not?" Sarah-Jane said peremptorily, for she knew she was making herself an object of infamy just by talking to him in such a public place and it angered her greatly.

"I beg pardon, Miss Williams, ma'am, but I fell on a boat an' 'ave knocked my head," he told her, hoping that the fiery red was draining from his face at least.

"Truly?" she remarked in a tone that evidently proved she did not believe a word of his explanation, but decided that this was not the right course to follow for she did most sincerely wish to thank him again, so taking a deep breath she expressed her gratitude in as mannerly a fashion as she could. He told her she had no need to thank him and enquired after her father, marking with concern the shadow that passed across her face.

"I am afraid he has suffered another setback, although he is beginning to improve again now, but my mother finds it increasingly difficult to look after him for she is not always in the best of health herself. So I have given up my employment with the Tregenza's and returned to live at home," she informed him, wondering if that was a wise thing to say for now no doubt the man would be forever kicking his heels in her kitchen.

"I'm some sorry to 'ear it Miss Williams but I should 'ope you wouldn' be offended if I was to call an' see you .... see you an' yer family fer I was made to feel mos' welcome in yer 'ome ma'am," he said, pouncing in on her remarks as she had presumed he would. There were a great many times in her life, she thought to herself in annoyance, when she wished that she had not been brought up to be quite so truthful.

"I cannot stop you Mr. Bolitho but I would tell you my feelings towards you have not changed and, tired as I am of repeating this information to you, they will not alter, so you will be wasting your time to come and call on me," she informed him testily.

"Well, I shall jes' 'ave come to see 'ow yer father is doin' then, won't I, Miss Williams?" he said, an amused smile on his lips.

"As you wish," she told him airily and then, spotting her brother coming down the street with the pony and trap, breathed a sigh of relief and made her farewells hastily, before leaving him to return home in her brother's company.

William John turned the equipage and set the pony at a fast trot but he had noticed to whom his sister had been talking and rebuked her sharply for conversing with such a man as Joseph Bolitho. She replied sharply, annoyed with his criticism of her, that she had felt honour bound to thank him, for on the day their father had been taken ill he had been of invaluable assistance.

"Pooh!" remarked William John, "an' what would Joey Bolitho know 'bout 'onour. Precious little I'll be bound!"

As she had no wish to defend the man, Sarah-Jane kept her pretty little mouth firmly closed, but she remembered with a small smile that the poor man had had the grace to blush after all, and she thought it had happened more out of respect for her than in regard to his own feelings.

Two days later, Barney Rickard faced his young henchman across the table and told him boldly he wished to have words with him of great importance to all of them. Joey kept his face impassive but his eyes were watching the smuggler intently.

"I'm listenin' Barney," he told him softly.

"I've decided that the smuggling trade is no longer the occupation I wish to follow," and he noted Joey's eyes widen in surprise although characteristically his expression did not alter one whit, "for I have been at the trade for a long time now and have made more than enough out of it for my needs. Phoebe has always had a hankering for a small farm and to that end I have used some of my money to purchase a small estate in Hampshire. A couple of tenanted farms and a reasonably sized manor house, for I have no wish to draw too much attention to myself. I appreciate that you have not been brought up to be a farmer but should you wish it, Phoebe and I would be delighted for you to come and share our home as you do here. You can have the rent from one of the farms for your income if you would like, or even to farm it yourself when it becomes free," he coughed and glanced at his wife swiftly before continuing with regret: "As you are well aware Phoebe and myself have not been blessed with children, as yet, and even if we do have the joy of bringing a child into the world we would always consider you a part of our family. Consequently, when we have passed to our eternal rest, provision would be made for you to receive the whole or part of the estate for your inheritance, dependant upon whether we are destined to remain childless." Barney looked up and caught a muscle twitch in Joey's face, but that and the warming of his cold eyes was all that he could detect in his countenance, so he drew breath deeply before asking: "Well, Joey? What would you wish to do?"

There was a prolonged silence until finally Joey asked if he could have time to think about their proposal, for it had come as a bit of shock to him.

"Naturally, Joey. It's a big decision so we would not want you to rush in to it," he replied and then, getting up, he brought out the glasses and poured out a Madeira for his wife, before getting the brandy down from the mantelpiece for himself and Joey.

That night in bed Joey could hardly sleep for excitement, for now when he called upon Sarah-Jane he would have so much more to offer her than himself alone. Surely now, she would see him in earnest, so willing and able as he was to change his life for her. He himself had saved a vast sum over the years, not enough to buy an estate with like Barney but certainly plenty to keep her well dressed and to provide for her in the style in which he thought she deserved to be kept. Almost laughing aloud he pictured himself on a bay, just like Captain Redvers, cantering across his land, ordering scoundrels from his property with all the authority in the world. Even if he dared not admit to himself that the life style he was imagining was not the sort of life he would have liked to have led, it had to be better than the only one he knew, for he was sick to his soul with the smuggling and he recognised that his dearest love would never look at him favourably if he should continue down that path. His head a jumble of thoughts and fancies he rolled over in his bed and soon fell asleep, still smiling softly to himself.

Redvers sat by John Williams' bed and talked quietly to him about the old days, and the delight they had all felt when the big lode at Wheal Sankey had come in; he was well aware that he owed a lot to his mine captain's firm belief in the mine.

"If you had not talked me into putting in my money that day John, I would not have been so financially well off as I am today," he admitted honestly.

"Well, you saw me right and no mistake, Cap'n Trevarthen, sir, for without your help my sons would not have got themselves such good places to go to," and went on to tell with pride the strides that his sons were making in their various occupations. Smiling at Redvers he added, "and thanks to your missus my girl got the best education for miles around and that's a rare thing for a maid hereabouts."

At the mention of Penelope, Redvers smiled fondly, and then informed John that he was off to pick up the mail in Penzance and was hopeful that Paul would have found time to write him, for he was kept so busy in London he seemed not to have a moment to spare. Promising to come again with any news and to visit with his old friend he quietly made his goodbyes and, with a few words to Mrs. Williams and Sarah-Jane, made his way into Penzance. He had almost arrived at his destination when he saw Joseph Bolitho coming towards him down the street and wondered if he still pursued Sarah-Jane, but imagined it an impossibility because any fool could see that at the mention of his son's name her face, as it always had, took on a completely different look. Wondering if he should address him or not his dilemma was solved as the young smuggler politely doffed his hat, murmured "Cap'n Trevarthen, sir," and continued on his way, his face as impassive on greeting Redvers as his own had been when he had in turn acknowledged Bolitho. Within a short space of time Redvers, with the mail stowed safely in his pocket, returned to the little cottage and passed over a letter from his son writ especially to the Williams family. Sarah-Jane's look of delight told him all he needed to know concerning the relationship between herself and Bolitho, for the man could not be such a fool as not to realise that her heart was taken by another. Returning to Trevu he headed to his office and placing his other letters on one side, broke open the one from his son and began to read contentedly.

Back at John's little cottage, Paul's letter brought equal delight, and to one member of the household in particular, although nothing in the letter merited such emotion, a look of ecstasy. When in the afternoon a knock was heard at the door, consternation broke out on that same face as, when she answered it, Sarah-Jane found herself looking up into the smiling face of Joseph Bolitho, clutching in his arms a covered basket. Unable to leave him standing on the doorstep as if he had been a delivery boy, he was invited in, and greeting her parents most warmly, presented Mrs. Williams with his gift of fruit that he had brought out from Penzance.

"Thought some of it might be of benefit to yer 'usband, ma'am," he informed her quietly, his lips displaying a smile of quite entrancing charm, or so Mrs. Williams thought. She thanked him genuinely and asked John pointedly if he would care for Mr. Bolitho to sit with him for a while. If he did not relish the prospect, even in his weakened state, her husband considered it to be impolite to refuse. However, when Joey sat beside him and offered to read to him if he should like that, he was most surprised.

"Well that would be mos' pleasant Mr. Bolitho, but I can't think what you could read that would be fitting," and then wondered if that sounded churlish; he did not want it to for the man was being most considerate. Joey, noting John's bible on the small table by the bed, asked if he would like a passage from the bible. At first surprised and then intrigued, he told his visitor that he would derive much pleasure from that, so Bolitho chose a passage from the Song of Solomon which he read quite beautifully, before turning to Corinthians and beginning to read from chapter thirteen. When he had finished, John looked up with a smiling face and told Joey that he had much enjoyed the pieces chosen; he was unable to go to Church as he would have liked and it was most pleasing to hear the words again.

"You know your bible, Joey," remarked John warmly, for he had appreciated the texts Bolitho had read and had enough of his own charity that he could not help but look upon the young man with a kinder eye. Catching sight of the look of regard Joey was directing at his daughter, he felt sadness for the young fellow for so desperately loving his Sarah-Jane, for her father knew she had ever a love for only one man and he was not the one who was sitting at his bedside

Joey, observing Sarah-Jane covertly, thought he had never seen her look more beautiful, for she seemed to him to have a glow about her, and her green eyes sparkled so finely that he felt his heart flutter at the sight of it. Remembering his manners, he considered it was getting time for him to leave and stood up to make his goodbyes.

Sarah-Jane appreciated that he had brought pleasure to the invalid and thanked him warmly before turning to her father and promising to read him Paul's letter again when she returned from seeing Mr. Bolitho from the premises. Something in the way she said Trevarthen's name and the smile that trembled on her lips as she said it gave Joey a sensation of fear, but he thought himself a fool. Probably his head had not recovered from its battering, he mused to himself, for surely she could not have set her sights on the boy Trevarthen of all people? They walked slowly to his horse and when they got there he asked to call again, for he had something of great importance that he needed to discuss with her.

"Why of course you may visit Mr. Bolitho. I cannot thank you enough for the pleasure you gave to father with your readings, for he loves his bible so. Whoever taught you to read in that way deserves much praise for I could see that father derived great benefit from it. Well, thank you again," she said and she held out her hand hurriedly as if in haste to return to the cottage. Placing his customary kiss on her fingers he smiled into her eyes, but had the distinct impression that the warm regard in them saw another man before her and was not meant for him at all. Despite the pain in his heart he determined to come again and broach the subject of their future together so he wished her farewell and set off. Towards the end of the lane he turned to catch sight of her for she always stood to see him from the property but the plot of grass was bare and of his beloved he could see no sign. He sighed and proceeded homewards with a heavier heart than the one that had accompanied him when he had arrived such a short time ago.

Within three days he had returned, and as her father was asleep and her mother visiting in the village, Joey seized his opportunity. Sitting quietly at the table with his beloved, he began to relate to her his wish to give up the smuggling, for he knew she detested it so. She made a favourable reply so he took a deep breath and proceeded to tell her that his circumstances were about to undergo a change. Explaining that if he accepted Barney's offer he would have to move away, he delicately informed her that he understood full well that she would not wish to leave her family during her father's sickness, but he would be quite prepared to wait for her until such time as it would be appropriate for her to do so. He quivered to see the blank look in her eyes for he, of all people, could recognise that such a look would be used to hide someone's innermost feelings, but he had come this far and so took a deep breath, and launched himself into the only proposal of marriage that he had ever made. When he had finished, he noticed that tears were slowly forming in her eyes, but his heart contracted in pain within him as he saw her slowly shake her head.

"I am most honoured Mr. Bolitho, that you should wish to so change your life for me, but I cannot accept your offer of marriage for as I have always told you it is not you that I hold in my heart and it never will be," she told him sadly.

Swallowing hard, he reached out and caught up her delicate little hand and held it in his firm grasp, before saying gently, "You 'ave also told me Miss Williams that this man 'as no thought of 'e. If that is the case then I would urge 'e to turn to one who loves 'e more than any other could ever do an' would love an' 'onour 'e all the days of 'is life," and he attempted a smile, although at her words his heart felt broken in two. She sighed and out of pity caressed his hand gently, amazed to find him tremble at her touch, but still she would not have him and repeated her vow that she loved another.

"I would knaw 'is name, Miss Williams," he said.

"No, Mr. Bolitho, for you have no need to know it, because he is not the sort of man that would ever cross your path, so different are you in your ways," she informed him quietly.

"I shall come 'gain Miss Williams an' try to make 'e accept my offer fer I am most truly in love with 'e an' 'ave bin' since ever I first saw 'e," he told her sadly, but at that moment John Williams awoke from his slumbers and Joey let go her hand and went to sit at his bedside.

"I should enjoy if you could read me from Ecclesiastes, Joey, Chapter three, do 'e know the one I mean?" and he noted that Bolitho nodded sadly but found the piece and began, in his soft voice, to intone the passage, reading firmly and composedly, unable to display his distress for others to see. John smiled as the familiar words were slowly delivered and the reader faltered only the once when Joey stumbled over the phrase, "A time to love, and a time to hate." When he had finished John smiled at him sympathetically for, ill though he was, he knew well that his daughter and Bolitho were both suffering the soul eating sadness of unrequited love.

CHAPTER 16

LETTER from Miss Sardi Brown to Captain Redvers Trevarthen

Clifton Court, London, 11th June 1804

My dearest Redvers,
Our son, you will be delighted to hear, has become the sensation of London society. After attending a ball held by Lady Wrothford in honour of her granddaughter, Miss Chloe Perriman, he became all the rage. Not only has he hardly had an evening in since that memorable night but we receive visitors on most days and he is forever finding himself invited to balls, routs, parties, soirees, any manner of entertainment. As he was a well known author in society before ever he appeared in London, his presence has placed him high on the list of the most desirable guest to attend whatever event the notable hostesses of this fair city are holding.

He has also become fast friends with Peter Fleetwood, the son of my old friend Colonel Fleetwood of whom you have often heard me speak, and Peter has taken charge of him as regards introducing him to pursuits which are for more likely to find favour with young men of their age. I hasten to add at this point that young Mr. Fleetwood, although full of life and gaiety, has a sensible head on his shoulders and will take great care of Paul so I have no fear that he will fall foul of the low life that unfortunately abounds in this, as in most other, large cities.

He has become quite confident about taking his curricle around London and yesterday took up Miss Perriman for a drive around the park. Lady Wrothford also invited him to make up the numbers for a visit she arranged to the theatre. As I was invited as well I was able to establish that, although he says nothing to me about it, he was most particular in his attentions to the said Miss Perriman. Whether it be because she is such a shy girl and he was trying to set her at ease or because he is beginning to feel a decided partiality for her I know not, and not wishing to discomfort him I have no intention of probing too deeply into his feelings. He has told me that he is missing his father and his home but he is kept so busy now he has not a lot of time for reflection.

If you would not object I would like him to stay until the end of July as I hope to take him with me when I visit Bristol next week and I know well that I will not be able to leave much before the end of June to return to London. Naturally he may prefer to stay on here, he will not lack entertainment after all, but I would prefer him to accompany me as I think he will find Bristol equally as interesting as London and I can assure you that the good people of my home city will be most impressed to have the famous author, Mr. Paul Trevarthen, in their midst.

My dearest love as always,
Sardi.

F J Warren

Letter from Mr. Paul Trevarthen to his father.

Clifton Court, 10th June 1804

Dearest Father,
What news I have to tell you. I am quite proficient at driving my curricle and Ebony, my horse, although inclined to be a handful on occasions is the most majestic creature. I have been to the opera again and the theatre twice and my friend, Peter Fleetwood, a cracking young blade whom I hope you will get to meet one day, has taken me to a cocking, which I did not enjoy - such cruelty, and a fight at Barn Elms, which I did. He has taken me to some wonderful inns, the food at some of the places is astoundingly good.

Sardi has been most kind and keeps buying me all manner of things. I am using the writing box she gave me to pen this letter to you now; it is made of mahogany with inlays of different woods and looks most fine. I seem to be doing something every night, dances and balls and all manner of things. It is very enjoyable but hard work to find something to discuss with all the people that want to talk to me. The people of London must be most bored with the entertainments to be found here for they are forever calling to see us and asking me to sign my books for their daughter, sister, aunt or just themselves, not just the first book either I might add, and when I go to their houses they insist on sitting so close to me I find it quite oppressive. I shall be glad to get away to Bristol next week because I presume that I will not be so well known there and will be able to live a quieter life for a while.

My love and respect as ever, your dutiful son,
Paul.

PS I am enclosing a letter for Hannah and would be most grateful if you would read it for her.

Letter from Captain Redvers Trevarthen to Miss Sardi Brown.

Trevu, 14th June 1804

My Dearest Sardi,
I am quite at a loss as to where to begin this letter. When, I ask myself, will you have the time to read it at any event? My dear this boy of ours seems to be winning hearts wherever he goes and I must admit he makes me so proud of all his accomplishments. Caroline has invited herself to stay next week and I shall be glad of her company for I am most lonely without the dear boy, but I shall have great delight in giving her all the details of the dances and visits that you have told me about. How she will be impressed. I fear the name of Lady Wrothford will be bandied about in most of the withdrawing rooms of Penzance for weeks to come!

Paul has written but not so frequently as yourself. He seems to be remarkably busy although I am not so sure that he is as fond of the balls and dances as you might like him to be. I am so glad you have found him a young man of sense to be his guide and mentor in London. One cannot help but worry after all - he has lived a fairly sheltered existence.

I cannot thank you enough for all your kindness to him, he is most grateful for it as he is always enthusing about his curricle and horses and all the other gifts you have given him. I do not want to disappoint you but he has made no mention of either Lady Wrothford or Miss Perriman in his letters to me, or to any other female for that matter, but he can be very reticent where matters of the heart are concerned so you may be in the right of it after all. I have told him that it is time for him to mend his broken heart and he has admitted that he can understand my wishes, but like you I think it wise not to press him on the subject.

Yes, my dearest Sardi, I shall make no objection to his staying with you for as long you wish even though every day without him seems to drag unbearably. I shall look forward to his return and at Christmas to welcoming you back to my home. I will have to end now to get this letter to Penzance in time to catch the mail. I hope that it arrives before you leave for Bristol and that you are not finding having a young man of Paul's boundless energy too taxing for you.

With my dearest love, I remain your ever affectionate,
Redvers

Letter from Captain Redvers Trevarthen to his son.

Trevu, 14th June 1804

Dearest Paul,

How delighted I am that you are enjoying yourself in London. The house is most quiet without you and your old father is missing his boy most dreadfully, but I am determined to be cheerful and to present a happy face to the world. I do not want you to come home on my account for I believe that all young men should go out and have some experience of the world. I do so hope that you will find Bristol to be as interesting as London has been. Your mother tells me that you have a very active social life and apart from being very busy during the day, with your riding and driving, are rarely at home of an evening. You appear to be making a lot of new friends as well. Perhaps your friend Mr. Fleetwood would like to come to visit some time before the end of the year? I am sure he will find Penzance quite dull after London and I am worried that you may have the same problem!

On a happier note, I have read your letter to Hannah and she was so delighted to have a letter written especially for her that she burst into tears and called you 'her dear little lamb' and insisted that I read it again so that she could tell Ned what you had said when she showed him the letter. The wet weather has not damaged the hay so we will be stacking [5]pooks all over this coming weekend. Beauty has had a fine heifer calf and Mrs. Pascoe

---

[5] Pook: a haycock, made up of sheaves of hay.

another girl - still no boy after four attempts and poor Davy has endured much joshing from the men.

I saw Sarah-Jane and she has asked me to send on all the family's best wishes and she hopes that you are enjoying your stay. Poor John has been unwell again so I went to see him two evenings ago and he said he was feeling much better, but Sarah-Jane was worried enough to call in Dr. Simcott. I will be visiting again soon and will, as you would want me to do I am sure, pass on your best wishes and kind regards to him. Perhaps if you could find the time a short letter to them would not go amiss. I am sure that it would be much appreciated, especially at this time.

I went down to the churchyard on Saturday and placed some flowers for Penelope. It was most peaceful and as I was leaving the sun came out from behind a cloud and bathed her resting place in sunlight. I cannot explain why but I found it most comforting. I am sure she would be most pleased to know that you and Sardi have become such good friends. She had the truest and warmest heart of any woman I ever knew. Time is beating me and I must haste to end this letter.

With my fondest and dearest love I remain your ever affectionate father.

Letter from Mr. Paul Trevarthen, written in Bristol, to Mr. and Mrs. John Williams and daughter.

Ambleside, Bristol. 23rd June 1804

Dear Mr. and Mrs. Williams and Sarah-Jane,
Thank you all for your good wishes and kind regards that father has passed on to me. I am writing a short note to let you know how I go on. I have seen a great many sights in London including St. Paul's Cathedral which is a very fine building. It is a very big city and seems to be all full of noise and bustle. The houses are very grand and I have been to a great many dances, and to the theatre to see plays and comedies and also to the opera. I shall have so much to tell you all when I come to see you after I get home.

I do so hope you are feeling better now, my dear Mr. Williams. I do so miss our quiet little chats that we used to have, even if Mouser insisted that one or the other of us had to hold him at the same time.

I am staying in my mother's house in Bristol at the moment and it is most fine, but perhaps not quite as big as the one in London. I have visited the docks and seen many fine ships.

I remain your humble and dearest friend,
Paul Trevarthen.
PS I would be most pleased if Sarah-Jane would keep an eye on dear father for me for I know he misses me dreadfully, as I do him, and I am so far away at this time.

Letter from Mr. Paul Trevarthen, written in Bristol, to Mr. Peter Fleetwood.

Ambleside, Bristol. 23rd June 1804

Dear Peter,
A quick letter to let you know how I go on. Sardi has introduced me to so many people that I find I can hardly remember my own name. I have been closeted with bluestockings from the literary societies for days on end, made to go to all sorts of parties and dances. Had to stand up with all manner of young women, some fairly pretty but all ninnies, and now Sardi has said that we will not be back in London before the 28th so I will not be able to go with you to the Golden Bear as we had arranged. Tell that saucy wench Mary Thomas that I will be willing to, as she so quaintly put it, 'ruffle up the feathers of her cuckoo's nest' when next I see her. I have no wish to visit Meg Barnes again, a nice enough baggage but I am bored with her. I am afraid that I become bored by such women quite quickly, it has always been like that for me. I do not mean to be so heartless with them but I cannot change the way I am. Meg will make no complaints for I paid her well and she probably expects no better.
I am missing my Ebony most dreadfully but hope the days will soon pass. I have told Matlock to exercise him well for I do not want to find myself on the grass of the park the first time I take him out. Also the same for the chestnuts. I shall look most foolish if I can not pull them up in time and have to go all the way to Brighton with them. I am afraid that my life here is as busy as it was in London for Sardi has always something for me to do. I must go my dear Peter as I am needed again! Sardi has sent Richmond to tell me that I am wanted in the withdrawing room, the Ladies Reading Circle has arrived and wishes to talk with me. They have been before and one poor woman has the most amazing growth of facial hair I have ever seen. I try not to stare but find it almost impossible not to do so.
I beg to remain your most affectionate friend,
Paul

Letter from Miss Sardi Brown to Captain Redvers Trevarthen.

Ambleside, Bristol. 24th June 1804

My dearest Redvers,
I shall not write a long note my dearest for I have very little time. Paul and I have been kept so busy. I have had a certain amount of work to do but have tried most earnestly to keep Paul occupied and for him not to get bored. It was found to be as I predicted and the knocker is never still. Several of the Bristol literary societies have called at the house for talks with Paul and in the evenings we are never at home. I shall look forward to returning to London for a rest. I have noticed that Paul has been most complimentary about the young ladies that have been introduced to him. He said that they were all remarkably pretty but I have not been able to

identify that he had his eye on any particular girl, or indeed that he had his eye on any of them. He is, as you foretold, most discreet about matters of the heart. I think he is enjoying himself although I am treated to a fit of the sullens occasionally when he decides to be particularly recalcitrant, but he knows I will brook no nonsense from him and he is a good, obliging boy for most of the time, so I have had very little trouble from him. I have had a communication from Lady Wrothford and we have been invited to another party at her house the day after we arrive back in London. She has informed me that Miss Perriman finds our son the most marvellous young man that she has ever met. Lady Wrothford indicated to me that she also agrees with this sentiment. She is quite a droll creature and perhaps if you can be persuaded to visit me some time you will get to meet her and you will see what I mean.

I must go my dearest for we are committed to the Heathcoat-Dawes this evening and I must ensure that Paul is looking his best. Edward, his manservant, although very able has not quite the control over him in matters of dress that perhaps an older and more experienced man would have.

My dearest love as always,
Sardi

Letter from Mr. Paul Trevarthen to Captain Redvers Trevarthen.

Ambleside, Bristol. 26th June 1804

My dearest father,
What a time I have had here, hardly a day has passed when I have not had to go to a dance or a party in the evening and entertain the literary people during the day. I did find time to see the docks but not for long as Sardi had some business to attend to at her shops. She has managers for all of her premises but she likes to keep an eye on them to see how they go on. I have not had a rest from dancing hardly at all, but the people have all been most kind and tell me how thrilled they are to meet the famous Mr. Paul Trevarthen and I try to be pleasant to them all. It is very much like London after all and I have not had the rest that I thought I was going to have. I miss my horses and my friend Peter and although she has my best interests at heart Sardi says that I must go to these balls and dances because they are all her customers and she does not want to offend any of them. Naturally I do not want to upset her for she has been most kind to me, but to be honest at times she reminds me of aunt Caroline and I have to try very hard not to get annoyed at having to go out all the time. I am enjoying myself but it is most galling to have to be so charming to everyone I meet.

I have written to Mr. and Mrs. Williams and will try to write again from London but I get so little time to do the things that I would like to do.

Thank you for telling me all the news from the farm. Please to pass on my good wishes to Davy and Mrs. Pascoe. Are you pleased with your new calf and did you manage to get all the hay in without having it all spoiled?

The churchyard does look most beautiful at this time of year and I would be most grateful if you would pick some flowers from me for mother out of her garden, especially lots of bright hues for she had such a love of them.

I miss you most dreadfully dearest father, but am determined to stay until the end of July as I think Sardi would be dreadfully disappointed if I decided to leave London early. She tries most hard to keep me from being bored but I would rather follow my own interests more and not so many of hers. It is to difficult for me to explain to her because everything is tied up with her business and I dare not offend her customers for fear that they will go to other establishments with their custom. It is not so bad actually but I have not had a chance to visit a book shop once! I think that sounds ungrateful for all she has done for me but it is most difficult to be something that you know you are not. Perhaps I am just being homesick and when I get back to London I know it will be better because I can go around with Peter again and go out riding and driving.

Sardi took me to her parents' graves yesterday. It felt most strange to be standing there I can tell you. They were both under forty when they died, is that not sad? She said that they loved each other very much and it was so strange for I was reminded of you and mother.

I must go and get ready for I have a dance to go to tonight and I have to look my best. Sardi has bought a new waistcoat for me and it is most beautiful.

I remain as always your ever-loving son,
Paul

Letter from Captain Redvers to Mr. Paul Trevarthen.

Trevu, Cornwall. 3rd July 1804

My dearest Paul,

Thank you for your letter which I have read with interest. I would point out to you that Sardi is not used to having to amuse someone of your age. It is probably difficult for her and I do believe that she is trying her best to see that you will have happy memories of your stay with her. She does not understand that you are of an age when you have your own opinions of what you would like to do and where you would like to go. She has to think of her customers and as you so correctly pointed out it would not do for them to be offended by a member of her family and so take their custom elsewhere. Sardi has had a very hard road to travel through her life and to become as successful as she has could not have been achieved without a great deal of hard work and sacrifice. I know that you will be a good and dutiful son to her while you are staying in her home and I think if you are required to follow the pursuits that she would like to do, or more correctly the pursuits that she thinks you would like to do, then you have to make a sacrifice and do as Sardi requires. I shall write no more of this but hope that you will try to show more consideration for your mother after you have read this letter.

F J Warren

John Williams is now much better but he will never be as active as he was before because he has been much pulled down by his illness. Sarah-Jane and Mrs. Williams are both well. They were all delighted to receive your letter and are looking forward to seeing you again.

The hay was not spoiled and I have five fine ricks and the heifer calf is growing by leaps and bounds. Davy's latest took sick Wednesday last and although I sent for Dr. Simcott nothing could be done. She did not thrive and died early yesterday and will be buried tomorrow. Mrs. Pascoe most affected but Davy more philosophical because he says a sick child is hard to raise and it is best they die young if they are not going to go well. Hannah visited and I think has been of some comfort to Mrs. Pascoe, and I heard her giving Davy a piece of her mind as well.

Hannah often talks of you and sends you her love and best wishes. I know she is missing you as much as I am. I hope your horses are doing well and that you are giving them enough exercise.

I have followed your instructions and placed a large bunch of flowers on Penelope's grave. They were as you requested full of colour and looked most beautiful. Keep yourself of good heart, Paul, and try for a little humility with Sardi for I think she deserves it of you.

Your ever-loving father

From Captain Redvers Trevarthen to Miss Sardi Brown.

Trevu, Cornwall. 3rd July 1804

My dearest Sardi,
I have written to Paul and reminded him to be well behaved whilst he is with you for I know well how temperamental he can be when he wants to get his own way. Penelope and I tried so hard not to spoil him but he was given a lot of freedom and I am sorry if you find him difficult at times. He does understand that you are trying to make his visit as full and exciting as you possibly can but I must confess that he can be difficult. Have we not had nearly three years of Paul being difficult? I have you to thank for bringing him back to us for well I know that nothing I said would make him behave as he should during that sad time. I am sure that when he comes home he will be full of all the people he has met and the dances and balls that he has attended and will bore us all with the exciting times he has had.

I have had a very busy time on the farm and this has helped to pass the lonely hours without him. I am comforted with the thought that he is with the woman who from the moment of his birth selflessly put his interests before her own. I do most humbly thank you for that my dearest and for what you are doing now for you have given him the opportunity to explore a bigger world than I could have ever done. Try for a little patience with him my dearest Sardi for he is so young and has never found himself inhabiting such an exciting and unknown world before.

I will finish now for I have business in Penzance and will take the opportunity to catch the mail with this letter whilst I am there.

With my dearest love, I remain your ever affectionate,
Redvers

Letter from Mr. Paul Trevarthen to Captain Redvers Trevarthen.

Clifton Court, London. 18th July 1804

> My dearest father,
> My apologies sir for not writing before but I seem not to have a moment to myself. I have taken notice of your letter and I am trying my very best to do as mother wishes without complaint and with as good a grace as I can. I am feeling so very tired, as busy as we have been and this afternoon we leave for Lady Wrothford's country house in Berkshire. Mother and I have been invited to stay for a week for Lady Wrothford says the country air will do me good after the hectic life I have been leading in the city.
> I would write more but my head aches, most likely with the all excitement of the last week! I will write and tell you more when I get to Berkshire and I hope not to be on the go quite so much.
> Your ever-loving son,
> Paul

Letter from Miss Sardi Brown to Captain Redvers Trevarthen.

Clifton Court, London. 18th July 1804

> My dearest Redvers,
> What news I have to tell you! Paul and I have been invited to spend a week with Lady Wrothford and I am quite overcome with excitement. To have an invitation to her country seat is unheard of, especially for someone of my social position but in truth the invitation is for Mr. Paul Trevarthen, author, for he is the rage of London and your social event will be made if you have secured the presence of this famous literary figure at it.
> He has been most attentive since he received your letter and has gone with me to all the events that I have accepted invitations for - my dear three in one evening last night! - first to dine with the Frobishers, then to dance at the Clairmont's ball and finally for supper at the Harvey-Pattersons. Such a whirl as our life is in!
> I have only had to remonstrate with him once. He would go riding the other morning when rain was threatening to come on and of course he was caught in the most tremendous thunderstorm and returned soaked to the skin. I was very abrupt with him as he was due to give a speech to Mrs. Booth's literary group and as he arrived home late from his ride he had very little time to get himself ready. Since that day he seems to be suffering a slight cold and complains of a headache but I expect all to be put to rights after he has had his week in the country. Lady Wrothford has been most kind and has told me that perhaps some rest will soon put Paul back to his customary energetic self.
> I must go now to supervise the rest of the packing but will write more after we get back and tell you how well we have gone on. I am hoping that Paul spending time with Miss Perriman on their own will give him the opportunity to appreciate her many fine qualities.
> Your ever-loving Sardi,

F J Warren

Letter delivered by hand from Lady Wrothford, of Hatcombe Hall, Berkshire, to Captain Redvers Trevarthen, of Trevu, Cornwall.

Hatcombe Hall, Berkshire. 20th July 1804

Sir,

My coachman has been instructed to hand this letter to you as he is the bearer of bad tidings. Your son has been taken ill whilst staying with me. I have had the doctor to him and he is suffering from pneumonia and is, I regret to inform you, most ill. His mother is constantly at his bedside and is blaming herself most bitterly for his illness. I have instructed her not to take on so but we are all most afraid for him for he is rarely able to know anyone. Come at once for the doctor has not said so in so many words but I know that he has a great fear for your son's life. My carriage will bring you here, all changes have been arranged for I fear there will be no time to stop upon the road.

Rest assured my dear sir that everything that can be done for the dear boy is being done but come now to be with him.

Geogiana, Lady Wrothford.

CHAPTER 17

REDVERS tried to refuse to leave his son's bedside but Lady Wrothford overruled him. He was exhausted from his travelling and, as her ladyship had correctly pointed out; the Doctor had great faith in Paul and was no longer calling as often as he had done previously. She did not inform him that the Doctor had told her that he felt there was nothing more he could do, that it would depend on Paul himself now and his constitution to pull himself through.

"Strong young fellow, your boy. He'll beat this, never fear. Good constitution, he'll do, Captain, he'll do. Got a room prepared for you. Call you if . . ." and she was momentarily lost for words but pulled herself together, "shouldn't need to though. He'll do as I told you. Off you go now," and he was shepherded out of the room rather in the manner of a reluctant schoolboy being sent to bed.

After he had gone she went over to the large bed and adjusted the screen that was shielding the branch of candles that lit the room. The young man stirred in the bed, muttering incoherently and trying to push off the covers but she restrained him deftly and firmly told him to rest. He seemed to understand for he went off to sleep again and slept peacefully for a long while. At the time appointed by the doctor, Turner, her butler and an ex army man, helped her to administer the medicinal draft. Soon overcoming his feeble attempts to resist, she swiftly tipped the contents of the glass down his throat. He coughed and seemed to struggle to get his breath but soon the effects of the drug took him back to the realms of sleep once again. She dismissed Turner and, taking a seat by the bed, regarded its sleeping occupant with a determined look on her face and, paradoxically, a softened light in her rather hard eyes.

For three worrying days Paul drifted between sleep and delirium. His body was hot and dry and he had a great thirst but had to be made to drink. He knew no one and rambled on about people and places in a confused state. Sometimes he called out for his mother and Redvers knew, as Sardi did not, that the mother Paul was seeing in his blank, unfocused eyes was the one who lay quietly in the little churchyard in Cornwall and not the one who sat and sobbed at his bedside.

On the evening of the third night the patient was more restless than ever and they were all present at his bedside, each of them praying in their different ways and all of them subdued. He started to struggle so violently that his father was forced to hold him down and when he heard his son cry out coherently and in great despair for his mother not to leave him he felt the tears run down his own face unashamedly. Paul relaxed and fell back on the bed and drifted back to sleep, Redvers gently removed his arm and as he did so he noticed that his son had begun to sweat profusely, he took it for a good sign and asked Lady Wrothford to send for the doctor. When the Doctor arrived he examined Paul and then turned to them with a smile of relief on his face.

"He will come through now. He will be very weak and his body has had to fight hard to bring him out of it but with much careful nursing he will fare well. I'll leave a medicine for him which will be of help," he informed them and then wrote out a list of directions regarding the nursing that the patient would require. With the household's grateful thanks still ringing in his ears he departed.

A week later the invalid was sitting up in bed, propped up with pillows and reading from a pile of letters that had been received for him as soon as it had become known that he was recovering from his sudden illness. He was still listless but his bright smile was beginning to appear on his face again and his voice and body were becoming stronger with every day. His mother or his father often sat and talked with him, if he wanted to talk, but most times they just sat quietly by his bedside and did not mind at all if he fell asleep in the middle of a conversation. Sometimes Lady Wrothford came to sit with him, but he felt quite in awe of her and did not attempt to say much. Chloe came and read to him when the others were not present. She had all sorts of books to read from and even read most beautifully in Latin for him from several different authors. He felt most rested by it and talked quietly to her about all sorts of writers and books and was most surprised to find that she had such a wide love of literature.

Slowly Paul began to win back to strength and health. However, it was to be another week before he was allowed to leave his bed and take a wobbly step or two about the room. Two days later he was dressed by Edward, who had been brought down from London by his mother, and was bemused to find that he had lost so much weight that his clothes no longer fitted. His mother set to work at once and adjusted his other suit, so that when he tried it on it did not hang off him quite so badly and he felt better for it. Slowly with every passing day he became fitter and stronger and by the middle of August he could manage a walk in the garden as long as he could sit down for a while. It was decided that he should recuperate at Lady Wrothford's for as long as was necessary and his mother and father were told that if they wished to leave him in her care it would not present a problem. His mother did not want to go but she had received various letters from each of her business premises asking for her assistance in sundry matters, so tearfully bade her leave of him. His father stayed for another week, but returned to Cornwall telling Paul he would reappear with his own carriage to transport him home when it was felt he would be robust enough to attempt so long a journey. Paul, finding himself with only her ladyship, Chloe and Edward for company at first felt that he would not be able to manage without the presence of his parents, but he soon discovered that Lady Wrothford's manner, although abrupt, actually had his interests uppermost and he could spend his days as he wished as long as he did not attempt to do anything that she felt would be too taxing for him. If the weather was fine her head groom took Chloe and himself out for rides in her Ladyship's barouche, and as soon as he felt strong enough he was allowed to pick out a suitable horse from her stable and to ride on the estate, but always with a groom in attendance. On other days he could go fishing or take out a gun and go shooting in the gamekeeper's company. He had the run of the library where he could read what books he liked and, best of all to Paul, he was encouraged to eat as much as he liked. He played Lady Wrothford's piano in the music room and often Chloe would join him; it was not unusual to hear their laughter mixed with the notes of a lively tune.

On discovering that her Ladyship played chess he assayed his hand at a game and discovered that she was even more shrewd than he had supposed when she soundly beat him. Fired, it took him three attempts to beat her and in his excitement he almost made the wrong move, which would have cost him dearly. The convalescent was surprised to find that he was no longer quite so nervous in her ladyship's company and she successfully began to draw him out, so it became quite natural to sit with her in her sunny withdrawing room and to chat away on the many and varied topics that interested him.

Sardi came to visit and was amazed at how much better he was looking. She informed him that she was making arrangements for his horses and curricle to be taken down to Cornwall so they would be there for him when he returned home with his father. She told him also that although she would love for him to come back to London, it was thought best that he return to Cornwall from Berkshire so he could recuperate in the quiet of his own home. She informed him cheerfully that she would be coming to stay in early December after all and would be with him for the Christmas and the greater part of the January, and she would return to see him again before he left for Cornwall so he could write and tell her if he wanted anything to be brought down.

Sardi was delighted to discover that his clothes no longer fitted quite so badly and, although still thin, her beloved son no longer looked quite so gaunt. Peter Fleetwood, on Lady Wrothford's suggestion, was invited to stay and so travelled down for a weekend and the two friends spent many happy hours shooting and fishing together. Lady Wrothford made sure that they were left alone so they could talk after the evening meal and, without the women around, they enjoyed themselves with some bottles of wine along with a quantity of brandy and port. So well did they indulge that it was late in the evening before both preceded somewhat unsteadily to their respective rooms, each trying desperately not to make a noise but giggling loudly all the while. The next morning at the breakfast table they were both subdued and rather heavy eyed, but to their immense relief Lady Wrothford appeared not to notice. That night they soon found the direction of the local ale house but were more circumspect here and returned home in a less befuddled state. Again Lady Wrothford made no comment and Peter declared to Paul that she was in fact a 'great gun and that she had probably been a bit of a goer in her salad days'. To his surprise Paul found himself in agreement, declaring she was 'a good sort' and informed Peter that she was not as bossy as he had first thought. Before leaving, Peter told him he would write and would try to come to Cornwall and see him before the end of November. He also told him he should offer for Chloe, for a nicer, sweeter girl he had never met and any fool could see that she was madly in love with Paul.

This last pronouncement stunned Paul for it had never occurred to him that dear little Chloe felt anything more for him than what he had thought, never having had a sister, to be a form of sisterly affection. He was so quiet the next day that Lady Wrothford barked her intention of sending for the Doctor again but he told her he was feeling quite well, it was just that he had something on his mind and he thought he needed to reflect upon it quietly.

She stared at him questioningly but said nothing, only telling him that there was a chill wind today and to dress up well if he was planning to go out. Assuring her he would do so, Paul retired to the library and took a book down from the shelf, opened it at the first chapter and never turned another page. After an hour he put the book away and went in search of her Ladyship and, finding her in her withdrawing room and solemnly asked permission to talk to her.

She eyed him unnervingly for a moment but only said: "Certainly you may, Paul. Sit down."

He sat down as instructed and after a moment's hesitation asked if Chloe had said anything to her about liking him.

"Yes, she has," replied the old lady succinctly.

Paul waited in anticipation but there was nothing more forthcoming, so he plunged on again: "If she has intimated that she is . . . that she . . .," he cleared his throat and tried again from a slightly different direction, "I have never intended to give her the impression that I have felt any more for her than I would have felt for a sister. If she is . . . if she has become enamoured of . . . of me I am sorry for it but I have . . . I . . . ," but here he was interrupted by Lady Wrothford.

"Had a chat with your father while you were laid up. Found out quite a bit about you. Told Chloe not to expect much from you. Not a silly girl, knows which way the wind blows. She is young, she'll get over it. Got a good heart, so won't spend her life mooning over something she cannot have," she said with a challenging gleam in her eyes.

Paul blushed and looked away and stared out of the window. After a moment he turned back to face her.

"I suppose you think I am a fool?" he asked.

"Yes," was the blunt response.

He lowered his head and stared at the carpet and did not say anything for a moment before saying, "I cannot make myself fall in love with someone. It would not be honest of me and it would be unfair to the . . . to whoever I was . . .," he stopped suddenly and then stated baldly, "I am not in love with Chloe. I am sorry for her if she is in love with me for I did not mean it to happen."

"No need to tell me that you don't love my Chloe. This girl that you are in love with, she will be married by now. Girls do not have the freedom of men. They have no place in society if they remain single. Your mother's an exception to this but she had to work hard to get where she is. Clever women with a talent to sell. Nothing would have lifted her out of the gutter else and so I tell you. I married a man I had not the slightest intention of being in love with, or he with me for that matter, but I assumed a married women's freedom. When he died I had the freedom to be a widow of consequence. I have lived well on it since. If I had determined to stay single because I was not in love with my future husband I would be some poor, patronised old maid now. You can spend your life in the single state if you will, but why should you stay single to appease your heart? 'Tis your family has to suffer for it, not you. Your father needs you to provide an heir to carry on the family name. Has he to be in his grave before you think fit to oblige him?" She saw him wince but continued unabated, "Got to summon up the determination to marry someone, Chloe or some other, 'twould be selfish not to do so."

"I would be a hypocrite if I asked some young women to be my wife an' I did not love her," he retorted.

"Why?" she asked abruptly.

Disconcerted by her brusqueness Paul sought for an explanation.

"Well, because it is not honest to offer that which you are not capable of giving," he explained.

"Fiddlesticks! How many wives expect their husbands to be in love with them, or if they are, to stay in love with them? Why, your own father admitted to me that if it were not for you, his son by another woman, his own marriage would have stayed loveless. He was lucky, so was his wife come to that for she got him back. Most of us do not have that good fortune," and for one brief moment she looked regretful. After a brief pause she continued: "Chloe knows what is expected of her. Her mother, my daughter ran off with an officer in the dragoons. Did you know that?" He shook his head but she did not notice and continued her tale: "Damn fool of a girl thought he loved her. Abandoned her before Chloe was born. Died in childbirth." There was a longer pause and she blinked rapidly before continuing, "Chloe came into my care. Did my best to bring her up sensibly. Marry her and you'll have no trouble, Paul. Stay in love with you no matter what. Not going to be poor. This estate is part of my son's properties and its income goes to him but my money, and I have rather a lot of it, goes to Chloe, when I die. Not that you will need money. Your mother is worth a small fortune, and your father is well off. You yourself have a substantial income from your own writings."

"You make it sound so cold blooded," muttered Paul awkwardly.

"Well, in the majority of cases it is. Good job too! Marrying for love did not serve Chloe's mother well, did it?" and in her customary fashion answered her own question, "No, by God! Marry Chloe, Paul. Plenty of money. Taking little thing. Won't cause any trouble. Too much in love with you for that. Family won't bother you, for 'tis only me to all intents and purposes and I'll soon be dead."

"Nonsense," said Paul with a hint of a smile, "You are too strong minded to die just yet, methinks."

She threw her head back with a crack of laughter but then looked at Paul seriously. "No need to rush your fences Paul. Think about what I have said. Chloe will wait until you make up your mind. I'll not marry her off just yet. Anything you want to discuss further?" she asked him abruptly and Paul, feeling as if he had been through a fiery furnace could do no other then shake his head dumbly.

"Well go away then," she said in dismissal and turned back to her needlework.

With mumbled thanks Paul retreated and spent the rest of the day deep in thought and was not at all talkative. Chloe was most concerned and asked him if she had done anything to displease him.

"No, of course, you have not, dearest Chloe. I am just trying to sort out a problem I have, that is all," he assured her.

"Well, I would not for the world displease you, Paul, you know that," she said earnestly, her hazel eyes searching his face worriedly. Smiling down into her concerned face he took her hand in his and lifting it to his lips placed a gentle kiss upon her fingers.

"Never by a look, or a word, or a deed have you ever displeased me, dearest Chloe. Remember that" he said softly and noted how beautiful she looked as she smiled with relief. Feeling himself unnerved by her delight he said, quietly: "If you will excuse me I have a letter I must write to my father. I will see you later at dinner and, perhaps, I will be in a better humour by then."

In the silence of his room Paul stared moodily out of the window for a long time, but then turned and got out his writing desk and, taking out a sheet of paper, jabbed his pen into the ink and began to write hastily. At dinner he was still quiet, but after they had dined, declined a port and dutifully joined the ladies, playing the piano with Chloe and a game of chess with her ladyship. Admonished for not concentrating he was beaten soundly, but declined the chance to square the match, promising to give more attention the next time he essayed a game.

"Don't like namby-pamby games, boy. Put more in to it when we play again," his mentor said, giving him a fierce look.

"Yes, your ladyship," he answered, but made an effort and smiled engagingly at her ladyship. She chuckled and told him he was a young rogue and a blasted charmer to boot.

"Grandmamma!" uttered Chloe, much shocked to hear her beloved Paul so addressed. Her exclamation amused Paul so much that he went off into a peal of laughter and her ladyship gave a hearty chuckle.

"Well!" said Chloe much offended, "You are both as bad as each other."

"Yes, my dear," replied her grandmother, "I do believe we are."

Chloe reluctantly had to smile and very soon the infectious good humour that she had unconsciously introduced into what had been previously a rather sombre evening meant that, by the time they retired, there was a much more pleasant ambience between them all.

A week later his father waited patiently for Paul to say his goodbyes before beginning their journey home. Edward was still looking bemused by the gift of an inscribed gold watch that Paul had had his mother buy on his behalf for him as a token of thanks and friendship. Paul was busy thanking the various servants, then he turned to say farewell to Chloe and to thank her for her companionship whilst Redvers, who had already thanked his hostess for his night's stay, was now engaged in thanking her for the care she had shown to his son during his illness and convalescence.

"I cannot believe him to be the sick, skinny boy I left in your care last month, so much has he prospered," he told her, his face glowing with delight and relief.

"Humph! Had precious little to do with that once he got his appetite back. Eats like a horse don't he? Still, tall lad, big frame to fill. Good boy, kind to Chloe. Treats her like a sister but you never know, he might see the light," she told him cryptically in her usual abrupt manner. " Send him to me again." Regarding the young couple she shook her head sadly and said, "Look at little Chloe. Breaking her heart with every smile. Damn shame. Had a chat with him. No good. Wrote to tell you he wanted to come home the same day. A little quiet reflection might start him off. You can never tell. I won't give up you know." She turned back to face Paul's father with a determined glint in her eye.

Redvers laughed and he too looked at the young couple, "No, I am most certain of that, but you have not reckoned with Paul for he can be most stubborn."

"Ah!," she cried and poked him in the chest with her ringed finger, "and so can I," and raising her eyebrows continued threateningly. "Paul can be as stubborn as he likes, but I would like Chloe to be as happy as possible. I won't last much longer. No one to look after the dear little girl then. He might not love her but he is fond of her and he will make her a good husband. He's the one I want for her and I am determined to get her what she wants. So I will get him. Warn him if you want but his bachelor days are coming to an end. Tell him he cannot win this chess game either."

Captain Trevarthen, much struck by her determination, laughed and continued to offer his thanks to this strange woman with the heart of iced gold, but she waved them aside.

"Trevarthen, if I was fifty years younger I would marry him myself, damn me if I wouldn't," and then in a soft, almost childlike voice she said pleadingly: "Do take good care of the dear boy. He has gripped my heart like no other man I have ever met," and then announced more firmly, "Mind me now, take care of him."

Meanwhile Chloe, desperately trying not to cry, was telling Paul how much she would miss him and that she would write to him and would he please to write back. He assured her that he would and told her not to cry and, yes, he would miss her dreadfully too because she had been so kind to him. He gave her a quick kiss on the cheek and hugged her briefly, telling her he would never forget her. He hoped silently to himself that she would not read too much into his last words. Stiffly and formally he shook his hostess by the hand and began a speech of thanks, but was cut short by her ladyship in her usual brusque manner. However, most unlike her normal fashion she proffered her cheek for him to kiss. As he did so she whispered quietly in his ear, "I'll have you in check yet Paul, you see if I don't," and she chuckled, rather wickedly he thought.

Their goodbyes over, they got into the coach and began the long, and for Paul, tiring journey home.

Barney regarded his wife across the expanse of the elegant and tastefully furnished room in which they sat. He had never seen her look so content and he was beginning to enjoy himself, for the life of a country squire most definitely agreed with him. To ride in the morning along the lanes and byways of your own land, and have your workman doff their caps to you gave him great pleasure. The quietness eased his soul for it had not been an easy life for him. In quiet reflection he thought back over his beginnings that had led him to this peaceful and quiet existence. His father, stricken by debt, had sought the only solution that could solve his problems and put an end to his life, but his death served only to multiply the troubles that his selfish act had left Barney's dear mother to contend with. Four children at home and no money to feed them with, so her eldest son left his schooling and fell in with some smugglers, the better to help his mother. Whether because of his education or his luck he was never to know, but soon he was leading a redoubtable group of men and making enough from the game to provide his mother with a good income for herself and the children. Financially secure at last, his mother caught consumption and swiftly died along with two of Barney's sisters.

His younger brother professed an interest in the military, so Barney bought him a commission in the Lifeguards. Then his sister married a local man so he had time to look about him for a wife at last and when he espied Miss Phoebe Gibbons, a young woman of modest social standing, the only child of ageing parents, he resolved to marry her. Her family had no objection for they had no knowledge of their future son-in-law's activities, and so they gave their blessing and they were married in the little village church. His lifestyle had come as a great surprise to his young wife for she had no idea he was involved in such activities, but she adored her husband and settled down to having him from her side on business in France for weeks at a time and, when in the county, out at all hours of the day and night, but in compensation he brought home a steady income. His dear Phoebe, ever practical, set about saving for the day when they could leave their smuggling life, for although she appreciated that it had kept her warm and well-fed she felt disgusted by the brutality of it. Her parents died soon after her marriage, but with her young husband to look after she put her loss behind her and carried on as before. When news came that the young sister had died in childbirth and her baby daughter with her it was a tremendous blow to Barney, but before that fateful year had ended the young brother, in his smart regimentals, could do no more than purchase himself a half broken horse and, convinced of his abilities to train it, had his head cracked open when he fell from it in the stable yard at his first attempt to ride the terrified creature. With no family left to provide for, he buried his pain along with his brother's young body and concentrated on expanding his activities in the smuggling field, confidently expecting that his dear little wife would produce his son and heir in due time. But to his deep regret, no progeny appeared. When Joseph Bolitho came into their lives they began to look upon him as their own child, but it was false for the boy served a different purpose and, because of his traumatic beginnings, he could not or would not allow himself to be like a son to them. For everything they did for him he expressed his gratitude, accepted their way of life, and grew up to be well-mannered and respectful to them. For the work the boy undertook for him; he seemed unconcerned to kill any man that Barney feared should pull him down, for he could not afford to lose his position in the smuggling trade or more importantly his life. Even then, it was known that Joey had a conscience for tales had often emerged of his generosity to his friends and to the families of the men he had so cold-heartedly murdered.

Now they had to sit and suffer as they realised that the young man they had uprooted from his life and occupation in Cornwall could not fit into the pleasant lifestyle that they themselves were enjoying to the full. They watched in despair as he became more and more reserved and withdrawn, and even for one like Joey, so inscrutable and impassive, it had come as a shock to them. Joey himself had agreed to go with them to see if he would like the life and they assumed that like them he would be overjoyed to find himself amongst green fields and little company, but the young man was fretted by it, as he had from birth been used to an existence that had a continuous parade of life in all its horrors running through it. That he had been disappointed in love did not help, they knew, so they set about introducing him to various females in the locality. But although politeness itself to the assorted young women that they introduced him to, as soon as he left their presence he had nothing to say in their favour and more often than not nothing to say about them whatsoever. So now they sat in despair and worried about the young man who they had come to think of as their son, even if he did not see either of them in a parental light.

"If Joey had been brought up differently from birth he could have been a great man, Phoebe, there is no doubt about that for he has many admirable qualities, but I shall regret to my dying day that when I took him in I saw only my own gain from it and not his. If I 'd concentrated on improving the boy, to fit him for a better life than the one I was leading, I'm certain that he could settle the better to being with us here," said Barney and gave a heartfelt sigh.

His wife, looking equally sad, sighed with him and shook her head before announcing, in her quiet way, "We will have to let him go Barney, although it is going to break our hearts, for he is not ours and he never was. If his mother had cared for him perhaps he would have learnt to care in return. When I think back to what he was like when he came into our household I think we should be congratulated for how he looks now; such a big strong young man and so handsome, but with all my caring of him I have never held him in my arms and hugged him as a mother would. We treated him from the first as a live in servant, Barney, and when he would not talk of his former life we maintained our silence. So he began his new life with us, hiding a past he couldn't talk about and beginning a role that requires secrecy at all times. When he fell in love what chance did he have, being who he was? After all the girl is from a respectable family like I was myself? My parents would not have allowed our marriage if they had known of your trade Barney, and in all honesty, I would probably have not accepted you either, although I have never regretted a day of our lives together," and taking out her handkerchief she burst into uncharacteristic tears.

Barney got up immediately and went to her, taking her in his arms he did his best to console her but he knew that every word she had said was true. So after they had dined they sat down and talked to their protégé and told him of their proposal, that if he was not happy in this life, they would help him to lead another. Their news was met with caution by Joey but relief as well, for he did not know how to tell them that he was so miserable. He knew he should have been grateful for the opportunity they had given him, but to Joey it was no opportunity at all for he was imprisoned by their delight and joy to be away from all he had ever known. As a boy he had experienced only poverty, hunger, filth and pain, but he had learnt to accept it and when presented with a house to live in that was clean, with plentiful food and good clothes to wear he had looked for no other.

Unused to affection he had not sought it from the Rickards; it was enough to know that they provided for his needs. In the beginning he had enjoyed his work for Barney and when he had to kill an informer he could do it coldly and efficiently, for it maintained his very existence by doing so, but his conscience pricked him for he could not bear the thought that the families left behind should have to experience a small part of what he had been put through as a child. In spite of his dislike of his new life, and miserable as he was, he knew if only his beloved Sarah-Jane had been willing to marry him he could have lived in this place, brought up his own children amongst the green fields and pleasant rural countryside. Blinded by love, to be with her was enough and his life would have been complete. He had come away from Cornwall to this place, after she had refused his offer of marriage, broken but determined to go back to her and ask for her hand again, unable to accept that her love for another man could hold out against his own feelings for her. Convinced she would weaken eventually he clung to that hope, but on arrival in Hampshire the freedom from the smuggling life that he had known since a boy was nothing without her beside him. Not having sight of her pulled at his heart and he would have written her, but could not bear the thought that she might not reply or worse; he feared that if a letter from her should say that she had no love for him, he believed to see the words written in her own hand would crush him completely.

Admitting to the Rickards that he would prefer to go back to Cornwall was surprisingly difficult for him, even though he knew they were aware of his unhappiness, for over the years he had developed a great regard and fondness for them although he had never been able to show it. Now, when it came the time to leave them, he would have liked to have told them of their worth to him but could not, for they had never spoken to him in such a way and consequently he did not have the ability to express his own sentiments to them. He merely thanked them awkwardly for their care for him, and with a list of names in his pocket and a letter of introduction from Barney to various people in his own county and in France that he would need to deal with if he was to continue in the smuggling trade, he set off by horseback and made his way back to Cornwall and to the woman who held his heart in her hands.

CHAPTER 18

"FIRST her father, then her mother. That poor maid don't 'ave no luck. Still she wen't 'ave no ties now. Can marry if she's a mind to," said Hannah. She directed an inquiring look at Paul, sitting in his usual chair in the kitchen and received a frown in return.

"An' don' 'e look at me like that either Master Paul. Sarah-Jane bin hangin' out for 'e ever since she first met 'e an' you knaw it," she told him, wiping the flour from her arms.

"I am not marrying Sarah-Jane and she knows it, Hannah," he said firmly, "even if you do not."

"Well," she said, "I think 'tis a shame. For you as well as she."

Paul stood up, stretched, leaned over and pinched one of a newly baked batch of cakes as Hannah turned to put the dough to rest. She turned back and, seeing the suspicious lump in his cheek, glanced down at the cakes and looked up again quickly.

"Master Paul, you idden sick now. I'll get 'e one day you wait an' see if I don't," she told him laughingly.

He gave her a quick kiss and hugged her briefly and then he was gone. She sighed contentedly. It was wonderful to have him back, wonderful to see his father without that dreadful look on his face, even to see Caroline Crebo with no tear stains on her face. Wonderful not to have tearstains on her own face. She turned and busied herself in her kitchen, singing a hymn to herself.

Thinking over Hannah's words, Paul put on his hat and left the house to stroll towards the familiar little cottage, remembering as he did so the hours that he and Sarah-Jane had spent together as children. He smiled to himself as he thought of the games he used to play as a child and how she had followed him everywhere like a faithful and adoring puppy. All the laughter that had echoed around the little cottage when he had visited there, and now, all would be sad and miserable. John Williams had died the day before Paul arrived back at Trevu and his first visit on his return had been to the St. Michael's Church for his old friend's funeral. Before a fortnight had passed Mrs. Williams was found dead in her bed one morning by Sarah-Jane when she went to take her in some tea before breakfast. The second funeral, coming so soon after the first, was by far the sadder, for Mrs. Williams, although not so robust as in former years, was not expected to die so quickly. Sarah-Jane, only just in her twentieth year, was left alone in the cottage. Redvers and Hannah had visited but until this day Paul had not put in an appearance. Truth to tell he had no idea what to say to her for, when he visited in the past, he had enjoyed his chats with her parents as much as he liked to talk with her. She was his oldest and dearest friend but he did not love her. If Sarah-Jane wished to see more in his friendship than there was he was sorry for it, but he could do nothing about it.

When she answered his knock she smiled sadly into his face and asked him into the cottage and made him a cup of tea. Sitting at the little table they talked quietly together, but when the cat began to meow loudly Sarah-Jane smiled mistily at him and said: "Poor Mouser misses father so," and softly began to sob. Paul thought he ought to have put his arms around her to console her, such an old friend as she was, but he felt awkward and afraid lest he gave her the wrong impression of him. He knew that she held him in high regard but, as he did not return her sentiments, Paul had always been most careful not to give her the feeling that he felt any more for her than friendship.

"I am so sorry, Paul," she apologised, wiping the tears from her eyes, "but it has all been such a shock, for father had appeared to be getting better and then for Mother to .....," but her voice broke again.

"I know it must be terrible for you dear Sarah-Jane," he said and impulsively he reached across the table and, catching up her hand, squeezed it gently in compassion. Blinking away her tears, she allowed her hand to rest in his but after a while drew it away and told him that she had decided to leave her home and go and live with William-John and his wife in Falmouth.

"They can do with the help for they have bought a bigger hostelry and need more staff to help run it. I will be paid for my services and it will give me some independence, for with no . . . no husband it would not be right to remain here," and she raised her green eyes to his face and looked at him questioningly.

He blushed and quickly lowered his gaze and sought for an answer. Finally he said, "I am so sorry Sarah-Jane for your loss, but I think it will be for the best if you are to go from here, for I have never thought of you in . . . in that way and old friends that we are I cannot lie to you." After another long silence he told her awkwardly that he thought that he should leave and got up and made his way to the door. She followed him and he turned and spoke again: "Find a man who worships you Sarah-Jane. Do not waste your love on me for methinks there is a better man than I shall ever be who would be the more deserving of your adoration," and wishing her farewell, he leaned forward and kissed her cheek swiftly before leaving the cottage and striding purposely away. Wretched in spirit he felt humbled by her love for him, but it did not alter the fact that she was not the woman that – still - he loved more than any other.

Emerging from the wood he crossed the road swiftly and headed back towards Trevu, so wrapped up in his thoughts that he was unaware of the rider approaching slowly through the little village that nestled to the side of the wood. The rider espied the man and stopped his horse. The blank look on his face registered no emotion, but he pondered the significance of what he had seen. Kicking his horse on, he arrived outside of the cottage so recently vacated by young Paul and knocked firmly at the door. When it was opened to him it was obvious that his beloved Sarah-Jane had been crying, but under the circumstances it could be presumed that was only natural. She looked surprised to see him, for she informed him, she presumed he had left for Hampshire, for William-John had told her so.

"I come back to see 'e," he said carefully, "an' when I 'eard of the loss of yer parents I come to offer 'e my condolences," and as she invited him into the room he noticed the two teacups on the table, but said nothing.

"That's very kind of you Mr. Bolitho," she said and offered him a seat at the table and, without saying a word, removed the cups before asking him if he would like some tea himself. His blue eyes studied her face, noting the blush that crept into her cheeks.

"Perhaps you wouldn' want another cup so quick, Miss Williams?" he asked and this time her blush became even deeper.

"Paul . . . ., I should say Mr. Trevarthen, has just been to offer his condolences for he had not come before; he has been ill and has not ventured abroad much since he returned from London," she told him nervously, but could not look him in the eye so turned away. Moving swiftly he got up and, catching her arm, swung her around to face him.

"Thas' the man stands 'tween us idden it, Sarah-Jane? Paul Trevarthen! An' there's me thinkin' must be some preacher fellow or somethin'. Bound think more of 'e than you would me with all 'is money. Some 'usband fer 'e, Master Paul would be, if you could catch 'en!"

"Stop it Joey! Stop it!" she cried distraught, and tears began to pour down her cheeks.

Unable, in spite of his pain, to see her in such distress he pulled her to him and cradled her in his arms. Dropping his kisses onto her soft curls he whispered desperately, "Don't cry, dearest, please," and then, "I love 'e, Sarah-Jane, I love 'e," over and over again, but after a while she put up her hands and gently pushed him from her.

"I am sorry for you Joey, but it cannot be for I do not love you and I never will. 'Tis best we part for I am to go away; Paul Trevarthen has no love for me and I must learn to live my life without him," she said resolutely.

"Sarah-Jane!" he pleaded desperately, "Come away with me, my dearest, fer I 'ave a place we can go far away from 'ere. A place where you could be 'appy fer I'll spend my life doin' all I can to please 'e," and he caught up her hand and took it to his lips, but she wrenched it away in despair.

"No! No Joey! Forget me! Find another wife for I am not the one for you," she told him coldly but then in a gentler voice added: "I cannot help it Joey, but you are not the man I love and I cannot marry you. Please leave me now for I wish to be alone," and she turned away unable to look at his pain, and said with a sob: "Forgive me Joey, forgive me but I cannot love you." She listened to silence for a long while, but finally she heard the sound of his footsteps crossing the room and then the door banged shut behind him. Picking up Mouser in her arms she went to sit in her Father's chair and finally racking sobs shook her whole body, and she felt great sympathy for Joey Bolitho for she knew he was suffering the same pain as herself.

Redvers was surprised to hear that Sarah-Jane was going to leave, but he understood that she would find it easier to go away then to spend lonely nights waiting for Paul, who would never be hers. He regarded his son fondly; sitting with his long legs stretched before him, his head in a book, oblivious as always to the chaos he was wreaking in the hearts of most of the women who came into contact with him.

"I have had a letter from Lady Wrothford," said Redvers conversationally.

Paul looked up and smiled, "She is well, I hope?" and he added with a wry smile: "She is a most redoubtable woman, full of energy and not an easy person to get one's way, with as I found to my cost often."

His father laughed and said, "She says she is well but the letter mostly concerns Chloe." Surreptitiously looking into his son's face for some reaction he was disappointed that there was no sign. "Lady Wrothford says that Chloe is missing you dreadfully and that she has become quite listless." At that Paul put down his book and gave his father a very direct look, but said nothing and his father continued his reading with impassive features. "She was delighted to receive my invitation and would like Chloe to visit with us. I . . . um . . . forgot to mention it but your mother has offered to bring her down with her when she visits at Christmas."

"Whose idea was it to issue the invitation?" he asked his father bluntly.

"Mine," said Redvers and then added with a smile, "after consultation with Lady Wrothford, of course."

"That woman is determined I offer for Chloe," remarked Paul bitterly. "She says it is not necessary for me to be in love with her for Chloe will understand and not expect more of me."

"Then what are you waiting for?" asked Redvers in an exasperated voice.

"Not what, father, who," he replied, "and well you know it!"

Redvers sighed. He pondered for a moment and then looked up at Paul and said determinedly: "She will not be coming Paul, for she will be married by now. If she is not then she will suffer a similar fate to Sarah-Jane. By not accepting any offers of marriage Sarah-Jane has to spend the rest of her life working for someone else's family and filling up her lonely nights with thoughts of you. Your Dorothea would not be in a position even to have as much of a life as that if she did not marry. To be a single male is allowed, to be a single woman is to be a social outcast, forever derided by other members of society. Take my word for it; she has married not because she wanted to, perhaps, but because if she did not she would have faced a life without respect and without position. Her father is younger than me, Paul. Can you imagine Dorothea spending the rest of her life content to spend her days with him, in his house? No, she would get herself a husband to avoid that at all costs!"

"What if she is married? Am I supposed to marry Chloe knowing full well that I love another and always have?" replied Paul, angrily.

"When you were so ill you often cried out for your mother. Sardi would hold your hand and tell you she was there and the tears would be pouring down her face. Be honest now, Paul, and tell me what I believe to be true - was it not Penelope that you called out to and not Sardi?"

Paul hung his head but replied firmly: "I think only of the mother that brought me up as my mother. Sardi is the woman who gave me life and who loves me as a son and who I love most dearly, but you are in the right of it. It is not the same."

"Then you can understand me when I tell you if ever I should marry again it would be Sardi, but for me also it would not, and could never be the same as the love I had, and still have, for Penelope. Sardi understands that the woman you think of as your mother is Penelope, even if during that terrible time she allowed herself to believe that it was her that you wanted and not my wife. When I lost my love for Penelope and found it again through you I was even more in love with her than before. I have been most fortunate because I was given the chance to love again, whereas you have denied yourself the chance to let what regard you have for someone to maybe blossom into love," his father told him gently.

Paul shook his head, "I cannot," he said simply.

"Then be prepared to watch poor Chloe suffer for your sake and see how pleasant that will feel. Sarah-Jane has had to suffer for you. Is it fair that this poor child should share the same fate?" Redvers muttered in annoyance.

"Lady Wrothford will marry her off to someone, never fear. She will not be left to spend her life alone," Paul predicted firmly.

"Listen, Paul! Listen to me! There has never been another girl with whom you have had such an affinity. She loves music, books, she has been well educated and seeks only to please you. I have watched her look at you as if you were a god come down to earth, and well I know you are not that Paul, but a wife to love you as sincerely as that would be enough to gladden any man's heart!" he cried in exasperation.

"It would be false of me to tell her I loved her! I could not utter such a lie!" returned Paul hotly.

"Then do not tell her!" replied Redvers brutally.

There followed a long silence, before suddenly Paul got up, wished his father good night and went to his bed. He did not sleep for a long time but lay quietly thinking, his mind going over and over the conversation he had had with his father. At breakfast he did not have a lot to say and Hannah asked him if he was unwell again but he smiled at her and shook his head. Paul retired to his room and took up his pen and wrote first to his mother, telling her how well he was and that he was looking forward to seeing her when she came down to Cornwall, then to Mr. Armitage to thank him for his letter and to tell him he was recovered from his illness. Two more letters followed; one to James Hoskin who had obtained a commission in the Light Dragoons, asking him how army life was suiting him, and the next to Peter Fleetwood telling him he could hardly wait for his visit next week and passing on his regards to the Colonel, and then, finally, he wrote to Chloe.

This was his most difficult letter and he did not know what to say to her, but decided that the best course to follow was the path of truth, so he wrote about the love he had for Dorothea, the brutality of their separation, and his subsequent behaviour that had so upset his family. After he had laid bare his soul, he asked her if she could still feel about him in the same way as she did knowing all that, for he did not love her and neither did he think that he ever would. If she wanted him she most know of all his faults and he could not believe that any woman would still feel the same way about him after hearing of them. He signed his letter only with his name and sealed it and took all his letters down to the hall ready for them to be taken to Penzance for the mail. Returning to his room he picked up his latest Latin text that he was translating and began to write; he was seen no more until Hannah called him for lunch.

A week later Paul clasped three letters in his hand, but the one he considered the most important he left until the last. Peter's letter informed him that he would be arriving on the following day, Sardi wrote that she was very busy, but not so busy that she could not send greetings from the many friends and acquaintances that he had met in London and Bristol. When he opened the third letter he found his hand to be shaking. Chloe started her letter hoping that he was well and that his health was improving and went on to say she was looking forward to seeing him again when she came to Cornwall with his mother. Thanking him for his honesty, she told him that she had fallen in love with him on seeing him that first day in his mother's shop. She realised and understood that he did not feel the same way about her. However, if he should wish to offer for her hand she would not refuse him, but if he did not she would accept that was to be his final decision and would have no complaint of him. She signed her letter as simply as he had done, with only her name. Paul folded the letter and placed it in the bottom of his little writing desk and remained thoughtful. The girl, although young was most pleasant to look at, she had even been described to him as beautiful. There was still time to make up his mind about her, he did not have to hurry into marriage even though his whole family and her grandmother appeared to wish for it. Paul frowned, but he was not the sort of person that could be pushed into taking any course that he did not want to take. So he determined to await her arrival in the December and to see what transpired over the Christmas.

The next day Peter's curricle bowled up the drive to the house, and he jumped down and smilingly introduced himself to Davy before passing him the reins. Shouting Paul's name he rushed towards him and hugged him whilst telling him how pleased he was to see him again and how well he looked. On being introduced to Redvers he shook hands with him in his usual friendly manner. Hannah dropped a curtsey and was delighted with Paul's new friend for he seemed forever smiling. Peter took it upon himself to ensure that Paul also was always smiling for he would not allow him to suffer from remorse. "A shocking bad habit of yours Paul!" he informed him which made Redvers laugh at his son's expression of contrition. So the two young men set off to explore the locality. They toured the taverns of Penzance, sampling copious amounts of alcohol as they did so, and they made free with some of the light skirts of that town, arriving home in the early hours of the morning. Captain Trevarthen was not so old that he could not imagine how the two young men were spending their time when he saw them at breakfast. Peter was delighted to attend a dance at the Squire's and made himself a success with the ladies for, whereas his friend was ever charming, young Mr. Fleetwood was not averse to flirting with the ladies, both young and old, and all seemed captivated by his easy, personable address.

When not chasing the ladies, Peter and Paul indulged themselves in a varied assortment of country pursuits. Hannah's son took them out on his boat and although Paul's guest was most unwell, as soon as his feet touched dry land he thought it had all been a huge joke and told everyone about his experiences, laughing all the while. If Peter had deliberately set out for society to like him he succeeded admirably, but truth to tell he was as the people he met thought him to be - a young man of friendly and engaging manners. Paul revelled in his company, for although he did not miss the excitement of London he had missed Peter's friendship and had found life in Cornwall to be rather dull, much to his surprise. Peter, forever talking would regale his friend with tales of life in London, as well as relating all the latest gossip about the people Paul had met during his time there. When he told Paul that Lady Wrothford had come to town with Chloe to buy her outfits to go to Cornwall and that they had all dined at Sardi's and how pretty Chloe looked, Paul was quite unprepared for what he was to say next. Suddenly serious he looked deep into Paul's eyes and said, "Marry her Paul, for she is the very one for you. Her grandmother would like it so and your family would be happy for you as well. Damn it I would be happy for you even if it meant that we could no longer roam, searching out our delights as previously," he added with a wicked laugh.

Paul smiled but as usual said nothing; however he was shocked and surprised by his friend's suggestion. On Peter's last night in Cornwall they forsook the numerous pleasures of Penzance and decided to stay at home with Redvers, so they sat in the parlour in front of a roaring fire, drinking brandy and talking companionably. The next morning Peter departed amid much merriment as Hannah had supplied him with an almost overflowing basket of food for the journey. He gave her a big hug and kissed her rosy cheek, for he had been introduced to the delights of Hannah's kitchen on his first day in Cornwall. She blushed and hid her face in her apron, giggling all the while. Shaking Redvers by the hand, Peter thanked him enthusiastically for making him so welcome, and then he said his good byes to Paul and whispered to him not to make a cake of himself over he-knew-what. Paul merely smiled but laughed aloud when Peter hung out of his curricle, waving at them all whilst shouting to Paul to come back to London again because life was so dull without him. His friend's visit seemed to have done Paul some good for it was noted in the household that he seemed to be happier; he was more talkative and he even made a visit to Mrs. Carter and sat and conversed most pleasantly with her for half an hour. In a short while his Latin translation was completed, so it was sent off to the publishers and Paul found himself with time on his hands. However, he was soon to find his mind preoccupied by quite another matter.

A few days after Peter's departure, Paul received a letter from Lady Wrothford, which he took to his room to read and never mentioned its contents to any member of the household, except to say that she was well and had sent his father her kind regards. However, apart from her good wishes her letter had told Paul that she now expected him to propose to Chloe. "For you cannot tell an impressionable girl like Chloe that you do not love her and not expect her to get all fired up about you," she wrote. She went on to tell him that she was changing her will and that if he married Chloe she would leave all her money to her. If he did not marry Chloe it would go to Lady Wrothford's son, "a nasty mean minded piece of work" ran her description of him and her granddaughter would have to throw herself on his mercy. If, however, Chloe did not want to marry Paul then the previous will stood and she would still inherit her ladyship's money. She had taken it upon herself to ask Chloe what her answer would be should Paul propose and her granddaughter had informed her that she would accept his offer.

Paul read the letter twice, unable to believe her temerity, before striding over to his writing desk and beginning to write furiously. Annoyed by her actions, he wrote that she was a "designing woman" amongst other epithets and that he would make up his own mind whether he proposed to Chloe or not and would not be pushed into it by her, signed it only with his name and took it to Penzance to catch the mail. Lady Wrothford wrote back by the next post telling him not to get so heated, for after all Chloe might meet someone else and change her mind about him. The poor child was, admitted her ladyship, besotted with him at the moment, but there were plenty of other men and quite a few of them had been showing an interest in her granddaughter. She was such a very pretty girl after all. Did he not think so? Paul, inflamed the more by each succeeding letter, was completely unaware of the silent delight his father took to see his son's determined face as he placed his latest epistle in the tray in the hallway.

Their letters raced back and forth. Lady Wrothford's were derogatory about him and every one of them managed to infuriate him in some way. His raged at her because her comments were goading him into committing himself and he took great pains to inform her that this was a feat that she would not accomplish. Also he wrote angrily, she had the presumptuousness to alter her will in such a way and was placing him in an impossible situation. "If I do not offer for your granddaughter I may blight her young life, an' if I do I may well blight mine!" he objected forcefully. The letter he received in return told him that "he was writing so much twaddle, and he such a famous author too!" Chloe could have the last word after all, she could marry another if she wanted to. He was not the only man in the world, and plenty of young men were showing an interest in her dear Chloe, wrote her ladyship.

"Good," replied Paul, his pen racing across the paper furiously, "I hope she marries one of them and that she will live happily ever after."

Lady Wrothford replied with, Paul thought, unnecessary detail, that Chloe's keenest suitor was almost forty but very rich, ten thousand a year and a title. This venerable gentleman had informed Lady Wrothford that the family was quite good and the girl looked well enough, but his most pressing reason for offering was to get himself an heir. He thought Chloe would be capable of that at least. Perhaps after all Paul would not have to commit himself to matrimony, her ladyship suggested, for surely such a handsome offer would solve all their requirements.

Seething with indignation, he replied that on no account was Lady Wrothford to give her permission for dear little Chloe to marry this uncouth beast, for he was sure that such a lovely girl could do better for herself than that. "I expect she can," wrote her ladyship, "but I must see her settled before I die, if not to you at least to a family of some repute and wealth. He would not want her to starve after all, would he? Chloe would be arriving next week, he would have to come to a decision soon." His final missive to her told her that was exactly what he intended to do, and he would make up his own mind and he would thank her not to interfere.

Two days later his mother's carriage pulled up and set down Sardi and little Chloe in front of Trevu. Sardi was all smiles for Redvers and for her son, but poor Chloe looked lost and not a little frightened. Paul, feeling his heart drawn in sympathy, smiled reassuringly at her. From the first, Hannah was enchanted with Chloe and all the servants smiled and fussed over her and she was made to feel most welcome.

Perched up beside him, he took her to Penzance in his curricle and she was introduced to so many people that her mouth felt stiff from smiling. Mrs.

Carter invited them for tea and Chloe blushed prettily when she was asked if Paul was her young man. They spent wet afternoons playing the piano together, laughing all the while. At local dances and parties they found secluded corners in which to talk if all the attention became too much for them, for the provincial populace was quite captivated with her, and to Paul's evident annoyance, not a few of the local lads were quite entranced by her beauty. On getting up in the morning Paul awaited her arrival at the breakfast table with unconcealed delight.

When Trevu held its usual Christmas Eve party the local people came to the big house and the tables groaned with food. Chloe delighted friends and staff alike, for she had always such a pleasant way about her and Paul found himself proudly watching her as she laughed and chatted with all the people introduced to her, whatever their status. Paul could not remember a more pleasant and happy party for such a long time. On Christmas morning the young couple sat together in the Trevarthen pew in the little Church, exchanging admiring glances, and afterwards Paul took her hand and showed her his mother's grave. She smiled shyly at him and told him that it was the most beautiful place in which to lie and she was so sorry that she had never met her, because everyone had told her that she was such a kind and lovely lady.

Studiously avoiding the household Paul sat alone with Chloe and they talked earnestly together. He was as honest with her, talking face to face, as he had been in his letter to her. If he did propose he thought it only right she should understand the true nature of his feelings. She studied his face with her large eyes but then smiled her entrancing smile and informed him that she did not mind because he appeared much fonder of her than she thought she had a right to expect.

The following day he wrote to Lady Wrothford asking permission to marry her granddaughter. Her ladyship wrote back that she was delighted to give it and wished them both well, but she would be obliged if Paul and Chloe would return to London for the wedding, for she did not think herself well enough to travel to Cornwall for the event. Detesting long engagements, she informed Paul in her usual authoritarian way that the wedding could take place by the beginning of the next month at Hatcombe Hall. When he showed her letter to her granddaughter, Chloe went off into a peal of laughter which encouraged Paul to join in. However, they agreed to Lady Wrothford's wishes and so Chloe returned by coach a week later. Paul was to follow with his father within the following week and they were to be married in the little Church at Hatcombe Hall at the end of the month. Redvers and Sardi could not contain their delight at the good news and his mother insisted on returning with Chloe, for she did not wish that she should travel all that way alone. Also she insisted that no one else would make her new daughter's wedding dress, so she would need to return to London. Peter Fleetwood received a letter asking him to be Paul's best man and replied that he would be delighted to perform the office and added, cheekily, that with Paul out of the social scene he would have his chance at last with all those pretty young girls. When they met again at Sardi's, Peter greeted Paul with his usual disrespect by clasping him warmly by the hand and saying "At last!"

They had little time to see anything of London, for father and son were packed off to the tailors for the fitting of their new suits. That they fitted so well was due entirely to Sardi's foresight in taking their measurements with her. Redvers, never having seen Sardi's London house, was most impressed and agreed to her suggestion that he return after the wedding to spend some time with her for, she informed him with a wicked smile, that once he had his son off his hands he could start to enjoy his life again. Paul, laughing at her words, advised his father to put up in a good hotel instead; Sardi would ensure he was to be invited to every ball and social event for she was such a gadabout. That Paul should become increasingly nervous as the day of the wedding approached was only to be expected, but Peter proved himself invaluable by making sure that the poor fellow had very little time to think of it. Colonel Fleetwood and Redvers were introduced to each other at dinner two days before the wedding and, although both men had a mutual respect for each other because of their military background, their respective sons enjoyed much amusement to see the way both gentleman attempted to monopolise Sardi. The Colonel sadly admitted defeat, for even he was not so blind that he could not see that the entrancing woman he had loved from afar on first catching sight of her had never, in all the time he had known her, glowed with such beauty as she did when in the Captain's presence. His disappointment was tempered by the fact that his rival was, in his opinion, a damn fine fellow and also he was not so sure that at his time of life he should be thinking of matrimony, for now that he had established himself on his estate in Herefordshire he did not at all want to disrupt his pleasant lifestyle and return to the social whirl of London.

Two days before the marriage ceremony they travelled down to Berkshire in a large group, the elder members sharing a carriage and Peter taking Paul up with him in his curricle. When they arrived they were met by Lady Wrothford and a blushing Chloe who took Paul to see the array of wedding presents that were assembled in the drawing room. He was somewhat stunned by the quantity of gifts that their wedding had attracted and wondered whether they would all find a place in Trevu, for he could not imagine that the house would have room enough for all of them. The wedding was a very quiet affair: On Paul's side of the family were his father and mother and of course Peter and his father. Chloe had her grandmother, her uncle, his wife and one of their daughters to act as bridesmaid. At the wedding breakfast a rather quiet and reserved Paul found a note slipped into his hand by Lady Wrothford. It had only one word written on it, but when he saw what she had written he gave her his brightest smile and she smiled back, rather saucily for such an old lady. Quietly, he folded her note and tucked it into his pocket.

The newly married couple were to spend their honeymoon in a house on the estate. After saying his farewells to his family, Paul turned to Lady Wrothford and noticed that she looked tired, but she smiled her tight, twisted smile and tilted up her chin at him giving him a bold look. "Well sir," she told him, "I congratulate you both and wish you a long and happy life together. Take care of my little Chloe and . . . love her the best you can Paul. I'll ask no more than that. And don't keep my horses hanging around! 'Tis a cold day."

He laughed and, pulling her into his arms, gently hugged her and kissed her cheek, then he got into the carriage, which had been decorated with flowers and ribbons, and the next moment they were bowling down the avenue to take the road that led to the hunting box on the other side of the estate. That night, as he disrobed before entering the bedroom where his young bride lay, his hand felt the note that he had hidden in his pocket. He looked at it again and smiled in spite of his nervousness. Lady Wrothford's clear hand spelt out the one word - Checkmate.

CHAPTER 19

THE following morning, Paul stared out of the window in the little breakfast room, not seeing the wintry sunshine rippling over the lawn and fields. He hardly noticed the scene before him for his mind was on his bridal night. He, Paul Trevarthen - Penzance's notorious young rake had found himself so nervous on his wedding night that the occasion had almost turned into a disaster. Such had been the state of his nerves that he could not even touch his young wife. Instead they lay together like the effigies on the tombs of the lord and lady of the manor in the local church.

"Paul, do you not want even to hold me?" asked his bride in a timid voice.

"It is not that Chloe," replied Paul gently, "I do not know how much . . . I would not hurt you for the world, my dear Chloe, you see." He mumbled on, saying more and more idiotic things. The infamous lover, found himself full of trepidation like a schoolboy attempting his first kiss. His wife, completely unabashed snuggled against his body and said boldly, "Paul, Grandmamma told me what I might expect. She was most forthright, Paul, I am not afraid of what is to happen."

"You might not be Chloe, but I think I am!" he said in exasperation, "Did Lady Wrothford truly tell you everything?"

"She said she did Paul, but you know Grandmamma! After she gave me all the . . . the details she lapsed into such a period of silence that I had to ask if all was well with her. 'Of course all is well, I am just trying to think if I have forgotten anything!' she snapped at me," said Chloe and went off into an irrepressible giggle. Her laughter broke the tension and before he knew it Paul was laughing as well, his shyness left him, he took her in his arms and they enjoyed their pleasures in mutual contentment.

As he turned away from the window, the door was opened and his wife ran into the room, her face delicately tinged with colour. She crossed the room to Paul and, throwing herself into his arms, and held up her face to be kissed, saying happily as she did so: "Good morning husband."

He smiled into her sunny, laughing face and, folding his arms around her, kissed her full on her mouth and then said, "Good morning wife," and hugged her again.

This situation continued throughout their honeymoon but even in the midst of his happiness Paul would find himself thinking of the girl he had lost and would grow quiet. If Chloe noticed the change in his demeanour she was wise enough not to mention it, whilst Paul was foolish enough to imagine that it would not be apparent to her, that occasionally, his thoughts were elsewhere.

When at last it was time for them to leave the hunting lodge they returned to Hatcombe Hall in the carriage.

At the end of the following week the happy couple were ready to leave for Cornwall but on the point of departure Chloe unexpectedly burst into tears and hugged her Grandmother, crying as if her heart would break. Paul, worried by this turn of events was unsure of what to do, but Lady Wrothford took charge as usual and told his young wife to stop crying at once, and pulling out her own handkerchief wiped the tears from the sobbing girl's cheeks.

"Come, madam, enough of that! Your poor husband will think that you do not want to go to his home with him. Now, stop at once! You are not unhappy! Would you rather stay with me or go home with Paul? Answer me?" she asked in her usual forthright manner.

Chloe sniffed, "Go home with Paul, dear Grandmama."

"Good! I'm glad to see I have managed to bring you up with some sense at least," she said severely, and without further preamble turned from Chloe to Paul; "Well come and wish me goodbye, Paul. Don't stand there dithering!" she announced in her normal dictatorial manner. He came at once to her and kissed her cheek, placing his arms around her as he did so. She kissed his cheek in return, hastily wiped away a tear but with her usual brusque manner hastened them into the carriage, told them both to write, directed Chloe to make sure the sheets were aired at the inns they stopped in and ordered Paul to look after her granddaughter, else he would be hearing from her. Finally she gave them both a firm smile and told them it was time to go. Chloe, smiling bravely, waved until the house disappeared behind the bend in the driveway, but then she cast herself upon Paul's chest and wept uncontrollably.

"Please Chloe, don't cry, please," he pleaded, "I cannot bear to see you like this."

"Oh Paul, I know I shall never see her again. She has been the only mother I have ever known," she sobbed desperately.

He comforted her as best he could, but in his heart he feared she spoke the truth, for Lady Wrothford had begun to look frail and tired and it was most noticeable that she no longer moved in her usual energetic fashion. Gradually his wife's sobs subsided and he kissed her gently. He told her to stop crying and she smiled mistily at him. So with a mixture of sadness and joy they travelled on to Cornwall.

At Trevu, Chloe blossomed and made friends with everybody, completely charming everyone from Squire Tregurthen to Davy from the stables. Paul found himself subjected to a whirl of social engagements, but with his wife at his side he found them an easier experience to contend with than they had ever been in the past. The house seemed always full of visitors and when they had time alone they seemed always to be laughing, for the delightful Chloe had the most wicked sense of humour and would tease her poor husband unmercifully. Paul, to his surprise, found that he quite liked the experience, for she was always so happy to be in his company. In June, Chloe took Hannah on one side and whispered in her ear. Hannah beamed and nodded but advised her to wait for a while, for she thought it best to be sure. However, when Paul had gone over to visit a local farmer in the company of his father, Dr. Simcott's pony and trap called and he confirmed both their suspicions. Chloe awaited her husband's return and told him while they were taking a walk around the garden. Paul was dumbfounded at her news for he felt unprepared for fatherhood, but Chloe settled into pregnancy with increasing confidence.

Their son could do no better than to put in his appearance in the early hours of Christmas morning, which caused the celebrations at Trevu's annual Christmas party to be even more convivial than was normal. Paul, beaming with pride, thought his son the most perfect being he had ever seen and straightway dashed off letters to Lady Wrothford and his mother to inform them of the happy event.

Within a week of his son's birth Lady Wrothford's letters to them, one for Chloe and one for Paul, arrived at Trevu. She was delighted that everything had gone so well for them and congratulated them both. She wished them all much joy with their new son and thanked them for naming him George, after his great grandmother and Redvers, after his grandfather. "Quite right too," she asserted. A week later her maid, going to wake her at her normal hour, found that the old lady had died peacefully in her sleep.

Chloe was heartbroken when Paul gently told her the news but he consoled her as best he could. Obviously, as they would not be able to attend the funeral, being unable to get to Berkshire in time, he could only send a letter of sympathy to her son in which he extolled Lady Wrothford's many virtues. He received a short letter in return with a list attached, detailing the effects his mother had willed to Chloe and her chess set that she wished to leave to Paul. In spite of his sadness, that small act made him smile. His wife was naturally distraught at the loss of her grandmother, but with her new baby taking up a lot of her time and her young husband's consideration for her, she was able to sustain the loss in a better frame of mind than at first she thought would have been possible.

At the end of January Sardi arrived to visit them. She was enchanted with her grandson and Chloe found herself with another rival, apart from Hannah, Redvers and Paul, who all insisted on laying claim to her son. When not fulfilling their roles of besotted grandparents, Sardi and Redvers seemed to be smiling at each other whenever they were together and Chloe noticed immediately how happy they were to be in each other's company. Paul noticed nothing, being far too preoccupied with his son, so Chloe gave him a hint of what was happening. They were all sitting in the parlour; Paul holding George - who was contentedly sleeping in the crook of his arm - and Chloe snuggled against him with his other arm around her. Redvers and Sardi sat chatting on the other settle, smiling and laughing with each other. Chloe, covertly studying the couple, gave her husband a dig in the ribs and when he looked at her she nodded her head in the direction of his parents. He smiled a slow smile but looked at his wife and raised his eyebrows. Later she told him that she was sure a marriage was in the air, and he replied that he was not so sure.

"Silly," she admonished him, "of course they are going to get married. It is quite obvious to anyone that they worship each other." Paul smiled his slow smile, and merely told her that maybe it was so, but they would just have to wait and see.

A week later Redvers proposed to Sardi and she accepted him joyfully. Chloe admitted to them that she knew what to happen all along and so had prepared Paul. This struck Redvers and Sardi as funny and they both laughed heartily, and laughed again as Paul protested that he had not been so unobservant as his wife had said he was but this remark did not impress Chloe at all.

The wedding was to be held in London as Sardi had so many friends there, but they had thought it best to build another wing on to Trevu, otherwise with two couples and one nursery all sharing the house they would all find themselves with very little room, so they had decided to marry at the end of the year. Redvers would take Sardi on an extended honeymoon and they would return, hopefully, after all the building work had been completed in the spring of the following year.

In the early autumn Chloe had cause to take Hannah on one side again and in the October Paul was informed that he was to be a father once again. They were able to return to London for his parents' wedding and were back in Cornwall well before the birth of their second child. Redvers and Sardi returned from their honeymoon to discover that the new wing had been completed to their satisfaction and to find Paul cradling a daughter, as yet unnamed.

After much thought, the baby's parents decided that they would like their daughter to have Penelope as her second name. Paul told Redvers and Sardi while they all sat in the parlour taking tea. George, a dark haired lusty child, was contentedly sitting on his grandfather's lap, playing with the buttons of his coat. Redvers smiled gratefully at his son and looked at his little granddaughter, who was being petted by Sardi. His mother looked up and smiled at Paul with approval.

"Why Paul, that is just as it should be," she said and she bent and kissed the little girl on the top of her head.

"Have you decided on her first name yet?" asked Redvers cautiously.

"Yes, we have," said Chloe, "I hope that it meets with your approval Sardi, but we should like to call her Grace after your mother." At her pronouncement tears filled Sardi's eyes and she was unable to speak.

"You are not displeased," asked Paul anxiously.

"Displeased - no," gasped Sardi, "so touched, so very touched. How kind of you both and how thoughtful. I think this little lady has two wonderful namesakes."

Paul breathed a sigh of relief, as he had wanted so badly to call his daughter after his beloved step mother but did not wish in any way to offend Sardi.

That night Paul and Chloe lay comfortably in each other's arms, savouring the silence, as their daughter Grace was fast asleep in her crib by their bed. When she was old enough she would join her brother and the children's nurse, Miss Clavering, in the nursery but for the time being Chloe insisted that she shared their room. Paul had no objection as, on becoming a father, he had discovered in himself a love of children that he had not previously recognised.

His had been a happy but lonely childhood and, although he had plenty of playmates in the village and an especial friend in Sarah-Jane, he had often felt the need of company of his own age. Chloe had found herself in a similar position, but hers had been a worse case as she had only servants and her grandmother for companionship. Marrying Paul and having children had given her a whole new world. She revelled in it, being a naturally maternal woman, and to find that her husband was equally as delighted with their progeny gave her immense satisfaction. Noting her sigh of contentment, her husband whispered into her ear and asked her if she was happy.

"More than you would ever believe," she answered contentedly, but she turned and asked Paul if he did not mind if she asked him a question.

"Of course not," he said but warily. Although contented with his marriage he and Chloe both knew that theirs was not a love match, at least not on Paul's part.

"I wanted to talk about the children's education," said Chloe and felt a sharp pang in her heart as Paul's body relaxed in her arms, but undaunted she drew a deep breath and continued: "I should like to start a village school for all the local children, ours included, when the time comes. I have often thought it is such a shame that there are so many local children with unknown gifts and talents, that are not given the opportunity to use them. As I have been well provided for by grandmother I should like to use some of her money in a good cause. What do you think?" she asked him after a pause.

"I think that it is a most clever idea. Why did I not think of it? I have a scholarship set up at my old school but I am afraid that I gave no thought to the education, or more appropriately, the lack of it that exists in local towns and villages. My mother taught me at home, but there were few women like her around" he replied, "but we will talk about it tomorrow, I am tired now. Young Grace will demand attention soon so we had best sleep while we can. I can assure you that there will be one member of our household who will have much to say on the matter, for Sardi will be enchanted with your idea I know and will probably set up a sewing school to rival your establishment."

"Why not both in the one school, and cooking, woodworking and . . . and, well I don't know but all sorts of things" enthused Chloe, pleased by her husband's response.

Paul laughed and remarked lovingly, "Madame Wife go to sleep, else you will have me talking through 'til dawn," and as she opened her mouth to contradict him he kissed her into silence, and as he did so, felt a wave of passion sweep over him.

She giggled and turned to him laughingly as she said provocatively, "Not so tired now, dear husband?"

"Hussy," he muttered in between kisses.

Paul arrived at breakfast late, looking tired, but smiled ruefully at his parents and offered his explanation: "Grace kept us awake for most of the night," he vouchsafed with a twinkle in his eye. Sardi beamed dotingly at him, whereas Redvers, knowing his son of old, bit at the smile that was playing on his own lips.

"Have you set a date for Grace's christening yet?" asked Redvers conversationally helping himself to a slice of cold beef.

"Not yet, but I will have a word with the vicar this afternoon, as Chloe and I want to see him about another matter," replied Paul, pouring himself a tankard of ale whilst piling his plate with cold meat.

Redvers raised an eyebrow in surprise: "Thinking of taking the cloth, Paul?" he asked mischievously.

Paul whooped with laughter at his comment, much to his mother's amusement. "No," he replied, "Chloe has had an idea that we would like to discuss with him, but as it is her idea I will leave it to her to inform you."

When Chloe entered the room Sardi said: "Chloe, Paul has been telling us that Grace kept you both awake last night. I expect all is well but I do hope that she is not sickening for something?"

Chloe, catching Paul's eye and blushing rosily, was momentarily lost for words. Redvers quickly rushed to the young couple's assistance by asking for the details of her idea that Paul had been telling them about. Smiling gratefully at her father-in-law, Chloe assured Sardi that Grace was very well and then started to explain her plans for the school.

Redvers looked surprised with her idea, and then impressed, but Sardi was even more affected and told Chloe that it was a wonderful idea. She immediately began to go into details regarding the size of the school, the ages of the children, and information on the sorts of trades that could be taught along side a general education. As she continued on happily in the same vein, Paul, catching his wife's eye, gave her his 'I told you it would be so ' look, but she frowned back at him and, turning her face away, continued to discuss her idea with his mother.

"I think that a school in this locality is a very good idea but it will need a lot of thought and discussion to set it up properly," Paul advised, not wishing to offend his wife. Redvers agreed and told them that the vicar would be able to be of some assistance in arranging matters. "You will need the services of a schoolmaster as well unless you intend to educate them yourselves," he added and then continued: "Methinks you will need more than one if this plan finds favour with the parents and if you wish to teach them trades as well you will certainly require quite a company," he pronounced.

"Quite right, dearest," said Sardi, "after breakfast Chloe, you and I will have a good discussion about it in the back parlour and this afternoon - if you have no objection, - I should like to go with you when you pay a call on the Reverend Sandys."

After finding no fault with this arrangement, Redvers arose from the table and told them he would see them later, as he intended to ride over to a local farmer who had a fine heifer that he was minded to sell. Paul hastily accepted an invitation to go with him, because the determined look on the two women's' faces prophesied an intense discussion on their part and he felt he would benefit from a ride in the fresh air more than a morning of heated discussion. On the homeward journey, the Trevarthen's discussion revolved around the proposed school and Redvers praised Chloe in general, as an excellent wife and mother and, in particular, for her plan to set up the educational establishment that the area badly needed. His son smiled proudly and nodded in agreement.

"Strange as it may seem, I am most thankful that you were taken so ill in London and had to spend time with Lady Wrothford and Chloe, for I do not think you would have chosen Chloe as your wife if you had not been thrown together in such a fashion. You look like a man who has found happiness in his marriage," and he paused for a moment, "I hope it to be so for Chloe's sake, for I think she deserves it of you."

A slight flush of guilt shadowed Paul's face and did not go unnoticed by his father. Redvers sighed and sadly shook his head: "Do not let your past ruin your future, my son, for well I know how lucky I was to keep Penelope's love in spite of my actions," he said shamefacedly.

"I have no intention of putting my marriage in jeopardy," replied Paul firmly, "and I have no desire for any wife but Chloe. It is as you said; the woman I wanted to marry is long gone and living her own life now. She is a ghost of my past."

"Then long may your world continue happy Paul, for such happiness is a joy in itself and should not be disregarded," pronounced Redvers.

CHAPTER 20

THE Reverend Sandys ushered Sardi, her son and his wife into the withdrawing room of the vicarage and, after they had all seated themselves and given details of the health of Grace and young George, they broached the subject of the proposed school. He was surprised at first, but then entered with enthusiasm into the discussion and gave them many useful suggestions as to how to go about putting their plan into action.

Most of the afternoon was given over to discussing the school; and mention was made of forming a committee and the Reverend asked if he should take it upon himself to arrange a meeting with members of the community that would be suitable for inclusion in such an enterprise. As to deciding on matters more directly involving the educational side of the proposed establishment; it was decided that they be best left in abeyance until such time as the members of the committee had been appointed. Chloe, feeling proud that her idea had taken such a positive route, agreed with her mother in law that they leave everything in the vicar's capable hands for the time being and to meet again on a date to be decided when other interested parties would be available to discuss the matter further.

The following morning Redvers returned from a visit to Penzance with the mail. Chloe was the only one not to receive any letters, but she smiled unconcernedly. Sardi had letters from London and Bristol, Redvers' letters concerned his business affairs and Paul's were from his publishers, two literary societies, and Peter Fleetwood. Peter wrote to tell Paul that he had accepted a position as a secretary to a British diplomat, who was taking up a post in Athens, and would be leaving for Greece in the first week of November. He wanted to visit before he left, so he had taken Paul at his word to come and stay whenever he had the time, and was notifying him that he would be arriving tomorrow night. He asked Paul to apologise to Chloe before his arrival so that she would not be too annoyed when he turned up. She smiled when Paul read that part of his letter to her and said that she could never be annoyed with Peter as he was a particular favourite of hers.

Paul raised his eyebrows at this comment. "Please to remember that you are a married woman, ma'am," he said with a smile.

"As if the children will ever let me forget," she answered with a mischievous glint in her eye. She waited with a barely suppressed smile for his reply.

"And what about your husband, pray?"

"Oh him," she replied archly, "I suppose he ought to be considered for propriety's sake."

"Your supposition is quite correct, Madame Wife," announced Paul, trying not to laugh, and added in what he thought was an undertone: "Hussy!" completely forgetting that his mother was in the room and was startled when he heard her say his name in a shocked voice.

Chloe went off into a peal of laughter. "Do not be offended, Sardi, 'tis only Paul's way of teasing me," Chloe told her.

Reassured, Sardi smiled at both of them and shook her head and sighed, which for some strange reason made them go off into hoots of laughter.

The letters from the literary societies were, as usual, requesting his presence at different functions in London and one wanted him to give a talk at Oxford University. Sardi was most impressed and desperately wanted Paul to accept, her forceful personality starting to assert itself. Paul's mulish expression began to settle on his face and he announced his intention that he would not go. Redvers, returning at that moment, noticed immediately that there was a certain air of friction between mother and son. Sardi immediately informed her husband about the invitation from such an impressive establishment. It would be such a shame if Paul should miss such an opportunity, she intoned.

"I think Paul must feel very honoured by such an invitation, but truly dear Sardi, perhaps it would be best if Paul and Chloe decided what they would prefer to do for themselves," he replied in an even tone.

For one moment there was a dangerous silence but he smiled an understanding smile at his wife and said disarmingly: "Would that Paul had inherited his mother's ability to grasp opportunities as they present themselves but, alas, I fear he has inherited my reticence instead."

Sardi recognised that her husband was attempting to ward off an argument between Paul and herself. She glanced at Chloe, who smiled understandingly at her, but the look in her eye was a warning not to press Paul any further. Paul, oblivious to the machinations on all sides, agreed with his father and stated that he and Chloe would discuss the proposition later, and then concluded that particular conversation by informing them of Peter Fleetwood's impending visit.

"Just remember that you are a married man now, Paul. Chloe, be warned! The last time Peter came to visit Paul several taverns hereabouts benefited greatly from their presence," Redvers informed his daughter-in-law jovially.

"Paul knows full well that I do not object to young men enjoying the . . . the fruit of the grape. Grandmother always said it added to their charm." Her husband raised an eyebrow at this remark. "And, besides," she continued with a tremor of laughter in her voice, "as she so wisely pointed out, their remorse afterwards can be used so successfully for obtaining much obedience from them."

"Pooh!" laughed Paul and his wife immediately went off into giggles that were so infectious the whole room was soon rocked by their merriment.

When Peter arrived he was greeted warmly by his hosts. He had brought presents for them all; tortoiseshell combs for Sardi's hair, a book on shooting for Redvers, another book for Paul by Suetonius, a green silk shawl for Chloe which delighted her, toys for George and a small gold bracelet for Grace. He had even purchased a fine woollen shawl for Hannah and lost no time in descending into the kitchen and presenting it to her. Hannah, lost for words, determined to cook for Mr. Peter as never before and it became quite a joke in the household that she was bursting her stays in order to provide her young beau with as many sumptuous delights as she could provide. Of course, Paul and Peter frequented some of their former haunts, but Paul had no intention of imbibing too great a quantity as, deep in the recesses of his mind, Chloe's echo of Lady Wrothford's sagacity had taken root, and he had no intention of allowing his wife to have control of him should he arrive home befuddled and apologetic. Peter enjoyed himself hugely, as usual, and did not mind whether he spent time with the children - at one time on all fours on the floor pretending to be a dog for George's undoubted amusement - or telling Paul and Chloe about life in London, or partaking in any other pursuit that his hosts devised for him. However during afternoon tea he had everyone's attention when he mentioned that he was responsible for the letter from the literary group at Oxford University.

"Happened to mention to old Fortescue's brother that I knew you and the next thing was they wanted me to get you to their next meeting. Told them you were not so fond of that sort of thing anymore but that if they wrote to you they would soon learn if you were prepared to do one of your speeches for them. Never seen old 'Deathly' White so excited in my life when he came up to dine with me last month. Seems to me you are still quite a prize in the literary world Paul. Ever thought of doing more about it?" asked Peter, innocently unaware of the effect his words would have on the assembled company.

Paul, aware of his mother's eyes boring into his back, replied that he was not fond of that sort of thing. It was the work itself that he enjoyed and not the discussing of it afterwards, he said flatly. "Fair enough," said Peter, recognising that Paul wished the conversation to be turned away from that particular topic, and promptly asked Redvers if he had had a chance to look at his book. Paul flashed his old friend a quick smile of thanks and in turn tried to avoid giving his mother any opportunity for comment by asking if there was any news about the school.

Nothing more was said about the invitation from Oxford that night as Paul and Peter were not to be present; they had arranged to visit a tavern in the locality and returned long after the others had retired for the evening. They were both not quite sober so headed for Hannah's kitchen, knowing full well that she would have left some tasty treats for them to find on their return. Sitting in the still warm kitchen they chattered away quietly for a while, when Peter again brought up the subject of the invitation to Oxford.

"Don't want to press you, old man," he said to Paul, "but if you could only find it in yourself to go 'twould do my career a power of good. The thing is the chap whose secretary I am going to be carries a lot of influence in the government. He is a cousin of one of the dons at Oxford and if you would go and give one of your talks, he would be able to puff off his consequence and could bask in your reflected glory. Whereas I would then be advanced up the career ladder because I had achieved such a coup on his behalf, if you see what I mean."

"Peter, you know me well enough to know how I absolutely hate that sort of thing. My mother arranged so many talks for me on my visit to London and then again in Bristol that I came to detest having to do it," protested Paul.

"I know old chap, I know, but it would just be this once. Swear I'll never ask again," he pleaded before continuing: "Say you'd retired from public speaking to devote yourself to good works or something," he added as an afterthought. This explanation struck his friend as so funny that he shouted with laughter and was immediately shushed by Peter in case anyone overheard them.

"I'll discuss the matter with Chloe and see what she has to advise," affirmed Paul after wiping his eyes, "but I make you no promises."

With that Peter had to be content and, making sure that they had eaten their way through Hannah's half hidden plates of delicacies, they both headed for their respective rooms. Chloe had thoughtfully arranged for Peter to have a room well enough away from Grace's powerful lungs to ensure that he, at least, would get a good night's sleep.

Paul broached the subject of the Oxford trip to his wife, who could quite see Peter's predicament when all had been explained to her. Chloe considered for a while but then surprised Paul by telling him she thought he ought to go. He would be accompanied by his friend, after all, so would not lack for company. Peter had also been at Oxford and would doubtless know many of the people who would be present at the event. However, as she told him it was for Paul to decide and if he truly did not want to go, Peter, as an old friend, would understand. She brought the conversation to an end with a swift kiss and the suggestion that he go to sleep to help nullify the effects of the alcohol that he had undoubtedly drunk that evening. Paul, smothering a hiccup, whispered to his wife that alcohol and passion were a potent mixture as she would soon discover. The laughter that followed this admission was soon smothered by her husband's kisses, who proceeded to prove his argument to their mutual satisfaction.

When Peter, along with Paul's family, were told that he had agreed to go to Oxford, there was a mixture of delight and dismay. For some reason that Redvers could not explain he felt uncomfortable about the venture and thought it strange that he should feel this way. Paul dashed off a letter to the university informing them of his decision and both the young men set off for Penzance in Paul's curricle to catch the mail. As the weather was pleasant he took the opportunity of tooling the curricle around some of the outlying villages, which caused no small sensation amongst some of the younger inhabitants. Peter waved admiringly at several blushing females, remarking that there were some damned fine looking girls in that part of the world.

"Well, look your fill, Peter. However, I am a respectably married man and I have no intention of stopping my horses in order that you may further your acquaintance with any of them," his companion told him bluntly.

Peter laughed and mocked Paul for the paragon of virtue he had become, which was so vastly different from the madcap he had met in London and with whom he had so much difficulty in keeping in hand. Paul laughed and said that was true. However, when they got to Oxford Peter would see what a conscientious husband he could be when not in the company of his wife.

Two days later young Mr. Fleetwood returned to London with Hannah's usual overloaded hamper for company and promised to meet Paul at Oxford the day before they would be required at the University. He would arrange lodgings for them and make any other arrangements that they would need. Paul would just have to do his speech, answer a few questions, have dinner, and spend another night in Oxford, then return to Trevu and his family.

Meanwhile plans for the school were sent to Trevu to be discussed. The Reverend Sandys tried to talk the Trevarthen's, father and son, into becoming Governors, but they refused and so the honour fell to Sardi and Chloe. Other names discussed included Mr. Samuels, Paul's old friend from the book shop,

Squire Tregurthen and his wife, Mrs. Inez Carter, Hannah's son, Gabriel Hendra, who had set up his own carpentry business in Marazion, Dr. Simcott, Mr. Murdoch the tailor, and various other trades people from in and around Penzance. Paul noticed that no farmers had been included and suggested that enquiries should be made around the district to see if any would be prepared to hold office.

"You will need farmers on your side before you take their work force away from them. Also the fishing and mining industries ought to be consulted. If your idea is to train the children in trades and crafts it will be best to train them for work that will be of use to their future employers after all," mentioned Paul.

His mother and his wife were inspired by his argument and decided that letters should be written to all the people already on the list and any others that they thought would be of importance asking them to attend a meeting to be held on the ninth of September so that they could hear about what was to be proposed and to give their own ideas about the school. The Reverend agreed to send out the letters and to see about setting up a fund in the bank for the school. Sardi then impressed everyone by asking if it would not be possible for Mr. Spargo, the banker, to be one of the governors as he could then be the treasurer as well. When the meeting broke up its participants were well satisfied with what had been achieved.

Left alone, Paul soon found himself in Hannah's kitchen and was roundly told off when he helped himself to two of her cakes when her back was turned.

"There's no filling 'e an' there never was!" she admonished him. "I shall tell that dear little wife of yours what a devil you can be an' no mistake."

"No you won't Hannah, because you hate to see me go hungry and you know it. Otherwise why do you bake all these delicious treats, were it not to tempt me with them?" he argued, flashing his most angelic smile at her.

Hannah shook her head in mock disapproval but she could not hide the smile that Paul's infectious glee had always brought to her face.

"Got some news for 'e Mr. Paul 'bout Sarah-Jane," she announced and nodded at him in her usual conspiratorial manner. Raising his eyebrows, Paul waited patiently for Hannah's announcement.

"Goin' marry a sailor over to Falmouth. He's quite old an' only got one eye but he was quite taken with her and bin' chasin' after she ever since he clapped eyes, well clapped his eye, on 'er so to speak. She wouldn' too keen but accepted 'is proposal after a while. William John's wife was visiting her aunt in Marazion and come into Penzance for some shopping. Well I met 'er comin' out the ironmongers 'cos I needed a bigger pan for me stew an' she said it 'twas so," and she nodded again with a slight lift to her eyebrows.

"Well I hope it is so, she deserves the love of a good man for she had such a kind and honest heart," Paul told her before continuing, "and as she is my oldest friend I should very much like for her to receive a gift for the wedding. Do you think that would be appropriate, Hannah?"

"Oh! 'Twould be a lovely idea, but 'ave a bit a sense and send it from the Trevarthens of Trevu and not just from yourself. Wouldn' want put more wood on the fire now would 'e?" she replied and eyed him speculatively.

"Hannah! If she is getting married then she has long since forgotten what she felt for me," he told her firmly.

"Humph!" returned Hannah, "tell that to the liddle people and see if they do believe it anymore than I do! She's marrying 'im 'cos he got a bit a money and no family to bother with. Set 'er up nicely that will. William John's missus said 'e do worship she so Sarah-Jane wen't 'ave no bother with 'en. Well no more bother than women do 'ave with most men 'til they get 'em trained."

The grin that hovered on her mouth after this remark made Paul's eyes dance with laughter and he retorted laughingly: "Hannah and you call me a rogue and a devil. Much have I to learn from you and your wily ways, methinks."

Hannah burst out into a loud laugh and Paul managed to pinch a forlorn looking cake before beating a swift retreat.

Josh Pascoe, dismissed from the navy because of the injuries he had received at the battle of Trafalgar, had no clear idea of what to do with himself when he returned to his home town of Penzance. Press ganged into the service four years before his twentieth birthday, he had discovered a liking for the life and had never wished to leave the sea. Working his way up through the ranks he had ended up a gun captain in charge of his own cannon, with his own gun crew responsible for loading and firing the weapon. At Trafalgar he was badly injured, the cannon shot that hit his position had succeeded in killing all the men, his friends every one of them, that worked under him. Dragged from the bloody mess he was taken to the surgeon, who ministered to him in a rough and ready fashion for he had many men to try to save that day. Lucky to survive at all, he reappeared in the town a year after the battle lacking money, and his right leg below the knee. The townspeople were most sympathetic but, although at the time of the battle, they had gone mad with the glory of Nelson's victory, their gratitude did not extend to financial remuneration for any of the injured sailors that were now appearing on the streets. If he received anything at all it was often only a handshake and perhaps a few congratulatory words. He had almost given up hope of ever getting himself paid work again, when he chanced upon Likky Skewes coming back from Newlyn and they fell to chatting. Knowing full well that Likky was working for his old friend Joey Bolitho in the smuggling trade, he asked hopefully if there was anything he could do to help for his meagre funds had run desperately low. Likky offered to mention the matter to Bolitho but told Josh not to hold out too much hope for, in his injured condition, he would be a difficult man to place. By its very nature you had to be fit to go in their sort of work and Joey could not afford to employ a man with Josh's obvious disadvantages, although he was only in his mid twenties. When a week later, he was thrown out of his cottage for having no money left to pay the rent, he thought he had lost all his dignity and would have no choice but to throw himself on the charity of the parish. Looking most dejected by the turn his life had taken, he sat amongst his sparse belongings and bethought himself in the trough of despondency at last, when a shadow blotted out the light and he raised his eyes to see a tall man standing before him.

"Evenin' Josh," said a familiar voice.

"Why, Joey! What you doin' up this way?" he asked in surprise.

"Come a callin' on me old mate an' sad I am see 'e sittin' 'ere like this, my old pard," Joey replied, "Still I reckon I found a bit a work for 'e. Start tonight can 'e?"

"Damn right! This very minute," returned Josh, hardly daring to believe his good fortune.

"Thas' good!" smiled Joey, before asking if he needed help with his belongings and bent down to pick up Josh's old sea chest, that he had acquired in Portugal and which had accompanied him on all his travels. Josh struggled to a standing position, and with the aid of a stick which he used as a crutch, hopped along behind Bolitho until they reached an old inn, named the Pelican, but known locally as Boscawen's after its former flamboyant landlord who, in the midst of a convivial evening, had dropped dead amidst his customers, much to their dismay. The door was open, and two slatternly looking woman were busily employed in cleaning the establishment thoroughly. Bemused Josh stood in the midst of the room and watched as kegs of brandy, rum and geneva were brought in by what seemed a veritable army of fishermen under Likky's direction.

"Ol' Charlie Maddern 'aven't stopped brewing 'is ale so there's plenty a' that to be drunk," Joey informed him with a smile.

"Am I goin' be yer barman, Joey?" asked Josh, in wonder, for he assumed correctly that Bolitho must have bought the inn off the Widow Boscawen and that he would need staff to help him run it.

"No," replied Joey carefully, and noted the look of disappointment on Pascoe's face. "Thought you could 'ave a go at runnin' the place for me. Split the profits fifty-fifty and no rent to pay. Do that seem fair to 'e?"

"Fair! Fair! Damn me Joey! Damn me!" Josh could say no more for he seemed to have been given a whole new life, but he hopped across the room and thanked Joey profusely, shaking his hand all the while.

"That'll do Josh! That'll do!", said Joey, embarrassed and turned away. "I'll be in tomorrow fer a drink with some a' me mates. 'Spect you'll a got the 'ang of things by then," and he made to leave, but at the door he turned to the bemused Josh, still standing in the middle of the room swaying slightly in an attempt to keep his balance. "By the by, Josh. There's a present fer 'e behind the bar. 'Ope 'tis the right size," and on that cryptic comment he raised his hand in farewell and was gone.

Hopping to the bar, Josh made his way behind it; there propped up against the side of a chair was a newly fashioned wooden leg complete with padding and leather strapping, along with a most fine walking stick the handle of which had been carved, most delicately, like a seagull. Josh picked up the leg and, getting himself to a chair, untied the string that held together his trousers below the knee, and after a slight struggle managed to fit it to his stump. He essayed a few steps with it and found it a perfect size. So, feeling more a man than he had done for a long time, he walked awkwardly but proudly back to a chair and sat himself down in it and, sinking his head in his hands, sobbed like a child.

Four months later, Josh Pascoe, landlord of the newly named Seagull Inn, placed a tankard of ale in front of Joey Bolitho as he came to the bar, but waived the payment as he tried to do every time the man entered the inn. Each month he passed over half of his profits, but it was noticed that Joey would turn up with some badly needed furniture or more casks, refusing payment for any of them. Josh would merely shake his head at him, whilst repeating over and over again, "Thankee, Joey, thankee!" Likky arrived not long after Joey and had his ale bought for him by his companion, who had slapped a handful of coins on the bar in his generous fashion, and told Josh to buy a drink for any one of those present who wished for another one. Moving to Joey's table in the corner of the room Likky sat down and began to converse quietly with his friend.

"Guess who I see'd day Joey? Looking most fine, too!" asked Likky, conspiratorially, but Joey would not be drawn and merely shook his head, his cold, blue eyes surveying every one of the men in the room, one after the other.

"I's over to Falmouth an' tried drum up bit trade in that big inn down by the harbour. Didden 'a no luck 'cos the Landlord knew we an' 'e wen't 'a no trade with smugglers," he watched intently to see if Joey's expression had changed, but it remained enigmatic, although he was asked sharply if Likky was going to tell him his news or dance around the may pole all evening instead.

"Yer maid," Likky said, quickly, "You knaw! That Williams maid over to Trevu! Thas' where she bin' an' gone to live," and he had the satisfaction of seeing Joey's mask slip for a brief moment. Turning his head, Joey searched his companion's face with his icy stare.

"You lyin'?" Joey asked, quietly.

"Strike me dead, if I should ever lie to 'e Joey," replied his friend worriedly, "I see'd 'er with me own eyes fer she do 'elp 'er brother William John an' 'is missus run the place. An' I'll tell 'e another thing, she didn't look none too 'appy to catch sight a' me neither. Soon as she noticed me she was gone like a rabbit an' I never seen 'er no more, but I asked 'round an' folks said 'twas due to 'er the place 'ad improved. She got more idea than William-John 'bout business an' they say 'e be pretty sharp." He glanced swiftly up into Joey's face and noticed the interested look in his eyes, but turned away quickly for his friend could be an awkward person if you probed him too deeply about his private affairs. There was a prolonged silence and finally Bolitho said he would be making an early night of it, for he had a lot to do on the morrow.

"Need me Joey?" asked Likky and coughed.

"No!" replied Joey firmly, "but I'll catch 'e somewhere in the evenin'."

"Right you are, pard," agreed Likky, relieved to have imparted his tale and still to have a whole skin at the end of it.

The following afternoon, William-John received another visitor from Penzance but this time the man boldly asked to see his sister. William-John told him brusquely that his presence was unwanted, for his sister had expressed a desire that should he appear she had no wish to see the gentleman. Her brother stood his ground as the expression on the man's face hardened. He repeated that he was adamant that Bolitho's presence was not required in his inn and would he very kindly leave

"Not 'til I seen 'er," came the cold reply.

"She won't see 'e Joey an' nothin' you can say or do is goin' alter that fact, and anyways," said William John, lowering his eyes and looking embarrassed, "my sister is to marry at the end of the month," he gasped out quickly.

"What!" cried Joey in disbelief, and his cold eyes burned in anger.

"She's gettin' married," repeated the landlord boldly, "an' she won't thank you fer turnin' up 'gain."

"I . . . I want a word with 'er! 'Tis most important!" exclaimed the smuggler angrily.

"Won't do no good, Joey. Sarah-Jane 'ave told me to tell 'e she won't see 'e. She bin' an' told this man she'll marry 'en and Sarah-Jane idden goin' change 'er mind. She couldn' 'ave Paul, an' she wouldn' 'ave you! So she left 'erself with two choices. Stay an old maid or marry an' get a bit a' security behind her. 'Er future 'usband got a bit a money so she'll never 'ave worry 'gain an' 'e's a lot older than Sarah-Jane so 'e won't give 'er no trouble. I'm sorry fer 'e Joey 'cos I knaw you tried stay out a the smuggling trade fer 'er, but she bin' in love with Paul Trevarthen from the minute she first seen 'en an' if you'd a bin' the 'ighest in the land you still wouldn' a done fer 'er," he informed Joey, not without a touch of sadness for the man looked deeply hurt by what he had said. After a slight pause, he added that his sister and her future husband would be moving away and that she would no longer be working at the inn. "Yer a young man Joey, with plenty a time find somebody else. Best fer you if you d' forget 'er, fer she won't look at 'e, an' knawin' what you bin' like all these years tidden surprisin' after all. I'll take a message to 'er from 'e if you wish but don't get yer 'opes up fer she won't change 'er mind," he offered and thought that Joey would have nothing to say, but lifting up his now impassive face with its cold eyes he simply said: "Tell 'er I'll wait fer 'er an' I will marry 'er meself, no matter 'ow many years got to pass afore that day do arrive," and then turned on his heel in anger and stormed from the inn.

Arriving back at his cottage late in the evening, he had hardly got inside the door when Likky arrived. Poor fool that he was he had the brashness to ask him how his day had gone and was promptly floored by Joey's hard punch to his jaw. Rubbing his chin he hastily departed, admitting to himself as he arrived at his own cottage that he must endeavour to learn that there were some parts of Joey's life that he would not have touched on and, the sooner his friend realised that, the better it would be for him.

CHAPTER 21

WHEN the letter of confirmation arrived from Oxford, Paul began to wish that he had not arranged to go and told Chloe he had a good mind to cancel the proposed visit. He had never felt comfortable giving speeches and if it had not been for his aunt Caroline he would probably not have had any skill at all in talking to complete strangers.

"You have promised Peter, 'twould not be fair to let him down, Paul," remarked Chloe.

"That's the thing. If I refuse to go now I will make Peter look a complete fool. He has probably made all the arrangements by this time. Damn and blast I wish I had never agreed to it! I shall miss you and the children damnably. I am not the sort of person who fares well at this sort of thing," he complained in despair, his heavy frown settling on his brow. His wife determined to make him see sense: "Stop it Paul!" she admonished him. "You will give a most accomplished speech, as you well know, for you certainly know your subject. As for a few questions afterwards; Pooh! You will have no trouble there for I have seen you do that time out of mind. It is a university audience so they will be all men, none of those sighing women that you find so disconcerting. You cannot disappoint Peter, so good a friend as he has been," finished Chloe firmly.

Paul writhed, but acquiesced. His wife was in the right of it; he had committed himself and could not with honour refuse to perform the office now. However, he tried to persuade Chloe to go with him but she refused, as she knew she would not relish the journey but more importantly, did not want to spend time away from her children.

As Chloe was determined that he should not renege on his promise he found himself talked into it and, when he found his wife supervising his packing for him, he made no demur.

On the point of departure he hugged Chloe and whispered his farewells, but he felt so alone and miserable; it seemed as if the years had rolled away and he was back at school. As the waiting horses became impatient and shifted in their traces; Chloe pressed her hands against his chest and told him it was time to go. For answer he pulled her to him again and kissed her fiercely, knowing only that he was going to miss her more than he could understand. Finally he wrenched himself away and entered the chaise. He put his head out of the window so he could say his goodbyes and Chloe smiled at him, lifting her chin proudly, for she knew that any sign from her of vacillation would mean that Paul would get out of the chaise and refuse to go. She noticed how unhappy he looked, but was determined that he should not leave with such a despondent expression on his face so, unseen by his parents she mouthed 'I love you' and had the pleasure of seeing him smile at last.

The university had arranged for the post chaise and Paul had nothing to do but sit back and enjoy the journey. By the time he got to Truro he was ready to get out and return home, even if he had to walk, but the thought of his wife and the bell that she would peal over his head if he dared to do such a thing deterred him. All the way to Oxford he found himself thinking of his dear little wife. On the road he wanted her beside him to talk with, when he took his meals he wanted her to tease him about the amount of food he could eat and consequently ate far less than he normally did, and at night in his strange and lonely bedchamber his body ached for her. Paul supposed he felt despondency at having to disrupt his comfortable lifestyle and to jaunt across the country to give a speech to a parcel of dry academics. He thought of Peter waiting to greet him at Oxford and felt almost angry that he was doing all this for his friend's sake and not for his own part. Then, immediately, he felt guilty that he should feel so about Peter, for had the positions been reversed he knew that there was nothing his friend would not do for him. How selfish of him not to make this small effort to advance Peter's career. He shifted uneasily on the seat, squirming physically and mentally at his egocentricity. When he finally arrived at his destination the sight of Peter's delighted countenance went some way to cheer him up, but he still felt low and his friend could not fail to notice that Paul was not his usual cheery self. With the object of improving his friend's disposition, Peter took him to the lodgings he had arranged for that night and sat him down to a sumptuous meal, which normally Paul would have had no difficulty in appreciating. He smiled warmly at Peter but it was apparent that, although he made a good meal, he did not eat with such relish as his companion had been accustomed to see him do. Peter hated to see his friend so despondent and tried his best to cheer him up by telling him tales of his time at Oxford and of the scrapes he and his friends had gotten into. Paul smiled at his companion's reminiscences but his natural cheeriness was missing and he had to summon up all his mental strength to make conversation.

"What is the matter, Paul?" asked Peter finally, "Afraid you will let yourself down tomorrow?"

For answer Paul only shook his head and a long sigh escaped him.

"I think I know what your problem is Paul," Peter remarked.

"Problem? I have not a problem that I am aware of," retorted Paul.

"Oh haven't you my young buck! You have no idea obviously, but I think that you are suffering a sickness," Peter told him with an amused smile quivering on his lips.

"Pooh! What sort of sickness have I got then, Doctor Knowledge? Will I require a revolting potion to cure me?" mocked Paul.

"Probably, but most assuredly a pair of spectacles."

Paul started and then laughed, asking what nonsense Peter was talking , had he been imbibing more than he should have before meeting the chaise? Peter shook his head and continued to regard his friend with amusement.

"Well, what is the name of this illness that I have contracted dear Peter? Melancholia, perhaps?"

"Hmm. Well sort of Paul," mused Peter. "A melancholia of the heart perhaps."

Paul regarded him suspiciously but made no comment. Unabashed by his friend's expression, Peter continued, but more seriously than before.

"You are lovesick, Paul," he stated baldly, "but methinks you are only just beginning to realise that the love you always thought you sickened after is not the one that is gnawing at you tonight. There is another woman on that pedestal now and deservedly so, for she has slowly gained possession of your heart by giving herself to you so unstintingly that you never noticed what was happening to you."

"Don't be stupid Peter," scoffed Paul, "Chloe herself would laugh to hear you speak so."

"Is that what you believe, Paul?" asked Peter in a soft voice. "Is it so hard for you to acknowledge that it is your dear wife who has become the love of your life?" he asked simply.

Abruptly changing the subject, Paul enquired about the arrangements for tomorrow and asked a great many questions about what he might expect, and more importantly, what was expected of him.

When they retired for the night, they were both completely sober, and Paul lay quietly thinking of what Peter had said, trying not to believe it. He had found himself in the same position once before, when Sardi had returned and his affection for the woman he even now thought of as his mother was placed in jeopardy by the conflicting emotions in his heart. Of course Dorothea was still the woman he loved more than any other, he reasoned. His dear Chloe held only a small part of his heart after all. Peter had mistaken his dislike of having to give a speech for a yearning for his wife. He smiled to himself in the dark: "Easily done," he told himself, but Chloe's face appeared before him, mouthing her final goodbye as he left in the chaise. He felt immensely heartened by the remembrance of her declaration. She was a most wonderful wife and she deserved a better husband, he reasoned guiltily. He adored his children and could not imagine his life without them, and then he realised he could not imagine his life without Chloe either. This thought gnawed away at his brain and it was long before he finally slept, knowing that it would be Dorothea's face confronting him in his dreams. That night Paul finally took his love in his arms and kissed her and sighed with relief, finding no fault in her hazel eyes and chestnut curls and that wonderful, irrepressible giggle that rippled from her throat. He awoke feeling such a lightness in his heart; he could not believe he was the same person that had plodded so dolefully to bed the previous evening.

At breakfast his companion was overjoyed to see Paul eating his normal large meal and, as he was more talkative and so much like his old self, Peter sighed inwardly. After they had eaten he took his old friend on a tour of Oxford. Paul was fascinated by the many old buildings and Peter had a busy time explaining their history.

However, it was only natural that Paul's nervousness returned when he was dressing himself for the evening. Peter, entering his room to see if he was ready, took responsibility for tying his cravat; such was the mess that Paul was making of his attempts.

"Calm down, Paul," he said reassuringly, "you have done this sort of thing time and time again. Why get into such a bother about it now?"

"I wish it was over and I was home again for I have come to detest these occasions. Sardi made me do so many of them and I felt so obliged to her that I could not refuse. I would watch her glowing with pride with every word I spoke, but for me it was agony. Forgive me Peter, but I should never have accepted this invitation for it will be a disaster I know. I shall forget my speech and they will make me look a fool. Damn! Where's my fob watch?"

and he turned away and started to go through his overnight bag in case it had been put away.

"Here it is Paul; on the table, where you left it," Peter told him softly. He studied his friend concernedly for a moment before continuing: "If you truly want to cancel this evening I can tell them you are indisposed," he said, trying to keep the disappointment out of his voice.

Paul took a deep breath, for he was being a fool and he knew it. Glancing at his friend he was aware of the concern in his eyes, so he laughed determinedly and, when Peter smiled back with relief, Paul told him that he was always a bundle of nerves before giving a speech.

"Take no notice of me. I shall settle down and start to act sensibly; my speech will take over and everything will be fine," he admitted with a brightness he was far from feeling. He looked at his watch and said abruptly and with decision: "I think we had best leave or else they will think I truly have turned tail and run back to Cornwall."

"Think of that sumptuous dinner that awaits you Paul," returned his friend with a grin of relief, "and after we will be staying with old Poulson himself. He is a crusty old duffer, much addicted to gambling. He married a young wife with a fortune so he could continue to fuel his passion so 'tis said. Perhaps we could have a turn on the town in some of the gaming houses?" he suggested, hopefully. Knowing full well that his friend detested card games he was not surprised as Paul shook his head, so he answered his own question by saying, "I thought not. Well, an early night and then back to Cornwall. Have you any fault to find with that?"

"No," replied Paul, "but why have we to stay with this chap Poulson? Can we not come back here instead? As far as I am concerned this establishment is perfectly adequate for my needs."

"My dear chap," said Peter, throwing his arm around Paul's shoulders and leading him out of the room, "they have almost come to fisticuffs, so keen are they to have the honour of putting you up for the night. It is part of the tradition around here to house the speaker in the house of the most influential personage. 'Tis an honour for them as well as you."

"Humph! What an honour to have me in their house," he said with mock pride and laughed out loud, and Peter, feeling more relieved with every passing moment, joined in and so in happy companionship they left for the University.

At first, on being introduced to so many academics Paul found himself overawed, but once he got into his speech he relaxed. The conspicuous lack of women made a considerable difference because there were no disconcerting sighs rippling towards him from the audience. As his subject he talked on Carthage, Scipio Africanus and Hannibal. He pointed out that, although history was viewed from the standpoint of the present day, it should be considered from a more geographical point of view in order to appreciate the complexities of it. After all, if Hannibal had not been defeated history would have been very different, because the inhabitants of Carthage were not European and therefore the possibility would have arisen that the balance of power could be situated, for a while at least, on the African continent. The questions that followed his speech were the toughest that he had ever dealt with. There were questions on his speech - did he think Scipio Africanus had a black skin? Probably not but Hannibal, employed by the Carthaginians- a North African people - might well have done. He was asked his opinion on 'The Noble Savage' and Voltaire's 'Ingénue' from his position as a coloured person, but he said any contribution that he made on that subject would be a disappointment, because he had been brought up in a white family with white values and it was only later in his life that he had given much thought to the problems of the coloured man's status in the white man's society. When he discovered that he had a talent that took no notice of the colour of his skin he had found it easy to progress through his life. 'His writings had made him a rich young man, whether he had a modicum of talent or no,' commented one embittered looking ancient, 'what future did he envisage for the rest of his life?'

Paul's brown eyes regarded the fulminating gentleman with some amusement.

"Well sir," he responded, "I think that Cicero had probably the best idea, when he declared *otium cum dignitate*."

There were shouts of laughter from the hall and a burst of applause; and even Paul's questioner allowed himself a grim smile.

After a speech of thanks for Mr. Trevarthen, the meeting was over and Paul found himself led off the stage and into a dining room with tables that groaned with appetising dishes. Peter noticed that his friend's smile was getting broader and perceptively relaxed. That Paul's performance had been a great success delighted him, not because he would have a share of the credit, but because he felt proud to have a friend with Paul's background who could impress such a gathering as this. However he made a mental vow never to ask him to do such a thing again, for he had seen what an effort it cost him. His friend deserved better than to have to answer questions on the colour of skin and not on his ability to translate Latin into such beautiful English, that he had made a flourishing career out of it.

They had little time to communicate because so many of the lecturers wanted to converse with Paul. Professor Poulson ambled across to Peter and asked him to introduce him to Paul for, as he stated, "If I am to be your host tonight 'tis only fair I should be acquainted with him before he crosses my threshold. Does he like gambling, by any chance?"

Peter shook his head, "Not a gambler sir."

"Oh well," sighed Poulson, "thought I could take him out for a rubber or two, but never mind."

When the introductions were made, Paul was not overly impressed with his host. His age was of no consequence as Paul did not seek the company of young men exclusively for companionship. Indeed Poulson was probably of an age with his father, but it was his manner that disturbed Paul. His host behaved rather in the fashion of someone who had won a prize and was intent on showing it to as many people as possible. Although not actually paraded about the room, young Mr. Trevarthen was left in no doubt that Poulson considered his position in the hierarchy of the stifled world of university life to be greatly elevated by the acquisition of the speaker as his overnight guest. What Poulson thought of his guest it was difficult to say. He was not overtly friendly for his cold manner did not allow him to be so. If anything he treated Paul more in the manner of an object than a living person. The thought that he would have to spend the night in this man's house appalled him but, as Peter had so wisely pointed out, the man would be playing cards for half the night in some gaming house and so they were unlikely to see much of him.

"It will be late by the time we leave here Paul, so we will not have to put up with his company for long. I expect his wife will have already retired by the time we arrive, so it looks as if we will be left to the mercy of the servants," whispered his companion in his ear. A smile that curled slowly over Paul's lips was the only acknowledgement that he made of his friend's remarks.

When the evening came to an end, Paul breathed a sigh of relief, knowing that soon he could turn his steps for home. He had no intention of making the journey last any longer than it had to and so had refused to countenance a suggestion from Peter that they head for London for "a couple of days recuperation" as that gentlemen had so quaintly put it. Peter jokingly told him he had turned into a dull old dog and Paul had laughingly agreed.

Poulson's residence was set a small step from the university grounds and, as their baggage had already been taken there, they had only to walk a short way with their host before arriving at his house. They were met at the door by a doleful looking butler whom his master ignored, passing him his hat and cloak automatically.

In the drawing room their host poured them all a brandy and proposed again that they should go with him for the evening. Paul politely declined and his friend was about to do the same, when Poulson pointed out to him that the house he would be attending belonged to Mr. Fleetwood's esteemed employer's cousin. Peter attempted to explain that he could not be so rude as to leave Paul on his own.

Poulson merely shrugged his shoulders and said pointedly that he would do his best to explain to his gambling host that, as Mr. Trevarthen was not a follower of games of chance, he could not very well take part, whereas Mr. Fleetwood, known to be partial to all such pursuits, had refused to accept their kind invitation. Peter, struggling with his conscience, desperately wanted to go, not to gamble so much as to ingratiate himself with the host. Starting in the diplomatic service with no connections whatsoever, he had soon realised that it would be necessary to do all he could to advance his position within the hierarchy that controlled his destiny. Paul, realising his predicament, smiled and asked permission to see Poulson's library for he had been told by one of his fellow dons that he had a most notable collection.

"Excellent idea, Trevarthen," the professor announced and taking Paul by the arm led him to a large room on the second floor and showed him into his well stocked library. Peter again attempted to protest that he should not desert his friend but only half heartedly, for Paul seemed quite content to study the shelves at his leisure and reasoned it would be far more sensible that his bookish companion should stay well away from gambling. Paul, if he should become at all partial to any activity, had an unnerving habit of enjoying his pursuits to the utmost. The thought of having to explain to Redvers that the fledging diplomat had succeeded in having his only son lose a fortune made him quake in his shoes, so he was quite prepared to accept the compromise that had been offered. He was not afraid to gamble himself but was wise enough to discontinue his game when he had lost enough money, so had no fear of finding himself in the position of explaining to his own father that the Colonel would have to sell his estates to pay off his debts. Within a short space of time Trevarthen found himself left alone and wandered admiringly along the shelves for, although he might find Poulson detestable, he had to admit that he did indeed own a most fine collection of books. Finding an excellent copy of Herodotus he carried it to a table and, sitting with his back to the door, began to read in delight. Lost in words, he did not hear the door open behind him and was unaware of the soft tread that walked so purposely towards the place where he sat. Only when she spoke his name did time pull him back at the sound of her beloved voice and he turned abruptly and looked into the grey eyes of his host's wife.

At first the shock of seeing her again made him immobile, but she seemed not to have changed at all for she was as beautiful as he remembered: her delicate complexion, her soft golden curls and her smiling, inviting mouth. In a moment he was on his feet with his beloved Dorothea in his arms and they kissed as passionately as if they had never been apart. His book forgotten, he followed her in a daze as she led him to his room and once there sense, caution, pride were all thrown away in the face of their unconsummated passion for each other. How they found themselves disrobed and in bed together he never knew, but to him it seemed the most natural act in the world for he had always such love for her and nothing in his life had been able to replace his heartbreak at losing her.

"My darling, dearest Paul. I have never loved another," she sighed and rained kisses down upon his face, covering his eyes, his cheeks, his lips, along with her tears. Suddenly her body was shaken by an uncontrollable sobbing and he found himself tortured into trying to comfort her, for with her tears he bethought himself of his wife and his heart contracted in pain as his love for Dorothea began to dissolve at the sight of his beloved Chloe's face.

"Please, Dorothea, please don't cry. You must not . . . you have to leave me for you know that this cannot be. We must . . . this is madness, Dorothea . . . I cannot . . ." but he got no further, for she kissed him again with such ferocity that he felt himself falling as if from a cliff. His heart and head told him he should cast her from him but his body responded to her passion. She was like a demon possessed, desiring only to consume him and Paul, helpless and hopeless in her arms lost all power and gave in to all those long, lonely nights of despair, when he had wanted so badly that which was now being given to him with such ardour. He closed his eyes upon the ghost of his past in her arms but the pleasure he received was merely physical. It was tainted by the picture of his wife's distraught face, which he was desperately trying to block from his mind. To him the lovemaking that they had just tasted was the bitterest of bitter fruit, but to Dorothea it was nectar. A taste of life itself for a woman so deprived of love that this small act was more than she had imagined would ever be hers. She continued to caress his body, all the time telling him how much she loved and adored him; how she always knew that one day she would possess him. Paul closed his eyes upon his tears and his ears to her trembling voice. He pushed her from him and looked at her in the gentle dawn light that was filtering into the room.

"It cannot be, Dorothea. This night should never have happened and it has to end now for both our sakes. Our families would not countenance it then and will not do so now, Dorothea. It has to end now. We have no choice. Do you understand me?" he told her in a hoarse whisper, with a strange dawning realisation that even if it could continue he did not want it to. The pedestal was cracked and the golden goddess fallen.

"I know it has to end my dearest, dearest darling, but I wanted one chance to have you as my husband for this one night. When I knew you were to attend the university I determined to get you to my home. So I took my chance, knowing that you wanted me as badly as I wanted you and suggested to my husband that if he could arrange to house you tonight he would be the envy of his fellows. He is a vain, proud man and a fool who has no more love for me than he would for a dog in the gutter. This marriage got me away from the father I had grown to hate and I accepted a husband who required only my money. If he desires my body it is only because he has lost badly at cards. I am rarely disturbed Paul," she murmured provocatively, and laughed, rather coarsely he thought; so unlike his image of an untainted goddess. She kissed him again and laid her head upon his chest, sighing with pleasure. "We have had a moment of deserved passion Paul, to compensate us for all those nights of longing," she whispered seductively, "I would it were more but it must content us our life long, for we shall never have the chance again, my dearest. I know that we have committed an adulterous act but I do not care, for surely we deserved to consummate the love that we have felt for each other all these years."

Paul sighed in despair, "Dorothea, Dorothea." She took it for contentment and kissed him again, calling him her heart's desire and showering him with endearments and kisses. But eventually, as the clock on the table gently tolled the hour of six, she slowly removed her arms from around his body and removed herself from his bed. She leaned over and, clasping his face between her hands, kissed him on the lips as she had done all those years ago at Trevu. He shuddered at the remembrance, feeling a loathing within him. Dorothea, blinded to his revulsion, thrilled with the feel of his trembling body and felt vindicated with the knowledge that he loved her still and slowly, regretfully, left the room.

Alone at last, her despairing lover watched the grey light begin to fill the room and let his hot tears fall disregarded down his face. He felt no more love for her than he did for all those woman he bedded with such coldness before his marriage. He could not believe it to be so but it was. The woman he loved now had won him and he wanted to be her prize alone. He felt consumed with shame at what he had done. Chloe must never know of this night, for if he admitted to her what had taken place he would surely break her heart and he could not bear to have that on his conscience. He turned his face into the pillow and gave in to the despair that racked him.

The next morning Paul sat at the breakfast table, the only member of the household in the room, and stared at his plate of food. The events of the night were still tearing at his heart, for even now he could not believe he could have sinned so completely against his dearest wife. Meeting Dorothea again had been the pinnacle of his dream, but now his desire for her lay trampled in the dust, mingled with the disgust of his own actions and the despair of realising that she was not the love of his life, that for so many years, he had passionately thought her to be. As the door opened he looked up guiltily and saw his friend enter, giving him a direct look that made his face darken in embarrassment the more. Nothing was said for a while as Peter busied himself with getting his food but, as he took his seat opposite his friend, he lifted his eyes to Paul's face and began to speak:

"Poulson and I had a most entertaining evening and arrived home in a most convivial mood. Our host considered that he required more brandy and took himself off to the drawing room, but I have not his head for the stuff and, politely declining his invitation, made my way to my own room," he informed him, watching Paul's face all the while. "You can imagine my surprise when, on reaching it, I heard your door open and, expecting my dear friend to come to see me on my return, waited patiently with my own door open whilst I searched for the taper to light my candle with." His friend was no longer looking at him, but sat dumbfounded with a bowed head so Peter concluded, "I was given the sight of our host's wife, barely robed, walking along the corridor as if she had not a care in the world. Strange was it not that she should be abroad at such an hour and clothed in such a fashion, for I had no idea that the lady was a sleepwalker." He thought that his companion would have nothing to say, but quietly Paul admitted that Mrs. Poulson had indeed spent the night in his bed, but gave no further explanation. They finished their breakfast in an awkward silence, until Peter coughed discreetly and then asked Paul sternly if he was ready to leave. "We can pick up our chaise at the Standard and travel on from there. I can imagine that you have no further reason to stay here."

They rose from the table and, picking up their bags, walked purposefully across the hallway, stopping by the door so that Peter could speak to the butler. He asked for some writing paper and, on being shown to a desk, wrote a short note of thanks for his host's hospitality and an apology for having to leave so soon without thanking his host in person, but he was sure he would understand they had a long way to travel that day and wished to make an early start. He signed his name and gave the note to Paul to read, who ran his eyes down the single sheet, nodded and passed it back. Peter sealed it with a wafer, addressed it to his host and passed it to the butler to be delivered. The butler bowed them out of the house and they walked down the steps that led to the road. Paul never turned his head to look back at the house, but Peter did and saw an upstairs curtain fall back into place. Arriving back at the Standard, Peter arranged for the post chaise to be ready to leave within the hour and, ordering some coffee, took Paul into the private room he had hired for their use. They sat on either side of the small fire that burned in the grate. The coffee arrived and Peter got up, poured two cups and passed one to his uncommunicative friend before resuming his seat.

"Well, would you like to talk about what has so obviously happened or shall we sit here in silence?" asked Peter, regarding Paul with barely controlled anger. He watched as his friend's face flooded with shame, but after a while he looked up and began to recount the events of the night that had led him to the position of an adulterous husband, that he now found himself to be occupying. His explanation; that their host's wife should have turned out to be the woman he had been in love with for most of his adult life made Peter snort in disgust and he commented bitterly that Paul had merely to send her away.

"Yes, I could have. I tried to but I . . . I gave in to her," admitted his shamefaced companion.

"Forgive me for not laughing," snorted Peter, "the great seducer seduced. What irony! What happens now? Secret trysts at discreet locations across the country? Or will you be setting up an establishment for her nearer to your home?" He looked scornfully at Paul, a slight sneer curling his lips.

"We will not meet again. Dorothea said she wanted one night after all the years of waiting and, for my part; I do not want ever to see her again. She is no longer the goddess that I have revered all these years, so the dream has finally ended," murmured Paul, and then he added in a resigned voice: "for me at least."

"Will you tell Chloe?" Peter asked in a more conciliatory tone.

Paul sighed guiltily. "She must not know how I have shamed her with my actions last night, for I do not think that I could endure for her to find out. I will have to live with the guilt and shame of it until my dying day." Glancing at his companion's angry countenance he pleaded softly: "Don't sit in judgement on me Peter. It was not my desire for her; it was pity, not love that may well have ruined my marriage last night." He took another sip of his coffee and Peter could find no words to say. Thinking Paul a fool for risking his marriage, he now thought that his friend had brought a tremendous suffering upon himself, for loving a dream so much that the reality of that passion had turned into a nightmare for him. Now the future beckoned and Paul would have to make the best of it if he wanted to keep that which he held most dear. They sat in silence drinking their coffee and, regarding his companion out of the corner of his eye, Peter found himself wondering what disaster would come of last night's coupling.

"I shall say nothing Paul, but what of you? That face of yours tells the world what you are thinking unless you make a great effort. Can you go through life hiding your guilt? I doubt it," he remarked and then, feeling angry with himself and Paul at the same time, cried fiercely: "You fool! You could have shown some restraint for God's sake."

"Damn you Peter, I know! You cannot torture me anymore than I am torturing myself. Don't you think I am not suffering for what I have done or, worse than that, will not have to suffer in the future," returned Paul, just as angrily. "I have no right to expect that Chloe will ever forgive me. I have lost everything for a moment's pleasure that was no pleasure at all. Now I have to go home and deceive my wife. I have never taken another woman since I married Chloe, never looked at another woman, never wanted another woman except for Dorothea. Ironic is it not Peter? I have bedded the love of my life and have awoken to the cold light of day to find she was not my dearest love after all," he cried. He shook his head, and closed his eyes as if to dispel the thoughts and images from his mind, but they would not go. When Paul got back to Cornwall he would have to face his family and pick up the threads of the marriage that he had shattered.

Their thoughts were interrupted by a knock at the door and the landlord's head appeared to say that the post chaise was ready for them. They left the room and after climbing into the chaise, the horses slowly pulled them out of the fateful city. They spoke little on the journey, Paul had become lost in his thoughts and answered Peter's questions with monosyllabic replies. When they arrived in London, Peter persuaded Paul to stop for refreshment and talked long and hard over the meal, trying to dispel the gloom that settled over his companion. If only he had known what was to happen he would never have embroiled his friend in the invitation to Oxford. He took on himself some of the poor man's guilt, knowing full well that it was his persuasive argument and Paul's wanting to help his friend that had made him alter his position and accept the fateful invitation. When they parted they shook hands and wished each other well for the future. Paul was going home, to his wife and family, and Peter was to start a new career in another country amongst a group of people he had mostly never met before - a challenge indeed, but Paul it was who needed the luck.

On his homeward journey young Mr. Trevarthen did not harry the driver into springing his horses. Indeed he seemed in no hurry to arrive at his destination. He spent long hours alone over meals that he barely consumed, drank little ale, ignored all company, tossed and turned in strange beds and always in his head was the image of Chloe's face, smiling. He shuddered to think of it. When he had left her at the start of his journey he could hardly bear to leave her, so great a pain it caused him. In his folly he thought it was the desire for the comfortable family life that she had given him. Now he knew full well that it was the love he felt for her that had caused his heart to feel so heavy all the way to Oxford. His heart felt heavier now, when it should have been so lightened with joy that he would have been unable to contain himself.

Slowly the chaise made its inexorable way to Trevu; taking him home, drawing him tighter into the net of his own construction and to the destruction of all he held most dear.

CHAPTER 22

IN the early evening Chloe heard the arrival of the chaise and Davy's voice raised in greeting. There was a low murmur from her husband in reply. By the time he had entered the dark hallway, Chloe had rushed from the back parlour and was upon him, throwing herself into his arms. She felt his body tense in her embrace and knew without asking that something had befallen her husband that he should respond so to her greeting. There was an infinitesimal silence, then his wife, summoning up her courage and all her pride, began to tell him about the children; the new words that George could say, how Redvers and Sardi were staying with the Trebilcock's at Bolijy for a couple of days, as their son had gotten leave from the navy and, on his arrival, they had hurriedly thrown a party in his honour and invited all their friends. Chloe laughed to say that she had never seen Mrs. Trebilcock so excited and continued: "but to be sure I should be the same if dear George decides to take to the sea for a career when he is of age, an' if I should be without him for half the time Richard has been away I am sure that I should burst to see him again." She prattled on, trying not to sound nervous, telling him brightly that his bath had been prepared to ease away the aches of the journey and took his hand and led him up the stairs towards their room. She called over her shoulder to Lizzie to bring more hot water to Mr. Trevarthen's dressing room and to get Daniel to help her if the pails were too heavy.

When the door of their room closed behind them, she turned to Paul and waited. He shifted uncomfortably and could not look at her or bring himself to say anything. A chill hand gripped at her heart, but she had suffered that before and surmounted the rising panic within her to say: "If you are tired Paul, retire after your bath. We can . . . we can talk tomorrow if you wish to do so." He nodded dumbly and withdrew to his dressing room.

So Paul bathed and washed away the grime of road and the aches of the journey, but his sin lay over him like a skin of shame and he could not wash that away. He dried himself before the fire and then returned to his room and climbed into the bed. Feeling no pleasure in its accustomed warmth; he eased himself down under the covers and turned his face away into the pillow. Later that night Chloe returned and he felt her warmth beside him as she got in the bed. Like a child he wanted to turn to her and hold her and pour out all the troubles that he had accumulated for himself since leaving his home, but he lay still, wrapped in his steel coat of disgrace. He felt a small hand travel down his arm until it reached his own and he clasped it tightly.

Her voice said softly, "All will be well, Paul. You are come safe home, now."

Her tormented husband let out a hard laugh that broke on a sob and cried out in a anguished voice, "No Chloe, I am home but no longer safe for I have imperilled all," and he turned to her and pulled her to him and pleaded for her forgiveness; his resolution not to tell her of his crime blown away like chaff in the wind. For such an enormous sin it took very little time for Paul to tell her what had happened. Only once did he hear her draw in her breath and sigh with sadness, for from the beginning of his confession she lay compliantly within his hold and never made an attempt to turn him from her.

He continued to lash himself with his shame until finally she placed her hand upon his mouth and hushed him.

"Sleep now, Paul. The clock will not go backwards no matter how much you torture yourself. Sleep, dearest and close your eyes and mind to your troubles. Tomorrow, we will talk again if you wish," she told him quietly, and she took her hand from his mouth and kissed him gently on his lips.

"I don't deserve you Chloe and I never did. I will . . . understand if you cannot bring yourself to continue as my . . . as my wife for I have disgraced myself and made myself unforgiv...," but she stopped his tumbling words by kissing him again and then said: "Sleep now, you silly boy. Let all rest quiet 'til tomorrow."

He felt his body relaxing in her arms as the sleep that had evaded him for so many nights overwhelmed him, he fell, unresisting, into a slumber that held him close and secure the whole night through.

When he awoke, he found his beloved wife looking at him with a soft smile playing on her lips. Paul stared at her, baffled by her calmness. Such a wave of love for her welled up within him that he wanted to cover her face with kisses and call her by all his pet names for her, but his shame held him back from putting his wishes into action. He watched in contrition and amazement as a soft, understanding smile lit up her adored face.

"Can you ever forgive me, dearest Chloe?" he whispered. Then, tentatively, he held her in his arms, and hiding his head in her hair, he pleaded again for her forgiveness.

He heard her firm, stern voice, the one she kept for George when he was being particularly naughty, say: "If you ever, ever take a woman who is not your wife to bed again, I will take the children and leave you without a moment's care. Do you understand me, Paul?"

For answer he nodded his head and she heard him mumble, "Yes Chloe." He sighed and continued hopefully, "but it was not all my fault, Ch . . ." but he got no further.

"I will listen to no excuses, Paul! Suffice it say you fell for your dream, but that is all in your past now. She wanted one thing from you under the delusion that you still loved her. If you could have been honest with the poor woman, you would not be lying here now so full of remorse. You gave in to temptation, not she! She wanted comfort from the man she loved. I know full well what that feels like Paul, for I have often wanted the same for myself. Dorothea it is that has my sympathy Paul, not you," she told him and turned her face towards him, her dancing eyes at variance with her stern voice, "but for this once and, mark me well Paul, only this once I will forgive you."

"My dearest, most adored Chloe," he said, "forgive me not only my indiscretion, but also my years of blindness, that I could not see that what I held was a gift that far excelled anything that I ever dreamed of and is more than I ever deserved." He watched her smile into his face but laughed with glee as she said archly, "Humph! Flatterer." Unbelieving that the torture of the shameful despair he had felt should be disappearing like fog burnt off the land by the sun's heat, he pulled her to him and, telling her of his love for her and only her, they fell into a passionate embrace that bore no resemblance to the disaster that had befallen him the last time he had held another in his arms.

Redvers and Sardi returned the following day, delighted to be reunited with Paul. Sardi had her son's ability to be unaware of subtle differences in people, and saw only Paul's smiling face. Redvers knew immediately that something had happened for his son was more than attentive to Chloe, but now and again there was a certain nervousness about him. He considered if he should ask Paul what was troubling him, but knowing his son of old thought the better of it. There was no one tighter or more prickly than Paul if you picked at him for an explanation that he was not prepared to give. Chloe showed her smiling, happy face to the world and gave him confidence, so he was prepared to accept that all was well. Hannah it was that mentioned innocently to Captain Trevarthen that: "young Mr. Paul had come home with his tail between his legs but that, is little wife soon 'ad 'n sorted. Bin good as gold ever since. Whatever 'e got up to when he was on 'is travels we 'aven't 'eard but she got 'en towing the line now and no mistake," and nodding wisely she left Redvers to enjoy his cup of tea in the naive belief that her words had been of comfort to him.

Upon occasion Paul was aware that his father appeared to be staring at him, but as always his face was impassive and Paul had no wish to jeopardise his new found happiness by letting his tongue run away with him, so nothing was mentioned between them. He had little to say about Oxford other than that the speech had gone well and that he had not enjoyed himself and could not wait to get home. His mother informed him somewhat severely that he was wasting his talent and he scowled at her. Redvers told her that she would have to abide with the knowledge that her son would not bestir himself in society if he could help it.

Slowly they settled back into their old routines; Redvers occupied himself with the farm and the mines, Sardi and Chloe with the children and the planning and organising of the school and Paul, when he was not stealing quiet moments with Chloe, and rather riotous and loud ones with his children, spent his time translating various accounts of the campaigns of Fabius Maximus Quintus for a work he was putting together on the subject of the Second Punic War. Although not of a military persuasion he found the whole subject of war, and particularly the Punic Wars, fascinating. He wrote his letters to his various friends, including Mr. Armitage, now a father in his own right, and asked his advice on an author he was trying to track down. His last letter was to Peter, who had just taken up his diplomatic post in Athens, reassuring him that all was well. Chloe knew all and had forgiven him and his marriage was more now than had ever been before. Paul had been granted the forgiveness of his wife and desired fervently to forget that dreadful night. There were no more dreams; his ghost had been laid for good and he desired only to spend his nights in the arms of his precious love, blissfully oblivious of any other woman.

Sitting at his desk a month after his return from Oxford, there was a gentle tap at the door; his father stepped into the room and crossed to his son's desk. He smiled at Paul and, glancing at the papers, asked him what great work he had taken on his shoulders now. Paul told him and Redvers replied knowingly: "Oh. The Delayer, have I that correct?"

His son was most impressed and said: "Quite right, sir. You surprise me with your knowledge. I thought not that you knew of him."

"Paul, Paul!" Redvers said teasingly, "I had an education too, you know. I may not have applied myself as well as you but surprisingly some of it stuck."

Paul grinned, "Your pardon, sir. However, I doubt that you came here to talk of long dead Roman soldiers. Is there something you wish to ask me?"

"Much," said his father and smiled grimly, "but I will not, for well I know that I will get no reply to my questions." His son looked instantly discomforted but tried to hide it under a faltering smile.

"Perhaps you will confide in me one day Paul, but in the meantime I thought you might like to see this," and withdrawing from his pocket an edition of the local gazetteer, he unfolded it and passed it to Paul, pointing to a passage half way down the page. It was an account of the famous local author, Mr. Paul Trevarthen, who had given a speech at the prestigious Oxford University. It gave details of the subject of the speech, the lavish dinner that was given in his honour and the fact that he was lodged in the house of the famous professor of mathematics, Professor Arthur Denby Poulson and his wife. The correspondent was at pains to point out that Professor Poulson was an especial friend of his and that he and his wife, the well known heiress Mrs. Dorothea Poulson, were most impressed with the charm and manners of their young guest and his friend, a Mr. Peter Fleetwood, now a secretary to the British Ambassador to Greece. It went on to list Paul's published works and the fact that he had been an old boy at Helston School, where a scholarship had been set up in his name.

Paul's hand was shaking as he put the paper down on the desk. There was an awkward silence until Redvers coughed and asked if he would like to say anything.

He shook his head but then said cautiously: "Has anyone else seen this?"

"Half of Penzance probably, but it would only interest the ones that can read. Let us hope for your sake that they can only read the words and not between the lines," said Redvers and, pushing some papers to one side, sat himself nonchalantly on the desk and regarded his son's face. All he noted was his son's shamed expression, then Paul quickly turned away.

"Now what was it Hannah said of you again?" Redvers mused, "Oh yes. I have it now. That you had returned from Oxford 'with your tail between your legs' as she had so quaintly put it. Strange that you should feel so despondent when this paper gives such a glowing account of your speech and the wonderful dinner that you both attended afterwards. Oh yes, and the correspondent's especial friend, Professor Poulson and his renowned wife, um . . . now what was her name?"

His son, discovered, sprang to his feet and, snatching up the paper ripped it into pieces. He turned from the desk and crossed to the window, observing the garden with a sightless gaze. He knew he had been a weak and foolish man but he would have to lift up his head now. If his father did not know what had happened precisely he was clever enough to make an educated guess. He whirled about to look his father in the eyes and said boldly: "We shared a bed but her husband knew nothing of it. I did not want to but I succumbed, I succumbed not to love, I knew that before even the act took place, but to pity and temptation," and proceeded to explain the events of the night to his impassive father. He sighed, "When I got home it did not take long for me, in spite of all my fears, to confess all. You see what a wonderful wife I have Father? Chloe made me face up to my wretchedness and despair, forgave me my sin and has never mentioned it since."

A soft, reminiscent smile slowly descended upon Redvers lips. "I of all men should understand that Paul, for I too had such a wife. Methinks at one stage you may have thought yourself cursed, as I admit I did, but when the light dawned into the darkness of my life I knew then what it was to be blessed."

Paul smiled a grim smile. "Will you tell mother?" he asked quietly.

"No," replied Redvers simply.

"What about Hannah?"

"Hannah knows you had something to hide when you returned, but she also knows that Chloe has sorted you out to her own satisfaction and that is good enough for her. As long as Chloe remains untroubled by you, Hannah will remain happy."

Paul gave a short snort of laughter and shook his head "It is over, father, my lost love is lost no longer, but she is no longer my love and cannot touch me now. Never again will Chloe have to fear another woman, for I have come too close to losing all to want ever again to find myself in such distress," he told him. He stooped and, picking up the pieces of discarded paper, placed them upon the fire. They flamed into life and then shrank and crumpled before they died. He thought he saw Dorothea's face in the flames but dispelled it, imagining it most fanciful of himself to think in that way.

Redvers got up from the desk and, looking into his eyes, said solemnly: "I have nothing more to say Paul. I'll leave you to your work, after all 'The Delayer' should not be kept waiting."

Paul smiled at his father's joke and they parted, each understanding the other more than at any other time in their lives.

A farmhouse had been allowed to fall into disrepair because two farms had been combined and the property was not needed, consequently, it was considered most suitable for conversion into a school. Although part of the Trevu estate, it was set a mile away from the main house and there was a good road for access. It was nearer to the village than it was to Trevu and had an ample yard, with substantial buildings that could be adapted into school and craft rooms. A small river ran near by and the house had its own spring fed well, so all in all it was considered a more than suitable site. At Lady Day Redvers and his tenant farmer signed an agreement, with effect that the rent should be cut for the tenant's farm and that the unused farmhouse, its outbuildings, and three acres of land surrounding it, the river rights and the access road should no longer be part of the farm. Captain Trevarthen resolved to accept no money from the funds and so signed over ownership to the School Trust; soon a veritable army of craftsman and workers were employed in renovating the house and outbuildings. The land was fenced off but nothing else was done to it, as it was considered best to leave the land empty until the school was running, and then it could be decided to what use it could be best put.

In the following February the school's instigator gave birth to her second son. An event that brought much joy to the Trevu household, and particularly to her husband.

The school committee expressed a desire to name the school after young Mrs. Trevarthen, but she politely declined the honour and instead suggested that they name it after the original farm; Treropy School was so named. By the September the school was now almost completed and the committee met to decide on enrolment of pupils and the final plans for the official opening day. They had appointed all the teachers and trainers that they would need, mostly local people so that the children would not find themselves amongst strangers. If Mrs. Pascoe taught them how to cook and Mr. Hendra showed them how to use a lathe so much the better. There had been a fair amount of disagreement about teaching the boys as well as the girls all the basic crafts, but as Mr. Murdoch, the tailor, pointed out tailors were men and if a young girl should show a natural aptitude for carpentry so much the better, for why should she be denied? Sardi was his ally immediately and she pointed out that accomplished young woman would be an asset to the community and the wider environs. Some of the matrons looked aghast at such a suggestion, but Squire Tregurthen considered this point for a moment and said in his booming voice: "Well said ma'am, well said. Quite a feather in our cap if our local youngsters are turned out to be more accomplished than the young men and women from other towns in this area. Methinks it will be thought to our credit."

The force of his argument was not lost on most of the people sitting at the table; and so it was agreed that the education was to be given to all and the children themselves could decide what they would prefer to study, after they had had some basic training. Pupils showing exceptional aptitude would be encouraged to study that particular subject if their parents so wished.

When the meeting drew to a close, it was decided that the school would open just after Michaelmas on the third day of October in the year 1809, and they happily left the meeting feeling that they had accomplished a great deal.

There was intense excitement on the school opening day, with lots of excited and nervous children, and an abundance of parents all wishing to be shown over the school. By the end of the first term it was considered that the school had become a great success and they were now having to turn pupils away because they had no room left.

Squire Tregurthen proposed a party to celebrate the opening of the school and the date of the second of January, 1810, was chosen because it would fit in with the beginning of the new term a week later. However, a month before the party Redvers sought out Paul, for he had heard news of an impending disaster that directly concerned his son. As usual he had not far to look, for Paul was sitting in his room surrounded by a pile of books and papers, looking calm and composed. But one look at his father's face dispelled all of that.

CHAPTER 23

"WHAT'S the matter sir? You do not look as if . . ." Paul started to say but his father cut him short.

"Paul! It is a most serious matter, Paul! I have had reports that Jeremiah Petherick has been seen in the area. Apparently he was drinking in the Ship at Marazion and had much to say of you and none of it to your credit. He made many threats to your person as well," he told him. "I stopped at the Squire's on the way home from Penzance. There's a company of dragoons sent down to Camborne at the moment to help keep the peace between the tinners and townsfolk, so he has written to their commanding officer and asked for a troop to be sent on to Penzance."

"Surely we do not need to go to all this trouble, father? The man was almost certainly drunk. He has probably come for a visit to . . . old friends or relatives or some such thing and . . ." but Redvers interrupted him again:

"Paul! This is most serious for God's sake. He is talking of killing you!" he shouted in exasperation.

Paul fell silent, and his father began to pace about the room, all the while explaining to his son that they would have to have a body of troops at the house and some stationed in Penzance. Mr. Ledbourne, the Custom Officer, was to be asked if he could supply one of his men to follow Petherick so that his whereabouts could be tracked.

"We will have to tell the woman, of course, and the household staff. There will be much talk but we must do our best to quell the rumours," he said worriedly.

"What did you tell the Squire?" asked Paul quietly.

"Well, not the truth, that's for sure!" snapped Redvers at him. He saw Paul flinch and then, realising that he could not continue so, sat himself on Paul's table, and put his hand on Paul's shoulder and informed him quietly: "I do not know how to tell you this Paul, for it is the saddest of news: Dorothea has died," he said gently. He heard a sharp intake of breath from his son. He waited a moment and then continued quietly: "Apparently she had been ill for quite a while. Perhaps her father, in his grief, blames you because she was never happy, never had a good marriage. I don't know all the details, but from the tales that have come back to me of what he has been saying he is determined to have you out of this world as surely as she has left it."

On the news of her death, Paul closed his eyes and sighed deeply, but he said not a word. After a moment he slowly got to his feet and said quietly, "I will go to Chloe and tell her. Will you tell, mother?"

"Yes, yes, of course," replied Redvers, "Not all of the tale but enough to make her realise the seriousness of it. I shall tell her only that because of the death of his daughter his sadness has refuelled his hatred for you"

They were both quiet for a moment and then left the room on their respective errands to their wives. Chloe blanched when Paul told her the news, but said only: "That poor, poor woman. I can even feel sympathy for her father in a strange way."

"So can I, Chloe," sighed Paul, "for he loved her deeply, as much as father loves me. He chose a life that made it impossible for him, and father as well, to countenance our marriage. Dorothea and I were young and blind to their view. She did not care about my colour any more than I cared about his past. We cared only for each other. I have often thought it most ironic that, of all the fellows she had chasing after her, she should have picked the one that her father would in no way be able to tolerate. It was a damnable mess for all of us, Chloe, and as you well know it blighted her life and, if it were not for you, it would have blighted mine." He covered his eyes with his hand and let out another loud sigh. Chloe took his other hand in her own and cradled it against her cheek. She had put all that tragic history in the past and now this new disaster had risen up to confront and chill her very soul.

Redvers, ever practical, told his family that there was no need to worry that Petherick should accost them in their home, because two of the farm hands had volunteered to take turn and turn about to guard the house. Paul nodded dumbly at his words, but he could not dispel the deep sense of foreboding that had settled over him since the morning.

Later that evening Squire Tregurthen and a military gentleman were shown into the withdrawing room. Redvers and Paul rose to their feet as the two men bowed to the ladies, before turning to them and shaking hands first with the father and then the son. Squire Tregurthen introduced Sergeant Blamey to them and told them he had been sent down from Camborne especially to form a guard for the Trevarthen household.

"Blamey has two men outside and they will take turns to guard the property, and the people inside it of course. I noticed you have set up some of your men as guards yourself. Damn good idea! Can't have too many precautions in a situation like this. Ledbourn's man has picked the blaggard up already. Staying in a farm cottage at St. Hilary apparently, so well away from you at the moment," the Squire informed them.

"If you have established his whereabouts would it not be possible to arrest him?" queried Redvers.

Squire Tregurthen sighed heavily, "Would love to Redvers, but what excuse have I? Apart from making a few drunken threats he has done nothing that I can arrest him for. We will watch him now 'tho. If he puts a foot the wrong side of the law we'll have him boxed up, right and tight, you can be sure of that. Ledbourn's man will keep him in his sights, never fear. He's been responsible for a lot of transportations and hangings from amongst the smuggling fraternity in the north of the county, so has been sent to this locality in order to watch or even to infiltrate the Bolitho gang. Ledbourn says that this fellow is his best man. So you can rest assured he'll not let you down. They pay him well for his secret work, for if ever he was discovered he would not live out the day once the smugglers got him. Down a shaft or over a cliff in the wink of an eye. They have too much tied up in their trade to allow any of his like to get away, don't you know?"

Squire Tregurthen exuded such confidence that they all felt much more reassured, especially Paul, who feared not for himself but for his family. Petherick would want to destroy Paul and probably all his line, for he had lost his beloved daughter, leaving him alone in a joyless world. Now with the Squire's robust assurances he had less to worry about. Petherick would be well and truly fenced about and would have no opportunity to do more than

Broken Bonds: The First Book Of The Trevu Trilogy

he had done already by issuing drunken threats. After the Squire had left, Redvers led the Sergeant off to find him some quarters for himself and his men. Blamey assured him that they could quite well sleep in the stables with the horses but Redvers was adamant that suitable accommodation should be found for them. Life settled down although it was irksome to be always under the protection of the soldiers. Happily for all of them, a week before Christmas a report came from Ledbourn that Captain Petherick had taken the morning stage from Penzance. His departure had been followed all the way to Southampton by a succession of agents and it had been assumed that he had given up hope of catching Paul unawares, having thought better of putting his threats into action he had gone home. The information was delivered by a beaming Blamey who had come back from Penzance that evening full of the good news. They all breathed a sigh of relief, but Squire Tregurthen had suggested that the military should not be moved until at least a month had passed. Sardi thought that this was too extreme, but Redvers overruled her.

"We can put up with their presence for just a while longer, dearest. If it means that we can all sleep safe in our beds over the festive season then I think it will all be worthwhile," he told her coaxingly, but with a recognisable firmness that she understood well enough to know that her husband would not be moved from his position.

"Very well, Redvers," she acquiesced, "it shall be as you wish," and reaching out, clasped her husband's face in her hands and kissed him tenderly. For answer he embraced her passionately and returned her kiss with fervour.

"La sir!," she said with a wicked look, "That impassive face of yours has a certain look on it tonight."

"And why not madam?" he replied with a grin, "The old dog enjoys his pleasures still."

"Humph!" she giggled, "Old dog indeed!"

Probably because of the relief they all felt, Christmas was special that year. Their party was considered the best ever, it even surpassed the birth of George four years previously. Paul was coaxed into dancing with a succession of females, from the not so sprightly to those who had only just learnt the steps. When he danced with Chloe people in the room cheered and laughed, giving them a round of applause and making poor Chloe blush rosily, whilst Paul's face was covered with his beaming grin, such was his delight. At the end of the evening they sang their customary carols and Gabriel Hendra lifted his fine tenor, singing 'The Holly and the Ivy' so beautifully that many a handkerchief was dabbed at eyes awash with tears, so touched were they at such a beautiful sound.

On the night of the ball as they prepared to leave, Sergeant Blamey took up his position to the front of the carriage and one dragoon was stationed to bring up the rear, the third having been left at the house. This was their normal practice for they thought it best that the house should be guarded at all times, the military gentleman had placed very little faith in Redvers men to be able to carry out their duties with the discipline that had been instilled into the professional soldier. The ladies were handed into the carriage by their men folk who then climbed in themselves and, after some noise and confusion, mainly caused by Sergeant Blamey shouting so loudly, that the carriage horses took exception to the noise and reared up in the traces, they left for the Squire's house.

As the Trevarthen carriage made its way from Trevu, in a small inn close to the harbour in Penzance, a placid looking gentleman who went by the name of Sam Jenkins was sipping a pint of ale. When he saw a face he recognised he made nothing of it, but did not linger over his drink and declined another. He left the hostelry nonchalantly and made his way slowly down the hill to where the road forked. Unable to stop smiling to himself, he thought 'Two birds with one stone. Quite a prize!' for well he knew that the smuggler's run was planned for that very night, when so many people would be at the Squire's party. Spotting Joey Bolitho, the ringleader walking and talking abroad without a care in that little inn would net a fine return. It had taken him a long time to piece together what was to happen that night, but at last he had all the information needed to catch Cornwall's most wanted smuggler and to end his game, and life as well probably, forever.

Waiting to tell Captain Ledbourn all the details he had discovered was by far the best scheme, for Bolitho was a most wily fox who could change his plans at a moment's notice, but Jenkins patiently accumulated all the facts and was now able to present them to his employer. The French cutter was coming in off Winnerd's Cove an hour after midnight, to be met by Seth Mankee's fishing smack. The illicit goods would be transferred in the shelter of the bay and brought ashore where a consignment of packhorses would have been assembled. From there they were to be taken to Bolitho's favourite store, a disused mine shaft known as Wheal Susannah. It would take very little work to apprehend them either on the beach or on the coastal path, and if Ledbourn could inform the navy in time, the French cutter could be taken as well. Jenkins could not forego a smile at the thought of all he had accomplished, for he knew that no other agent had been able to accumulate such detailed information as himself. Hours of patient observation and listening had finally presented him with the prize that he so justly deserved and, as for the man from Southampton who had returned so unexpectedly, well that was an unlooked for gift. Not suspecting that anyone had noted his reappearance, the gentleman sipped his ale in the inn that night, seemingly without a care in the world. Whistling tunelessly to himself, Jenkins made his way to Ledbourn's little house, thinking of what he could spend the forthcoming largesse on that he was assured of receiving.

How well a new coat would become the soon to be famous Mr. Samuel Jenkins, or perhaps a fine pair of new shoes? His whistle and his thoughts stopped simultaneously as his skull was cracked open as the result of the vicious blow struck at him from behind. His body collapsed in a heap and, still warm, it was picked up and nonchalantly thrown across the back of a pack pony.

"Where to Joey?" hissed a voice in the dark.

The murderer fitted the bloodstained iron bar down the back of poor Sam's coat, tied the hands and feet under the unresisting beast's belly, and then straightened up, wiping his bloodied hands on his luckless victim's rump.

"Don't care Likky," he said softy, "plenty of old shafts roun' these parts. As long as it's deep we 'em got no worries. Be back in yer place by eleven mind."

"Right you are, Joey," said Likky and turning the pony walked off into the dark, the muffled hooves making barely a sound.

Joseph Bolitho allowed himself a smile in the dark and set off in the opposite direction, whistling the curtailed tune far more melodiously than the unfortunate Sam had done. He was well aware that he had taken a gamble in waiting so long to dispose of this particular agent, but he had watched him most carefully and knew full well that he had not informed Ledbourn of the details of that night's run, for the customs officer's mistress most obligingly kept Joseph Bolitho supplied with all the information that she had so expertly gleaned from the poor fool during their hours of bliss together. As soon as the ignorant Ledbourn had left her bed to stumble drunkenly towards his home, a sober individual with cold blue eyes would take his place and, for this gentleman's largesse as well as the delight of having him in her bed ,'Salty Mary' would repeat word for word all that her previous lover had told her concerning his attempts to catch the smugglers. The accommodating Joey was as generous with his payments as he was with his caresses and the delighted lady spent many a satisfying hour in his company.

The Squire's party was an enjoyable occasion as he never stinted the food or the drink available. Paul, aware that his wife and mother had their eyes upon him, was most careful not to consume too great a quantity of alcoholic beverages. Redvers talked with old friends and acquaintances about his many interests and even escorted his wife onto the dance floor. She laughed merrily at his heavy footed attempts and told him he lacked his son's finesse; he laughingly agreed with her. When it came time for them to leave, they said their farewells, thanked their hosts for a memorable evening and got into their carriage. They had only travelled less than a quarter of a mile before Sergeant Blamey's attention was drawn to the fact that the rear trooper's horse was lame.

"Permission to fall out, sir. Have to go back and get another, sir. This poor beast won't go much further, sir," called out the soldier.

"Very well. Permission granted - and be quick about it!" Blamey snapped, annoyed.

"Yes sir," he answered and tried to turn his horse and salute at the same time, but was not entirely successful.

"Sorry about that sir," said the Sergeant falling back to draw alongside the carriage.

"Are you going on Sergeant, or will you wait for Stevens?" asked Redvers.

"Best to wait for him, sir, or at least walk on slowly," replied Blamey, "for fear he gets lost on these country tracks more than anything."

They all smiled to themselves and, so as not to let the horses get cold, they walked on slowly towards Trevu. The night was cold and a crisp frost lay on the hedges and road. It twinkled in the moonlight and gave the air a sharp feel that toned up the skin on the Sergeant's face and made his gloved hands tingle. In the coach they had warm cloaks and blankets with hot bricks for the ladies, but even they were aware of the chill of that night.

Sergeant Blamey, negotiated a bend in the road where the hedges on either side had crept down to the road and turned it into a narrow pass. The road itself shone silver and the hedgerow looked like so much ruffled lace draped elegantly along the sides.

"Damn pretty sight," the sergeant said, half to himself and smiled. He was still smiling when the shot exploded in his chest and took him clean off his horse, leaving him lying in front of the rearing and snorting carriage horses. The coachman tried to settle the terrified beasts but could not go forward unless he drove them over the sergeant's body, and he could not turn for the road was too narrow.

A figure swathed in a cloak came out of the hedgerow and grabbed the lead horse. His cloak fluttered free in the wind like sinister wings. Under his hat he leered gleefully up at the coachman, still attempting to placate his team.

"Got a firearm up there son?" the man asked, almost warmly.

"No sir," said young William, incurably truthful, and another shot rang out taking him cleanly in the shoulder. He dropped the reins and pitched forward, but did not fall from his seat.

The horses reared and stamped again, but the lead horse's head was being pulled down by an iron grip and inexorably it had to give in to the greater will.

"Get out, all of you!" commanded the rasping voice.

Slowly the occupants of the coach descended onto the roadway. One look, in the silver glow of the moonlight, had shown the array of firepower with which their assailant had armed himself. Having no time to reload he had thrown away his first two pistols, but the butts of two other pairs could be seen plainly, shining from each pocket of his coat.

Paul stood in front of his wife, his arm firmly holding her behind him. His mother stood to his left and he stretched out his other arm, in order to keep her out of harm's way as best he could. Redvers stood in front of her so that they provided a united front and as much protection as two unarmed men could to their womenfolk. Slowly their attacker took a pistol from his left pocket and, releasing the now quiet horse, another from his right.

"Leave them alone, all of them," said Paul in a clear, cold voice, "they are not the ones you want."

"Shut your filthy mouth, you dirty scum!" came the abusive answer.

There was a moment's silence, and then Sardi's firm voice said distinctly and without a tremor: "You are the scum, here! You and all your kind. You filthy slaver, you!"

Petherick laughed harshly, and said cruelly: "I had sluts like you aplenty on my ship. Good bodies, nice teeth and skin the colour of chocolate. Glad to give me anything they could just to save themselves from the chains."

Paul swore and moved towards him but his mother and Chloe held on to him tight and restrained him, but they could not stop him from shouting out to the man. "How dare you!" he cried, "Your daughter would be ashamed to hear you talk so and well you know it, for she had a gentle heart and . . ."

"Ashamed!" Petherick screamed, cutting in on Paul's words, "Ashamed! She lost her shame when she fell in love with you and lost her life pining for you, you scum. Dying in my arms, she was. Not a word of me, not a mention for her poor father who loved her so, who loved the very ground she walked on. The only tears she shed were for you, her beloved Paul! Her filthy, stinking, beloved Paul. My precious girl, crying all the time in her delirious fever for her dirty black heathen. I'll pay you back for ruining her life, you black bastard, you! You took her from me, not her illness. 'Twas the love of you that killed her, you bastard! As my sweet darling has gone from this world I'll see you out of it. Go to hell and rot where you belong," he cried in despair and, levelling his gun, he fired a single shot. A flame of gold burst upon the silver moonlight and momentarily lit up the faces of all present.

CHAPTER 24

WHEN trooper Stevens heard the shot he spurred his new horse into a full gallop and came across the carriage, and the scene of chaos, as he rounded the corner. Pulling up his horse, he jumped to the ground, running towards the man who was beating senseless his opponent against the side of the carriage. One of the women was crying and imploring him to stop and, as he got nearer, he recognised him. He caught hold of the fighting man's arms and pinioned them behind his back, and watched as his beaten victim slowly slid down the side of the coach and crumpled on to the floor. Young Mrs. Trevarthen's look of horror was accentuated by the cold gleam of the moonlight, but he watched as the small, shaking female pulled herself together and, walking towards him, reached out her arms to the struggling man, crying softly: "Paul! Paul! It's over Paul. He cannot harm you now." As she caught hold of him, the soldier released him and went over to look at the beaten man on the floor. So badly battered was he that he was unconscious and, even if he came around, it was unlikely that he would be able to stand, so the soldier turned his attention to the other couple.

A grey haired man sat on the road, rocking the lifeless form of the other woman in his arms. Tears were running unheeded down his face. Beyond him lay the body of Sergeant Blamey, smiling at the moon with the innocent look of a child on his face.

"I'll tie up that man sir, and go for help," said the trooper and, after he had quickly strapped Petherick to the carriage wheel, he thoughtfully removed the remaining guns, mounted his horse and rode hell for leather for Penzance.

Dr. Simcott slowly shook his head, "A bad business, Mrs. Trevarthen, a bad business."

Chloe nodded her head dumbly, and muttered softly: "I know. I cannot get the horror of it out of mind," and she let out a stifled sob, but heroically wiped away her tears, and continued stoically, "Will she live?"

"She's ... um ... she's strong. Not so young but very fit for her age. It's a bad wound 'tho - she'll never be the woman she was. I've stopped the bleeding but there has been a lot of damage done and one lung has been so badly destroyed it will never be of use to her again." He sat beside the young woman and caught hold her hand in a warm clasp, "Can you bring yourself to tell me how it happened?" he enquired gently.

She gulped, "Yes, yes of course. Captain Petherick shot the sergeant first in front of the coach. Poor William had not a chance and he shot him as well. Then he had us get out of the coach and he called S..Sardi and Paul such awful names and he said such filthy things about them," and she glanced up apologetically. "I cannot repeat them Dr. Simcott, I truly can't," and her voice broke on a sob.

"Of course not, my dear, of course not," he soothed.

Chloe shook herself resolutely and continued in a breaking voice, "Paul had pushed me behind him and was holding out his arm to protect his mother. Redvers was standing in front of her. They were both unarmed and doing their poor best to defend us. When he pointed his gun at Paul and made to fire, Sardi reached out for Paul's arm and pushed him so violently to one side that he fell against me and she . . . she was . . .," she stopped again to wipe away the tears, "hit with the shot meant for her son."

"As she fell, Redvers caught her in his arms and Paul sprang forward and caught hold of . . . of that hateful man . . . and started to hit him. He kept hitting him and hitting him. There was no way he would stop for he . . . he would not listen to me. He seemed like a man possessed. When trooper Stevens arrived he caught hold of Paul's arms and restrained him. Our attacker was on the floor covered in blood and . . . and then . . . Trooper Stevens tied him up and went for help. Then they got us home and then you arrived." She lowered her head again and began to weep silently.

"I think I should give you a sedative Mrs. Trevarthen. You must not fret yourself like this. There is nothing any one of us can do now. Time will decide," he said gently.

"No. No thank you, Dr. Simcott," she answered firmly, "I must stay strong for Paul. Is he still with his father?"

Dr. Simcott nodded, "Putting him to bed I think. I talked Redvers into taking a sedative because there was nothing he could do. If, God willing, his wife will last the night he will need all his strength for the morrow."

They both turned as the door opened and Paul trod heavily into the room. His face registered a blank despair. There was blood on his coat and his hands were cut about and bruised and very bloody. Chloe got up immediately and went to him. She took him in her arms and tried her best to console him.

Dr. Simcott, observing the young man's distraught face, coughed and suggested that Paul, like his father, take a sedative but Paul shook his head.

"I will see to Paul, Dr. Simcott," said Chloe resolutely, and continued, "If you would like to stay the night, in case you might be . . . needed, I can have a room prepared."

He thanked her and accepted her offer as he did not wish to leave his patient, for her life was balanced most precariously, but told her not to bestir herself on his part. He would find Hannah himself and she would see to the arrangements for him, making to leave them, he caught himself up as he was about to wish them 'Good night' and quietly let himself out of the room.

Chloe led Paul to the settle and made him sit down. She found the brandy bottle and with shaking hands poured him out a glass of brandy and, returning to his side she placed it in his hand. He looked down at it dazedly and took a sip. It put heart into him, for a little while, but it could not stop the tears from falling down his face and she removed the glass from his limp grasp and rocked him gently in her arms.

To the amazement of Dr. Simcott, Sardi survived the night and slowly, very slowly with every passing day began to win back her strength. That she would be an invalid, they all knew but they were none the less thankful that her life had been spared. Redvers spent long hours with her, talking quietly and softly. Paul sat by her bedside and thanked her over and over again for saving his life. She dismissed his words with her gentle smile. As she improved he gave her news of the children, brought the baby in for her to see how he had grown, carried Grace in so that the sight of her smiling face would evoke an answering smile from her grandmother, and even boisterous little

George was allowed a few moments with his grandmother as long as he was very quiet, like a mouse, so his father had warned him.

As the local magistrate it was Squire Tregurthen who brought them the news they were expecting of Petherick. He had been sent for trial at Bodmin and was tried for the murder of Sergeant Blamey and the attempted murder of William Pascoe, the coachman. He had pleaded guilty and Redvers, Paul and Chloe were asked to provide statements as to what had happened on that night. William Pascoe, with his arm in a sling had his statement taken down by the local constable and it was forwarded to the court along with those of the Trevarthen's. Dorothea's father did not dispute any of their words, signed a confession, pleaded guilty and went into the court hoping for and expecting to receive the death penalty. He was not to be disappointed. Refusing his lawyers to make any appeals on his behalf he sat out his time in the prison, waiting defiantly for the hangman to perform his duty.

When the date of the execution was known, Redvers would not leave his wife so it fell to his son to attend the execution, for it had been agreed that for the pain that had been caused to their family a member of it should be in attendance. Redvers did not relish the prospect of sending his guilt racked, sensitive son to such an occasion but Paul, distraught with remorse, considered it his duty to go. Squire Tregurthen would be attending, so Redvers asked if he could oblige him in the matter and take his son with him.

"Certainly, Redvers, certainly," he said nodding sadly.

As the Squire thought of the journey he proposed that they leave the night before and stay over with some friends of his. It would be a long day to travel to Bodmin in time for a midday hanging and no doubt the roads would be packed, for such an event always drew a big crowd. Redvers nodded dumbly in agreement, aware that one member of the proposed party would be looking forward to the execution with undisguised relish. When the time came Chloe packed her husband an overnight bag, then Paul hugged and kissed her and said his farewells and turned and climbed into the Squire's capacious coach. The journey was not overlong for they were to stop the night with acquaintances of the Squire who resided near Truro, but Paul felt his destination was rushing to meet him like an eagle swooping on its prey. The Squire's friends greeted their guests with much merriment, but they looked at the dark skinned young man askance and found little to say to him. He would have found little to say in return himself, so downcast did he feel. At dinner he ate little and in his strange bed he slept less, but when the sun rose the following morning, bright and clear, he dressed himself carefully before putting in an appearance at the breakfast table.

"Come here lad," shouted the Squire from behind a plate piled high with a vast amount of food. "Get some of this down your neck. It will be a little while afore we sup again."

Paul took a seat beside Tregurthen, but ate sparingly and hardly touched his ale. The Squire could not coax him into eating more so, after their meal, they thanked their hosts and once more resumed their journey. In the coach the Squire regarded the young man pensively before remarking: "I've sent word you will be in attendance. If he wants to see you or . . . send a message the warden will let us know." He looked at his companion, who was looking blankly out of the coach window. "If you wish . . . up to you, of course . . . you could always see him yourself if . . . if you have anything you want to say to him," he told Paul nervously. For answer Paul only shook his head and continued his unseeing gaze.

When they arrived at the town it was full to the brim for such an occasion. Traders had set up their stalls, the hostelries and inns were doing a roaring trade for a large crowd had already gathered, although they would have to wait until noon for the show. There were various bands of musicians and some of the people were passing the time by dancing and singing. One toy seller was pulling in a good crowd and a large income by selling his toy doll. He caught sight of the tall, dark skinned young man and demonstrated just what it was the toy could do. Paul's eyes registered his disgust and he turned his face away from the sight of the hanging doll, jiggling its death dance.

Squire Tregurthen led him off to a hotel and took up residence in the private room he had bespoke a week earlier. A harassed looking waiter brought in more ale and prattled on to the two occupants that it was a fine day for it, although it was disappointing that the Pengelly woman had only been transported for stealing some bread from her employer, and was not to be executed, as he enjoyed seeing a woman hung.

"The crowd get more excited by it too," he added with a grin. "The ladies do moan something fierce when the noose is put round their necks. You should hear the crowd cheer then," and he rubbed his hands together in glee before remembering himself and asking them if they required anything further. The Squire shook his head and flipped a coin at him, which he caught expertly, then he touched his forelock and, still grinning, left the room. Tregurthen filled a mug for Paul and passed it to him. He tapped his coat pocket and informed him that he had his brandy flask if young Trevarthen felt the need of it. Paul quietly declined and moved to a chair by the table.

"First hanging, Paul?" asked the old gentleman conversationally of his young companion.

"Yes sir," said Paul softly.

"Nothing to it!" he told him jovially, "Soon get used to it. Some last longer than others of course, but they mostly all give a good show. The crowd can get a bit raucous but I've got a good place reserved for the coach. Arranged for a few fellows to stake it out for us. See plenty from there, or at least all you'll need to see," and he shot a quick look at Paul from under his bushy brows.

"Yes sir," replied Paul mechanically.

"The landlord has got his wife to make up one of her hampers for us. You'll truly enjoy that my boy - that woman makes an apple and pork pasty that will make you think you had died and gone to heaven," so rapt was he in the contemplation of the feast that he forgot where he was and for what reason, his thoughtless words were lost on him.

They sat on in silence until the clock struck the hour of eleven. The timepiece seemed to Paul to tick faster than normal and he tried desperately to compose himself for what he was about to witness. His fault it was that had caused the tragedy that had assembled them here today, all the tragic players had to take their places on the stage until the scene had finished. He had invoked the crime and would have to pay the price.

The Squire stood up and told Paul that it was time to go. They had to pick up the hamper and get to their place at the execution site; then all they would have to do was sit back and wait for the hangman and his victim to take centre stage. Tregurthen's eyes widened in appreciation as he was given a sight of the contents of the hamper prior to the lid being fixed in place, but Paul could only shudder at the sight of such plenty.

Tregurthen laughed gleefully like a child, "Strange, haven't been to a hanging for three years. I'm getting quite excited at the thought," and slapping Paul on the back they went on their way, the Squire with genuine anticipation and Paul with the dragging feet of a condemned man.

When they reached their chosen spot the Squire got out and decided that they would have a better view if they occupied the coachman's seat. Consequently, the poor servant was abruptly ordered to get down and to go to the front and hold the horses whilst Tregurthen directed Paul to get himself seated. He shouted up to ask if Paul wanted anything from the hamper, but he silently shook his head, so the Squire picked himself some delicacies, filled his pockets with them and then proceeded to heave his bulk up beside his companion. Spotting various acquaintances he waved cheerfully and shouted his greetings, but contented himself in the main with the consumption of his food.

As the appointed hour drew near the crowd began to get restless. Some of the more drunken members began to sing bawdy songs and to call out to get on with the show. Paul, even though he felt it was his duty to be present, wished himself a thousand miles away, feeling his skin crawl at the attitude of his fellow man. Sounding now like a howling mob of rabid dogs, he noted in despair that even the young children in the crowd were jumping up and down with the excitement of it. Suddenly the noise trebled as a door opened and the chaplain, the pinioned prisoner and his guards stepped out and made their way to the scaffold. When they all stood on the top the crowd fell silent as the prisoner was asked if he had any last words. Petherick stepped boldly forward and surveyed the crowd dispassionately before his eye alighted on his victim, perched high on the Squire's carriage. In a resonant, loud voice he began to speak, the sound carrying clearly across the now quiet gathering, but he was oblivious to them, for he had sight of only one person's face in the multitude.

"I am come here, at this time, on this day and to this end for no more reason than the rightful love of a father for his daughter. For her I would have died willingly if I could have saved her, but I could not, so now I die willingly that I may be with her and keep her safe throughout our lives eternal. Let the . . .," and he paused for one moment, "black demons in this world be cast into the fires of hell and there burn for ever more. Amen," he concluded and he stepped back to meet his fate, his defiant glare still burning into Paul's very soul.

His last sight on earth was of Paul's blank face, which registered neither triumph nor despair. The screaming of the crowd reached fever pitch and Paul heard the Squire shouting excitedly into his ear: "Here he goes!" and the poor, proud, prejudiced man dropped to his doom. His desire for death was not reflected in the way his body responded to the assault upon it. It danced and jerked, fighting on for several minutes, much to the delight of the crowd, who roared their approval, even Tregurthen stood up and shouted gleefully at the sight and clapped. Paul watched every movement, every twist and jerk, right through until the body merely swung gently at the end of the rope like a dead fly dangling in a spider's larder. They stayed until the body was cut down, an hour after the execution took place, as was the custom. Paul, his duty over, got down from the coachman's seat and returned to the inside of the coach, his face impassive. The Squire joined him, still smiling, and commented jovially that he had seen better, but it was a good day out for all of that. He had not left much in the hamper but suggested that if Trevarthen felt the need of anything he could help himself. Paul declined again so, hiding his disappointment, Tregurthen shut down the lid and, banging his cane on the roof of the carriage, told his coachman to start for home.

So directed, the man holding the reins carefully picked his way through the crowds still thronging about. Paul's eye was caught by a child in her best dress, with little white shoes peeping through under the lace. Her blonde hair, grey eyes and pink and white complexion so forcibly reminded him of Dorothea that a shudder ran through him. She turned and smiled a most winning smile at him and then, in her glee, held up her new toy for his approval, and the little dancing doll of death went through its private agony for her delight and to his distress. He turned away and, leaning his head back against the squabs of the coach, shut his eyes against the gruesome image, but it hung in his mind like a black, avenging angel, and he could not free himself from the sight of it.

Less than a mile from the town he asked the Squire to stop the coach. Tregurthen looked surprised, but did as he was asked and leaned forward to look into his companion's face, most concerned at the expression on it.

"Anything wrong, Paul?" he asked solicitously.

"I beg your pardon, sir, but I have to . . .," gasped Paul and he swallowed quickly, "have to cast up, sir," and descending from the coach, ran towards a low wall that bounded the road. Leaning over it he was violently sick, and continued to be so until he thought he could be sick no more. He stood up and wiped his face with his handkerchief, before slowly returning to the carriage and got back in. The Squire looked at him worriedly for a moment and then reached into his pocket and, taking out his flask, opened the top and passed it to Paul.

"Thank you sir," he said gratefully and put the flask to his lips and gulped down a mouthful of the liquid. It burnt its way down his throat and burst into flames in his empty stomach, for all the world like the fires of hell engulfing him from the inside.

"Better now, lad?"

"Yes thank you sir," replied Paul and returned the brandy to its owner.

The cane was again employed to give instruction to the coachman and they continued their journey. They stopped once upon the homeward route but again Paul could not face the food supplied for them at the inn. The Squire said it was a pity and advised Paul to get about to a few hangings to harden himself to it. Busily employed in ripping the flesh from a chicken leg he said, between mouthfuls: "You're too sensitive Paul, always have been. Get your head out from between those damn books of yours and get yourself about more," and he winked at the young man as he continued: "Might have another one soon. Got a new man after the Bolitho crowd."

"What happened to the last one, the one who was also employed when . . . when he . . ." Paul began to ask.

"Oh him. God alone knows? Down some shaft somewhere. Nobody's seen sight nor sound of him since New Year's. This new man's keen 'tho. Wants to make his mark. He'll get him; you see if he doesn't and I'll tell you another thing," he affirmed as he gulped down a mouthful of chicken, "that Joseph Bolitho will make a pretty picture, dancing about for the crowds to see." He laughed jovially at the thought. "And if we are lucky we'll have more than one of them; hanging out like their mother's washing, jerking and flapping in the wind," and he laughed merrily in anticipation of the prospective treat.

They arrived at Trevu quite late and upon entering the dark hallway they were met by Redvers, his expression impassive as usual and Chloe, frightened but trying hard not to let her feelings show. The Squire refused refreshment, but entered the withdrawing room with them for a short while and asked after Sardi. Redvers face could not quite hide the concern in it but he merely said: "Dr. Simcott says it will take a long time, providing there are no setbacks."

"Let's hope she continues to progress. Give her our best regards and tell her we are praying for her," Tregurthen said. Redvers clasped him by the hand and said simply, "Thank you Joshua. She will appreciate that and thank you for what you did today."

"Pooh!" he said, "that was nothing. I enjoyed it but a . . .," and he turned Redvers about and whispered in his ear, "young Paul took it bad. Barely ate a thing; surprised me that did, knowing your boy like I do. Then we had hardly left Bodmin when we had to stop the coach for him to be sick. Not too late to get him hardened up, Redvers. Don't want him going through life as lily-livered as that now, do you?"

He did not expect an answer to his question and informed them briskly that he had best get home, for he had someone calling on him, so he bowed to Chloe and shook the two men by the hand. Paul attempted to thank him, but the Squire waved his thanks aside and only told him that the next hanging was going to be a lot better, and winking at Paul like a conspirator added: "You'll enjoy that much more having got one under your belt, so to speak."

When he left, Redvers instructed Paul to go to his mother as she was awaiting his return. Chloe gave his hand another squeeze and then unclasped it, and Paul rose from the settle and headed towards his mother's room like an automaton. He knocked and entered to cross to her side. She opened her tired eyes and looked at him, studying his face before telling him to sit down. Reaching out her hand she squeezed his own gently, much struck by the sadness in his face. They continued to sit without any words but with an unconscious understanding between them.

The tall man sat with his long legs stretched out before him in the library, and studied the book he had in his hand most carefully for it was one he had not read before. He was disappointed that he would not have the time to read it and could not ask to borrow the book, for he knew its owner would not consider him the sort of fellow who would be capable of reading. Wondering idly if he would be able to purchase it at some time in the future, he read on for a little while, until he heard a familiar booming voice in the hall way and swiftly replaced the book in its correct place on the shelves. Moving himself to stand with his back to the fire he waited, his face impassive, as the door swung open and Squire Tregurthen erupted into his library, surveying Joseph Bolitho with a smiling face.

"Dammee Joey," he cried, "I am sorry to have kept you waiting for I presumed I should have been home by now, but the town was packed an' we had to stop for a supper on the road. I had to go in to have a word with Redvers and to ask after his wife," and in response to Bolitho's question, merely said: "What! Oh yes, still alive although Simcott says 'tis a miracle, for he did not expect her to survive for as long as this." He walked to the table and seeing the bottles there picked them up one by one, studying them carefully. Opening one of them, he poured himself a glass which he held up to the light, thoughtfully admiring the colour of the liquid, before sampling some of the brandy.

"My God! That's a good one Joey," and he drank the contents before pouring himself another glass and, taking a seat by the fire, he pointed to the chair opposite him and Bolitho, correctly interpreting the signal, sat himself down, regarding the Squire with his usual enigmatic countenance. Tregurthen, loosening his neck cloth, then proceeded to regale the young man with an account of the day's happenings, all the while staring into the smuggler's face to see if his expression would alter as he described the gruesome events. The mask like features did not change until he gave an account of young Trevarthen's reaction to what he had seen, and Tregurthen noted a softening of his visitor's look, but almost immediately it disappeared and his inscrutable expression was restored. "Never seen anything like it for young Paul was sick as a dog. Had to give him some of me brandy to restore him," the Squire laughed reminiscently, "still 'twas his first hanging so I shouldn't have been so surprised. You'd have enjoyed it Joey, for the inns were doing a roaring trade," Tregurthen informed his guest and, raising his eyes to the impassive face, enquired quietly if he had much trade thereabouts. Bolitho merely looked at him inscrutably and replied that he never divulged with whom he conducted his business for it would not do to inform one upon the other. The Squire, after very little thought, appreciated the force of his reasoning.

"No by God! That would never do Joey, for I should not like our little arrangement known hereabouts; for as a local magistrate I cannot afford for this sort of thing to be broadcast abroad," and he raised his glass as an example. Joey allowed himself a grim smile, but imagined if he should ever find himself up before the man no mercy would be shown to him, for who would believe a common criminal like himself against the power and might of the local squire? Tregurthen chatted on for a while longer about various hangings that he had witnessed and the pleasure he had derived from them, before bringing his talk to an end, paying off Bolitho and seeing him from the premises by means of the back door. Shooting home the bolts behind him, he returned to the library and sampled some more of his brandy, considering that it would be a shame should anyone ever catch the man for then he should lose his opportunity to acquire some of the finest brandy around. Smuggler he might be, but Bolitho knew the value of good alcohol and never failed to supply him with the best.

Outside in the street, Bolitho seemed to nod his head at the opposite wall and of a sudden Likky Skewes appeared from a recessed doorway, falling into step beside him as they made their way to Josh's inn. Joey felt a deep sympathy for young Trevarthen for the fellow was a sensitive man and not the sort to appreciate the hangman's art. That he himself did appreciate it was most apparent, for he had spent his life from boyhood onwards studiously avoiding getting himself into any predicament that would have entailed him becoming a recipient of it. As they walked into the Seagull Inn's yard, Joey, uncharacteristically informed Likky of the Squire's comments about the day and his enjoyment of both the spectacle and the hanging.

"Tcha! Bleddy 'ipnercrat!" announced Likky in disgust.

"Hypocrite," corrected Joey softly.

"'Ess!" intoned Likky angrily, "an' 'e's one a they as well!" and continued on his way, muttering his annoyance of a world in which the rich appeared able to get away with everything whilst the poor struggled so hard to even exist. Still spouting his philosophical comments, they entered the inn and made their way to the bar amidst much laughter and shouted greetings.

That night at Trevu all was quiet in the big house until Paul awoke screaming from his nightmare of jiggling corpses, all with Petherick's contorted face. Struggling to free himself from the sights of hell forced into his mind he heard his wife's soft voice, soothing him gently, and slowly he responded to her calming words. Redvers, in the new wing, cringed to hear his poor boy so tortured but got up to go to Sardi, for well he knew she would be fretted by her beloved son's cries. Chloe was with him, he told her softly and gently wiped the tears from her eyes, she it would be that had the job of rebuilding their son's world for him.

Paul suffered nightmares for weeks, awakening all with his tortured screams. His appetite deserted him and the weight began to fall away from his tall frame. Chloe called Dr. Simcott to him despite his protests. The good doctor's advice, apart from rest, was that Paul must try to put it all behind him. After all, the doctor told him, he had a wonderful wife, loving children and a good home. Paul smiled in agreement, but he knew like no other that the devil inside him was gripping him fast in an iron hold and would not let him go. He dreaded having to go to sleep at night and often Chloe would find him in the morning in his room with his head dropped over his books and the candle burnt down to its end. She sighed over him and cried when she was alone, but she would have to continue painstakingly building him back up to the man he had been. The great, foolish, handsome giant that she loved so dearly and that she felt had not deserved the half of what he was suffering now.

One day, as he sat reading softly to his mother by her bedside, Sardi reached out her hand and, catching hold of the open book, pulled it down and softly spoke his name.

"Yes, mother," and he turned his thin face to look at her with a semblance of his old smile.

She looked at him for a long while, noticing the sad eyes, and the hollowed out face with its nervous smile, wavering on his lips. Paul could not hide his emotions like her beloved Redvers for he was like his father only in looks. Then she bethought herself of own dear father, and knew then where Paul got his sensitive nature from; for in spite of all the ills the world had thrown at the ex-slave, his compassion and sensitivity to his fellow man shone through him like a beacon of hope. Redvers had told her that on that dreadful night Paul would have beaten Petherick until dead if he had not been stopped. He it was who had rushed forward, unarmed, upon an armed man. Paul would have stopped the shot that hit her if she had not taken it upon herself to try so desperately to save her beloved son and to have pushed him away. Sardi knew what she was doing then and why. She had wanted to save her son from harm and now he was being destroyed by the sight he had witnessed and she lay powerless, unable to help him, unable even to take him in her arms in a loving embrace.

"Paul," she said softly, for her voice was very weak. "When we have seen the bad in life we must counterbalance it with the good to make sense of living. Look forward now, my dearest, and put the past behind you for it cannot be altered no matter how much we would like it changed. My own father, your grandfather, would be suffering now as you are, for you have his temperament, not Redvers. I cannot tell you how proud I am to recognise him in you for he was a man worthy of more than he was able to achieve in his short life. The mantle of that responsibility is on your shoulders now, my darling. Please to wear it proudly for his sake," she whispered and then added with an encouraging smile: "and for mine."

"Oh Mother," he smiled grimly, and caught up her hand to his lips and she smiled in understanding as she felt his tears falling on to her skin. They sat together for a long while in silence, having no need for words and finally her son realised that enthroned beside his beloved Penelope was this remarkable woman, of whom he was so justifiably proud at last.

His wife noticed a change for the better in Paul almost immediately, but kept her own counsel and never asked either the mother or the son if anything had transpired between them. That night, for the first time since the hanging Paul slept the night through without a murmur and awoke to find his little wife snuggled into his side. He sighed with relief at not having awoken to the sound of his own screams ringing in his ears.

CHAPTER 25

SLOWLY, life began to return to some semblance of normality at Trevu. Paul and his father spent long hours in Sardi's company. To Redvers she talked quietly of her pride in her son and of the love she had always had for his father. That he could not return that love in the same measure she minded not, she told him, for he had given her so much for which she was grateful. She was determined that he should know that, without his dear Penelope, she did not believe that the son of whom they were both so proud could have become the man he was. She laughed as she agreed with her husband that her darling boy had not the ambition that she could have wished for, but she considered he had better qualities by far than the need to see himself ranked the highest in his field. To her son she talked little but seemed content to have him sit with her, holding her hand in his gentle grasp. He often read to her and she expressly asked that he should read his first book of poems, for she found them most comforting. Smiling in appreciation of her pride in him he did not mind, however much she wished him to read; as he could give himself freely to her now for he read for her pleasure alone and not for an assembled mass. Sardi, gaining strength from somewhere, expressed a wish to come downstairs in the summer and Paul had the responsibility, being by far the strongest member of the household, of carrying her down to the withdrawing room. Neighbours and other friends were soon dropping in and helped her to pass the time. Soon much laughter and gaiety could be heard coming from the room and Paul was relieved to see his mother getting back to her old self. She was even strong enough to take some steps herself and, leaning on Paul's arm and with Redvers arm around her waist, she walked out into Penelope's garden and, seating herself in the midst of the glorious colours and scents, she told them brightly how she appreciated to be at peace at last after her former hectic life.

Consequently, on a gloriously sunny morning, her son was not prepared to hear his wife calling frantically for him from the top of the stairs to come immediately to his mother's room. From her place at the side of the bed, Chloe's frightened face turned towards him as he came rushing through the door.

"Oh Paul," she cried, "I can't wake her up. She will not respond to me."

By this time he was by his mother's side and it was he that noticed the small drop of blood at the corner of her lips. Slowly the blood became a trickle and it dripped slowly upon the white of her night-gown. He felt fear clutch at his heart, but he strove to conquer it and informed his wife he would go immediately for the doctor. Taking Ebony from the stables, for he was his swiftest horse, he rode for Penzance at breakneck speed. Meeting his father on the road from the village he sent him home at once, the look on his son's face was all that Redvers needed to see to understand the seriousness of his wife's condition. In Penzance Paul threw down his horse's reins and, taking the steps to the doctor's house two at a time, hammered on the door. When it was opened to him he disappeared briefly and returned pulling Dr. Simcott by the arm in his desperation. The doctor's stable lad appeared with his horse, for Dr. Simcott knew he had no time to wait for his gig to be harnessed.

A look of fear crossed Paul's face for his own horse was not where he had left it, but hearing his name called loudly he turned to see the smuggler Joseph Bolitho running towards him with Ebony's reins in his hand.

"Took off, sir, when you went fer the Doctor," he explained, but Paul had no more time than to offer a brief word of thanks before heading off in the direction of his home. Bolitho watched grimly after the galloping horseman as he disappeared from his sight. By rights he should have hated the man, he reasoned, for it was to him that his beloved Sarah-Jane had given her heart, but he could not for there was something about the young Trevarthen that he admired. He had never forgotten the kindness shown to him when the Captain had saved him from the baker and neither had he forgotten his small son's mischievous smile, for in his bleak little world at that time it had seemed to light up his life. Turning on his heel, he made his way slowly towards his own home. Once there, he took out his bible and found again the passage from Hebrews that he had quoted to his rival's mother all those years ago and hoped most sincerely that she would be restored to health, for having his own mother murdered had given him great sympathy for the Trevarthens in their time of trouble. His eye was caught by the proceeding verse and he smiled ironically as he read 'Let brotherly love continue' to himself. Brotherly love was something few people would ever consider the cold, dispassionate smuggler could ever feel for any man, but for Paul Trevarthen's plight Joseph Bolitho felt it then.

Dr. Simcott and Paul arrived at Trevu and dismounted from their horses before ever the waiting stable hands could catch hold of them. As one they rushed for Sardi's room, but on reaching it Redvers' face and Chloe's sobbing told them that their haste had been in vain. Dr. Simcott confirmed that Sardi had died and, whispering his condolences, quietly made his way from the room. Paul, frozen like a statue, could only stare in disbelief at his mother lying so serene in her bed, looking for all the world as if she had fallen into a blissful sleep. Her lips had even a gentle smile upon them. Redvers bowed his head and kissed his wife's cheek, whispering her name softly. He looked up after a while and gazed compassionately into his son's distraught face before he stretched out his hand towards Paul, who came to his side and placed his arm consolingly around his father's shoulders. Chloe wiped her eyes and, slowly rising from her seat, quietly left the room, leaving the two men alone with their loss.

A week later, Paul and Chloe stood side by side in the little churchyard. Paul had placed the two bunches of flowers, one for each of his mothers, on their respective plots. His tears fell equally for in the end there was no difference between them; he knew that both had made him the man he was. His beloved wife held fast to his arm and smiled comfortably at him and he recognised that he would have to shrug off his despair and go on, although the pain of Sardi's loss, when mother and son had come to such a point of understanding, was almost more than he could bear. Slowly they walked away and retraced their steps to Trevu, seeking out Redvers in the parlour. He looked up as they came in and smiled at them and his son observed that, in some strange way, a sort of peace lay about him. His father had told him that Sardi's suffering was over, she was free of pain at last and for that they should all be thankful. Paul had sighed his agreement but he had been hit hard by the shock of her death. Redvers had always known how badly injured his wife had been by that fateful shot - for he had been a soldier after all - and had never expected her ever to get out of her bed. When she did, his heart swelled with pride for her. His had been a lucky life in lots of ways he reasoned, for he had been endowed with the love of two wonderful woman. One so quiet and gentle but with an inner firmness that he had lacked, and the other determined, strong-willed and able to take her life and make out of a disaster a marvellous success. They had both given him this one son, this poor young man who had suffered so much for so many different reasons, but for their gift he knew himself to be eternally grateful.

A month before Christmas Redvers returned from Penzance soaked by a heavy rain shower that had come in off the sea and rushed up the valley. He contracted a severe cold but would not take to his bed although Paul remonstrated with him most forcibly. Three days later, having some business to conduct with his lawyer concerning Sardi's estate in Bristol, he refused to take out the coach and had his horse saddled as usual and rode into the town. A chill November wind froze him to the marrow as he walked back towards the stables after the conclusion of his meeting with the lawyer. As the discussion had worn on he had found it more and more difficult to concentrate on what the lawyer, Bosence, was saying to him for his head was beginning to ache atrociously. When finally he had reached the stables the ostler had to help him mount his horse and, worried by the Captain's condition, offered to find someone to ensure he made it safe home. Redvers summoned up a grim laugh and told him he was quite well enough to make his way back to Trevu, for he had made the same journey for most of his life. In spite of his bravado, hardly a mile out of the town the Captain pulled up his horse, to try the better to get his breath. The pain in his chest was almost tearing him in two, but he would not give up and determined to get himself home. He was dimly aware of a cantering horse on the roadway but had little energy to turn in the saddle to see who it should be. An excitable roan stopped beside him and sidled up to his horse, and he heard a young man's soft voice enquire if he was in need of assistance. Turning his head slowly, with beads of sweat on his brow, he found himself looking into the concerned blue eyes of Joseph Bolitho. Grimly he shook his head and gasped that he was quite well. The young man, aware that Captain Trevarthen was shivering, removed his own cloak and placed it around the sick man's shoulders, gently removed the reins from the man's almost lifeless grasp and slowly led his horse along the road to Trevu. They ambled along in silence, for Redvers had little energy to do more than breathe. Just outside of the farm yard Bolitho stopped their horses and carefully placed the bay's reins in Redvers' hands. Nodding his thanks he looked up into the young man's face and thought his memory playing tricks on him, for he was sure he knew the face the smuggler wore from somewhere in his past, but the person would not come to him.

"I think you'll be all right now sir, but best t' get yerself in out a this bitter wind," and he made to go, but was presented with Redvers' shaking hand outstretched towards him. When he grasped it, the young smuggler looked into the Captain's face and noted his puzzled expression and the way the sick man's eyes studied his features.

Discerning that he was trying to speak, Joey leaned forward to hear what Trevarthen was saying and heard him state, in a rasping voice: "I know you, Bolitho, but who are you?" and assuming that he could not remember from where, told him that he had been the young boy who had stolen the bread in Penzance all those years ago.

"You did me a kindness then sir," he said softly, "an' I'm returning 'en to 'e now," and had the satisfaction of seeing a smile on the Captain's drawn face. "Now, c'mon sir, in with you, fer this be no weather fer you to be out in," he told him gently, and with a final smile he slapped Redvers' bay mare gently on the rump, so as not to frighten it, and the beast moved slowly forward towards Trevu's yard, her master on her back still swathed in another man's cloak. Redvers, almost at the entrance to the yard, stopped his bay and turned to see again the fellow with the terrible reputation patiently waiting on his horse to ensure that, even so near to Trevarthen's home, he should still arrive safe. It took an immense effort but slowly Redvers raised his arm; unable to do more than wave him a salute and smiling as he saw his helper's face break into a smile of its own, before the infamous smuggler lifted his hand to touch the rim of his hat in acknowledgement.

Once in the yard he was met by his son; on the point of having his own horse saddled to go and look for him. Exhausted, the Captain collapsed into Paul's strong arms and was taken semiconscious to his room. Paul sent for Dr. Simcott immediately who, after his examination, prescribed rest. Redvers, awake but weary in his bed, smiled at that, but for once he did not disagree, for it had been a most interesting life and he thought he deserved a rest at the end of it. After two days, as Redvers condition gradually worsened, Dr. Simcott took Paul on one side and prepared him for the worst. Paul protested that it was only a cold and his father would soon be up on his feet again.

"Listen Paul, and listen well. It is not a cold, it's pneumonia now. He won't survive it because he does not want to," Dr. Simcott informed him gently.

"I have had pneumonia! Lady Wrothford had me take horrible medicines and they cured me. You can do the same for father," he cried desperately.

"Paul you were a fit young man. He is over sixty and this last year has put such a strain on him. Don't be selfish Paul, if he wants to go you have to let him," said Dr. Simcott sympathetically.

"No!" cried Paul in distress, for he could not bear the thought of another loss so soon. In less than six months he had lost his mother and now his father was to die. Paul turned to his wife in despair and she consoled him, but told him that he would have to face up to whatever the world had decided he should have to deal with and, if Redvers was to die, than so be it. He shook his head, but she made him listen and made him resign himself to it.

Redvers let the threads holding him earthward slowly unravel and was quite content to do so. He slept for long periods of time and saw again his past life played out before his closed eyes. The young boy with his brothers riding around the estate, his sister with her proud ways, his short life in the military, meeting his beloved Penelope and being so besotted with her timeless beauty. The friends and acquaintances he had made jostled against each other in his mind. John Williams with his cheerful optimism, Hannah's joyful laughter, Squire Tregurthen and his booming voice, the young Inez Carter on his brother's arm, her pretty face wreathed in smiles. Even the young smuggler found room in his jumbled thoughts in all his guises, sometimes as the impoverished boy, or as the insolent trespasser intent on courting Sarah-Jane and at the last as the concerned young man who would not let him make his final journey to Trevu alone. The more shameful side of his life did not hide itself from his presence either, but it did not prick his conscience as before. The many woman in his life danced before his eyes, laughing and smiling. The black haired girl in Sennen, the brown eyed beauty in Portreath, too many to name, - even if he could have remembered their names - but their faces he could see as clear as day. The schoolteacher's wife from St. Buryan with her auburn tresses and nervous smile, the laughing prostitute from Penzance, who had entertained him night after night, with her heavy mane of glossy brown curls and the finest blue eyes that he thought he had ever seen in his life; and then finally his dearest Sardi. Possibly the most beautiful woman he had ever known with her entrancing smile and soft brown eyes. With all that she had suffered in her life, she had chosen him to love and did so unreservedly her life long and he felt so humbled by it. She it had been who gave him the prize he valued above all others and for his beloved Penelope, with her kind forgiving heart, to be brave enough to make him realise it. On his last night he sent for Paul and, summoning up the residue of his strength, told him of all the things in his life he had a pride in, he was the most proud of Paul for he had been to him as no other son had been to any father before. His distraught son tried bravely to hold back his tears, but Redvers smiled at him and gently squeezed his hand and said softly: "Paul, my beloved son, let them fall. I am proud to have them as my own." After that he seemed to fall asleep, but his son refused to leave his side. Chloe came and, finding the discarded cloak that some kind soul had wrapped Redvers in on his last journey home from Penzance, placed it around her husband's shoulders, to warm the son as it had the father, but made no attempt to take him away from his post. Hannah and Dr. Simcott found him in the morning, still holding his father's cold hand in his warm clasp, with his tears glistening on his cheeks.

Redvers funeral was almost more than his son could bear, but he had to support his Aunt Caroline through it and made an effort for her to be proud of. Towards the end of that day, when everyone had left Trevu, he returned alone to the graveyard, sank on his knees on the cold, damp grass and shed his tears, without care if anyone should see him.

Life had to go on, however, and so in spite of his sadness one of the first acts Paul wished to make was to establish ownership of the cloak. The more to thank the kind person who so obviously had tried to help the Captain on his final journey home than to return it, but he met with no success for the ostlers at the inn were the last people in the town to have spoken with Redvers and they had no information to impart. Mr. Murdoch could not help either, other than to inform Paul that the cloak was of exceptional quality and that it had originated in France. Dumbfounded, Paul made his way slowly out of Penzance, puzzling as to whom amongst their many acquaintances would have a cloak made for them in a country they were at war with, but he could think of no one. The chill wind bit into his bones and he wrapped his own cloak well around himself to ward off the cold as he headed back to Trevu.

On the outskirts of the town he espied a small group heading along the road towards him, battling bravely against the force of the wind. The sight of a barefoot young woman with two small children clinging to her skirts and another babe in her arms all wearing, clothes that had seen many a repair pulled at his heart, for all looked so impoverished and undernourished. To be out in such cruel weather dressed in such thin garments appalled him, so he passed over the unknown owner's cloak into the mother's unbelieving hands and, searching in his pockets emptied them of what was to Paul, a small amount of money that he was carrying on his person. The woman, unable to believe what had befallen her, gazed at him, with her eyes wide open in shock. Seeing her expression, something stirred in Paul's memory and, he remembered the young thief with the bread in Penzance all those years ago. He smiled fondly for immediately his own father's kind actions on the impoverished boy's behalf sprang to his mind. Smiling down into the woman's face, he asked politely who she was and whither she was bound. She replied in her strong dialect with her name and that she was a widow, evicted from her cottage when her husband had died in an accident on the farm where they had lived and that she was going to Penzance to look for work. He told her to continue into the town and to use the money to feed and clothe herself and her children and to find themselves some lodgings. On the Monday of the following week she was to present herself at the offices of Bosence and Rodda, the solicitors, where she would be informed of work suitable for her to undertake on another farm if she should wish to accept it. If this was not acceptable to her, he assured her he would charge Mr. Rodda with the task of finding her another cottage in which to live whilst a solution should be found for her problems.

"Do you understand, my good woman?" he asked with a smile and she nodded her head vigorously, so he doffed his cap and continued on his way. The widow wrapped the cloak about herself and her children and stood to stare after the departing gentleman, unable to comprehend her good fortune, for there was only one man in the district with a skin that colour and he was well known to be an honest, generous soul and as good as his word, for like his father before him he did not make a promise that he would not keep.

That night, for the first time in her life, the young mother lay in a warm bed, with well fed children nestling against her and gazed in wonder at the new clothes placed so carefully on the chair at the end of the bed and at the shiny new pairs of boots arranged in a neat row on the floor. Sighing in wonder at the turn in her fortunes, her hand caressed the cloak that she had so carefully thrown over their bed. She determined to keep it always in her possession, for the gift of it had brought such comfort to her.

Paul was now the master of Trevu and, not only was he the heir to his father's estate, but also his mother's estate came to him through Redvers. So in a short space of time he had become one of the richest men in the county: not that he cared. The Trevarthens had always employed a manager for the estate, but just before his father's death the old one had retired and so the young master had to look about for a new one. The man he took on was young for such an important post, but he had impressed Paul with his ability so he had been appointed to the position, but the young master kept an eye on things for he had not spent his whole life with his head in a book. Wheal Sankey had a good mine captain in charge so he had no worries there. His problem was his mother's various properties and businesses, for he had no knowledge whatsoever of that trade, so he visited the family lawyer, and asked him to look into it for him.

That year there was to be no party for the Christmas tide at Trevu, for they were in deep mourning and it would not have been appropriate, but they invited Aunt Caroline to come and stay in the New Year and she wrote back to tell them that she was most pleased to accept their invitation. She stayed for two weeks and her forceful personality was of great help to Paul. Caroline knew instinctively that her nephew would need help and guidance to enable him to take up the responsibility of running the estate. She was impressed with what she had seen him do already and told him so. When he told her that he had set the family lawyer on to sort out Sardi's estate, she nodded in agreement. She encouraged him to visit all the local farmers with his new estate manager, Jonas Hampton, explaining as she did so: "That way you will know them and they will know and meet Jonas. He will be the link between you and them, but your neighbours will know you as the man who makes the decisions and they will respect you the more for it," she said solemnly.

Paul accompanied Caroline on her various calls to her friends around the locality even though he had found it a great strain as a young man. However, he was the head of Trevu now and with it he had an, albeit unwanted, status. The men of the households, if present, would engage the new Master of Trevu in conversation and more often than not they made sure that they were present. Gradually it was borne in upon Paul that his position in the locality as the biggest and wealthiest landowner carried a certain responsibility. The charm that he had instinctively used amongst the ladies was altered slightly to polite interest amongst his male acquaintances. He was, as always, civil and prepared to sit and listen to all their ideas and opinions and never offended anyone, but he did not alter his own convictions to suit anyone either. The result of this was that he was respected for his wisdom and sincerity and it was impossible to find a family with whom he had dealings that would have a word said against him. On the way back from one of Caroline's social calls she found herself watching her nephew closely. His face was not unlike her late brother's, but whereas Redvers had a very closed countenance Paul's was as open as a sunny day, but she had no fear of the Trevarthen's losing their position in society because of Paul. In company she knew that Hannah called him Mr. Trevarthen because she could bring herself to do no other, but in her warm, cosy kitchen she was never allowed to be so formal with him and he made a point of only answering to his name. He was the same with the farm hands but he never lost their respect for it. She smiled to herself at her efforts at trying to turn him into such an estimable man, that he would be able to stare down his nose at anyone who even as much as raised an eyebrow at the dark-skinned young Paul Trevarthen. Paul had won their respect with his honest and open personality, not with her pretentious wiles. She sighed, but proudly. He had taught them all a lesson: even his proud and silly aunt.

"Something the matter, aunt?" asked Paul, his face immediately registering concern.

"No Paul, dearest. Nothing at all. I was just admiring the view," she said simply.

He smiled back, reassured and their journey continued, each in complete harmony with the other.

In the February a curricle bowled up to the house and a smiling Peter Fleetwood got out. He exchanged a few pleasantries with the stable lad, who took the reins of his horse and led it away, and then he picked up his cloak bag and bounded up the steps to the front door. When Chloe was told who her visitor was she rushed from the parlour and held out her hands with delight to see him.

"None of that Chloe," he said, regardless of Lizzie's astonished stare. He gave her a hug that lifted her quite off the ground and planted a large kiss on her cheek. "How are you dearest Chloe? And where's that scamp of a husband of yours? Don't tell me he has got his head in a book again?" he enquired with a laugh.

"I am very well, Peter, and no, Paul has not his head in a book. He is away in Penzance at the moment, but I expect him back quite soon," she answered, "but come into the withdrawing room and I will send Lizzie for some tea."

In a very short space of time, Hannah was in the withdrawing room with a tray piled high with treats for her Mr. Peter. There was much jollity between them and Peter told her he would be down in the kitchen later, just to make sure that everything was in order. Still laughing, she left Chloe and Peter chatting away happily over the tea tray. Within five minutes Paul had returned and joined them. He was delighted to see Peter and when his friend asked would he be allowed to stay for a couple of nights, Paul replied in the affirmative and informed him that they would be most pleased to have him. They sat and talked all afternoon. Peter gave them his condolences in person and was surprised to find that his friend seemed to have more maturity, and reasoned that his wife was probably the cause of it. Paul had accepted his losses as Chloe had told him he must and had grown through the experience. The responsibility of managing the estate had also given him an air of authority, but with his friend Peter he soon reverted to his usual open personality. Quizzing the infant diplomat on his sudden appearance, he enquired if the young gentleman had been dismissed from the service and laughed rudely on being informed by his friend that he was most highly thought of.

"I was due to come home for some leave and I could not resist the thought of seeing again the most entrancing woman I have ever met," announced

Peter with a wicked smile and he caught hold of Chloe's hand and kissed it. Paul could contain himself no longer and hooted with laughter, Chloe collapsed into giggles and Peter smiled broadly.

"Well to be honest, I am employed as a mailman," he announced. "When I turned up at Father's he remembered a package had been received for me from before Christmas. He eventually found it and when I opened it I found this." Picking up his cloak bag, he rummaged about and produced a small parcel addressed to Paul Trevarthen, Cornwall, and passed it over.

Paul turned it over in his hands and looked at it in surprise. "Why was it sent to you and not the publishers? It must be a book or something by the weight of it," he reasoned.

"Well open it, dear Paul, and then we will all find out," Chloe told him.

Taking out his pocket knife he cut the string that bound it and some papers, and a small book, bound in white vellum with a letter attached, fell into his lap. His face registered his dismay at once, for he knew immediately just what it was that had been sent to him. His hands shook as he picked up the little book, but his wife had all his secrets and she it was who bravely said: "It is Dorothea's book is it not, Paul?" before continuing serenely: "Perhaps if you would like a moment to read the letter on your own, I can show Peter to his room."

They both got up, but Paul asked them to sit down again. "You know all there is to know of me, both of you. I will hide no more from you now," he said with composure. So they waited patiently as he opened the letter addressed to him and began to read it. His wife and friend knew that he had received news of a most serious nature for the expression on his face registered dismay and disbelief in equal measure.

He cleared his throat and stated, "This letter is from Poulson. It states that he knows what happened the night you and I stayed in Oxford, Peter. After, he sent Dorothea away and told everyone that she had gone into the country for her health. When she came back, at the end of the following July," he looked quickly at Chloe and saw the dread premonition of what she was about to hear fall across her face, "their marriage resumed as before. However, Dorothea was no longer well and within a year she had died. He informs me that she wished for me to have back the book that I had signed for her all those years before along with the address of the orphanage where the . . . where the baby was placed." He sighed deeply and continued: "Poulson wishes me to note that his wife's estate has passed to him. The child has never been acknowledged by him and no provision was ever made for it, nor does he intend to pay for the upkeep of the said child because, as he states: 'by her very colour it is obvious she is no child of mine.' He goes on to say that he bears me no ill will as his wife had no love for him, nor he for her but, because of my actions, I have inadvertently been the cause of making him a very rich man indeed. He does not wish, nor does he expect to receive a reply to this letter."

As soon as he finished speaking, Chloe got up and went to him and placed her arms around him, and he leaned his head against her and apologised softly that he should bring such shame upon her.

"Nonsense, Paul," she said firmly, "I have no reproach for you. You have borne enough."

Peter asked after the child and what he proposed to do about it.

"It is a little girl and it was placed in an orphanage in Bristol," his friend replied quietly and, looking at the dates on the notes continued: "on the day of her birth apparently."

"Oh the poor things," said Chloe, her sympathy for mother and child in equal measure.

Peter coughed discreetly and then said: "Well, it's probably for the best."

"Nonsense," Chloe cried, "such a little child to be abandoned like that!"

"Chloe they had to, Poulson could not pass it off as his own unless it had a white . . .," her husband began and then stopped and looked guilty.

"A white skin, Paul?" Chloe finished his sentence for him, and glared at him. Paul hung his head and then said: "It has happened. I can change nothing now, but I will see that she is adequately provided for and it might even be possible for some couple to adopt her."

His wife released him and stamped her little foot angrily, before crying, "How dare you talk like that, you of all people, how dare you!"

Peter tried to calm her, by saying in his reasonable voice: "Chloe, Paul can do no other, don't you see?"

"No, I don't see," she cried, her eyes sparkling with temper. "All I see is the father who, but for the bravery and love of a good woman, would have grown up unwanted and unrecognised in an orphanage himself."

"Chloe have some sense, we cannot take it into this family. Think of the scandal, woman! How would you hold your head up ever again?" he asked.

"The same way the mother who took you in did, I should imagine," she told him in proud defiance.

Her husband sighed and shook his head before putting the notes and the letter back into the envelope. "Excuse me, for a moment," he said quietly, as he got up, "I'll put these in my desk for safekeeping, for I do not want them found by any of the servants." Making his way towards the door, his wife ran to him and caught him by the arm, "Paul, please," she pleaded.

"No!" he shouted angrily and shook her off and left the room, slamming the door behind him..

Dinner was a quiet affair and Peter announced them he would leave on the morrow, for he did not think it right he should stay longer, as he had all unknowingly brought them such bad news. He left after two rather strained days in the couple's company, but was adamant that Paul would be doing his best for the child by sending money for its upkeep. Paul made the necessary financial arrangements, and refused to listen to his wife on the subject. When he returned from Mr. Rodda's office his she would not offer him her cheek to kiss, and that night he found his clothes in the passage outside their bedroom, and the door barred to him. He sighed, but accepted his punishment and moved back to his old room. Hannah demanded an explanation of him but was told not to interfere most abruptly, so she went immediately and asked Chloe, but she could get nothing from her other than that her husband was an obstinate man and she would make him see sense eventually.

At the beginning of the following week, the family lawyer sent Paul a message to call and when he arrived in Penzance he was stunned to be told that he would have to go to London and Bristol to tie up his mother's affairs himself. "Surely they will accept my instruction's through my lawyer?" he told him.

Mr. Rodda sighed and looked at Paul over the top of his spectacles. "I am afraid that if you wish to complete your business with them than you must present yourself in person and instruct them accordingly," he announced, much to his client's annoyance. He pointed out that Sardi's various concerns would need to be overseen and that, as he did not wish to sell any of the properties, he would have to establish what he would wish to do with the households. He continued placidly: "Your late father relied upon his wife's abilities to run her establishments and never sought to interfere. His sad demise, following so soon after your poor mother's, has unfortunately meant that to you falls the problem of initiating his instructions."

Paul swore in frustration, and immediately apologised, but even he could understand that his mother's estate would need far more of his time to be spent on it than the mere passing over of the Trevu lands from father to son, for that had been done in their family ever since the first Trevarthen had set foot on the land. He thanked Mr. Rodda for the work he had done on his behalf and returned home in a very bad mood indeed, for he did not relish the thought of having to leave his home, especially as his dear wife was pointedly making her poor opinion of him obvious to his household. Some time to win back her affection was his ambition, not to have to travel around the country discussing a business he did not understand amidst a company of people of whom he had barely any knowledge. When he informed Chloe of what the lawyer had told him she showed little interest, so he asked, in his most persuasive manner, if she would like to accompany him as he would be gone for at least two weeks and perhaps, he thought, she would enjoy to visit her old friends in London. She looked up from her embroidery and asked him abruptly, if, when he was in Bristol, he would be visiting his daughter.

He scowled and replied sharply: "Of course not, Chloe, don't be so absurd."

"Then I have no cause to go, and I will stay here and await your return," she told him coldly. Swearing under his breath he regarded her in frustration, but he determined he would try again to placate her for he was convinced that she could not hold out against his will for ever. Crossing to her chair he put his arms around her, but she rebuffed him and told him in no uncertain terms precisely what he would need to undertake to regain her former high opinion of him. Annoyed by her reaction, he studied her seething expression for a while until finally; he sighed, moved to the door and slammed it behind him as he departed.

Three weeks later, with his business concluded to his satisfaction, he sat in Sardi's carriage ready to begin his homeward journey. It had been boring, frustrating and annoying but finally he had everything set in train to complete the business arrangements as he wanted them. Something, he did not know what, had made him direct the coachman to the next address but he did so nevertheless. When he arrived there they were most surprised that he should visit, but showed him what he had asked to see. He neither moved nor spoke but climbed back into his carriage and returned to Bristol. After lodging a complaint with the authorities, he was kept busy for another two days before he returned with a member of the governing body and they made a complete tour of the building. The gentleman hurriedly made notes as the tall young man at his side rapped out a series of commands and instructions. As they were about to leave he asked him a question which almost made the governor drop his notebook.

"No problem at all, sir, if that is your wish," he told him obsequiously. "Follow me to the office and everything will be put in order according to your instructions."

So barely a half hour later, the carriage finally began its homeward journey and Paul Trevarthen relaxed with a small, proud smile quivering on his lips.

It was a beautiful day and Chloe and the children were all sitting in the garden. George and Grace were playing with a litter of puppies and Bessie, the farm dog and their proud mother, kept a maternal eye upon her offspring but was glad to have some relief from their perpetual bickering. Little Ben was more content to toddle around the flower beds smelling the flowers, and then to amble back to his mother with some that he had picked before running off to get some more.

The sound of the carriage wheels coming up the drive heralded the arrival of her husband, but she did not move and would not go to greet him, so he found her in the garden with their children. His youngest son saw him first and stopped with a limp flower dangling from one fat hand and pointing with his other. "Look, Dada, Dada," he said simply and smiled with glee, just like his father.

Chloe had no wish even to acknowledge him for her opinion had not altered during his absence, but the sight of George's surprised face intrigued her so she turned her head and saw her husband standing tall on the grass. On his face was his usual beaming smile and in his arms was a little brown haired girl, with a scowling expression on her face that so perfectly matched the one her father would wear when he was not in the happiest frame of mind.

"Oh Paul, Paul," she cried, and with tears almost blinding her she rushed towards them. In a moment the little girl was transferred to her welcoming arms and found herself caressed and cosseted for the first time in her young life. She smiled at her husband through her tears and Paul considered himself a man blessed beyond belief to have such a wife. They all sat on the grass together and the children came and greeted their father and it was explained to them that the little girl was to be their new sister. After a while George took the child by one hand and Grace held the other and they led her over to play with the puppies. When one of the puppies licked her face she began to giggle and, turning her head to look at Paul and Chloe, she laughed loudly and they joined in with her obvious delight. Chloe turned her head, her eyes shining, and studied her husband's profile. He was watching the children and smiling softly to himself.

"Why did you do it, Paul?" she asked gently, nestling against him.

He turned and looked down into her adored face and smiled happily, but as he began his tale he sighed. "I visited the orphanage and asked to see her. The place was dark, unkempt and smelly. God knows what the money sent for her care was spent on! Certainly none of it found its way to the poor child or to any of the others either by the looks of them. She was in a room on her own, wearing filthy rags for clothes and chewing on a piece of dry bread. They did not even have a name for her, just a description. 'Female child, dark complexion, light brown hair, brown eyes - from birth'. God knows how she survived the privations that she has undoubtedly suffered, but she did. I left immediately, went to the authorities and purchased the property there and then. Once I had signed my name I set about to have the place altered. The people running the orphanage were packed off, when they had sobered up enough to know what was happening, and new people were appointed of my choosing. When I left, I made sure that an army of builders and decorators were employed so that the place becomes not only habitable but suitable for the children to live in with dignity and happiness. I have appointed a cook and left the governing body with a list of instructions concerning the welfare of the children and the standards that I wished to see implemented and maintained. The money will be there for it to be run properly, but I have pointed out to the members with great care that I will not tolerate any mismanagement and should I, or my agents, find any such then they would be replaced by more competent people. By that time I could not bring myself to abandon her; I determined to bring her home with me and filled in the necessary papers. I entered the hovel that was her room and when I did she ran towards me and caught hold my hand and," he smiled tenderly, "my heart as well. I bought some clothes for her on the journey home and a matronly landlady at the first hotel we stopped at washed her for me and got the tangles out of her hair." His proud smile lit up his face as he watched his children at play, but of a sudden he turned anxiously toward his wife.

"Have I done right, Chloe?" he asked, searching her face with a worried frown," for there will be a deal of talk for you to face."

"Pooh! What of scandal, it will not bother me. Your daughter is where she should be and where I hope she will learn what happiness is at last," replied Chloe contentedly.

"Amen to that," sighed Paul, and then as a thought occurred to him he said: "I should warn you, Madam Wife, she certainly takes after me in one respect."

His wife looked enquiring.

"She has my appetite," he said with a twitch of his lips.

"Well, no matter, as long as she leaves me enough bread for my dry toast I will be content," his wife replied with a gentle smile lifting the corners of her own mouth. It took a moment for the implication of what she had said to register with him, but when it did he let out such a whoop of joy that all the children turned their heads towards them and watched spellbound as the two adults proceeded to kiss passionately.

George was the first to speak and told the little girl not to take any notice because they were always doing that sort of thing. Shyly he told her their names and then, as she did not respond, asked if she had a name. His newly acquired sister shook her head so he looked around for inspiration. His eye alighted on a pretty flower that he knew the name of and asked if she would like to be called: 'Daisy'.

The child thought for a moment, carefully studying the flower he had pointed to and then nodded, so he picked one for her and placed it in her hand. She took it to her nose and sniffed cautiously before smiling happily at him. George smiled confidently back at her and then, looking at his parents, he caught up her little hand and led her back to them. Firmly and solemnly he informed them, much to their amusement, precisely by what name his new sister that they had been given was to be known.

Printed in the United Kingdom
by Lightning Source UK Ltd.
113794UKS00001B/138